Praise for the Novels of Andrew

A Climbing Stock

Andrew Hiller's first novel was about as good a debut as any author could ask for. The world and the lore behind it certainly draw our attention, the story is captivating, engaging and takes many surprising directions, thanks in no small part to the fact that it's populated by such a radiant and distinct cast of characters.

--Yakov Ben Efraim, Quick Book Reviews

This updated version of Jack and the Beanstalk is a clever and fun ride. If you like double entendres and fairytales, this is a great book for you. It tells the story with a modern perspective - corporate greed, trading stocks, etc. - but includes an entire world of fantasy as well. Check it out if you like the feel of an alternate universe that melds current day America and fairytale land.

--Jessica Piscitelli, Caged

A Halo of Mushrooms

It almost strikes you more as a foodie fantasy (eat your heart out, George Martin). It evolves past that, of course, but Hiller begins his tale with plentiful, savory details. His words are crafted with an unfamiliar cadence that makes even something as mundane as preparing (and eating) food seem magical and full of whimsy.

--Michael DeAngelo, The Tellest

Joe, May your stocks always rise

"Andrew Hiller in *A Halo of Mushrooms* presents us with a mouthwatering fantasy story of wonder about the power of another of our five senses, taste.

The only other fiction I've read of comparable appeal to taste was *Like Water for Chocolate*."

--Geoff Hill, *The Life Well Lived*

"Wonderful read – engaging, enjoyable, fast moving – the author does a great job of crafting the characters and story.

Highly encourage everyone to pick up a copy"

--Henry Sienkiewicz, *Untangled*

"A really good read, and a fun one, too!"

--David Daumit, *The Oval Tome*

"*A Halo of Mushrooms*" is a brilliant read. Truly refreshing and unique in the realm of modern Fantasy."

--Mike Gagnon, *Marvel Handbook*

"*A Halo of Mushrooms* was an intriguing read filled great characters and a captivating plot. Andrew has a beautiful style of writing that displays the time and effort put into this novel. This book is certain to impress you.

--Marissa Reads

A Climbing Stock

A Novel

by

Andrew Hiller

A Climbing Stock is a work of fiction. Names, characters, places, and incidents are the products of the author's imagination. Any resemblance to actual events, locales, or persons, living or dead, is entirely coincidental.

ISBN 978-0-9969582-2-6
eBook ISBN 978-0-9969582-3-3

www.andrewhiller.net
First Edition

1. A Climbing Stock

Once leprechauns sang just within earshot. If you ran fast enough and could knot the rainbow around the old maple, the golden pot was yours. Once, but not this time--

Today, John strode past his visiting mother, knotted his tie around the doorknob, snapped open the briefcase, took out a ledger filled with red numbers, left, and came back with a tray full of Mother's cookies and lemonade. He turned on the calculator and took a drink.

"You're an idiot," Mother said helpfully.

John pinched the bridge of his nose and sighed, thumbing through the pages.

"Thanks." He answered distractedly, setting this month's disaster down on the piano's music rack. The walnut fallboard covering the keys gave a pleasant thrum as his fingers drummed on it.

"Your father was the same way." Mother continued. She crossed the living room with a hammer snap of her heels. Her dress stayed still as she walked, every line displayed exactly as in this month's Vogue. No wrinkle dared reveal itself. It would remain proper. It would know its place. She smiled. The bright red slashes emphasized power. The ruffles at her wrists failed to soften the look. Her diamonds looked primed to cut glass.

John sat down on a corner of the piano bench. The wood looked dark against his skin. This month's tallies glared at him, daring him to play them into harmony or improvise them into something beautiful. He shuffled pages, flexed his fingers, and then slumped his shoulders, turning instead to gaze at the offered cookies on their silver tray. A rip in one of the curtains distracted him. He swirled lemonade hoping that would be helpful.

"It's good to be home." John mumbled.

"Harrumph." Mother harrumphed. They watched each other.

Mother downed her lemonade like whiskey in a shot glass. Then, she stood very still and turned her head. A white linen tablecloth dared to flutter on the dining room table. Hands went to hips and she nearly took a step. The fabric froze… caught. She glared it into submission. It fell straight and resisted the breeze from the damnable air conditioner vent.

The most remarkable thing about the Fasola-Sprat home was that it was completely devoid of perpendicular angles, not by design, but because the foundation had sunk… given in. From the outside, it glistened with a new coat of paint, its granite walkways were freshly scrubbed, and its lawn so meticulously kept that people often wondered if a gardener had at it with a toenail clipper, but inside despite Mother's vigilant efforts wear began to show.

The prestige item of the living room was a deeply burnished grand piano. It vibrated and glistened with the need to put on a show, but like the house it was a bit of an illusion. The thing hadn't been tuned in twenty years and hadn't been played for at least five. Its bench didn't even close properly, but that was because John Fasola used it as an in-box.

Overall, the house had the feeling of a scrapbook. It was definitely one that "was". Even the windows sagged, milky and foggy. John glanced at Mother through the reflection of his glass and toasted her with the lemonade.

"Did you put any sugar in this at all?" John said, dipping his finger into the glass. It came back puckered.

"The way you look I'm not sure if your blood pressure could stand the sugar."

John looked up and smiled.

"Then why the cookies?"

"Sell the business, John."

He choked.

"I can't sell the family business"

"It's not a sacred cow, John." Mother sternly informed.

John looked up and smiled. He swept a few hairs off his jacket and stared at the twenty-year old marketing texts neatly stacked and freshly book-marked in a corner of his living room. The bookcase he walked to practically bulged with mail and forgotten recipes for success. He pulled out an assortment of papers, charts and letters as if they were proof that he knew what he was doing. After all, look how much paper he had accumulated. The endless stacks had to mean something.

Mother stood over him. Her arms crossed. John looked past her at a photo of his father that hung askew on the wall. His voice was resolute, even though it cracked.

"I can't sell the family business," He had been saying that sentence a lot recently. Mother didn't harrumph which made John exceedingly nervous. Taking a deep breath, he walked over to the piano, lifted the fallboard and plunked out a few notes, before realizing it was the beginning of a blues song and stopped immediately. "It would be like selling the family."

"Sell it now while the pieces are still worth something."

"God, this lemonade is bad."

"I gave birth for this?"

John lifted the lid of the piano bench and thumbed again through the reports filed there. Desperately, he searched.

"It's here somewhere!" he growled.

Mother released her white-knuckled grip from a slatted chair and checked her texts. Menace filled her smile. Then, she glided towards the ledger. Her son, alarmed, hurried with a poorly disguised attempt at nonchalance to intercept her.

"Aha!" he said, pulling a sheet. "We claimed a profit in the third quarter of…"

"Son" she said patiently, "You make rotary dials. No one dials anymore."

"I've expanded the business, Mom."

"Oh yes, I forgot. You make turntable needles."

"Dad would never sell the business."

Mother picked up the tray and ground the uneaten cookies into dust. She turned and picked up a photo of Dad and John.

"Your father loved to take you fishing. He loved that old fishing pole. Man refused to use bait." She studied her son before continuing, "'Digital is the devil,' he used to say. 'Analog is the only way.' Your father was an idiot too."

"Digital only records the high and low registers. True music lovers can never be satisfied by digital. It's a fad, Mom. The idea of an album is too important. Everyone knows the best music is always on side B." John countered, rubbing away more hair. He only shed when she visited.

Mother nodded, took the ledger from his grip, and nodded again. She walked to her suitcase. John winced when she pulled out her tablet. She tapped out the numbers and made some projections. A few pie charts, a few line graphs later, she took off her glasses and closed the ledger. John took a step backwards.

"But, Mom," John tried, "Remember when we sold 40,000 slide rules..."

"Y2K was a long time ago, Johnny," she shook her head, "I will not go through bankruptcy. I will make some calls and set up a meeting. 'Slide rules,' he tells me. The factory has got to be worth something. Can I trust you to sign the papers?"

"Mom. The family business."

Mother shoved the graphs towards him.

She would never understand. Not the mother who bought her clothes straight out of Harper's Bazaar all the while complaining that the magazine was falling behind the times and needed to work harder at following the micro-trends. Not when she budgeted hundreds of dollars every week to tint and poof her hair so she could look more like a TV reality housewife. The Corporation of Ordinary Wares had never been fashionable enough for mother.

John willed away a headache. That too, had become all too common.

When John turned sixteen his father put him in a car and showed his son what he called "the starving towns." He drove slowly to give his boy a chance to memorize the faces of people idling on broken stoops staring out as blankly as the residents of a nursing home. There wasn't much light in their eyes.

"They were abandoned, son, some of them twenty years ago." Dad rolled down the window to let the dust in. The ghosts of worn town houses with boarded windows, broken boards, and cracked sidewalks filled his memory.

"A factory is like a heart, boy. When it dies or is chopped up, everything around it dries up." Father slowed the car to drive by a washed-out family in grayed clothing. "Look at them, John. The Corporation of Ordinary Wares is more… She kept folks fed in the depression and she keeps their blood warm now. Without the Wares…" His father looked away, "Look how long it's been since these houses were painted. How long do you think it's been since their Corporation betrayed them? Every town needs its heart. We must do everything we can to keep it beating."

Mother slammed the ledger closed.

"I'll make the call tomorrow," Mother decided.

Dad affectionately called Mother "the clog."

John turned away and went upstairs. It took all his strength not to slam the door. Mother smiled and shook her finger at her husband's photograph. "Idiot," she said and turned to the liquor cabinet. From behind the door rose a sulky shout.

"Nostalgia is in. You'll see."

Mother looked at her husband's image again then turned her attention to the closed door before downing a shot of bourbon.

"He's your son," she told the ghost.

The man tried hard not to laugh when he looked over the assets. He complained of restructuring costs, severance pay, retraining fees, the useless backlog of inventory. John grabbed the cuffs of his best navy suit and sat through it all. In his mind, he sailed back in time to a time when… actually, he traveled to a place that never existed. A time of noble businessmen who sat around an Arthurian round table where each man was equal and worked towards a fair and just… for some reason in his mind's eye his mother looked a little like Morgan Le Fey just then. These men and women then, with their ironically round boardroom table and standard of black and pinstriped gray, were the black knights.

They cared nothing for the heart of a town.

Worse, they even had the effrontery to deny him the Grand Hall. This meeting was held in a regional office. The Mid-Atlantic office. The Corporation for Ordinary Wares deserved better.

On the ride over, leaves fell. Not in a rush of gold and ruby, but a cascade of brittle brown. Each crunchy step felt like the breaking of bones, like he was walking over a field of corpses. The building was suitably tall, 17 stories, but when he told them who he was, they didn't even offer to park his car. They told him to take his Volvo down to the basement lot. He complied, took the elevator (the faux marble walls were nice) to the ground floor and was told to go to Conference Room L on the thirteenth floor.

Conference Room L? The thirteenth floor! He huffed. *The Corporation for Ordinary Wares deserves at least a Conference Room B!*

A stout receptionist in a gray skirt and an oversized white blouse greeted him. She got him a cup of coffee with sugar and apologized when he asked for cream.

"We have non diary creamer." She offered and closed the door.

The conference room was half full. The men looked like they had been part of a semi-successful cloning experiment. Only their hairlines differed. The table sparkled, all glass and aluminum while the light fizzed down from a series of small spotlights on the ceiling. The air stiffened. Champagne was nowhere in sight.

Their offer was nearly a hundred pages long, but half the men in the room weren't even listening to the presentation. They just gleefully tapped away at their smartphones and occasionally nodded. The lone woman of the room had the grace to cover her mouth as she yawned. John played the role of a supplicant. They were doing him a favor.

Six fountain pens lay in the center of the table. John was sure they were filled with blood. Some of the pages already looked signed.

This was not a foregone conclusion! John would have a say! He took a deep breath and straightened up. If he had to sell he would get the best price he could.

The man in the grayest suit repeated his last point, dramatically punching the table. John jumped.

Unnoticed, a little man seated on the water cooler laughed. One might imagine he sprang from a dew drop of color clinging from the faucet. The kind that refused to let go. He was not quite natural. For one thing, his head was barely the size of one of the cooler's air bubbles. For another, he was enjoying himself. His heels kicked, causing tiny ripples in the water. His hands clapped. Yet, the sound never carried. It might not have occurred to the little man that this was certainly not a place to have fun. John certainly bore a grim face. Even his counterparts in their stiff gray suits all wore dour, bored expressions. Yet the little man smiled. Why even hair curled like a toddler's laugh as it crept out from his broad-brimmed hat. Plainly speaking, the nonsense and blather these gray suited office sirs prattled on about tickled him. On and on, they kept going ignoring the glazed eyes and nodding heads. It was as if the plan was to bore John into submission. When the gray man pulled out the same chart for the fourth time, the little man stuck out his tongue and made a face. No one stirred or noticed and so he turned and waggled his buttocks at them, then giggled again. When someone finally turned to locate the source of the sound the little man wiggled down the spigot.

They made their offer.

It would have been a fair offer in 1929 after the crash, unless you consider inflation. John stammered, tried to rise and felt his legs give way. The rumpled, heavy man in the Brooks Brothers smirked as he presented his Indigo pen.

John trembled. His color became yellow. The offer actually made him physically ill. The woman offered her hand to help him up; he refused to take it, afraid it might signify agreement. He excused himself.

Outside, he kicked a water fountain. Then, remembering some old rule kicked it twice more. The little man materialized behind him. John turned. The wee man stepped lightly to the side. He stood exactly behind John's narrow shoulders and shadowed the larger man's movement to ensure he remained unseen. John massaged his temples and slapped himself lightly.

"Think," John urged himself. Behind him, the wee man vigorously rubbed his hands together. With each stroke, the little man grew a foot. He stopped when he reached his fourth foot.

"Jack," he finally said. John turned around and jumped. There had been no one there. The wee man waited. John smiled uncomfortably and pinched the bridge of his nose, then smiled, trying to ignore his start and the sudden pounding in his heart, so as not to appear rude.

"It's John, no one calls me Jack."

"John then. It's a shame what they do. I knew your father. Hard worker, good man, your father," the little man began.

"You think I should take their offer?"

"Oh by the… Well no, your father wouldn't accept a poor deal like that. Your father made one hell of a deal with my kin. He wouldn't have told you the story. It was part of the deal."

The small man circled the fountain, and when he caught his reflection, groomed himself smoothing his hair and straightening his collar.

"John," he continued, then paused, "I can't call you that. Are you sure I can't call you Ja… as you will." He pursed his lips and hummed a strange bouncy tune, then raised a finger. "Johnny, then." He clapped in approval of the compromise and looked back over his shoulder at the boardroom. It was silent inside, almost as if the men and women ceased to exist the moment John had left. The wee man nodded and took a step forward, thrusting out a hand. "You were shrewd to leave, Johnny. If you come back they'll sweeten the pot…" the wee man choked. "Offer," he amended quickly.

"You've a better offer?"

"I told them you'd be shrewd. Just like your old father. A Johnny to the core." That seemed to amuse him. "You know how they are mapping, just finished mapping, the human genome, Johnny," John nodded. "You're a talker, Johnny. I like that. My family has the new company. You've heard of BEAN, haven't you?"

"Bean?"

"Biomicroscopy Endoscopic Arterial Neurosurgery. BEAN. You've heard of it."

"I'm afraid I…"

"Not much of a player are you, Johnny. Don't watch the news either, I bet. BEAN is big, as big as the rest of all of biotech put together. I'm authorized to offer you a substantial share in the company."

"BEAN, I don't know."

"We IPO in a week. Everything is set. The only problem is we need plastics. We need a factory to make the bottles to put the medicine in. You've got space and you've equipment designed to handle heavy plastics, light plastics… Do you see what I'm offering?"

John stared at the little man. He looked polished. Emerald cufflinks twinkled. A pressed Armani suit accented with a silk bow tie so green it smelled like a spring garden. Even the wrinkles in his broad face looked pleated. His voice was warm and seductive. John backed away from him. If something sounds too good…

"You're offering me a partnership. A share of your company for…"

"Oh no," the man laughed with a laugh that would have embarrassed Santa Claus. "I'm offering you 3, 000 shares of BEAN for your company."

"You're offering me 3k of BEANS for my company?"

"Sounds familiar doesn't it, Ja… Johnny. We've done this dance before. Your family always makes out well. I get what I want and you get to take care of your mother in style."

John turned towards the door to go back to the conference room. A sudden stiff, dry, air-conditioned gust made him shiver. His heart still had not settled.

"Your father had the balls to throw the dice, Johnny. This is your chance to choose a road. You take a step into that room and I will rescind my offer. Oh, you just take their offer and continue down your safe path with your mother looking down her nose at you. You were willing to hold on, weren't you? You were willing to hold for love or faith. Your father would be ashamed of you for taking the pennies they're offering."

John hesitated. His fingers urged him to turn the knob and take the deal Mother had arranged, but there was something in the little man's stance, some cockiness that he longed to echo.

"I need to call my broker" John said.

"Sure, call your broker," the little man sneered. He said nothing for a moment and just stood there as if he were searching for something inside John. John took a step backwards. A wistful smile widened the wee man's cheeks. Then, he took one of the emerald shamrocks off his lapel and handed it to John. "There was a time when family meant something, my boy. I came here to do you a favor for your father's sake, for old time's sake, but you're right. You are no Jack. Take the pin. It's worth more than the trifle they're offering you. I have to give you something for all the times your family gave me." The twinkle faded from his eyes. "I never thought I'd see the day when a Jack turned down an offer of beans. I suppose luck is truly dead."

John felt the weight of the pin. He opened the door, stared at the dour, rumpled faces in their sterile off-white room, they turned slowly as if time was defrosting, and then back at the slumping, suddenly old man walking towards the elevator. John turned and ran.

"Wait," John said, putting his arm around the man's shoulders. The leprechaun perked up.

"You've made the right choice, Jack," he said, snatching the pin back.

"My mother's going to kill me."

"She always does, Jack. She always does." The wee man giggled as Jack signed the papers.

Needless to say, John's mother packed up her things and left. Not only did the contract offer only 3,000 shares, it subsumed none of the company's debt. The offering price was set at 15 dollars. That meant that John turned down an offer that would have given him $250,000 clear for a stock speculation that put the family $2,700,000 in debt.

Mother was too angry to even call him an idiot.

In the morning, John watched CNBC eagerly. BEAN opened poorly and by the end of the day was only worth ten dollars a share. John listened to the self-assured, pompous advisors laugh about how this nowhere stock was the most unready company to go public that anyone could remember. "What do they do? No one knows," Martin Brotheau laughed. "Plus, what serious issue engages in the takeover of a bankrupt company riddled with debt and horribly obsolete machinery a week before going public. I really feel sorry for the people who underwrote this."

John turned off the TV. He went upstairs and called his accountant.

"If I sell everything, Terry. Yeah, the house, too, if I sell everything, can I come out of this?" Terry didn't answer. John heard his breathing so he knew Terry was still there.

"There are a few tricks, John. We can hold off the wolves for a little while, but yeah, I would start liquidating your hard assets. I figure we have to the end of the quarter before... how are you at picking lottery numbers, John?"

John slammed the receiver. He pictured his mother living on the streets. He could get her a good cardboard box. One near the best hot air vent in the city. He could at least do that much.

His liquor cabinet was empty by morning. He passed out. During the next two days, he only recovered long enough to stumble to the bathroom before collapsing somewhere in the living room. The smell of vomit and gin permeated the house, especially between the keys of the piano. When he could see and stand, he saw his answering machine held 127 voice messages.

"Hello, John... this is Terry. Something's going on with that stock. It's got a good pop on no news. It hit 20. I think you should sell before the money managers start taking profits."

"Hey John, Terry. I hope you didn't get around to selling. This stock is shooting up like a weed, man. It's at 50. Jesus, 30 points in two hours. What do you know about this? Can you tell me anything?"

"John. Where are you? I think there's something wrong with my computer. This just can't be right. I'll give Ferris Baker a call and see if they can verify..."

And the BEAN stock kept rising and rising for two days until...

"Hello, John, we've got to consider some tax shelters my man! This stock is higher than W. Buffet. I don't know why you haven't called back yet. We're still… I'm still your guy, right? Come on, just 'cause you're a multi- multimillionaire is no reason (beep)"

"Me again. We've been through a lot. I knew your father. Come on, pick up. I didn't hold it against you that you never tipped me off about this BEAN stock. I mean, shit, this stock is rising through the roof… It's sky high. Okay, I know what you're thinking, but I've some big clients. I can handle you. Maybe I could've done more to save the business. I admit that I made some mistakes, but you know I've worked hard for you… How many honest accountants do you think there are out there!"

John scratched his head and wondered if he was still drunk. He rolled off the piano bench, crawled to the antique wicker sofa to lever himself up, and went to the front door. He picked up the three morning papers piled there and a gift-wrapped bottle of champagne. The champagne was from Terry. BEAN was on the front page.

Stock Soars. From 15 to 5,000 in Two Days. Will the BEAN Stock Ever Stop Growing? As John started to faint, he saw his mother open a cab door. For the first time he could remember, she looked happy. Dimly he heard his mother shout, "Tell me that for once in your life you were smart. Tell me you didn't sell. Fifteen million dollars! Fifteen million dollars!"

2. A Glimpse of the Castle

"Excuse me."

The woman looked up from pumping gas. Her nose wrinkled from the fumes and she stood on a stain formed from countless drops of fossil fuel. She wore a pursed expression that was closed and not prone to handouts. With her free hand, she tightened the belt of her dark overcoat cinching away her money. If her body language was a bank, the security guard had just drawn his pistol. Wind knotted her blonde hair. Her breath, like his, came out in clouds. The meter pinged happily. She chose Unleaded, not Plus or Super.

"Excuse me." John repeated. Her eyebrows twitched. Her lips were painted slightly purple. She took a step to the side to put the hose between her and the stranger and inclined her head.

"I've been trying to find out," John began again, "If you came into money, some serious money, what would you do?"

She let out a breath.

"What are you trying to sell?" She grumbled. The man took a half step back and put his hand on her fender leaving fingerprints that faded after a moment.

"No. No." John said, waving his hands. He showed her the paper he had been taking notes on. "I'm just trying to find out. You see I've… and I don't really know what to do. So, I've been asking people. What would you do if you just made fifteen million dollars?"

Her eyes widened and then drew narrow.

"Is this some kind of pick up…?"

John interrupted her and brought out a newspaper. It had the story of the sale of the Corporation of Ordinary Wares and subsequent rise of the BEAN stock. The picture of John in it wasn't very good, John thought, (Surely, he didn't look that old or out of shape.) but people who didn't know him seemed to think it looked a lot like him.

She took stock of him. There was an earnestness about him. Maybe it was his unkempt hair, a brown thatch that seemed like it had never known a gel and that the wind made into an overturned haystack or maybe it was because his tie was loose around his neck and even though she could barely see below the collar-line she could tell it was stained and dull from years of use.

"I don't know." She said, suddenly feeling shier. "I think…" The handle lurched telling her that her tank was full. The driver behind her was already on his horn and looked sulky and impatient. "I think I'd go on a trip." She said, finally answering his question. Her eyes widened a little bit, "Maybe a cruise to Alaska."

John nodded and turned.

"Wait. Don't you want to talk about this some more?" she asked.

John paused. He turned away bashfully and then waved. The woman watched him approach another driver. She bent to study herself in the mirror. Then collected her receipt, got in the car, and drove off feeling put off as if she had blown a big opportunity.

John continued conducting his make shift poll.

After surveying thirty-nine people in book stores, gas stations, in front of the movies, supermarkets, electronics stores, and a K-mart, John discovered three things he should do with his sudden money: buy a car, go on a vacation, and quit his job.

None of these satisfied him.

It wasn't like he was a lottery winner or his great aunt died and he suddenly had all this money. John S. Fasola had owned the Corporation of Ordinary Wares, a factory that did millions of dollars in business every other year. John knew money. According to the IRS, John had been rich.

And yes, John shared some of the trappings of wealth. He lived in a large house next to neighbors he couldn't name. His car squandered gas inefficiently and he knew almost none of the most popular slang of the day. Still, the truth was that

John was always worth more than he was worth. Most of his money went back into the business and he lived a life barely better than most of his factory floor workers.

Being actually rich confused him. Worse, it played havoc with his moral compass and sense of duty. And so, he got in his car to continue his quest. John sought a place full of wisdom and answers. He wound up at the mall.

The Beddinger Mall was the largest shopping center in the state. Once an open air mall full of Mom and Pop shops, it now was a Mecca for everything mass produced. John nodded to himself. If retail was the cultural hub of America, surely this place contained its answers… a large measure of its soul. With a clang of metal, he slammed his car door shut and headed into the Mall.

A blast of warm air hit him as the doors slid open. The mall denizens, a pale, unearthly lot wore their coats buttoned despite the twenty-degree difference in temperature. John took off his gloves and placed them his pockets, then noticed that everyone else seemed to still have theirs on and followed suit.

The mall possessed everything he would ever need. At least that's what the ads promised. Someone offered him a smoothie sample which he was sure had no fruit, but as he was a fan of slushies he took it. He asked a few more random people about what they would do and scribbled their thoughts. They really offered very few variants.

He quickened his pace as he passed the Victoria Secrets window before succumbing to an urge to linger. The women in the store never looked like the women in the windows or on the posters. Sometimes he wondered if that was cause for a lawsuit.

Turning from the lingerie, he focused his attention back towards his list.

He didn't want to own a new car or go on a vacation and you can't quit a job you sold. Still, it was obvious that people expected him to do something extravagant with the money. John looked over his survey again. Sighing, he crumpled it.

He shot the paper ball at a wastebasket and missed. Bending, he saw a word. He unfolded the ball and read that sentence. Hurriedly, he scanned the other sections. Only six percent of those polled had felt that way. He considered the ramifications of going for such a minutely considered proposition. Still, it was a legitimate idea. It might even be barely socially acceptable. John pinched his nose. He slapped his thigh. He looked at the tiny scrawl. "Buy something for my family," he read.

"I'll do it," he said, and ran out of the mall.

"Can you believe it, Mother?" John said, stepping out of the new car and handing her a set of bow-tied keys. "Cruise control. A cassette player in the car. Boy, you should have seen the looks I got for that! I had to pay extra, believe me. The dealer said he didn't know people even had cassettes anymore." John hurried and opened a metallic silver door. "Windows you don't have to crank and I got this especially for you, Mom." He lowered his voice and looked around conspiratorially. "A CD player. I think we can afford the fads now."

"I was hoping for something red and Italian," Mother said, but she took the keys anyway. She returned to her seat on the porch.

They both swung. The air was chilly, but pleasant enough in the sun. The grass was just beginning to take on its winter hue. The neighbors' fences were all closed, but they wore decorative things like twinkling lights and through the slats they spied the flash of TVs through the windows. The new car, Mother's Honda, sat in a circular driveway. Why mother wanted two seats when four was more practical distracted John, but only a little. He measured a car's true value by its trunk space. He stared happily at the gift. Above geese scrawled curious omens in the sky. Cars honked in return, but the geese didn't seem to understand their dialect.

He fidgeted with his pockets and felt the list. It had one item crossed off. The gift was bought. Now what? A cloud dissolved into frayed pieces of cotton. John followed the tendrils and started humming until Mother disapprovingly patted his thigh.

What was he to do? The list proved pretty useless so he surveyed his memories. When was he happy? What did he need? What did he want? A smile crested his face, but he dismissed it. Really, what would he do with Indiana Jones' whip? He twiddled.

"Mother."

"Yes, dear."

"I want to get back into business."

"You're a man of leisure now, son."

"I miss working, Mother, and I think I've found the perfect business."

"Really?" Mother smiled indulgently.

"Rabbit ears."

Mother smirked. John took her arm and pointed towards the horizon. She squinted at John's vision. "Cable is just a bunch of repeats and 3rd rate programming." He explained, "I figure any day now people will decide to cancel their subscriptions. Think about it, Mother, all those people suddenly needing television antennas. It's perfect!"

"Son," mother laughed gently, opening a brochure on plastic surgery, "you're still an idiot."

"But," he stopped. Mother glanced up. Her eyes softened momentarily as she saw again the new car in front of them. She considered lecturing him about how TVs were no longer made to hold rabbit ears… how in fact there was no analog television anymore, and even worse, people downloaded shows to binge watch, but instead she took a shot of lemonade, shivered in protest, and held it in. John grimaced as if he wanted to convince her, wanted to argue, but in the end they both leaned back, kicked higher on the porch swing, and stared at the new car.

As for the Honda itself, Mother would trade it in, but it still pleased her, just as the crude kindergarten paperweights he made long ago used to please her. John returned mother's smile and walked to his old Volvo. Clouds swirled in his head, but the breeze that carried them only brought more clouds. He wanted sun or rain. His hands drifted over the cool metal. He loved every bump and ding. Each represented a sign of movement, of progress. Was there a way here to read the future? A phrenology for cars? Could a mechanic study the bumps on the Volvo's body and devise a plan for its driver in the way some could read the bumps on your head? It was worth a trip to the library. He could… he stopped and kicked the tire.

How could he tell Mother that this money made him feel terrible? That three days each week he left at three in the morning to drop off cash to each of his former employees to make sure they'd be okay? He used to make things, used to help people. Now he was supposed to have things and he just didn't know how.

He considered offering his managerial expertise to BEAN, but no one seemed to know where its headquarters was located, not even the major shareholders. As far as anyone knew, John's factory was the only physical proof that BEAN even existed. That and that somehow tons of these drugs kept being produced. But they were being produced without patents, without chemists, or even FDA approval.

Well, all the drugs had FDA approval, but according to an article John read, no one could remember doing the actual approving. Some corporate giants reportedly were getting very frustrated with BEAN and its endless fast track approvals. Doctors were also nervous because they found themselves prescribing drugs they had never read about in their journals. No one had any research about efficacy, side effects, or anything. Even stranger, nothing coming out of BEAN had anything to do with its name; nothing endoscopic, nothing arterial, and certainly nothing having to do with surgery. John, like everyone else, wondered what BEAN was up to.

His cell phone rang. John sighed. It was another 202 number. Taking a deep breath, he flipped it open.

"Mr. Fasola?"

"Hello." John agreed.

"This is Daniel Cerrato with Senator Schuster's office. We've been doing a little bit of research on Biomicroscopy Endoscopic… about BEAN."

"Yes, sir," John said affably, staring up at the sky. Two clouds kissed.

"We were wondering if you wouldn't mind flying down to Washington to be a witness on a hearing we are arranging about stock manipulation."

"Me, sir?"

"Well, you are listed as the first private investor in the company."

"But,"

"Don't get me wrong. You aren't in any trouble, sir. This is purely exploratory."

"Do I have to?"

"Do you have something to hide, Mr. Fasola?"

John sighed. It seemed every organization in the country with an "F" in their name wanted to speak with him. Besides this call from the Senate, he had three meetings set up with the FTC, who wanted to discuss how the stock could have possibly climbed from 15 to 5,000 in two days, and how he became involved. More important, they wanted to know why, since reaching 5,000, the issue stopped growing. Every day, it attracted just enough buyers and sellers to return to exactly 5,000. Then, there was the FDA who wanted to know what it was that these approved drugs actually did and how many people they had been tested on.

"Do you at least have copies of the studies?" a frustrated FDA man asked earlier in the week, "My computer freezes every time anyone types in 'BEAN.' Heck, today I swear it froze when someone in the office talked about going to a barbecue this weekend!"

John worried more when the FBI called three times and questioned why he was the only American investor listed amongst the initial investors and why he was the only investor with an address.

All of it made him very nervous.

John drove to his old rotary factory. Some of the old hands waved hello, but the security guard didn't.

"Mister…" The guard began checking his list.

"You know me, Bruce."

"Do you have an appointment?"

"I own this factory."

"BEAN owns this factory."

"Well, I'm a major owner of BEAN."

"Sorry sir, no one enters the BEAN. There are industrial spies everywhere."

"Bruce…"

"Go home, John."

John waited, but Bruce just put his hands on his hips. The gate remained shut. Only a handful of cars sat in the parking lot. It looked deserted, especially for a Thursday. Surveying the building, he found most of the blinds drawn. Every top floor office appeared to be dark. Out front, stacks of large crates blocked the main mechanical door making it impossible for goods to travel in or out and even the front door remained inaccessible because of a large crane someone parked inches from entryway.

"Is it okay, Bruce?"

Bruce glared at him, then looked around and leaned forward. "I don't know what it is, John. Look, I wouldn't even talk to you except everyone knows you been playing Santa Claus." He paused and added with a guilty expression. "They kept me."

John looked quickly at his shoes as his cheeks started reddening. No one was supposed to know he was helping out his ex-employees. *Bruce couldn't know*, he thought and shuffled his feet before turning turned to study the burly security guard. He wore Corporation of Ordinary Wares' colors still: a soft denim blue shirt and khaki pants. An old fashioned walkie talkie hung from his belt. His holster looked so new that one might guess the gun had never been drawn. John certainly never remembered any security guard ever needing to. The attention made Bruce stare off into space. He squinted as if trying to figure out something he'd been trying to avoid.

"They kept about twelve of us, John. Twelve out of a hundred and twenty." He stopped to let John digest that. "None of us go in. We just load the trucks. It's like we're window dressing. I know we weren't chemists, but hell… we're not even allowed to use the bathrooms in there."

"Bruce…"

"I'm getting paid more than I ever was. I'm not going to let you in. Get an appointment. No offense, John."

"Bruce…"

"Hell, John, I don't even let them in." He pointed towards the windows. I don't know when they get here, but no one goes in and no one leaves. Least not during my shift."

"What about the trucks, they have to be delivering raw materials."

"First thing they built was that crane thing and a sort of hangar door on the roof. Stuff gets lowered in. Hey, John, you trying to cost me my job?"

John rubbed at his temples and turned towards the fence. The chain links looked imposing. The blacktop seemed too open a space and the gray factory walls loomed steep and menacing.

"Look, go on home. From what I hear you don't need this place anymore. Plus, I'm figuring you don't want to know. I don't want to know. Why open up the goose that lays the golden eggs?" Bruce frowned, scratched his chin. "Why the hell did I say that?"

He gave John a shove and closed the gate. John stared at his people. They were still his people. People he and his father took care of and… he ducked his head as he heard the roar of a helicopter.

It hovered low to the ground and in front of the gate. A little man with the emerald cufflinks sat inside. A broad smile lit his features. He wagged his finger admonishingly at John, pointed upwards, and the copter flew up and deposited him on the roof. Then, the wee man leaned over the ledge. He pointed to the clouds. John looked up. He saw sky. When he returned his gaze to the roof, the man and helicopter had disappeared.

3. A Problem with Cows

Emerging from a rainbow, the wee man sneezed. A smile touched his lips at the sight of the familiar room. It felt like weeks since he last returned home. He unstrapped a glass disk from his back before plopping down on a straw chair to catch his breath. All appeared normal. The lumps and indents of the pillows still held the shape of his head, a swirl of silks eddied in an endless twirl of unseen air, and sunlit dust thickened the dirt floor. More importantly, the clay chests still lay closed, woolen bags remained hung on their pegs, and a small barrel that smelled disturbingly of water leaned sealed, against the far wall.

Into the larger of the clay chests, Jeremy placed a wide concave lens. It glinted with colors. He winked at them and they twinkled back. From the third woolen bag, he wiped clean and ate a stick of zucchini. With a *tsk* and a loosening of his tie, he set to work with a broom. He had been away from home too long.

Outside, his goat Bernie bleated. The wee man frowned. It was unlike the black and white billy to be needy. He stiffened his grip on his broom and waited. The wood felt solid in his hands. Soon enough, a sound like sizzling eggs followed by a large thump entered through the window. Jeremy Tucker, the wee man took a peek outside and then grabbed a lump of coal from the smaller chest for that is the best thing to do if you spot a dragon in your garden.

After all, dragons have a terrible sense of smell. In fact, after blindfolding many dragons at various birthday parties over the years, Jeremy realized that many dragons couldn't smell the difference between a lemon and the ocean. They could, however, locate sweet things like a hawk sees a rabbit. This was precisely why Jeremy always challenged dragons to wine tastings using dry wines.

Shrugging, he massaged the coal against his skin. Dragons also ignored anything really dark, figuring that the dark thing was something that they had already burnt.

Lastly, before leaving, Jeremy Tucker, wee man and leprechaun, lifted the lid to a gourd and dropped in a pair of emerald rings and the shamrock pin just as another goat squealed. Frowning, he grabbed his shovel and a jar of the cherry preserves from a silver tree-shaped stand. He covered both with coal dust and then walked outside.

"Hey! Dragon!" he called. The dragon turned its long snout towards the voice, but couldn't find the coal-covered man. It finished swallowing the goat. Jeremy Tucker slapped the dragon's hind leg with his shovel.

"Scat!" he said.

The dragon's eyes widened. It smelled charcoal. It nodded as if that made sense. Before it, the great beast saw a fence of twelve-foot zucchini and something that looked like a rabbit burrow.

The next thwack left a dull pain that shivered through its scales. The dragon craned its neck and looked down, seeing nothing that could be hitting it. After a third strike, the dragon backed away breaking a fence post. It looked about nervously.

"You're not a ghost," it declared uncertainly.

The leprechaun said nothing. He turned the handle of his shovel and this time prodded the beast with its edge. The metal clanged against scales.

"What are you?" the dragon demanded, hissing steam. Again, Jeremy didn't answer. This time, he stabbed the dragon with a thrust. The dragon, unharmed, but unnerved, backed away. It roared and flame arced over Jeremy. Fire touched down well behind the wee man setting alight Jeremy Tucker's poor marshmallow field. White puffs smoldered blackly and crisped on the vine. Jeremy fumed like his crop. How dare the dragon set flames to lick his crop? This was no lollipop orchard! He was not even behind on his taxes… well, not too far behind.

An armored tail's arrival brought him back to the present as the great beast turned this way and that trying to spot the ghost. The wee man jumped over it and then ducked under it.

The tail's jagged barb spiked several holes in the ground both to the wee man's left and right. A gopher popped up from one of these to shake its fist. The dragon stared through wisps of black cloud. It stomped towards the gopher.

"Are you the ghost that keeps hitting me?" it asked imperiously. The gopher squeaked and dove down. Debris puffed upwards even as a clawed foot smashed town on the earthen tunnel that marked the gopher's escape route.

"There," the dragon nodded. "Done with ghosts!" Just as the flat of the shovel struck again. It rang like a warped bell. The dragon leaped.

"Ghost," it said, "Are you still there?"

Jeremy grinned seriously and popped a smoldering marshmallow into his mouth barely remembering to puff it out. The taste surprised him.

Not bad, he thought, *these might sell well at festival.* He must remember to give dragons credit for inventing toasted marshmallows. His fingers plucked one more burnt treat, causing the dragon to spin towards the motion, but again, it saw only earth, plants, and charred material before it. Jeremy held his breath. The dragon's great golden eye mere inches from the wee man's face. Luckily, the charcoal held even when his hand did not. A flap from the dragon's wing tore the shovel from him. It clattered against a rock once before the dragon's tail thrashed towards the sound. Jeremy winced as the shovel shattered.

The dragon took one step away. Could it smell Jeremy's sweat? *No*, Jeremy assured himself. T*hat would be impossible.* Sweat's not sweet. He waited a beat, then deciding the dragon would not be chased away, carefully loosened the lid to the preserves before flinging it as hard as he could towards a tree beyond his zucchini gate. The dragon darted towards the preserves. The jar shattered. Yellow eyes narrowed. Nostrils flared. The dragon patted its stomach. It purred. With a slice of its tail, it mowed down a section of the zucchini, then slowly got up on its claws and tiptoed toward the cherry preserves.

"This is fine preserves!" the dragon said, scooping up the contents with its furry tongue. Chuckling, the beast scooped the pieces of the jar with its claws and launched itself in the air. It licked each clay fragment clean. It roared once and then circled the garden. When it soared above the roof of Jeremy's house it shouted.

"Good-bye, ghost! Next time remember, I like apple preserves better."

Jeremy shook his head.

Trumpets blared. The sound travelled over hill and river from the south. The pink trade road restricted to the width of a path as if shouting, *You're not welcome!* Some trees, much to their shame, lost a coat of leaves. Apples deserted their orchards unwilling to be part of trees lacking the proper machismo. They rolled towards farms looking for a bathtub to bob in. Jeremy covered his mouth. It was impossible to tell if the fruit was committing suicide or just looking to relieve stress. The horns sounded again. *Feather and spit! Someone must have spotted the dragon.* Jeremy turned without washing and ran, charcoal colored, towards the village, only slightly annoyed at having caked his Armani suit with coal dust.

When the wee man arrived, the local folk were already busy gathering up maidens. They were fools. Most dragons didn't care if their food was male or female. Rather, the perfume or garland of flowers placed around the sacrifice's head attracted them. If only they would just put the perfume and garland of flowers on a stalk of broccoli, everybody would be better off.

The process was well under way. A greasy haired, slack jawed regent measured the prospective townswomen with a concerned look. He lifted an arm, pinched a waist, and continued. Three women he ordered placed under guard for inspection and cleansing. The midwives turned their backs. They felt responsible for each life they brought into the world and would not witness this. Only one, a farmer named Gaebil Henry, protested.

"I say we go after the dragon." He shouted. "Show it the strength of our arms and the vigor of our hearts."

"Say that when you gain a son," Fran May answered. Gaebil lowered his head. He had but three daughters, two of which were on the cart to be taken away.

"We shall have a festival to honor the maiden chosen by week's end," the regent announced, ignoring all.

"A week under a dragon's wing?"

"A short enough time to pray for a soul and give proper homage to one who would surrender her life for you, Fran," a midwife answered.

The regent paused and nodded. This was enough of an explanation. Townspeople shifted and fretted, but no one wanted to be the one to prove his heart empty to the midwives and parents. A blast of the horn later, the village gates pulled open, and maidens, regent and guard left.

Jeremy Tucker watched the carriage pass. Unhappy, but proud women stared out the windows at him. A tightness filled him.

"Stop," he yelled. "You don't have to… the dragon won't, if you…" Horses trotted briskly down a paved trade road. The whip beat an inconsistent pace. Jeremy chased. By the first curve, they stopped. The little man caught up, jumped and placed both hands on the window. Silk curtains brushed his hands. Then, strong hands grabbed his wrist. A man wearing tinkling silver ringed chain mail hauled him up to glare at him. The man's moustaches barely hung lower than his frown. One of the sacrificial candidates shrieked. The man tutted at Jeremy.

"Now, you see what you've done. You've upset them."

Feet dangling, the wee man faced the driver. He worked at a charming wink, but the driver interrupted him.

"Jeremy Tucker," the driver called out, "you're lucky no one ever found the cow." Jeremy sagged. The chain mailed man shook him. Jeremy opened his mouth trying again to speak, but before he could get a word out or spin a tale, they threw him at a tree. The wee man struck, thudded like a bag of flour, and sputtered.

"No, Jeremy. Never again," the driver said and with a flick of his whip, the carriage rumbled onwards. Jeremy rubbed his head and rump.

The wee man stared for a moment, charcoaled hands on charcoaled lapels, then turned and went straight to the house of Gaebil Henry.

Gaebil was a pretty man with prettier daughters.

"It is the giant Corp O'Rat's doing." Jeremy accused. "He controls the dragons. You know it. There's not a reason to sacrifice anybody if we take up arms against Corp O'Rat."

"Oh, aye, probably," Henry sighed, "but a giant is worse than a dragon by a fair step. And O'Rat's the worst giant anybody's ever heard of. Feathers and spit, man, I hear he's even starting to go after the other giants. If O'Rat can take them on… Better to ignore him and deal with the dragon. A dragon you can reason with, but the giant Corp O'Rat…"

"Corp will eat all the crops, ruin the land, and turn the dragons wild and you'd do nothing but pine for a daughter not even dead yet."

"It's your fault, Jeremy."

"My fault?"

"You bought the cow from Jack."

"I've tried to make…"

"You took the milk of human kindness away from us."

"That cow was nearly dry. She gave little milk."

"And did you try to milk her, Jeremy? And did you try to mate her? No, you cut her up and cooked her up for a family dinner."

Jeremy turned and kicked Gaebil's cooking pot. The pot shuddered and coins began bouncing about inside like boiling eggs.

"I chased the dragon away," Jeremy said finally.

"That'll do no good. The regent'll just call it back and try to make a deal."

"But…"

"It's tradition. No one argues with tradition. Why do you even try?" Gaebil's eyes widened as Jeremy's cheeks reddened. The coal-covered man turned away. Absently, he pocketed the gold he had conjured.

"Why did you never tell?" Jeremy asked.

"And risk the hangman's noose myself." Gaebil shifted a curio. "I'll warn you again. Stop. You'll end up doing no one any good."

"I feel guilty."

"You!" Gaebil dropped the curio, "I didn't think it was allowed."

"I know! It's a terrible sin," the leprechaun paused and studied a gold coin with an odd nostalgic glint, "We were becoming cold, hard. Like these, Gaebril." He flipped one of the coins from his hand into his pocket. "I thought eating the cow would do us some good. Do you know I've even started collecting beans again?"

"No."

"It's true. Beans."

"Jeremy have you forgotten what beans are?"

"Protein and fat, Gaebil."

"Nay, Jeremy. They are sustenance. Sustenance."

Jeremy Tucker turned and walked out the door and back towards his burrow. If even a father about to lose his daughter wouldn't listen…

"Beans! What are you planning, Jeremy Tucker!" Gaebil had come out of his house. Folks stirred. Jeremy's name roused them.

"What are you up to?" Fran May repeated.

"Beans! Did he say, beans?" Another fretted.

His name was enough for most of the locals. His name combined with the threat of beans was too much to ignore. They grabbed hayforks, sticks, rocks and whatever else they could find. With a whoop and a roar executed with the fury of a well-practiced mob, they charged after the little man. Jeremy hopscotched the cobblestone road and bounded onto a street post, an old glee bubbling up inside him as he ducked in and out of hills and between the boles of trees. Ah, how he still loved to be hunted. Too few bothered these days. Townsfolk roared and chased, tripped and stumbled, and slowly thinned as the hours passed.

As the chase dwindled so did his smile. They dispersed. His problem did not. He frowned as the last of his pursuers gave up the hunt. He turned and glanced at a youthful moon. Looked at the beans in his hand. He had already planted one. He had two more.

"Well, Johnny, you've climbed the stock and grabbed some treasure, but there's still the girl, the harp and the giant. Ah lady, am I mad? Still planting seeds in other people's gardens when I've got all my gold and not a threat to it." He looked at a rainbow. It stared back as if it were frowning at him. "I… curse that cow."

A registered letter came.

So, Johnny, the BEAN stock has grown as promised and I see you want to join us. We do need you. One of the big boys, a real corporate giant, is after us. If we're not careful he might swallow us whole. Believe me, neither of us want a hostile takeover of BEAN. I can't get you an appointment. There are too many at BEAN who are concerned with your family tree to do that, but I would like to see you. We could use the help. By the way, you are not a major shareholder, Jack. You shouldn't tell people that. It'll make people expect more out of you than you're ready or able to give.

Yours sincerely,

JTL

John reread the letter a couple of times. He wondered which giant was after BEAN. It could be Pfizer, Merck, Johnson and Johnson, or maybe Elan. *Elan might make some sense, since the little man looks Irish. Little man?* He paused. *Why little man.* He couldn't push away the description. Somehow size seemed integral to the person. It was a particularly un-PC thought.

John scanned the letter again. For the life of him he couldn't remember the little man's name. He must have said it. John wouldn't have signed away his company without even knowing the man's name, would he? JTL? John smiled suddenly. Jack. His name must have been Jack. He was sure he had heard the little man say the name Jack.

4. It Ain't Worth Beans

Looking at his watch, John realized he was late. His appointment was set for now. He straightened his tie, took a deep breath, and ran down the blacktop to the misnamed one-story building called the Wicket Watch Towers.

Cars, mostly SUVs, stuffed the parking lot, but every so often a hybrid snuck its way in. The larger cars beeped menacingly as John brushed by them in an effort to squeeze between spaces. *The hybrid owners must escape through sunroofs*, he thought, noting the claustrophobic spacing. He didn't linger though because, as Mother often chastised, *not being early is being overdue.*

He tried to ignore the odd inscriptions beneath him. Several of the lines here appeared wrong. The road was filled not just with yellow parallel stripes, but several enclosed boxes and even a circle or two. The circles fielded X's inside them. John dutifully skipped and jumped through one set that hopscotched in front of a staked out area of naked earth that come spring might host a garden. Slightly out of breath, he reached the towers. The old office building was squat and longer than it was high. It had the feel of an old elementary school with its white cinder block walls and red metal doors.

John opened the front door and searched for the directory. He couldn't believe how many businesses had taken up residence in the Towers. The air smelled of ammonia.

Someone bustled by wearing a green sweater and bruised blue jeans. The building lacked a staircase, but there was a ramp to the lower offices where Lisa Fischer of Baron's awaited him. John thought it a little strange that Baron's was not listed in the office directory, but the address was right and the suite number seemed to jive.

The first time John had been interviewed had been part of a high school writing project, but back then he got to interview his questioner too. That made it easier and even though he was no longer a media virgin, being in the spotlight didn't suit him. These past weeks had taught him great sympathy for Richard Nixon's infamous sweat.

Mother tried to help. She insisted he needed more suits. *One oughtn't be photographed wearing the same jacket twice.* He compromised and bought two new ties. Today was a red tie day.

Many of the rooms seemed to bare quasi-governmental names like the Institute for Wiretapping Surveillance Overlook Advocacy Foundation or the USRCAITTVA which boasted so long a name that when he asked no one knew what it stood for and most people couldn't even remember the full acronym. They just called it the U.S. Cavity. The office workers all had shifty eyes. He was tempted to enter the Flying Monkey Institute, but when he saw pictures of cosmonauts, astronaut monkeys and the model gyroscope kept under glass, he kept on going. Besides, he really was late.

Baron's took up two rooms in the WW Towers. The logo looked really sharp and made John feel proud. That he would be in Baron's made this a hallmark day.

The lobby was furnished with metal and glass coffee tables, low stools, and a male secretary who looked entirely too perfect. His suit was so deep in color it seemed objects would get sucked into it. His smile was neither large nor small and yet somehow seemed both formal and sincere. His tie made John glad that he had bought a new one. The flag pin on his breast was oddly comforting and perfectly perpendicular.

"John Fasola." He announced as if they were old colleagues. "Welcome to Baron's. Ms. Fischer is just finishing up a phoner and will be with you momentarily." A moment later, a light flashed on his phone and he nodded. He rose so smoothly there wasn't a single visible ripple in the fabric of his suit.

John nodded, impressed. Then again, this was Baron's. Lisa Fischer's interview would certainly be different.

She sat behind a mahogany desk, with only one folder on it. It looked thick. Her 26 inch flat screen monitor had several windows open simultaneously. A quick glance revealed one open to the Corporation of Ordinary Wares Website (Apparently, no one had shut it down), one opened to a recipe page that read "Legumes for every day" and, of course, the BEAN website. The S&P ticker flowed across the top of the screen. Every light on her phone was flashing, but she ignored them all to focus on John S. Fasola. For a long time, she did nothing but stare. John felt measured and thought back to his previous interview experience. He sincerely doubted she would want to know what his favorite color was or which musical act made him want to dance.

His heart pounded.

The office was utilitarian. One desk, one chair, one metal lamp, a file cabinet that looked empty, a bookcase lay empty, devoid of books, tchakas, family or vacation photoss, and apparently Lisa Fischer did not believe in pencils for there were only pens in the office. Along the back wall rested a stiff leather couch. The cushions looked like black bricks. John sat himself there because it seemed the furthest polite distance. The GQ receptionist entered and poured two glasses of lemonade.

John drank and made a face.

"Your mother's recipe," Miss Fischer intoned. She tapped her lip with a pen. "For a sweet man you sure do like sour things,"

"I'm sorry. My mother…"

"Your mother lives with you." She stated.

"No, she…"

"That's sweet. Taking care of your mother." She placed a hard disc recorder between them. She pressed record. "This is so I don't misquote you. Do you mind?" John shook his head. "Would you mind saying it out loud, so I can record your permission?" John did.

She dusted her blazer and unbuttoned a sleeve. A heart dangled free from a bracelet. John wondered whose it was.

The little charm was gold even though everyone knows that silver is better luck.

"John," she began. His attention flicked away from the bauble and returned to her face. Her dark hair made her face appear almost ghostly white. Oddly, her teeth were imperfect. They were too yellow and somehow looked raw. A pen tapped against her cheek. There was no notepad or even a sticky anywhere in sight.

"John how do you feel about the fact BEAN has just been indicted for tampering with the FDA and is accused of producing fraudulent documents for its many drugs?"

"What?"

"Are you aware that BEAN broke into the FDA, tampered with its computers, and illegally deposited forged documents giving themselves approval to distribute four drugs?"

"They did?"

"Can I take that for affirmation?"

"No, I…"

"Further, are you aware of the danger you are in? Distributing thousands of pills with no proof of short term or long term side effects?"

"I am? Wait! What do you mean…?"

"Then you admit it! You are BEAN."

John shook himself. Her focus was predatory.

"No!" he stuttered, "What do you mean I'm responsible?" he stuttered.

"Come now, Mr. Fasola, we both know that you are BEAN. You are the only person who can be linked to the company in the world. Besides, you don't expect us to believe that you just stumbled onto it?" She stood smoothing her blazer, "Oh, it's a pretty story, John. They just came up to you and exchanged the shares for your company. You didn't check them out, didn't have your lawyers or accountants research them. Oh no, that's not how you do business, you just shook hands and exchanged a concern whose raw materials were worth 1.6 million dollars for 45,000 dollars in stock. Is that really what you expect us to think?"

"I… It's the truth," he said. "I was…" he thought of his mother, "an idiot. I got lucky."

"Really, Mr. Fasola, the pen tapped loudly against the mahogany. You got lucky." She rose to pace the room, her heels clacking on the floor. John wondered how she managed not to leave any marks. The tile was as smooth as an ice rink after the Zamboni. Suddenly, she towered over him. "Well, who was it you made the deal with?"

"Jack." He whimpered.

"Jack what?"

"I don't know."

"You don't know." She sounded deadly, not at all like he imagined a reporter for Baron's should sound. Dimly, a part of him noted that there were no articles on the wall and the lobby had no copies of the newspaper. He pushed himself back into the couch as she pressed closer.

"You expect America to believe that you signed away your company, your life's work, for $45,000 worth of a stock you never heard of and you didn't even find out the man's name"

"I…" He thought for a moment. "Look, I have a letter from him. He's real." John passed her the registered letter from a folder he'd brought. She looked at it hungrily.

She stepped back. Turned her back on him to read. She had a nice back.

"It's addressed from your factory." She said, still facing away from him, "And what exactly is a JTL?" The scanner buzzed and an image of JTL's letter appeared on the monitor. John hadn't noticed the watermark before. It kind of looked like a cauldron. Overdramatically and insincerely, she sighed.

"I had hoped you would be cooperative. There was nothing in your history to say you wouldn't be." She left a red mark on her cheek with the pen. "For God's sake, you never even cheated on your tax forms. Personal or business!

That's why you nearly went out of business before you saved yourself with this BEAN scam."

John rose and made a face at her. The lemonade really was sour. He smoothed out his red tie, his power tie. Clearing his throat, he undid a length of thread from the sleeve. She studied him. Her hands were perfectly still.

"This is not an interview." He said quietly. It wasn't. Once he said it, he was sure he was right. This was certainly not the profile piece about a man suddenly made good that they had pitched to him.

"This is not happening." He said with a bit more force. He stared at her pen. She had never scribbled anything down, couldn't have scribbled anything down. With ferocity he slammed the lemonade down. The liquid splashed. Lisa blinked. It felt like a jump. Quickly, John untucked his shirt and tried to dry the liquid, to erase the stain he left in the immaculate room. The lemonade burned his fingers. He somehow doubted (despite its lemoniness) that it was very much like Pledge.

"Well," she said, studying his hands. John sat down again and stuffed JTL's letter into a scuffed brown briefcase and dramatically turned the combo lock.

"You're not a reporter," he accused.

She pivoted.

"Look at the very least we need to discover how this cyber terrorism was accomplished, John. How did BEAN hack into so many federal computers? You must know something." She paused and looked directly at the middle plaque on her otherwise Spartan wall. It had a strange glass eye on it. "You weren't very forthcoming with the FTC or the FDA. What I said was true. They are filing charges and you're the only one they have to file them against." Her expression softened and she hung her dark blazer on the chair. She sat down on the couch and patted the cushions.

John instinctively held his briefcase to his chest. Her eyes and teeth smiled. The change was too quick, too abrupt. "There's no question that BEAN is guilty of fraud and computer tampering. You are the only person in the world who has made any money off BEAN."

"That can't be… true"

He looked at the exit only to see the shadow of the GQ receptionist hulking there. John pinched the bridge of his nose. Like she was stalking a nervous animal, Lisa rose and took his hand and led him back to the couch.

"Take this opportunity, Mr. Fasola. It isn't always offered."

"I'm not even a major investor," he said lamely. "BEAN's marketcap… I should have… look at the car I drive. Lots of people have made money off of BEAN."

Miss Fischer rose and turned towards the door.

"This was supposed to be a friendly meeting, John." She shook her head. "You'll be receiving a subpoena by the end of the week. I was hoping you would be reasonable. If you are an honest man, a good American who cares about the hundreds of thousands who might be poisoned by BEAN products, help us. Here's my card. If you help us, it'll make it easier to believe your story."

All the abrupt shifts made John feel dizzy.

"Who are you?" he asked. She smiled and shook her head, tapping the card.

"I expected better of you, Mr. Fasola" She steered him outside.

"Wait! This makes no sense."

The door slammed. It reverberated with the memory of Bruce's voice. "I don't even let them in. I don't know when they get here, but no one goes in and no one leaves." John felt like a pharmacist's scale. In his mind he weighed the registered letter against the business card from Lisa Helen Fischer, Special Agent- Department of Homeland Security. She'd made it clear. It wasn't really a contest. Somehow, he would have to scale the fortress. Somehow, John would have to break into the giant's castle, er… factory.

5. Not a Military Depot

Clouds sealed the sky. Shadows spread. Winter's hand tore, leaving skeletal branches. Houses crouched in a tight circle, their aluminum siding bent like worn frowns. The ground beneath John was all patchy mud mixed with gray and brown grass except for the small barricades of fallen leaves that fronted each. The wind held its breath. Nothing made sound except for the odd hoot or speculative howl.

Darkness enfolded the cul-de-sac interrupted only by the tiny halo of streetlamps, porch lights, and a few premature Christmas lights. Well, that and the light that leaked from living rooms and the passing cars. Fine, it wasn't really dark at all, but it was night and John thought it was spooky.

John opened the passenger-side door of his silver Volvo hatchback. He was dressed in a black t-shirt, dress slacks, and black dress shoes. In the glove compartment, he removed a black ski mask. Carefully, he covered the collection of James Bond films he used for research purposes in the back seat with a black blanket.

A few old reports and a collection of pens, from his factory days littered the space under the seats. The pens and stationary had his old company's name misprinted on it: "The Corporation for Ordinary Wares". The typo still grated. Once COWs were important. Now, his C O W vanity plate could almost refer to the Corporation of Obsolete Wares.

There was enough dairy in the state that John didn't worry that he could be ID'ed by the license plate, but the pens worried him. He scooped them up into a Hefty bag, feeling the weight of his actions, and ditched them in a lump of loosely raked leaves. The pile looked suspiciously asymmetrical to him. He considered going round back to see if he could find a rake, but checking his watch, he decided to leave the piles for later. Instead, he grabbed a briefcase full of cash out of the trunk, put it on the passenger seat, and turned the ignition. A gust of hot air hit him. The heat felt good.

He popped the briefcase and took out his target list. The next nearest man lived twenty minutes from John's home. He drove. The clock reminded him it was 3:00 in the morning. He refused to yawn. He pressed his lips tightly together and slapped his face. He even began driving faster to try to force himself to be more alert.

He parked on Cheshire Street, opened the glove compartment, and pulled the ski mask over his face. Soon now, he would reach his goal.

Burt Acrimony's house was at the bottom of the hill. John headed towards it. He crouched behind bushes.

"Does everyone in this neighborhood need to use those stupid lights," he complained to himself as another motion detector lit the street around him.

His briefcase hit him as he moved. It would leave bruises. Last week's collection were just starting to fade.

He saw a cop car, ducked down, and covered the brass initials on his briefcase with his hand. Looking up, he scribbled down the policeman's license plate number. The car had a broken taillight. John felt it his duty to report it.

Acrimony's house was surrounded by a tangle of thorn bushes that pretended to be a garden. If he had to break in, he doubted he'd ever find his way through. Luckily, Burt had his mailbox on a post near the curb. John opened his briefcase and took out one of the envelopes. He opened it to make sure the money was still there.

The mailbox creaked open. John dove to the ground. He swallowed mud. The briefcase thumped him in the head and envelopes flew causing motion sensors to pop into life. He froze. His watch showed it to be 3:37.

Stealthily, rolling and tumbling, John collected the envelopes while managing to stay beneath the top of the thorn bushes. His heart pounded. His lungs demanded. He kneeled down and tried to ignore the lights.

A woman appeared in the window. He remembered her from company picnics. He smiled a *hello* then hit himself in the head. She screamed. He heard it through the closed window. John stood. He thrust an envelope into the Acrimony mailbox and ran up the hill. Motion sensors tracked him like spotlights following a dancer.

He dove against the car door.

"Ow," he said, hitting his head. He glanced at his watch, fumbled the keys, slammed the briefcase into his knee, tore off his ski mask, picked up the keys, opened the door and listened for sirens. "Behind schedule," he groaned as his tires squealed against the sudden acceleration.

Someone is getting paid off. That was what Lisa thought when she saw John S. Fasola place the first envelope. She waited for him to leave and verified that John left money. *Not much though. Only a few hundred dollars.* She left the cash and hurried back to her car just in time to see John driving off. She slipped inside her Valkyrie 280Z, turned on her flash recorder and watched him.

"Vanguard Ave. and Chimera Way. Fasola seems to be repeating the same procedure. Man does the best Jerry Lewis impression I've ever seen," she paused and stared at him again, "maybe Peter Sellers… no, not really Jim Carey at all." She watched him sprint back to the car, chased by the sounds of neighborhood dogs. After the fourth house, she opened her thermos and poured a cup of coffee.

"Maybe it's blackmail. Maybe these people know something? Ooh, he hit another tree. Should have named the guy George." She stared at him and then resumed talking into the mic. "When's he going to BEAN," she sighed, "Guys, it can't be him. Unless he's… I've been following him for the last five miles with my lights on and I swear he still hasn't noticed me." She placed the recorder down. "I'm going to give up for tonight." She clicked it off, turned the ignition, and made a U-turn. From a short distance away she heard an "Ow."

"Twenty-five more," he sighed. Twenty-five who hadn't found jobs yet, twenty-five whose families were struggling because of his good fortune. John would not let them starve. John would not be the one to let Tiny Tim die. He would not scrooge his money.

He grimaced as he passed a post office. It would be so much easier to mail the envelopes, but then someone might find out who was giving the money away and he didn't want his former employees to feel guilty about accepting it. Bruce and some of the others might suspect him, but he didn't want it confirmed and he certainly didn't want credit. After all, it was John who had cost them their jobs.

He ended his journey at the Home Depot. Lisa Fischer's threat still haunted him. He had to find out about BEAN. He glanced at the James Bond collection in the back seat and smiled craftily.

Two hours later, he entered the hardware store. A forklift hefted crates of lawn mowers to top shelves where no one could reach or buy them. He passed by the customer service desk, rows of lumber, over 700,000 nails of differing sizes and densities, six screw driver displays, a set of hibachi grills, paint thinners, paint, and aluminum siding before he found his target… the man in the orange apron.

"Excuse me," John said.

"Yes," the clerk answered.

"I was wondering if you could help me. I'm looking for a grappling hook and a harpoon gun."

The clerk stared at his customer. John was still clad in black from head to foot with a mud-stained black briefcase clenched in his right hand. The guy was certainly dirty. Mud also smeared his face and shirtsleeves. A few leaves even lay matted to the muck. Over the loudspeakers the musak station choose that moment to play the theme song from Mission Impossible.

The salesman sniggered.

"What?" John said angrily.

"You planning to rob Rushmore? No, Fort Knox, right?"

"Listen…"

"Is that briefcase going to explode? Sorry, sorry."

"This is not how you treat a customer. I came in here with..."

"Well," the clerk said, "I don't know where you can find a harpoon gun, but you might be able to find a grappling hook in a sporting store. Maybe an outdoors shop that sells to mountain climbers. But there's not much harpooning around here. Just tell me one thing."

"What?"

"Are you Batman?" and the clerk aimed an imaginary harpoon grapple up at the ceiling beams.

John stifled an urge to hit the man. He turned stiffly around and shook his head. As he was leaving he heard,

"Do you know who that was?" a customer asked.

"No, who"

"I saw him in the paper. That's Mr. Bean."

"You mean that English guy?"

"No, the guy who runs the BEAN factory. Guy's supposed to be worth millions and millions."

"No shit, really." he said, "I just… a millionaire."

"He looks eccentric. What was he like?"

John left the building.

He drove past the BEAN factory again. Three stories of brick and cement defied him. How could he climb that? His dress shoes would never give him enough traction. He thought about, but refused to buy black sneakers. "Never buy something you'll only wear once," he heard the ghost of his father say, "It's wasteful and a shame. Now if you can get someone else to buy it for you…"

He cleared his mind. He could do this. He studied the best. The song in his head confirmed it, "No one does it better!" he mouthed, building up his confidence. He considered tactics.

John knew wearing black was a prerequisite to do this sort of thing. One had to wear black. That was the rule. Occasionally, one could wear a drab green, but John was nowhere near the jungle, so black t-shirt, slacks, and dress shoes would have to do. He felt quite the bohemian, though he had hoped to feel like a cat burglar.

That night, he returned to the Corporation of Ordinary Wares' factory site ready to break in. He parked in the parking lot across the street. The owner, Harvey, wouldn't mind… especially after hours. Crouching, he peered over the dash. A truck rumbled by and he froze. The driver didn't even tap his brake lights. John was James Bond… no, ninja invisible. Counting to thirty, he waited before daring to sit up. He had to admit… this was fun. He wondered if he missed his calling. And then, he saw the gate.

He forgot to buy wire clippers. How was he supposed to get past the chain link fence without wire clippers? Beyond the fence, he noticed an open second-story window with a metal trashcan placed only a few feet away. He considered using it.

"Too easy. It could be a trap," John said, fingering one of his James Bond videos. Still, he looked at the open window. It certainly looked more inviting than scaling his way to the roof with a grapple and a harpoon gun. Revving the engine, he frowned. "…Probably a trap," he repeated and smiled. He rolled up the window.

The best way to get into a guarded factory is with a beautiful woman. The second best way is with a pebble. Both methods work with about 95% accuracy according to the James Bond collection. John didn't want to involve a beautiful woman, though he had called a modeling agency earlier in the day to find out how much a decoy cost per hour. They suggested he call something called Central Casting and hire an actress. John immediately vetoed that plan. He knew from his factory days to avoid hiring someone associated with a union for a day job. Therefore, the pebble would have to do.

He looked dubiously at the small gray pebble in his hand, flipped it a few times, and held his breath. *Don't worry. This always works*, he thought comfortingly.

The security guard leaned against the fence. He stationed himself about three feet to the right of the gate's door. An aluminum card-table chair with a thermos on it stood by its side. There wasn't much cover, if you disregarded the used car lot on the other side of the street.

John hid behind a 1976 Buick, a black Buick. He peered through the cracked windshield and waited until the security guard looked the other way. John lifted the pebble, cocked his arm, and…

"What if they find out he was on duty when I broke in? Will they care? They might fire Sam. Sam's got three kids, John. How can you do that to Sam?" he asked himself. His rational side argued back.

"Well, maybe… but surely they can't fire him for succumbing to something as trial tested as the pebble gambit?"

"Shut up before someone hears you," another inner voice reminded him.

Sam leaned forward. John ducked down. A cool breeze made him shudder. *Coward,* his father's ghost called. *Just cooking up one damn excuse after another. I'd have been in there by now, boy.* He peered above the glass once more. Sam was facing him. *Idiot.* Mother's voice joined the chorus of people criticizing him in his head.

"I'm a bloody schizophrenic," John sighed, but the cacophony of voices seemed to harden his resolve. He waited, but heard no sounds of boots crunching. A wind whipped by him, but it travelled in the right direction. The security guard's nose couldn't scent him. John waited, trusting that the opportune moment would show itself. Then, the chain link groaned.

John peered over the edge. Apparently, Sam had decided this was a good time for a coffee break. He leaned back against the fence as if it were a vertical hammock, twisted the top of his thermos, and poured himself something that smelled like chicken soup.

"Okay," John said and crawled towards the trunk of the Buick. John got to his knees and saw Sam was still drinking. Holding his breath, he flung the pebble. It clinked off a dented hood. Sam ignored it. John stared at the security guard in amazement. Sam was good, very good. He was proud of himself. He had hired the man. Still, he knew that this would work. All those movies could not be wrong.

He picked up a stone and tossed it to Sam's right. It thumped against the fence. John ducked. The fence creaked.

"What was that?" Sam asked.

"Yes," John said, pumping his fist. He heard a squeal of iron. He flung another rock, further in the same direction.

"Who's doing that?"

John looked up to see Sam aiming a flashlight down the fence. The man looked agitated. This was it. John started sweating. Sam was obviously a pro. Who else would require three pebbles? John heaved the last rock straight into the fence. The fence rang. Sam jumped up and began walking towards the sound. John pulled down his ski mask and ran towards the unattended gate.

John flattened himself against the concrete wall of the factory wondering if it was a mistake to wear black when trying to scale a sand-blasted white concrete wall? He looked above him and saw a street lamp. Once again, he felt caught in a spot light. He edged towards the garbage can. Sam stood over a rock embedded in the chain link fence. He scratched his head with his flashlight, then bent to examine the rock from the underside.

John picked up the trashcan. It was lined with some kind of grease. His grip slipped. The can dropped. It struck his foot. John screamed. Sam turned. John spun. The can tipped and rolled. A beam of light shot towards him. John's foot throbbed. The beam moved closer. John dove against the fallen trashcan. Sam yelled, "Who's there?" John answered, "A cat" and then struck his head against the trashcan in frustration.

"Oh a cat," said Sam, relaxing. John looked up to the heavens and mouthed a *thank you*. The light beam began to turn from him.

"Wait a minute!" Sam said, and the light twisted around. "Who said it was a cat?" John closed his eyes. The gate creaked. He heard boot-steps.

"Idiot. Idiot. Idiot." John whispered to himself, then aloud he said doing his best Bruce, "It's Bruce!"

"Bruce?"

"Came early, Sam."

"Yeah? You came real early, Bruce," Sam said suspiciously.

"I…"

"You're not allowed back there. Why are you back there? Stand up."

"Ah… You caught me taking a whiz. You know those BEAN guys won't let us go in and I really had to… you know sometimes you…"

"Why don't you stand up?"

"Come on, Sam. Turn around. Let me finish. Give a guy a break. Would Mary want you looking at me?"

"Geez Bruce." But the light slowly made an arc. John sighed, relieved that he had insisted on writing all the company Christmas cards and knew every worker and their spouse by name. He looked at the window. It stood tall as Rapunzel's tower. Carefully, he righted the can.

"Are you done yet?"

"Too many beers" John laughed ruefully. He turned around to see the back of Sam's head nodding.

The slick bottom of his dress shoes threatened to spill him. Still, he balanced himself like a surfer on top of the lid and looked up at the window ledge a floor above him. He took a deep breath.

"Hey! You're not Bruce" called Sam. "Come down now!" John turned towards the voice. Sam removed his gun and stared at him.

"Sam, it's me." John called.

"I don't know who you are, but you will get down now!"

John remembered the black ski mask. He looked at the gun and then at the window and then back at the gun.

"It's me," John said again.

"Get down," Sam ordered.

John took a step to follow instructions. His dress shoes slipped on the lid. His arms pin wheeled. His feet danced to find balance. Sam took a step forward. John pitched forward. He closed his eyes. A shot rang out. John opened his eyes. Somehow, his hands were on the window ledge. He tried to scramble up. The shoes gave him no purchase. Another shot rang out. Flecks of stone dusted him from where the bullet impacted with the concrete.

"Get down!" Sam ordered again. John kicked off his shoes. His brown socks and feet grabbed at the texture of the concrete. Pulling and pushing, he levered himself over. He fell into blackness. Outside, he heard,

"Shoot."

6. Have You Ever Tried to Fit a Cow Through a Rainbow?

John remembered there being a file cabinet on the right, but when he reached out he felt wood. An earthy smell suffused everything. He stood and reached for the wall. More wood got in his way. The low thrum of a fan carried heat into the room. He tried again to navigate the darkness. Clunk.

"Ow."

He smacked into another wooden rectangular thing. He closed his eyes, figuring it would be easier to find his way in the dark that way. Probing in a circular motion, his fingers eventually found the light switch.

The room was full of crates. They read: kidney beans, pinto beans, green beans, lima beans, castor beans, soy beans, horse beans, broad beans, asparagus beans, hyacinth beans, butter beans, navy beans, civet beans, and phaseolus limensis. Staring at all the crates of beans made John feel a little gaseous. They also made him nervous, which made him wonder why there were no jumping beans in this collection.

"Why is there only one crate of each type of bean?" he further wondered, staring at the haphazardly stacked boxes. "If they're used in production, wouldn't they need… and shouldn't they be refrigerated?" John opened one box and found that it did indeed contain nothing but beans. He picked up a handful and sniffed them. The beans smelled rich and slightly salty. Returning them, he turned to the door.

Out of habit, he typed his old security code into the door. It was the only room in the whole factory that had a security lock. At least it was when John owned the factory. The door popped open. It never occurred to him how odd that was. He entered a narrow hallway with windows that overlooked the main factory floor. Cautiously, he edged towards the window.

Everything had been removed. Every vat, crane, conveyer belt, forklift, mixing station, press, and mold, was gone. Instead, in the exact center of the empty factory floor stood three standing lamps (the kind a professional photographer might use) and a concave mirror. John whistled.

He edged down the hallway, opening doors as he went. Three rooms were empty. The fourth room was not. Hundreds of paper airplanes littered the floor of that room. Rifling through them, John noticed that some were requests from the FDA, some were from the FTC, others were old inventory lists, and accounting sheets. There were letters from competitors and companies who wanted to provide BEAN some service or other. All were treated equally. Well, not exactly equally since the floor was littered with several different paper airplane designs.

It was the oddest organizational strategy John had ever heard of. Looking at the mess of folded paper, John wondered how BEAN was going to compute their taxes. No, he decided. This will never do. He sighed and began sorting them, creating neat little stacks.

A siren wailed. John stopped sorting. He remembered suddenly that he was in the middle of a crime and not responsible for what happened at the Corporation of Ordinary Wares anymore. *At BEAN*, he corrected himself. He rose and took another glance at the room. What he was looking for was not there, or if it was, it was not among the sixty airplanes he had unfolded so far. What he found would not placate Lisa Helen Fischer or the Department of Homeland Security.

He sighed.

Outside, John overheard an argument brewing. Carefully, he cracked the window.

"I can't let you in."

"We need you to let us in, sir," a policeman said.

"There's a burglar inside," Sam growled. He bounced agitatedly. "You have to do something."

Calmly, the officer answered.

"Unless you let us in or have the authority to let us in the building, we are not permitted to enter."

John ducked, but kept watching.

Sam scratched his head with his flashlight and looked nervously up at the windows. The guard seemed lost and searched for direction amongst the broken cars in the lot next door. They didn't answer which left him stuck. His prime instruction was to allow no one in the building and yet he needed to let these men into the building except that he had no way of getting into the building. No one ever provided him with a key!

It was a maze of thought too complex for poor old Sam. He wished he'd poured something stronger into his thermos. The officers looked disinterested.

"Can't you break the door down?"

"Not without permission or a warrant."

"I saw a burglar break in." a frustrated Sam screamed, "There are his shoes."

The trashcan sported a good-sized dent in it. John noted that he would have to replace it. One of the officers shined a flashlight and fingered the compression in the rim.

"I'd say about 180. Definitely, under 200 pounds." He announced. John felt affronted. There was no way he weighed a hundred and eighty pounds. Maybe one-seventy-five. The other officer put on some plastic gloves and retrieved one of John's black shoes.

"A second story man who uses tassels?"

"Will you give us permission to enter?" the first asked.

Sam walked towards the front door. It was well barricaded. Man-sized wooden crates and old factory equipment jammed against each other. He put a hand on a pipe and experimented with the idea of climbing. One of the policemen took off his hat to watch. Sam got about 4 feet off the ground and tried to reach for another window. His fingers stretched. An officer clambered up too, but neither could reach the ledge or anything that would gain them entry. Eventually, Sam sat on a wide wooden box with a broken slat and looked out across the parking lot.

"I suppose it doesn't matter. I'm not supposed to let anyone in."

"Can you call someone with the authority?"

"I… Don't you have probable something or other… can't you just…?" He pointed back at the building.

John closed the window. He tried to think of a good place to hide or a good way to escape. Silently, he blamed himself. He had hired too good a security guard. Sam had not been stymied by the pebble gambit as long as the security guards in the movies. *Of course*, he grinned, *knocking over the trashcan didn't help either.*

He watched a moment longer, then shrugged, and continued searching.

The third floor smelled oddly of burritos. A shiver ran up his spine as his stocking feet stepped from concrete steps to blue and beige commercial carpeting. He rubbed some warmth into his toes and felt tears in his socks.

Someone was playing the Chieftains in his old office. John listened to a reel updated with electric guitar and synthetic harp and frowned. *The drummer plays too strictly in four-four time. In fact,* a part of him groused, *the entire band clearly didn't understand the lyrics. It was obvious by the way they strum instead of pluck. I hate when they redo classics. If a song survives hundreds of years, why does it need to be modernized?*

A trace of light trickled from under the door. Suddenly, John couldn't move. Ahead of him, he heard bad singing and a stronger scent of burrito.

"What am I doing?" He asked, fingering the black ski mask. This was no time to play critic! The music stopped. From behind the door, a muffled series of claps could be heard, as if the man in his office ecstatically approved of the music. John retreated, and shivered again as his stocking feet hit the cold concrete. Suddenly, he noticed how dark it was. The hallway. The stair. The factory.

His eyes had adapted somewhat, but he was obviously unwelcome. He had broken into a place he had no business being in.

"JTL invited you," he reminded himself, but he didn't feel comforted. He had studied James Bond. He had broken the law.

"You might as well come in, Johnny," said the voice behind the door. Eyes dilating, he did.

JTL still looked polished. He wore a double-breasted tweed vest with a gray shamrock pinned to the lapel. Italian suede shoes stood under gray wool slacks. A tie as brilliantly orange as a jack o lantern, somehow managed not to be shocking. John took off his ski mask and held it against his chest like a supplicant.

"Have you ever had one of these, Johnny?" JTL said, holding out a microwaved burrito. "Of course, you have. Would you like another?"

John stammered.

"Course they would be improved if they added a little potato to the thing, but what meal couldn't stand a bit more potato?" JTL waited. He looked about and placed the burrito down and picked up three cans of barbecued beans. "It's an amazing country, Johnny." JTL began juggling the cans. "Imagine, acres of beans. Farmlands full of them. Do you even understand the implication of it all? No, I can see that you don't. You're used to it. Spoiled, I guess. Too used to farting away your own luck." His green eyes closed. "Johnny," he said seriously, "Have you ever tried to push a cow through a rainbow?"

"What?" John said.

"Have you ever tried to push a cow through a rainbow? You can't do it. They don't fit."

"You're…" but politeness stopped him from saying crazy.

"Think Johnny. Remember the stories? In just about half the stories, magic is either dying or fading. And do you know why?"

John shook his head.

"What are beans?" the leprechaun demanded.

"Vegetables?" John offered.

"No," the leprechaun slapped the desk, "they most certainly are not. They are sustenance." The wee man leapt on top of John's old desk, spun, kicked a metal file cabinet drawer closed, then hopped on top of it. John followed him mesmerized and alarmed. Papers tore and flew in the air. Then JTL winked and hopped back onto the table. With a high kick, he booted a lamp so that it spun six times before stopping at an angle that shone a light directly onto the wee man's his own face.

A glow shimmered from JTL's eyes to his teeth. His hands spread in a grand gesture.

"Think of it, Johnny. You can survive on only beans. They sustain you. Feather and spit, but they're magical stuff. Beans are sustenance. They give a land, a world its sustenance. The more beans… the more life. The more life…" he became quiet, "… the more luck, both good and ill."

"Would you mind if I called a doctor?" John said, thinking that the man needed a white room.

"And you have farms of it. Where I come from, if you had three beans in your hand you could name your castle, but that's not what's important right now, Johnny. What's important is that the Hindus were right."

"Hindus?"

"About the cows, Johnny. Listen to me. The Hindus are correct about cows."

"Cows?"

"Yes! That they are a higher type of good. Keep up, Johnny" JTL wrung his hands a little nervously. "Look. The less cows, the more apathy. You can see it in your own life. Is the world as caring a place with bison almost extinct and oxen completely gone?"

"Bison aren't cows." John complained.

"Johnny," the leprechaun said, shaking John by the shoulders. "You see my point don't you? A world that would devour its last cow, why that's a worse world than one that chops open its geese." A look of intense guilt filled JTL for a moment.

John was confused. John was more than confused; he was flabbergasted. This man was BEAN? This lunatic was JTL? A man who thought three beans could buy a castle? A man who tried to push a cow through a rainbow? What kind of man was he? He understood that the man was a genius. He had to be. After all, wasn't there a rule that all geniuses were a little loopy?

"And that's what the giants want, Johnny. They want us to eat all our cows. They want us to eat all our cows, so they can take over."

John stopped. He leaned against his old swivel chair and sat down. The bookshelves looked different, but that was because they were emptied of books and papers, and filled instead like a grocer's shelf with beans. The floor was covered by the same calm blue carpet that had always been there, except it was spotted with brown stains. Jeremy turned and loudly chomped down on his burrito. John tried to grab sense and spouted the first thing that came to mind.

"You're a vegetarian, aren't you?" John said, finally. The little man stared at him. He looked up at the fluorescent lighting and then back down at John.

"I used to be," he said, then turned suddenly, "Are you sure I can't offer you a bean burrito? It's got cheese."

The phone rang. John moved towards it. The little man waved him off. After the fourth ring, the answering machine took over.

"You have reached the offices of BEAN. Here to provide a better life for you and yours. We're sorry, but all lines are busy. Please wait and your call will be answered in turn." John stared aghast. He had always suspected that companies did this, but to see it in his very own office. JTL shushed him. "Or press 0 at any time to leave a message." The answering machine finished. JTL smiled.

"Hello," a deep voice said, "This is Officer Vader, from the fourth precinct. We've got a call that the um Biomicros… enderial… your factory on Jersey Street has been broken into." There was a pause. John and the leprechaun heard Sam yelling to the officer,

"Tell him that the crook's got a size nine shoe. Tell him that the crook's got a size nine shoe."

"We're setting up a perimeter, but if you want to make sure your intruder is caught, please authorize someone to enter the building."

"Setting up a perimeter with one squad car?" Sam demanded loudly.

"Shut up!" Officer Vader demanded. The leprechaun snorted, but John looked pale. JTL merely winked and started juggling cans of beans.

"Johnny, there are two giants after us." JTL said, performing double-flips from the top of the desk. The paper blotter hardly shifted. John edged towards the window. He considered leaping to get away from the madness, but JTL stopped him with a warning of—

"If you're going to do that, please put your mask back on, Johnny. You really don't want the giants' servants to identify you, do you?"

"Giants?"

"There are two giants." JTL confirmed. "Are you any good at maps?"

"Not really? What does this have to…?"

JTL unfolded a paper airplane. It contained a map that almost looked like the United States except the Floridian peninsula was a bit too small, and the Rocky Mountains were far too wide and tall. Heck, there were so many topographic squiggles around the Rockies that they made Everest look shrimpy.

"There are two giants who are after BEAN, Johnny. There's Buir O'Cassey who lives in the west," looking at a confused John, he added "to the left. Now, Buir used to be the biggest giant around and he still controls a lot, but over the years he's gotten older and has given more and more of his power to another. This giant feeds Buir all sorts of treats and lavishes him with luxuries, so that the giant Buir O'Cassey doesn't meddle. See, the second giant realized that it's next to impossible to kill Buir O'Cassey, so he decided to make him bigger and fatter so he would become slower and more tolerant."

The leprechaun fiddled with a letter opener and began to tidily slice his bean burrito into mouth-sized pieces. John wondered what a stroke felt like. Could he be asleep? He raised his hand, but Jeremy continued at a fiddler's pace allowing no time for disagreement or questions.

"Now this second giant, the Giant, Corp O'Rat, lives to the East." He drew a map of the United States on the back of an unread letter and pointed towards Boston. John stared at the twin maps, wondering why JTL required two maps. The little man stabbed at the new map, making John jerk forward.

"Are you listening, Johnny. This is important information. The second giant…"

"On the right." John said, sheepishly.

"Yes, Corp O'Rat lives to the right. The far right. He's the one who's really out to destroy us. We've got to stop him."

"Well," said John, giving in and finally trying a burrito "couldn't we just get this Buir O'Cassey to stop him. All you have to do is prove how unfair O'Rat's been?"

That evoked a deep breath and made the creases in Jeremy's face sag. Then, as if that was too much against his nature he dramatically jumped back on top of the file cabinet. The lamplight followed him.

"Oh no, Johnny. Can't do that. Tried that, Johnny. Been trying that for a while. Before I resorted to the use of beans. Buir is too content. The most that Buir will do is put a few limits on him for a while. Send him to his room, so to speak. Then after a while, Buir will forget about his edicts or decide that O'Rat has been become a good boy and remove his penalty. I've seen it time and again, feather and spit, but there are even those in the clan of O'Cassey who tell Buir O'Cassey it's not his affair at all to meddle with what Corp O'Rat does. Drives me mad sometime."

John agreed. JTL was mad.

He wished that JTL would climb down. The problem was it wasn't his furniture anymore. The metal groaned and scuffmarks scarred the 19th Century desk like a tap dancer held a competition on it. He wasn't sure that polish could fix it, but found his hands itching to try. He remembered his father behind that desk on the rare days the man kept still. Idly, he wondered if Jeremy had found the secret drawer yet. Father told him to always keep candy bars there in case of emergencies. It would be a bad place for beans. Jeremy leaped back to the desk and stamped on it, sensing he was losing John's attention.

"The problem is, Johnny, that the giant Corp O'Rat is eating all of us out of hearth and home. That giant is wasteful and without the cows to keep him in check… Do you see what I'm saying?"

John had an epiphany, *Bean and cheese burritos taste great,* but he answered, *No.*

JTL looked over his shoulder and mouthed something. He jumped down. The maps flipped into the air before fluttering away from the wee man. JTL ignored it and spoke even quicker.

"Let us say that you have a product like beans, Johnny. The product can be very helpful and can be made and sold inexpensively. O'Rat won't let you sell it. He gets Buir to tie you down and hold you hostage with his bloody tape. He keeps you like that so long, you're afraid your families are going to starve. So, you concede. You stop selling your beans or you give your product away. Oh, it has Buir's name on it and you'll curse him, after all, it was his tape that held you, but it wasn't his doing."

"But… You were held you hostage?" John interrupted, unable to keep up.

"The pudding is… O'Rat will start up business right after you've given up the shop. And if Buir's left anything of you other than bones, you'll see that O'Rat will sell a sicker bean and at twice the cost. It kills the luck, that does, Johnny, it simply kills the luck."

"So, what can we do?" Johnny asked, a bit swept up in the story.

"I've been watching you, Johnny. The way you killed your father's business was amazing." The little man whistled and slapped the tabletop. "I need you to help me do battle with Corp O'Rat. After what you did with the Corporation of Ordinary Wares, I know you could do damage to a giant."

The wee man stood in front of John and took his hand. The well-manicured hand was slick from burrito and cheese. The chatter finally stopped and John felt himself studied and weighed. The smile grew slowly tooth by tooth. John tried to retreat a step from JTL's cocky emerald eyes, but something deeper gripped. Something that seemed almost real. Almost sane.

"Johnny, I need you. Will you do it?"

7. Look, Look for the Rainbow

When Lisa Fischer's phone rang, she pulled her pillow over her head. The short fleece blanket kept her curled, but warm. In the distance, the TV she fell asleep to droned on. She yawned, turned, and tried to ignore the world, but the phone insisted. Blearily, she tried to find the alarm clock. It was too early for her eyes to focus. The caller was persistent and annoying- Three rings, a pause, then three more rings, a pause, then three more rings; whoever it was would not allow the answering machine to save her. Finally, she picked up the receiver and croaked "Hello."

Her director was irate. John Fasola was seen driving towards the BEAN factory. Where was she, he demanded to know. Lisa answered something, but even she didn't understand what she said. She thought she said something about three days of stakeout being too much for one doofus. She smiled. That sounded reasonable.

With a few well-enunciated comments, the boss woke her up. She pulled on a pair of jeans, a shirt from a pile of clothes on the floor and staggered to the bathroom. She allowed herself one swish of mouthwash and a corn muffin. Then, she was out the door.

She drove to the Bean Factory on Jersey Street and found John S. Fasola crouched behind a Buick throwing a series of rocks at a fence. Unbelievably, the security guard fell for it. After a moment's hesitation, she saw him run, narrowly miss a trashcan, and try to hide in the light of a streetlamp.

"This has got to be done for my benefit," she said, sipping on a convenience store coffee she had grabbed along the way. Then somehow, between gunshots and more slapstick, he entered the building. Lisa Fischer shook her head and leaned against the steering wheel.

The security guard rushed to the far corner of the building and entered a small booth. He picked up a phone. Lisa nodded. The guard was obviously calling the head of

BEAN. She looked at her watch and recorded the time of the phone call. They would finally be able to track him. She speed dialed her office and told them to locate the number for the BEAN parking lot security booth. "*Find out who was just called*," she told them.

She got out of her car. Scrunching her lips, she reached back in, opened the glove compartment and reluctantly pulled out a revolver. The thing felt cold in her hand. She balanced it with a grimace and aimed at the window and sighted someone on the third floor. As soon as the figure appeared, he vanished. He applauded her and then vanished. She gripped the gun tightly.

The COW factory loomed in front of her, a three story bland box that somehow looked like a prison. *Who else was in there,* she wondered, *how many*? "Might be too many," she said to herself. A feeling of dread shook her. Without understanding why, she locked the gun in the trunk.

She walked parallel to the gate, watching the security guard the whole time. The man was still on the phone animatedly talking to someone. He flung one out hand dramatically, stabbing the air to make his point, then turned to look back at the open window. Lisa smiled and slowed her pace. Someone must have said something disagreeable because Sam looked up, gestured wildly again and slammed the receiver down. After, he hunched his shoulders and covered his face with his hands. Lisa ran through the gate and shot around a corner.

The factory wall was rough and off white. It stretched down the sidewalk maybe a hundred and twenty yards with windows spaced every 30 or so feet on the second floor. A cluster of debris was jammed in the center of the front probably blocking a door. Around back, she thought she could see an exit sign illuminated behind a mess of pipes and beams and broken machinery. The windows on the ground floor were boarded up and amazingly free of graffiti even though the sandblasted wall sported vibrant signatures and dazzling bits of street poetry.

Lisa nodded. It was just one more sign of how successful BEAN had been at keeping everyone at bay… Until today. Until the day John Fasola decided to show up. She fingered the boards. One guarding the fifth window hung loosely. Going against protocol, she decided to enter. She looked around and found something like… no, she actually found a crow bar in the debris guarding the door. She slapped it against her hand and stared at a window. She was not supposed to be doing this.

Prying, she loosened the first board. It landed with a soft thud. She tensed. The light from the street lamps made her feel too exposed. Each sound felt explosive, but no one came around. She stared at her reflection wondering what to do.

She should at least call for back up, she thought. Why didn't they wake her partner? The guy was too good looking to need beauty sleep. Between thoughts, she levered the next board off. Lisa frowned, knowing she should report what she saw, but somehow found herself compelled and began tracing the window's ledge with her finger. She'd gone too far, was too curious, had been blocked too many times. Tonight, a door had been opened for her… or at least a window.

She waited a moment longer. Uncertain. *Do it or don't!* She demanded of herself.

She wedged her pocketknife under the weathered wood. It slid under the peeling paint and beneath the crack of a first floor window. She smiled crookedly.

It budged. The off and on red glare from the police car quickened her pace, but no one ever came around to check on the sound she was making or to look at anything other than the front of the building despite the loud protestation from a police officer that a perimeter guard was being formed. *Was everyone in this town an idiot?*

The window squealed.

Working the blade back and forth she pried it further under the pane. Huffing, she levered it open until she could get her fingers under. The wood groaned. Lisa held her breath, but the security guard was arguing too loudly for her to be heard. She quickly cut a wide opening in the screen behind the window.

Slipping inside, she closed the window behind her. The floor was amazingly empty. Someone stripped it of all machinery. *No signs of inventory either.* Above, she saw a row of offices and a hallway with a set of windows where managers would have once looked down on factory floor production. The only light in the building came from the streetlamps outside and a light that leaked out of the centermost second floor window. Taking a moment to let her eyes adjust, she made her way to one of the three doors marked "Stairs."

"Something is actually locked." she was shocked. The place had been such a fortress so far, she thought wryly.

Something creaked. She ducked into a shadow and stayed still. Her breathing felt controlled, calm, but still way too loud. The sound moved on with a soft door thud.

What is going on?

Before today, supposedly no one had been able to hack or break into BEAN. Her heartbeat increased. All the reports said that BEAN was impregnable. She looked back at the empty factory and a shiver ran down her spine. *What was happening today? Why did John Fasola choose today and why was the path being cleared?* She listened. Dimly, she could make out an electric hum and the voices of people outside. Above her, she heard clanging steps.

Her fingers itched with the need to hold something comforting. *What made me put away my gun?* Something odd was definitely about to happen. Every instinct said so.

She crossed the smooth gray floor at a jog and made her way to a second staircase. Her pulse continued to escalate. Another door unlocked. There was a sudden shock of light upstairs and then it was gone. She made her way up the stairs. Today, her employers would get answers.

JTL stood. His nostrils flared. In a bound, he leaped the desk and pressed his ear to the wall.

"Feathers and spit," the leprechaun exhorted, "Someone's broken in."

"The police?" John asked.

"Smells like someone with O'Rat's stink," he said. *Smells a bit like a dragon*, he added to himself.

"You'll tell them I didn't break the law? That you invited me?"

"I'm afraid I've a bit too Irish in me to have a green card, Johnny. My word won't mean much." JTL pulled a convex lens out of a closet. It stood about two feet tall and was lined with silver. "Grab the tripod, Johnny."

"What are we going to do?"

"Against a dragon?" the leprechaun smirked, "You're no knight, Johnny. I hardly expect you to take up arms. Just remember, when the time came your dad was a great hero."

"My dad?"

"Killed one of the French giants. Chopped his foundation right well, he did. A Monsieur Au Paulet, as I recall."

"Mon. Au Paulet," John repeated.

"You have it in you," he paused for a second, then added, "Jack."

Resolutely, John grabbed the tripod and followed the little man into the hallway. They dashed down two flights of stairs. JTL hobbled under the weight of the large lens. He sweated and looked just a little bit unpolished.

"If I'm right, Johnny," he said gently, then seemed to change his mind "When we get through run. Run hard and fast. Don't wait for me. If you trip, roll. Keep moving." He took hold of John's arm. "Remember, my boy, you have a lifetime of beans in you."

JTL placed the tripod on three chalk dots drawn on the floor. Tripod, mirror and tungsten lamps formed an acute triangle. JTL looked at the triangle for a moment and then edged the tripod to the right less than an inch. He removed a set of gels used to reduce the greening of fluorescent lights since the overheads were off and nodded. The lens was set on the tripod. The leprechaun rubbed his hands together. John turned and saw Lisa Fischer on the second floor.

"Mr. JTL. I have some questions," she called. John turned to run. Suddenly, the front door fell off its hinges. Lisa turned.

"Freeze!" They all heard. The police burst in.

Jeremy Tucker, Leprechaun switched on the power, producing three light beams that shot toward the concave mirror. They bounced off the rounded silver and struck the concave glass which exploded with sudden color... Color as pure as an infant's first thoughts sprang forth. Six unified beams ranging from ROY to BIV dazzled and raged.

Lisa staggered.

John felt dingy.

A three-year-olds' joy swept through John, Lisa, Jeremy Tucker, a startled police officer, and even Sam as a rainbow gathered itself. It launched soundlessly. The woman backed away and fell as the colors launched at her like a friendly fist. It exploded through her and bounded upwards. John reached out in wonder, trying to touch it. The colors were cool below and warm above. He smiled and took a step forward. A look of surprise lit his features. JTL watched the rainbow embrace John. John accepted the embrace and vanished. Jeremy grabbed the lens. He wrenched it free from the light. The rainbow disappeared.

"Aww…" The police said, disappointed, feeling somehow left out.

Jeremy smiled at the man and gave him a friendly wink, then rolled up his sleeve to reveal a gold Rolex. The brilliance of light faded, but somehow remained in a twinkle of the wee man's iris. It was enough to light the room. The officer advanced with a questioning expression. The room echoed with each step, but the wee man put a finger to his lips and shrugged. Sam began to back out unnerved by the small man whose curls formed thousands of mischievous smiles.

"I said freeze," the officer called out again. His gun shook in his hands.

Carefully rotating his wrist, the wee man stared at his watch. It flashed in the darkness. The officer was almost upon him when the wee man stopped. They both looked down. A prism shone in the glass above the clock face. Jeremy treated them with another wink, propped his lens under his arm, smiled once more, and jumped into his watch, disappearing neatly into the reflected colors.

The police… stared at no one. The room was empty except for three tungsten lamps, a concave mirror, a tripod, and a falling gold Rolex watch.

8. John

John knew only one thing. He didn't know anything.

9. Somewhere Through the Rainbow

Lisa felt awash in power. Strings tugged at her. They strangled and stretched her. She bit at them. They refused to let go. They wrapped and clung to her. Strings… no, snakes gripped her. Serpents, great fiery worms, wrapped their fangs about her, bit into her forearms, neck, and legs. She tore at them with her hands. She tore at them with her claws. Her hands. Her claws. Her hands. Her talons. Her sword.

Color consumed her. It peeled her eyelids back and scratched her irises. It pressed her down. The strings, the colorful strings… the snakes pulled her down. She couldn't breathe. She choked on violet.

Newsprint and smocks spun in the eddy, battering her with their soaking weight. Up disappeared. Wings, her wings, beat. The strings drank. Paint? Blood? She roared. Massive foreclaws tore. A ripple of blue collided into her and pulled her forward.

She scrambled onto the blue and surfed. Her lungs burned. She coughed red and orange. Her cough burned a string. It snapped. Flung off balance, she drank a sea of green.

One arm was hers. The other was some foreign scaled wing. With her human arm, she grabbed at her neck. She scratched at the metallic bits beneath the slurping string. Her reptilian arm no longer wanted to respond to her. Her human hand felt the pulse of the string drinking.

She lost consciousness for a moment. Desperately, she pushed herself over a cliff of gold and emerald. She began descending. Something lingered in her oxygen- deprived mind. These strings were old. They were a part of her. They owned her.

With one last effort, she forced her entire body to fight. Claw, talon, nail, sinew, tooth, fang, sword, scale, flesh, tail, toe, finger, wing, and leg thrashed. She tore scales from her body, from her face; wrestled for the sword that was somehow also her nails, her claws and with that sword swung wildly. She struck everything near her. Her muscles burned. The last oxygen slowly bubbled out of her. A shock of verdant kicked her. It used her as a springboard and leapt upwards.

Then, the whirlpool. Colors mixing and blending. Hungrily, it gargled her. The strings tried to pull her back, but the whirlpool's tug increased. The strings strained against their pull. They tried to rip her limbs off. Lisa screamed in yellows and orange.

A face appeared. A sharp, arrogant face. It was her own face. With the last of her strength she flailed at it, cutting light. She closed her eyes. Then suddenly, she smelled maple syrup.

10. Rocks, Mud, Run, and, Roll

His hands were thinner, muscles less developed. His stomach tightened, as if it had never known beer. A peach-smooth face met his searching hands. The ground smelled minty or was that the grass? A quick taste confirmed that the verdant blades did indeed have a nice zing. Sadly, the ground did not resemble nor taste like chocolate or coffee, but it was rich, soft, moist, and warm with the consistency of damp bread pudding.

Overhead, trees towered like skyscrapers and the further he looked the bigger they seemed to get. He stood. He wobbled. He sat. All five senses flooded with heightened stimuli. The gurgle of water tinkled through the air like a glassware symphony. A wave of shadow swept over him and he ducked. It wore colors that made a peacock look like a penguin. He shook with vertigo. The colors brought memories of the rainbow he had just fallen through.

"This can't be real," John said to no one in particular and no one in particular answered.

"I quite agree. A reel is a lovely dance and I hear no foot stomping music."

John spun, but except for a small chipmunk saw nothing near him. He quite missed the critter's backpack and walking stick. Still, John nosed towards it and it jittered its nose in return. After a bit though, the chipmunk found the exchange boring and tottered off leaving John alone on the minty hill.

He gathered his wits as best he could. *Think*, he thought, but the effort failed. So, he tried another approach and closed his eyes. He counted to twenty *(This hallucination requires far more than ten!)*, dug his fingers into the rich earth, and slowed his breath. His heartbeat slowed to the pace created by a heavy metal drummer getting his first solo. His breath smelled of car fumes and burrito. He shook his head. A breeze tickled his nose with the promise of pie. One eye peeked. Paradise still remained in front of him, but at least the dizziness felt less.

"Let's explore then," he decided.

John crawled down a hill, afraid that the vertigo might return, but the scents and too real textures calmed him. Everything around him expressed itself like it was printed in bold. Below, a lake shimmered. Fish leaped with a crescendo of sparkle and splash. He licked his lips. The water temped. It reached out in a wide bowl that seemed to stretch for miles. The hills and forest that framed it put postcards to shame. He quickened his pace.

A paddling of ducks fluttered away from him. He cupped his hands and shouted "Hello!" One turned to quack, but he was ugly and a bit of a loner. It slowed down as if to offer advice, but then realized it lost its flock in a cloud and hurried off! John stumbled forward to catch up, only stopping when his feet splashed in the lake.

How had he gotten there that quickly?

A wave of dissonance struck him. He bent to drink. His arms appeared strange. Not only were they thin and tight, but they were naked!

"What happened to the hair on my arms?" Even stranger, its familiar pop was gone. At fourteen, John broke his arm in a fight with Sean Smith. After that, whenever he reached out the arm clicked. He massaged his arms slightly alarmed at the range of motion.

"Okay," he said, "Simple. This is simple, John. You are dreaming." He exhaled. From a distance, the quacking became a beautiful honk as if a duckling had got its driver's license… *or pilot's license*, he supposed.

He steadied himself on a root and drank from a lake as blue as a movie starlet's eyes. He felt better. He enjoyed the cool. The water seemed ordinary, if a little too bright. He closed his eyes and took another steadying breath.

When he opened them, the lakeside grass was still the color of Christmas tinsel. The wind practically chimed.

Slowly, he stood and stumbled over a berry the size of his shin. John smiled as he took it all in.

"I must have hit my head again." he reasoned.

He relaxed and decided to take a stroll around the lake. It was a rather pleasant dream after all.

Berry scented air lulled him. Leaves crunched behind him. He imagined children jumping in piles. Leisurely, he turned around and looked up to see a gently sloping hill speckled with wild raspberries and mint grass. A slow smile spread across… *What is that?*

Eight-foot tall creatures stamped down the postcard colored hill towards him. Mosaics of quartz, mud, and thistle, glared at him angrily. Massive corded legs made of shale and granite, mixed with clay and what looked like slush, spiked the ground with each stride. They left a pockmarked trail behind them. John pointed. They pointed back. One of the monsters raised a truncheon. John turned as if to say, *Do you believe this?*

The whatsits should have moved slowly, being great stony creatures that hopped on spiked legs. The berries should have tripped them, or spattered making their going messy, but they seemed unaware of physics and sprung with ease. John stood fascinated, wondering if he was watching a mudslide or an avalanche.

Suddenly beside him, one of the monstrosities swung. John fell backwards clutching his arm. Pain! It too felt too real. He struggled to his feet, his arm on fire.

"Wait," he shouted, "what did I do?"

The things didn't wait, but continued their assault. John looked about. He called for help. None came. One lifted him. Another grabbed him. They stretched him like he was part of a taffy pull. Suddenly, he remembered JTL's words. He was supposed to run.

He reached for and grabbed a tree limb. Two rocky and weedy things pulled. They stretched him out while the third one practiced its truncheon swing. They stretched him out for batting practice. John desperately didn't want to become a piñata. He pulled heavily on the tree branch, trying to free himself.

The tree limb snapped and the jerk loosened the monstrosities' grip. For a moment, they let him sag beneath them. Then they pulled him taut again. The third creature, the one with the truncheon, pierced the ground beside him with its spiked foot. Slowly, it raised its heavy weapon above its head, letting it linger at John's eye level for a moment just so John could smell its former victims. Frantically, John threw the snapped broken tree limb still in his hand at the rock thing with the weapon. The truncheon wielder batted it away.

The broken limb, however, jammed itself into an ear hole of one of the other rock things. Surprise and annoyance sounded in its howl. It swung an arm to dislodge the stick. John dropped, discarded by the first creature. His head and shoulders struck the ground, but the other still held onto his legs. John flailed wildly. His hand found something soft and his fingers gouged. A shriek of horror echoed over the lake as John somehow scooped some clay out from his remaining captor's knee.

The creature shook, lost its balance, and began to topple. Wailing, it released John and stumbled backwards into a tree, denting it. John landed on his head. *If you trip*, John suddenly remembered JTL advising, *roll.* He did.

A truncheon pulverized the ground where he had just been. It left a dent in the soft ground so deep that a wise man could not climb out of it. Grass, rocks, and clods of dirt catapulted into the air. John saw this as his body ripped round and round gaining momentum. Mud clung to him. Sticks jabbed at him and leaves matted into his skin plastered there by the thick lakeside loam.

It never occurred to him to stop his momentum and make a dash towards the water.

The monsters chased. John collided with a tree at the bottom of a hill and limply climbed to his feet. Disoriented and covered in mud and rocks and fallen twigs, John stumbled towards the monsters.

The creatures stopped. The mud, grass, and stones that clung to John seemed to confuse the creatures, but didn't help to clear his vision. They paused as though they saw one of their own staggering at the bottom of the hill. John grabbed his head. Now, he saw six things rumbling down the hill.

"No," he shouted, pointing at the monstrosities. They misunderstood. The one with the truncheon saluted. It went in the direction John had pointed. The others followed.

John began to faint. He really wanted to, but then he remembered JTL's warning.

He ran. The question of where bothered him. Still, he ran.

He passed flowers that smelled of blueberries and raccoons that didn't quite fly, but seemed able to dig their paws into hidden footholds in the wind as they ascended. The trees that grew truffle-shaped leaves, he hardly noticed, though a field of wild licorice weeds drew his attention. Next up, John caught sight of a squirrel pressing a doorbell with a bouquet of flowers in its paw. That slowed him down. But what eventually stopped him was the statue of his father.

The statue was of a freckle-faced man with a hatchet standing on a broad leaf. The leaf was the size of a flatbed truck. The engraving below his father read:

"To Jack, in honor of making amends for selling the cow."

Breathing deeply, John thought, *the FDA* was right, *BEAN's are dangerous!*

Ever since he sniffed the products inside the crates, everything had gotten weird: the talk, the smells, the sights. Suddenly, he realized he shouldn't really be surprised. BEAN, after all, was a drug company.

"Their drugs do create a pretty place though." He mused. "And the colors …" he paused as a flash of rainbow vertigo made his knees give. The ground gave out a soft "wuft" as it caught him. His hands clutched his head. "Whoa!" He cried out with alarm, "The colors looked like tie-dyed t-shirts. All swirls and… and I liked it." He realized and cried out alarmed. A brilliant green frog hopped vertically up a cinnamon colored tree. John gasped. "I still like it! What do I do? I don't want to be a junkie!"

His father's statue had no reply.

He tried to calm himself again. Having delved deeply into James Bond recently, he believed that the BEAN beans must be part of a megalomaniac's plan. This thought disturbed him, for he had also seen Danny Kaye and Jimmy Stewart movies and realized that when an everyman accidentally discovers a plot for world domination it was his duty to end the threat. This was doubly true, since he had already broken into BEAN and was about to have an encounter with the police, not to mention the megalomaniac… if he ever woke up.

He frowned and climbed onto a leaf next to his father's statue in order to think. The leaf was done in gold leaf. John heard a giggle.

"Hello?" he said, before recalling that he should be running. A woman emerged from between two bushes dressed in rags. Politeness prevented John from making a face, but her appearance startled him. The woman was the first ugly thing he had seen since the rainbow spat him out. Well, the duckling had been kind of ugly too, but in comparison it was more ungainly and kind of cute. Her visage was so off putting, it made him completely reconsider the very definition of the word. The rag woman ignored this and adjusted her rags primly. She glared at him. Her eyes traced the marks his grimy hands and feet had tracked on his father's statue. John felt a blush rise up his neck as he realized what a mess he had made. She tsked at him with brows lowered.

"What are you doing?"

"I'm high." John answered, despondently.

"Not very," the rag woman observed. "Are you scared of heights?"

"I'm…"

"Well, you're certainly scared of baths. Climbing up all over our statue caked with mud and all that filth."

"You're…?" John swallowed his observation. It felt wrong to disparage her. It likely wasn't her fault that she was a rag woman. Her corporation may have failed her.

The woman watched him carefully even as he traced a finger along a clump of mud on a gilt leaf. She smudged it against one of her many rags and then tasted the mixture. This seemed to confirm something. Squinting at the mud on John's clothing and at the mud on the statue, she picked up a branch and held it like a switch.

"Well." She pointed fiercely. "I'm certainly not going to clean it and we're not going to wait here 'til it chances to rain."

She peeled a coarse rag of her body and threw it at him. John caught it puzzled, but the woman just pointed at the statue. "Oh, and don't give me that look. I see your arm and I've seen worse hurts on a bird learning to fly." She leaned imperiously towards him. Somehow, her scent of acorns basted with honey fit the patchwork assembly of her rag clothing. John hesitated. The rag squished in his hand.

"Do I have to make you, now?" she said, drawing tight the rags around her wrists. "I swear the young today…"

"Young?" he said, "I'm at least ten years older… oh, that's right, I'm high."

"High? You're still standing on the ground. Get to work."

John stared at her like she was an idiot, but she continued.

"Did a rat nibble on your brain while you were sleeping? You barely look old enough to sharpen a razor. Get to work!" She waited, tapping her foot, then after a pause ordered, "Clean."

He rubbed at the statue with the dirty rag. The gold leaf felt like crushed eggshells. She watched him with the fixed attention of a guard dog. His arm began hurting. She removed a bottle from her bundle and began drinking. He looked at her, looked back at his filth stained scrap of fabric, and then back at her again.

"Don't you dare ask," she said, putting the bottle away. A beam of sunlight bright enough to get an A on a pop quiz barged between them. Wind jostled after trying to crib notes. The rag woman ignored both and stood sentry, planting hands on hips. Sighing, John turned back to the statue. He continued rubbing the stone with the muddy rag. His polishing was making more of a mess than his climbing had. He took a step towards a puddle to dip the rag in, but she faced him down and he returned to polishing the statue with his even dirtier rag.

A shuffling sound startled John and he nearly fell. Branches parted and with it came a creaky, wizened voice.

"What's this?" A man emerged wearing a long robe dotted with stains that looked a bit like constellations. His beard dragged the ground though he stood over six feet tall. The rag woman lifted an eyebrow and barely turned her head to answer.

"Just someone who thought he could defile our Jack."

"And you made him clean it?"

"Yes."

"He's not doing a very good job."

"No, he isn't." the rag woman agreed. She sounded pleased.

"Well, I think you should have made him stand on his head a bit. Since he stained it right side up, he needs to be upside down to fix the problem."

"Typical wizard nonsense," the woman groused.

"If I could have some water?" John tried again, pointing to the muddy rag. They both stopped. The man clenched.

"Greedy, isn't he?" she said.

"He's a child." The wizard, for what else could he be, told her. "He thinks only of himself. Doesn't realize that people have to clean up their messes." John felt condescension drip like hot honey. "Well, it's fitting anyway." The wizard continued with a glance at the statue, "The thing being covered in mud, I mean."

Spit gathered around the rag woman's jowls.

"Don't you get political on me, I've been working too hard!" She scowled, her hair spiked outwards like a porcupine.

"She's been working?" John complained incredulously, earning a withering glare. A finger redirected him back to task and the former CEO of COW continued to spread and smear. His fingers hurt. Nothing at all rubbed clean. His nerves continued to fray until he blurted, "This is bull!"

The air stilled. A cloud opened its mouth in shock. A rabbit covered the ears of its children. John felt the change in an absence of shifting rags and chatter. Slowly, he turned around. The rag woman and the man turned grim.

"Did you hear what the boy just said?" the woman asked.

"Took the name of the bovine in vain. Did it without a thought." Both sounded enraged. The rag woman took a length of cord out from her bundle. The other circled to John's other side.

"Oh yeah," John said suddenly, "I'm supposed to run."

He jumped off the statue. The wizard made a grab for him. His long sharp fingers clutched mud and slipped off. John swung about and aimed a fist, but missed, tripping instead on the legs of the rag woman. The wizard made another attempt to snag him, but he got a face full of fraying rags instead. Dirt clods broke off.

"My eyes!" Cried the wizard, rubbing and flailing.

John felt a jerk. A cord wrapped around him. The rag woman smiled at her prize. She pulled tighter. John lurched backwards into her clutches when suddenly he was saved by a heavy hand striking. In his blind fury, one of the wizard's elbows caught him in the chest. The blow forced him backwards into the rag woman and they fell in a tangle of limbs.

For a moment, John's father appeared to reach down. His cocky smile glinted with gold. John reached up and grabbed his father's arm and sprang into the air. The rag woman screamed "Scandal!" but John was already past her and running. He still had no idea where he was running to, but his feet knew enough to keep going. He took one last look back at his father's statue and the rag woman. She spat with hands planted on hips indignantly.

"Come back. Come back with my rope."

Her raggy cord whipped against his neck and arms like a thing alive, tangling and tightening… Tangling and tightening. Branches and leaves whipped at his face. He tried to extricate himself, but while one end refused to let go the other snagged several times on trees, spinning him around. Somehow, the dizziness differed from vertigo. His wobbles befuddled the cord. It reached and reached until finally it grabbed too heavy a branch and stuck there. Firmly anchored, John found himself cartwheeling around the mighty tree so wildly that even the rope lost its bearings.

In the end, the branch bent far enough that it launched the poor raggy twine high into the air. The hapless thing landed on a bear trap with a hungry metallic snap. Leaves flew upwards as the hinges closed. This whipped the cord's ends to one side. The rope thrashed in frustration, striking everything in its reach. Its tantrum revealed a tiger pit. John continued through the scatter of leaves even as he heard a crackle of electricity. Behind him, the wizard had had enough comedy and decided to end it. He launched a spray of lighting towards the fleeing lad, but a broad maple leaf took the brunt of a spell and its brothers and sisters absorbed the rest. The air hissed in pain as the leaves blackened. Oblivious to everything but the fact that he needed to run, John ran around the pit.

Twigs grabbed at his soon to be shredded socks. He stumbled and looked back. The two had stopped chasing.

They turned towards the statue, then pointed at John, then looked back at the statue of Jack. Perhaps, they saw the family resemblance.

John ran.

A lifetime of beans is a good thing, he thought, glad he had eaten that burrito before becoming high, before his arrival.

The wood thickened around John, forcing him to squeeze between boles or climb over limbs. Some trees felt buttery, others wore a rough, serrated coat, while some felt as raw as iron. The mud continued to suck at his feet while sharp stones poked at his arches. Birds called unheeded warnings, but John stumbled on and clawed through brush, splashed through creeks, and leapt small ditches. His feet burned and bled. He ran until he couldn't breathe or for about forty minutes.

Finally, he reached the crest of a hill and his legs stopped. He fell onto a cushion of onion grass.

"Oh," he said.

Stretched out before him was a mile of cleared land. Hundreds of proud, antlered deer grazed and jousted on the field. Graceful does leapt. Behind them, stood a white wall. White like teacher's chalk, white like a new snow before rush hour, white like the whipped cream in a Norman Rockwell painting. So white it would have amazed a dentist. At each corner of the wall were spires that twisted like soft serve ice cream. Stone reliefs lie finely carved on the wall face. Even from this distance, the marbling of the veins looked exact, the gems of the eyes shone with intelligence and wit. The arms gripped with strength or tenderness. The leaping feet knew gravity. He sat, listening to his heart trying to catch up with him. Only one thought emerged in his dazzled mind.

"These are really good beans."

11. Lisa

"Something's hatching." The dentity announced.

"A plan?" Corp O'Rat mused, "One of ours, I hope."

"No, an egg."

The giant turned his attention to his dentity. She was sleek with a silver skin so reflective that the giant couldn't quite make her out. Looking at her, he saw only himself... which was something he quite liked. He peered closer and stroked his face approvingly.

Corp O'Rat sported a cleanly shaven squarish mug with graying temples. The cufflinks he wore on a starched white shirt appeared big enough and golden enough to buy food for a village for at least a year. His slacks ended in cuffs. His tie fielded so much silk that it put thirty-eight spiders into retirement. The biggest and perhaps only flaw in the giant's appearance were his hands. They were rather short and stubby... Well, short, if you could call anything on a giant short. Currently, his ringed digits were occupied with tally sheets. The profits may have out-sized even the giant himself. Still, the thought of a new egg caught his attention.

"Really? Is it golden?" he asked.

"Smells like a dragon egg."

"Like buttered toast?"

She drew a deep breath, "More honeyed."

"A wild one then."

"Oh Corp, do you need to control all the dragons?"

"Dragons are a useful commodity." He scratched his broad chin and itched his sharp nose. "Martha, my dear," he said at last.

"Yes," the dentity said, uncurling.

"I want that egg." Corp O'Rat gingerly opened a mother of pearl box and removed a monogrammed rapier. With the sword, he cleaned his nails.

"What if it's not a dragon? Do you still want it?" The dentity climbed onto the plate. She pulled a wing in front of her. With her fingers she began flicking feathers. Bell-tones pattered like spring rain. Her wings made sounds like a xylophone. The giant leaned back and discarded the rapier. She smiled when she saw she had his attention. Her music made him stretch.

Corp O'Rat stood and strode to his accounting sheets. A group of accountants scuttled to the corner awaiting judgement. With a peaceful smile, the giant began to flip the pages. Martha continued clicking her feathers with a steady beat. A calm so deep settled over the room that the roast fowl started snoring. Corp O'Rat leaned back. He used a jeweler's loop to read the accounts. The numbers lulled him just as much as the music until he found the clinker. Corp O'Rat turned abruptly, his toe no longer tapping.

"You forgot to carry the 2." The giant told the bookkeeper and then ate him. Martha stopped playing. He sniffed deeply and frowned.

"Only three things hatch, Martha," Corp said hungrily to the room, "Dragons, plans, and stories. Each has value."

"What about chickens?" Martha corrected.

"Chickens? The sky will fall before that concerns me." Corp said, dismissively, "If it is a chicken, you may leave it."

The dentity said nothing. Corp O'Rat dismissed her. He was lean for a giant. He dabbed bookkeeper off his lips with a linen and began his daily exercises with bicep curls. He hefted the tree trunks with little strain. After a moment, the light sharpened in his eyes. He motioned her back. "We are at war, Martha. At war for control. The easiest way to lose control is to ignore the details. Does one dragon matter?" He paused dramatically. Martha knew what he would say and so did not answer. "Of course it does. The reason we call enterprises "concerns" is because they may grow into something to be concerned about. If, however, we control everything we are aware of and make our best efforts to become aware of everything..." Corp O'Rat resisted the temptation to gesture emphatically. He had broken too many pieces of furniture recently and the woods around him were getting desperately thin. Instead, he lowered his voice, "Get the egg even if it is a chicken's."

Martha decided it was in her best interest to take her legs out of the cupboard, sew them back on and go. She carefully avoided O'Rat as she stitched patches around the areas where he had left tooth marks.

Jeremy twisted in a rip tide of yellow. His feet gripped the lens. Surfing, he crested a wave of brown and skipped off a torrent of gold and rose. Something had torn the rainbow apart. *John*, he supposed. *Who else could make this big a mess?* Wispy bits of canvas hungrily stretched for his hue. He prepared to bat them aside when he realized they were not canvas. They were marionette strings. Someone tore them, leaving vampyric shreds to crawl for scraps.

Jeremy leapt. A string snatched away the lens. The leprechaun reached for it. Another snaked around his wrist. It smelled of giants. Jeremy frowned. The string took a taste of him and shrieked.

"That's right," Jeremy shouted angrily, "I've been eating beans." He put his hands together and called to his kin. The rainbow responded. Color vanished. Jeremy swam fiercely in a sea of white light. The string knotted. It blistered. It burned. Up, down, and sideways, ignited in the purity of wavelength. Strings wriggled out of his way, but the light ate them.

Fingers clasped, eyes closed. Jeremy felt he was a part of something. The light embraced him and curled through his being. It whispered lullabies in his ears and chanted heroic songs and urged him to open his eyes. Jeremy offered coins to the rainbow. Its brilliance seduced him. It loved him. It asked for so little… only gifts of a little coin, a little luck. Jeremy instead offered his life. It considered the offer, but in the end fingered the gold disdainfully. The coins transformed from gold to not quite silver. Jeremy could not understand, but it felt glorious and for the second time he reached into his pocket prepared to give away all his magic, all his being. Then the white light slowly resolved itself.

The harsh light turned into a gracious, kindly ebony. The ebony approached and embraced him. He lifted a palm full of coins to the black. The color closed his hand. Peace rose. Then, black split into blue, red, and yellow. He was appalled and delighted by the colors. The three blended to form life. A wash of conflict stormed through him. The colors warred with each other to form reality. The white and the black were of the same coin, both aspects of the infinite, two perfections.

Blue thrust him forward. His understanding of the infinite disappeared, but his memory of it also stayed within him, just like the cow. He knew he would rue this too. Carefully, he emptied the beans he had smuggled through the rainbow. They were too much for him.

Gripping a reef of violet, he climbed until it became indigo. Squinting, he saw remnants of the disturbance. With bovine determination, he dove into the aqua and raced the wavelength back towards home.

Lisa did not like the fact that she was not in a factory. She did not like the fact that her wings were puny and could not produce enough lift to get her airborne. Did not like the fact that she had wings. Most importantly, she did not like the way the guy under the bridge was licking his lips and sharpening his knife.

The guy had major problems. He stood about seven feet tall with gorilla-like arms, and thick hippopotamus legs. Currently, the acne-covered fingers of one of its five hands gripped her neck.

"It's a nice place."

"I live under a bridge." he groused.

"It's a nice bridge."

"Are you kidding me? They were supposed to repave ages ago. Every time it rains… do you know what it's like for all that horse poop, road dust, and the bovine knows what to fall on your head when you're trying to sleep."

"City workers." She agreed.

"Tell me about it. Only thing they're good at is coming around and taking their share. You ask for service, you know what they do, send some accountant to check if you're all paid up, and let me tell you, no one's ever all paid up. Curds and whey, why do you think I live under a bridge. "

"I'm with you," she tried. The guy turned and smiled. Pus leaked from his mouth.

"No, but you'll be in me soon enough," he laughed, spraying her with foul smelling spittle. The knife threw off sparks as he drew it against the whetstone. Lisa stared at the rust. She swallowed. She tried to stand. Her wings feebly flapped. The guy clamped harder on her neck.

"None of that, hear."

She nodded weakly, wishing she had brought the gun. She wiped his spit away with a claw and pushed weakly at its arm. The guy laughed, picked her up and then thrust her into the water. He held her there. Her wings thrashed. Her limbs stretched. Bubbles escaped her. The water tasted like spoiled eggs and feet. An itch began building in her throat. She dug her claws into his bony gorilla sized arms. The grip loosened. She flapped harder.

"Stop spraying me!" The troll-like guy protested, and then shoved her under again. She gasped. The itch began to throb. She clamped her teeth against his arm. Salt burned her throat. Water stifled her thoughts. Pressure dulled her. The cough demanded to be released. She clamped her lips tight. Determined to hold onto her last air. She clamped them nearly through the guy's arm.

"Ow!" he said, "You are not nice!" and he threw her against a bridge support. Lisa gasped for breath, his blood dribbled from her mouth. She tried to spit it out, but swallowed some. She coughed. The itch delighted. A torrent of flame escaped her. The guy covered his eyes. Lisa hiccoughed. The fire died.

"Whey!" he cursed.

Seeing an opening, Lisa head butted him and raked him with her claws. The guy dropped the knife. For an instant, she felt like herself and instinctively spun and kicked him. The martial arts move surprised him. Lisa's foot landed square in the guy's stomach and his eyes bulged. She struck him again. He stumbled backwards, smacking his head into his cracked cooking pot. The itch returned, so she lit the fire. The hippopotamus legs thrashed. Having gained separation, Lisa crawled up a mossy bank, and turned to see if he would chase. The guy was searching the water for his rusty knife. Then she caught a glimpse of herself in the water.

Gecko arms hung folded over an alligator's torso. Emaciated thin human legs wobbled beneath her reptilian waist. Human eyes and forehead led to fangs and scales. Ruby studded wings stretched a foot to either side of her.

Something inside her crumpled. She slumped to the ground and touched the water near her image. The world disappeared; she could only see her rippling image.

"Aha," the guy said triumphantly. She didn't look.

"What am I?"

The splashing didn't make her turn.

She felt a hand on her shoulder. She tossed a pebble at the water distorting her image. The splashing grew nearer. The hand was warm.

"What am I?" she repeated.

"You are you," said the voice belonging to the hand. It was a new voice not belonging to the troll-like guy.

"You're crazy." She answered it. The voice grew more intense.

"You are beautiful. You could be beautiful." The hand gripped her tightly. It shook her firmly. The splashing climbed closer.

A shadow spread over the distorted rings of her reflection, a shadow with a knife. Fiercely, the hand pulled.

She turned. Jeremy Tucker, JTL, smiled kindly down on her. His grip told the lie about his patience. He stroked her scaled neck. "You had a good bath in the light. You don't stink anymore." He said to her. His eyes darted past her. She looked. The troll-like guy's thick feet were finding it hard to find purchase on the moss, but he was getting close. Jeremy Tucker put his hand on her claw. She shivered and pulled away. He leaned close to her.

"You said you had some questions for me?" and then he jumped backwards with a yip. Lisa balanced herself and struck out at the troll again. Her kick landed solidly and he slid down. Lisa lost her balance, but stayed atop the bank. Jeremy paused and smiled.

"What beans won't do?" he said, admiringly. "Come." He waved urgently for her to follow. She struggled to get her feet under her. The wings flapped futilely. Finally, Jeremy turned back and gave her a hand. He looked down with sympathy at the troll. Angrily, he reached into his pocket and threw the guy a coin.

"Feather and spit, what have I become?" Jeremy Tucker said. A tear spilled down his cheek at the sight of his coin in the troll's hand.

The guy accepted it, flipped it once, turned it over, bit it, and then heavily sat down. The toll paid, he planted his knife in the ground and with a stick began stirring his upset cooking pot.

Without another word, Jeremy led Lisa away.

Jeremy wrung his hands. So, what was she? That was what she asked of him. Weak as she was she did not ask him to save her. She asked what she was. His muscles tensed. She still smelled of giants.

Lisa faltered after only a few steps. She grabbed at him and pulled them both down. They landed on a bed of sunflowers that rained seeds on them in protest. Lisa covered her head and closed her eyes. Jeremy opened his mouth and enjoyed a crunchy snack. He gave a slight bow in thanks and dusted off his tweed jacket without rising. The shells he spat to the side. Lisa's hide pinged as the seeds bounced off her. The woman shivered. She held herself closely despite the warmth of the sunflowers and their flare of seeds.

"Color fever," Jeremy worried and threw his jacket over her. She smiled slightly and leaned back. The shaking subsided. The wearing of clothing comforted more than the warmth it provided. The leprechaun placed a hand tenderly on her still human forehead.

"Fever," he confirmed to himself. Lisa looked up at him.

"Fever?" she responded hopefully.

"No, not a hallucination, I'm afraid." He answered. She reached for his hand. Her claws cut him. JTL winced and backed away.

"What am I?" she asked again. He looked at her and turned, catching sight of the troll. The two hadn't gone far.

Downhill, the troll looked despondent. It continued stirring its empty pot and looked for a shoe to add. Perhaps leather would sweeten or at least thicken its soup. Jeremy considered his old friend… well, acquaintance. It was hard to call a troll a friend.

"Sammy?" Jeremy called over his shoulder.

"What?" came a sulky voice from under the bridge.

"Do you have any soup?"

"Would have." He answered, even sulkier. A chill blew towards them. Jeremy patted Lisa.

"Ah, you're making a mess of my jacket. Just sit still. It's good material."

The woman had obviously struggled in the rainbow. She fought with everything she had and the rainbow had taken almost all her strength. Her weakness and underdeveloped legs were proof of that. He sat down and hummed a lullaby. Lisa resisted, but ultimately closed her eyes.

"Sammy is only a troll at the bridge." The wee man gently informed. "Think of him as a guard, same as the guard in front of BEAN's gate." he said soothingly, "I paid the toll. He won't come after you." He massaged her claws. "I need to get you some supper, girl"

"Not a girl," she murmured.

"Course you are. You're still you." he answered, misunderstanding.

Poor thing, Jeremy thought, rising. *I'm hardly a suitable protector. I'm best at running and hiding, dipping in and out of trouble.* "I'm not responsible for you, you know," he said aloud, but too quietly for her to hear. "I need to find you a wolf or a bear. A bovine knight, but who besides me would take you in? Half made as you are."

He looked up at the sky.

"You would have thought that cow would be gone by now. How long does it take to digest one miserable… Oh dear."

He smelled money.

With barely a thought, Jeremy worked himself down to the size of an acorn. Branches rained down shorn from their mothers and fathers. The wee man dove under a leaf and hid. Silver fingers lifted the tweed coat.

Corp O'Rat's dentity calmly overlooked the scene. Her silver legs braced in a wide stance. The thing was hard to see as it was filled with the reflections of bridge and water and road. Imperiously, her wings flared and blinded them all.

"My," she said, "Someone is trespassing in Buir's Wood." A hawk's head turned and looked down. The dentity laughed. "I can taste your shadow from here." She said, "What brings you to such a dim place. Not a rainbow anywhere in sight." Metal scraped metal as the dentity licked her lips. Jeremy withdrew deeper under the leaf. The leprechaun closed his eyes.

"What are you?" Lisa said.

The dentity leapt. She landed astride Lisa.

"You must be the egg."

"What?"

"Leave her alone." Jeremy shouted. Martha leaned to one side and with fingers like quicksilver speared the ground around the leaf, caging Jeremy, but at that, the wee man smiled.

"You've made a mistake." He chuckled.

"Have I?" the dentity asked.

"Do you feel a cough, lass?" Jeremy removed a coin from his pocket. Lisa nodded. The dentity looked over. Lisa coughed. Blistering flame washed over the hawk headed silver woman. Jeremy expertly twiddled his coin between the fire and the dentity's silver hand. Unfortunately, metal doesn't blister as easily as skin.

"Do you think you're clever?"

Jeremy didn't answer. The dentity sniffed. The leprechaun was no longer there, having vanished through a rainbow made from egg fire and dentity silver skin. "I suppose you are," she answered for him, smirking at the colors bouncing from her palm. "but," she continued, "I didn't have any interest in you."

Lisa screamed.

12. How Come I Always Have to Rescue Myself?

The dentity towered over her, mostly because she was lying down. Her throat burned. Smoke dissipated. She smelled turmeric. It smelled bitter and angry and (she thought for a moment)… good. It smelled right.

There were trees. Really big trees in the distance and a road that was more of a path with ruts that lent it a sense of permanency. This compactness of the earth declared the road had been here forever. This road knew what it was about. It only hesitated at Sammy's Bridge and then continued on absolutely sure of where it was meant to go. When she studied it, she saw so many footprints that she could make out none.

Water popped from the stew or soup that she was supposed to have been the meat for. It made her stomach rumble. The smoke from her cough dissipated quickly. For a moment, the rings of black clarified the bird-like woman in front of her. She had the appearance of a hood ornament or maybe an Egyptian god. The dentity, where had that word come from, turned to study her. The silvery thing intimidated her in a way that the troll-guy never had. It remained silent which left her room for thoughts that startled her because of their ordinariness. *Had she ever been this hungry? Where did JTL go? Where were her answers!* She looked again at the road. Its solidness grounded her. She took a calming breath and saw… well, almost saw the dentity.

The silver terminator-like being stood facing her. So far, it had made no move towards her. Its mirror skin revealed to Lisa the worst thing in the world. Her reflection. What she had become.

What in the world was she? Some kind of lizard freak, kind of like a naga, but not really, because didn't those have snake bodies and no legs? At least she still had legs! For the first time in her life, she wished she had been into those stupid role-playing games her little brother was always going on about. She tried to think back. Surely, she had remembered something from one of those Monster thingamajigs he was always thumbing through while laughing maniacally at a sheet of graph paper.

The dentity cleared her throat.

"You choose poor company."

Lisa backed up. She was so tired, so scared, so confused.

"I'm sorry I didn't like your movie." Lisa said pitifully. The dentity stepped closer.

"Movie?"

"Sorry. I'll download it and watch T2 three times in a row, okay? I love Arnold movies!"

"I doubt that you'll see your love, Arnold Movies again." Martha paused, "Then again, who knows? Maybe he'll use you as a messenger."

"Why are you after me?"

"Corp O'Rat."

"Corporate, thank god. Tell them I need…"

The dentity slapped her.

"How dare you make demands of Corp O'Rat."

Lisa rubbed her jaw and cut it. The dentity lifted her. Its metal skin was soft. It stretched its wings and… it folded its wings and stretched them out again. It pointed up with its free arm. The silver wings jerked, seemed to strain. A breeze buffeted beneath them. They started flapping so hard that they blurred and strangely became easier to see. After minutes of effort, the dentity leaned against a tree, puffing.

"You have got to lose weight." Martha complained. "I've lifted dragons with less heft than you." Lisa burrowed her head under the jacket. The dentity shrugged, picked her up, staggered a step, and then began walking away from the bridge towards the road. The silver woman took only a few steps.

"You've got the…" her wing massaged her back, "Are you sure you're not human. You've got a heavy conscience for a wyrm."

"Worm!" Lisa said, "You're a worm." Frustration surfaced like an itch. Something filled Lisa's hand. Something she couldn't keep hold of. Martha's ears lifted.

The creature sprung lithely into the air. She looked odd. Silver hawk head with bunny ears. To make matters stranger, Martha began to hammer her beak until it looked like an elephant's trunk. The silver thing looked absurd.

Lisa tried not to. It didn't feel right, but she laughed. She laughed at the hawk faced, bunny eared, elephant nosed, silver woman. The dentity did not take it well. Its golden eyes narrowed angrily and Lisa instantly regretted the laughter.

"You would laugh?" she said icily, and before Lisa could respond the bird woman sliced a tree limb from the trunk of a tree with her wing. Then, she dove at Lisa. The dentity struck her three times, each time from behind. No matter where Lisa turned she wasn't quick enough. The feeling in her hand faded, but did not leave her entirely.

Lisa shrank herself into a ball, trying to shield herself with her gecko arms. The dentity made one more hostile gesture and then forcibly calmed herself, then it sniffed with such suction that Lisa's hair shot towards her trunk. Lisa winced, her legs shivered.

"There is something…" Martha began and perched in a tree. She took another sniff. It lifted Lisa off the ground.

"You smell of the light." Martha said, finally. "You do not talk like the light."

She sliced through the top of a tree and launched it away from Lisa. "… You smell of many things, hatchling. Yes, you do smell of the wyrm. You stink of dishonesty and treachery and something else... Something with an earthy smell and… Feather and spit, you've known cows. There's… I've never smelled such a thick scent of cow."

Lisa moaned in response. She thought of McDonald's. Martha looked around.

"Are you calling to them? Have you… Do you … have you been around so many cows that you can speak their tongue?" Lisa moaned again from the pain of Martha's beating. The silver of the dentity's body gleamed more brightly. She landed with a buttery flutter on the ground. "Please. Do you know where the cows are?"

Lisa moaned a third time. The dentity studied her carefully. Her face furrowed with such deep concentration that her features became visible. A melody fluttered from the breeze through the metal wings. The tune was uplifting, but strangely dissonant and sharp. The silver being nodded. It agreed with the melody. A decision was made. It frowned at its own decision and its sigh, rang in counterpoint to the melody.

"Do stay here," she said tenderly, "I must find a chicken. Corp O'Rat must get something." She lifted Lisa's head and put her soft trunk against her cheek. "You, I think, I should keep for myself." Martha studied the reptilian thing before her. Lisa moaned and nodded. The dentity took one last whiff. "So many scents. Even Corp O'Rat's. So many experiences," she added with admiration. Soft, cool, delicate fingers twined around her neck. They tightened abruptly. "Stay here." Martha ordered and took off.

Lisa waited, waited until the light beams fell through the trees at a different angle. Then, she rose and stumbled forward. Strangely enough, it was the thought of JTL, not the dentity that scared her most, that made her move.

Well, that and hunger.

She could accept Martha as a robot, a really, really advanced prototype. If not a robot, she could force herself to believe she was an alien something or other. She could believe the guy who lived under the bridge was some diseased insane homeless guy, but JTL had shrunk in front of her. Had shot down to the size of a peanut. He was Alice in Wonderland. No, he wasn't. He didn't need any pills. Worse, she didn't eat any mushrooms.

"I have to, have to take a bath," she thought, "buy perfume. Do something. Got to change the way I smell." Lisa, unlike John, didn't need to be told. Though her wings were sore, still she flapped them, it was the only way she could stay upright. The only way she could run.

She ran.

Knee sized strawberries lined a broad field. One of the berries jiggled. Its seeds exploded. The farmer dropped his plow and ran over towards his berries. From the cracked seeds leaked a fine dark chocolate. It coated the berry. Within moments, it hardened to a fine lacquer shell.

"They're ripe," he called. Wife and children grabbed sacks. Berries puffed with chocolate pollen. The farmer tasted one.

"Pudding, as fine a kirsch chocolate as I've ever tasted." The berries popped in order. The family allowed themselves one each and picked. Clouds thickened above them.

The farmer clutched the bag protectively even as a stone fish fell from one of the clouds. Its ridged flippers battered the air. Next to it, parchment floated on a tiny wisp of cloud. With a flip of a flipper, the parchment unrolled and shot out, draping the farmer. Parachuting without 'chutes were mottled things of twig, obsidian, quartz, and clay. They speared the ground with such impact that the farmer and his family stumbled.

"Your harvest has been ripe for over five minutes," condemned the flying stone goldfish.

"but…" the farmer began. The eight-foot tall things stamped behind him.

"You are in breach of contract. Corp O'Rat leased you this land with the expectation of prompt and full payment. You are in violation not only to Corp O'Rat, but to Buir O'Cassey. A tardiness in distribution of five minutes means tax revenues stalled. This penalty unfairly assessed to Corp O'Rat, will in fairness be passed on to you."

The farmer gaped, but knew better to complain, especially as the massive corded legs made of shale and granite of the golems violently spiked the ground. Rippling arms snatched sacks. "Your obligation, therefore, will this year be counted at eighty-five percent of harvest."

The eight-foot things stood one by one behind each of the family members. "You may state any objections now." It surveyed the family. "You have none. I shall report your willingness to accept the blame for this delay to Corp O'Rat."

The goldfish paused again. It dared the farmer to speak. His calloused hands clenched, but his head fell. The stone goldfish nodded to the clouds.

Immense shadows fell. They were hollowed out and from the top looked like a wheelbarrow. Eight-foot things shoveled dark chocolate strawberries onto them. The farmer stared at his nearly barren fields.

"Wait!" He called. The stone goldfish turned.

"Yes."

"It's the dragon's fault."

"What dragon?" said the goldfish dismissively.

"That dragon," he pointed. Lisa lay in an area of just cleared field. Berry juice and chocolate stained her face. Snores softly fell from her. The farmer tried to act indignant. "I must protest. Everyone knows the honorable Corp O'Rat controls the dragons. If a dragon has been here long enough to eat and fall asleep, then certainly I am not guilty. One of Corp O'Rat's people was informed and received payment. Can you put the blame on me?"

The fish flew over Lisa.

"This," it declared, "is not a dragon. You have tried to interfere with a proper business transaction. That, compounded with your outrageous delay of five minutes..."

"No," the farmer said, "look at her. From here, she looks like a…"

"You have wasted our time." It checked a series of scrolls. "That will incur an additional penalty of fifteen percent."

"That's my whole crop."

"Are you filing a complaint?" The farmer threw his sack against the ground. The goldfish nodded dispassionately, "You have attacked the ground proving that you are a poor tenant. "Golems," it said, addressing the things, "salt this land."

"No," the whole family shouted.

"Do you have something of worth to offer instead?" The stone goldfish leered. The farmer shook his head. It tsked, "I see." and wafted forward. The farmer watched his chocolate strawberries float upwards. "You must vacate. Without your farm you can offer nothing productive to Corp O'Rat. You are a drain on Corp O'Rat's resources."

"Curds and whey," said the farmer shocked, "I have always worked. Always paid my taxes."

"But you cannot continue to do so, isn't that right? Do you think we should bear the burden to support someone who has become useless?"

The man embraced his family. The stone goldfish patted each of them with its flipper. It paused and then with malice made a decision. "Take them," the fish told the golems, "Corp O'Rat will make productive use of them in the stables."

"Daddy," said the littlest one, "Is the giant going to eat us?" The fish swiveled in front of the girl.

"Not to worry, little one. It'll be years before you are seasoned well enough to be eaten." The fish nodded and the granite things advanced.

The girl screamed. Lisa woke.

Giant rock-like things tossed the farmer's daughter into a cloud. Lisa rubbed berry and chocolate from her mouth. A chocolate rush filled her. Before she thought, she stood. The stone goldfish swiveled. Father took a step towards his girl. A heavy obsidian arm pummeled him. The man fell. Lisa roared.

Chocolate powered wings took her into the air. She disregarded the itch.

"You are interfering with the business of Corp O'Rat." The stone goldfish said, placidly. Lisa's claws sent sparks across a golem's arms. It clubbed at her, but she ducked under, then rolled to her feet and coughed. Flames melted the slush in its knees and baked the clay of its joints.

"I told you it was a dragon!" the farmer cried, sprinting towards his daughter-girl.

The golem blinked. It flexed and the clay shattered. Stiffly, it raised its foot.

With a sweeping motion, Lisa tried to knock the thing off its spike. Her scales clanged.

"I warn you," said the stone goldfish, re-rolling its scroll.

Lisa's tiny arms caught a massive cord of rock and wood. Her arms trembled. Her palms itched.

"Will you defy Corp O'Rat?"

It was a question she had asked herself a lot. Would she betray corporate? She was never a part of DHS. She hated the ruse, hated lying... *Was corporate worth supporting no matter what?* What right did she have to spy and break into businesses and steal for them? The corporate, the one she worked for anyway, was not doing what it promised to.

The thought spun from her head as a cudgel caught her from behind. Lisa spun forward. One of the golems grabbed her. It squeezed the air from her lungs. Another battered at her dragon scales. Sparks set fires.

"If you do not obey Corp O'Rat," the stone goldfish nattered.

She bared her fangs. The thing was strong. She felt a scale shatter. She roared pain and fire.

"I do not belong..." she began, and staggered under a blow. A thing pulled back her neck. Two held her down. It aimed its spiked foot at her. The itch burned. A gecko arm ripped free.

"Yes," the goldfish contradicted, "You belong to us." It nodded to the golems. The spike crashed down. She swung desperately to try to catch or deflect the spike. The itch broke free. This time her claw disappeared.

Pressure vanished. She opened her eyes. The stone goldfish was flapping hurriedly. Golems shook. She took a step forward. One of them was missing a leg. Her wings swirled dust. She clenched a fist, a human fist, but it didn't register.

The golems fled. Lisa roared. Flame blistered the ground between them. Rising, she spun with the itch in her hand and charged the nearest thing. Instinct moved through her. She sliced with a quick rip. Orange streaked downwards. Her blow cut. It wedged halfway through its mass. The thing ground its limbs. Masses of rock, twig and vine pressed together to keep her from retrieving her itch, but within moments, her itch set the vines ablaze.

The clouds began floating up and away. A little girl screamed. Father and mother reached up.

She pulled. Her arm lacked the strength to unwedge the itch so she left it inside the golem. Dust trailed down its face like tears. Lisa ignored its pain even as her mouth hardened with a mercilessness expression. She flew without realizing what she was doing. Her scales shimmered like a prism. She had drunk from a rainbow. It had nearly consumed her.

She scratched with her claws, shearing pieces of rock. Desperately, the golem struggled. It swung. A blow caught her in the chest. Lisa staggered back. It stabbed with its spiked feet. Her fingers ripped at the burning thing, cracking the burning mud loosening its hold on her itch. With a mighty wrench, the itch flew free and spun towards the ground.

Groggily, the golem stood on its one spike. Lisa dove towards her itch. The thing retreated, grabbing a fence post for defense, but years of self-defense classes readied her for battle. The golem tried to hop backwards. Lisa took a step forward. Her itch flared even more brightly, blazing like a forest fire until it solidified into a blade. A sword as orange as lava smoldered in her hand. She had a hand! She felt her arm then. Tears gathered at the sight of it. Her human, gym fit, arm flexed. She brought her left arm forward for a double handed grip, but saw black, fire bit claws that still curved. That hand remained a stranger's. It distracted her. It lessened her and suddenly she felt her bruises, her shattered ribs, a broken cheekbone, and tears in her muscles.

Lisa gripped the itch, the sword. She felt it fading, hiding like smoke. She tried to will it back, tried to fuel it with her pain. Her claws closed against the heat. Something was failing. Then the flame became a hilt of charcoal that barely glimmered. After that, it vanished. The sword fled from her grip. She crumpled.

The remaining rock and mud thing didn't wait. It spiked the ground in angry hops trying to get to Lisa before she could recover her strength. The woman backed away, looking for escape. A stone fist clenched. She put her arms up to shield her. They were still her arms. Somehow, she found that comforting. The blow…

Rock sheared. The golem broke apart into pieces cut smooth as a pound cake. Lisa glanced up. Martha glowered at her.

"I told you not to move, hatchling." A fine dust touched her silver wings.

"I'm sorry." Lisa said.

"See that you learn to be more obedient."

"I'm not…"

"Not what?"

"I don't belong to Corporate." Then she hugged her wounds and moaned.

The moan seemed to stagger the dentity. It scanned the farm, the lost crop, saw Corp's goldfish, and then finally settled on the family. The farmer ran up to Lisa and clasped her wrists.

"You saved us, thank you." Then, he swallowed, hesitant to ask for more. "Our daughter…" he cried, pointing up.

Martha stiffened. She hissed at the family. The father advanced, raising a pleading hand. The dentity spread her wings. Farmer and wife fled.

Lisa looked different, but smelled the same. Was the egg more herself or was this part of her chameleon quality. Was she dragon? Bovine? Champion? Innocent? No, she was not that. Clearly, she was not that, but she was… Those memories were too painful to revisit. She kicked Lisa, but without intent to injure. The woman had the temerity to moan again. The fleeing family looked back and Martha caught their pleading eyes. The wind struck an angry chord.

"You don't belong to Corp O'Rat? Well," she said to Lisa, "we shall see."

13. A Less Satisfying Way to Save the Virgin Sacrifice

John walked, and then ran down the hill. Deer snapped to attention. The alpha deliberately bent his head and chewed grass disdainfully. It nudged others around it. They too, dismissed John as a threat and continued eating, playing, and jousting. Beneath them, the grass sprang buoyantly while overhead the sun dazzled with kind warmth. A breeze of roasted apples, spiced meats, and honey lofted from the castle.

John approached slowly, and as he neared the first of the herd, he paused. A fawn to his right skipped over to him. A doe paced behind. The males carefully watched. John fell to a knee and stuck his hand out palm up. The fawn delicately presented itself. Its nose twitched nervously. John gently stroked its fur. Mother and father relaxed. Alpha put its nose in the air and sniffed. Delight, deeper than an order for rotary dials, washed through John S. Fasola when the fawn nuzzled his hand. When Mother Doe placed her head on his shoulder, John felt all his tension loosen inside him.

Well, if I had to run," he told them, "this was a good place to run to." Twelve deer nodded and circled him. The fawn pushed herself against his knee. Instinctively, he patted her head. Alpha advanced. Kingly grace and confidence attended each stride. John felt a pressure on his neck. It was the doe. Relenting, he bent his neck and found himself bowing. Alpha paused, and then, dipping one foreleg, bowed in return. A wave of relief loosened the rest of his fear.

"God, why didn't I try beans in college? No wonder kids get hooked on the stuff."

Alpha looked quizzically at him. He pawed the earth. John smiled. The doe returned her head to his shoulder and leaned him towards the ground where Alpha was scratching.

"Why have you returned, Jack?" Alpha wrote in the earth. John backed away bumping into the doe's foreleg. She held him still and when his eyes met hers, he didn't feel as easy anymore.

"It's John," he said, out of habit, "no one calls me Jack." The doe took a quick, disapproving breath. A number of other deer turned their heads. He had the impression they were laughing at him. John lowered his eyes and chuckled too. Alpha walked up to him and put its antlers under his chin. It lifted John's head. They stared at each other. Alpha studied him then snorted. The circle dispersed.

John reached out and realized that the circle was still there. He was simply not its center anymore.

He walked through the herd of deer towards the scent of food. A cobblestone road began a few hundred feet before the castle wall. It stretched towards the sun and away, parallel to the herd of deer. John stayed off the road. The cobbles hurt his practically bare feet. All too soon, he reached the gate house.

"Hello there," a man wearing a hundred linked rings said.

"Hi," John responded.

"How high?" the man asked, confused. John looked around at the pristine lollipop orchard and the deer and honestly replied.

"Quite high."

"What is your name?"

"John Fasola."

"By permission of the gate barer of the castle gate of the fourth minor castle of his Lord, Buir O'Cassey, I bid John Fasola welcome."

"Thanks." John said. The gate barer ground his teeth.

"Not much into ceremony are you?" he asked. John mumbled something, "Well, did you at least bring a gift?"

"A gift?"

"Do you enter a home expecting your host to treat you with all courtesy and feel no need to give any, John Fasola? It is the custom of all people of good standing to give a gift to show their cordiality and manners."

"Oh." John said, and dug in his pockets. "A tip." He pulled out his wallet and removed a dollar bill. He handed it to the gate barer who took it. He turned it over. His features brightened.

"Certainly, you are welcome John Fasola. I have never seen such craftsmanship. You must know an excellent lithographer. Is this your father's portrait?"

John glanced at George Washington.

"Sure," he said, "he's the father of my country."

"Ah, this explains the quality. You are a prince."

"Sure," John laughed, "couldn't you tell." He lifted one shredded sock.

"Is this your house on the back?"

"Well," he said glibly, "I've heard it said a lot that it belongs to my people."

"Amazing. Truly. Ah, John Fasola, I have spent my wage buying woodcuts to make a good impression, but never have I seen a master who could produce this. The parchment is so thin. There is a print of fine quality on both sides, yet done so well that not one drop of ink bleeds from one side to the other. Truly, you have presented a proper gift of entry. Please, if you would condescend to see again a man of lowly rank come sup with my family sometime."

John couldn't tell if the man was being sarcastic. He looked honestly overjoyed.

"It's only a buck."

"Ah, thank you." The gate barer said.

"What?"

"Why now I know the engraver's name. When I show this to my fellows I shall proclaim this the work of Master Buck. Thank you. I am ever your servant."

"You're welcome," John said, coloring. He took a step inside. Then three back out. "What is that?"

The gate barer stiffened, then removed a long pole from his gate, removed its top with a quick twist, and tossed the cap to the side. The bar became a spear in his hand. Then, with an about-face, he turned to face the threat, but relaxed as he saw nothing out of place.

"What in the world is that?" John goggled.

The gate barer looked.

"What?"

"That."

John pointed to a blue buffalo. Its chest stood eight feet off the ground. It wore a collar of raven feathers. Great spiraling horns aimed themselves inches from the gateway.

"Oh that," said the gate barer proudly, "that's Geramir Busooli, our cow. Only six left in all the land," he added proudly, "Buir entrusted us to guard the welfare of Geramir. It is the greatest honor imaginable. Besides," he added confidentially, "Keeps the crime rates down."

"Your cow? That's not a cow. That's a…"

"It is one of only six cows left," the gate barer said rather sternly. More cheerfully, he added, "Have you, a prince, never seen one?"

"That's not a cow."

The buffalo turned its head and winked at him with lashes the length of a piano virtuoso's fingers. John leaned away. Someone had put green eye shadow on the buffalo. The gatekeeper patted him on the shoulder and smiled.

"Every year, many make the pilgrimage to see Geramir to taste real milk, so that they can know kindness. I hear they come from very far. Some even have to travel by boat to reach us. Do you know what surprises people most? There's no crime here. How could there be when we have a cow? It helps keep the peace."

John stared in awe.

"I understand how you feel. I remember my first time being in the presence of the bovine." The barer said, sympathetically. John barely heard him.

"No wonder he couldn't fit one through the rainbow."

"What's this?" the barer said, turning serious. "Someone's trying to steal cows."

"JTL," John nodded dully, "he said he tried to push one through a rainbow. He said that when we were back on Jersey Street. In the factory."

"By the bovine, someone's trying to kidnap cows." His hand gripped the spear whitely. "Who could do…? No one would…!" The barer walked to the castle's cow and put his hand protectively on a blue tuft of fur. Slowly, his eyes widened until they became wider than his slotted visor. "Did you say JTL? Was that the name of the man?"

John raised his arms defensively.

"That's what he called himself."

"Jeremy Tucker." He cursed, "I don't believe it. That crow is after cows again." With a mighty swing, the gate barer struck his spear against the other poles in the gate. They reverberated with a low tone.

The buffalo looked up. John felt an itch in his arches. All chatter in the castle village beyond the gate ceased. Metal rattled. Doors slammed. Coins stopped jingling in midair. Six more men wearing wedding bands across their legs and chest advanced to the gate. Four of them held spears; the other two short swords. The itch increased in John's feet. It climbed to his calves too.

"Take this lad to Buir! Take this lad to the regent! Take him somewhere!" The barer shouted, "Jeremy's at it again and this lad has overheard his plot."

"Lad?" he said, "Buir, the giant!" he said after-words. He started to run when he caught his reflection in a polished shield.

They were not his eyes.

Not his hair.

Not his nose.

Not anything.

He was fifteen with bowl shaped red hair. His eyes were almond shaped with irises painted colors that only a drunken dynamist would have chosen. His nose was aquiline. His body didn't seem to have an ounce of fat. He looked like a runner, a long distance runner, except he was too short. His mouth was wider, more expressive. His fingers were no longer stubby, but long and slender. Unconsciously, he began to stretch for keys he'd always had to roll over to reach. He looked nothing like himself, but it was undoubtedly him. A him he never was, but always was. He began to laugh. The guards and gate barer gently took hold of him. Dimly, he heard.

"Treat him carefully. He's a prince."

"Do you blame the lad? He held it well to get his message this far."

"Aye. Overwhelmed, he is."

"By the bovine. Jeremy Tucker."

They led him past the cow and through the village. They climbed the steps to the castle and placed him on a velvet divan.

"The regent will speak with you." Someone said. John didn't hear him. It felt too right to be this other person. It scared him. Somewhere inside, a part of him nodded.

"There, there, lad. The barer didn't mean to bring up Tucker's name. That boogey man won't be able to get at you in here. He wouldn't dare." A breeze that smelled of spring cut in front of them before playing tag with each candle in sight. Apparently, it was determined to make every flickering flame "it". "Just tell them what you know, lad. Tell them what you know."

John stood as soon as the man left. He lifted a pitcher and looked into it. It confirmed his suspicions.

"I look like a Jack." He said. He covered his mouth.

"You are not a Jack," the memory of his father argued, *"You are John Jr. Don't you ever let anyone call you that! You are nothing like a Jack. Do you hear me? You are not a Jack."*

"But Dad, look at me." And John's childhood shadow threw a cup of water up in the air, twirled, and caught the water back in a pitcher without spilling a drop. He crowed like Mary Martin in Peter Pan.

"You are not a Jack. Promise me son you will never be a Jack."

"Yes, sir."

John found himself placed in a marble floored room where gold striped the moldings on the floor and ceiling. Velvet curtains filled a window, tied off by a sash of fabric. Lavender and sandalwood scented the air. Warmth and the smell of baking bread rose from a vent in the far corner. An unlit fireplace filled nearly a whole wall. Dressing stands, tables, and a bed all stood taller than the former CEO of COW. When he turned around, a beautiful maid stood by him with a ready smile and a bucket. He smiled back, and taking that for ascent, she threw the contents on him, drenching John from head to foot.

He gasped, though the water was warm. The dried dirt became mud again despite his best effort to wring the fabric out. Brown puddles gathered on the perfect floor below him. Without a word, the maid curtseyed and skipped from the room to leave John. In her wake, three entered with grave expressions. Their eyes held questions, but they held their peace. John looked this way and that at a loss for what to say. They wore overlapping chains of gold and their clothes were polka dotted with huge gemstones and pearls. John gestured politely to sit, but the one in the middle gently shook his head with a small smile.

"Thank you," he began, "for your hospitality."

The woman on the right bobbed, but remained silent. John suddenly felt very tired and his legs began to sting from all the running. He motioned for them to sit, hoping they would so that he could do. Mud dripped into his eyes which he tried to wipe away with his hand.

The velvet sofa across from the bed looked soft and welcoming, but he stood where he was remembering how anal about cleanliness people in bean dreams were. His eyes fell on his footprints. Then cleverly, he stared at the sky. He figured if he stood there looking up, everyone would have to look up to try to see what he was staring at. The cold and wet worked their way into him.

"Look at him," a voice said sympathetically, "he's shivering."

That seemed to open up a dam, but John wasn't falling for it. He concentrated on looking up.

"The poor prince. Imagine what he must have gone through to get here. I hear he escaped from Tucker himself."

"The man who bought the…"

"Stole the." The other corrected.

"Oh dear," the first said.

"And he's so scuffed." John took a peak. There were more maids, at least one had a silver tray with dried fruit on it and the other was cleaning John's mess. The one with the tray gave him a considering look.

"It's not fair," she decided, "not fair at all. The prince is shivering and dirty and hurt and not presentable at all. He shouldn't have to face the regent like this."

"No," the other said. John watched the other clean. She looked at him and slyly said, "But there's nothing we can do. Of course, should a prince ask us to make him a bath and fix his garments, why we would have to do it!" The other caught on.

"It's true. Courtesy demands it. The regent would have to wait. Why…" the first said, watching him shiver, "he could even request soup be brought to him."

John couldn't stand it.

"Could I really?" he said. The two maids feigned a shocked look that he overheard them. They were more genuinely shocked that he had admitted that he would take an idea from one of their rank. They appraised him suspiciously. "I would really like some shoes too." He added.

"Do you need help getting undressed," the maid asked. The maid was a child, sixteen at best.

"No," John said, blushing. She turned and walked out. He bit his lip and pushed a dirty thought out of his mind. He felt ashamed of himself. *She's a child!* He reprimanded himself. *Then again, it might not have even been a come on.*

Stripping quickly, he stepped into the water.

It was Baby Bear right. Warm enough to relax his muscles, but not hot enough to burn. Spiced water seduced his nerves. He thought it might be floral. He reached for a lump of fatty soap.

A maid of honey hair walked in. She stood over John. John covered himself with the soap and turned his head. She smiled at his modesty and poured a pail of steaming water in the far end of the tub.

"Ah," he said.

"Too hot," she said, turning.

"No, it's fine" he lied and dismissed her. The water scalded. He watched her go. The door closed.

"Okay, so I'm not James Bond." He splashed unhappily.

Toweling off, he dressed himself in a pair of green tights the first maid had brought. He looked like Errol Flynn, he thought, and then staring at his skinny legs protested, *No, I do not look like Daffy Duck.*

The shirt was also green and fell to mid-thigh. He belted it with a fine thin rope. Hands on hips, head cockily posed, it still didn't look right. The belt should be leather. Black leather. And he needed a rapier.

"This hallucination is falling down on the job," he groused. Still, he looked better in tights than he thought he would have. He would sweep maids off their feet yet.

The shoes they provided were boots with hard wooden soles. They were harder than the marble floors. Flexing, he could barely bend them. He looked around the room for Dr. Scholls. The boots seemed to be made of leather, but was snake patterned. His eyes fell to the floor. Putting his back against the door, he tore pieces of towel to pad his boots.

He opened the door. His heart stopped, then restarted at triple time.

"Wow." He said.

"Who are you?" the woman asked. She was dressed in a golden gown. Silk sashes of rainbow hue laced the top. Her hair was a lustrous bronze, the kind of brunette that made blonde look bleached out and faded. Delicate features, smoothed from soft clay, tilted expressively. Her body curved exquisitely. He jerked his shirt lower. There were definite negatives to wearing tights. Her only imperfection was the heavy iron wrought shackles placed on her wrists.

"Wow." He said again. She blushed and turned away. He pinched himself hard. She was young enough to be his daughter. *So what*, he reminded himself, *you look twelve. Shut up*, he told his libido. *Give it up*, added his brain, *since when would a girl like that even look at you. She's blushing*, continued his libido. *Oh my god, what do I do. What I do! Run, John, run*, shouted his adrenaline.

"Do you have a name?" she inquired softly.

"John," he croaked, immensely pleased that his voice did not crack.

"Would you sit with me, John?"

"I…"

"They told me I would be denied nothing. I have only one more day."

"One day?" his heart pumped.

"I… it is pleasant here, isn't it?"

"Are they… what are they going to do to you. Are they going to execute you?" The thought disturbed him deeply. It wasn't just that she was beautiful. There was something profoundly wrong with the idea that she would be killed. *Stop being sexist! She could be a monster for all you know*, but something in her smile and bearing argued against that. He bit his lip in concentration, disliking the new turn his hallucination was taking. *What happened to the deer? The deer was cool. And the bath… I liked the bath, but…*._he thought, *this is starting to be a bad trip again.* Then he smiled inwardly. He knew he was right not to do beans in college.

"No." she said. He let out a breath.

"Good." He said. She smiled. His heart constricted. He looked away from her. *Daughter*, he thought, *she should be in high school. You can get arrested for dating*... but aloud he asked, "Are you sick. I once heard of a guy that was really sick; the doctors told him that he would last a week or two. Guy lived another twenty years."

"You are kind, John." She said and put a hand on his arm. "But it is certain. I have only one day more."

He turned towards her. Her face was very close. He stood and coughed.

"Why?"

She looked away.

"They took me here." She said instead, "It was my first time in a carriage. It was so exciting. Have you ever been in a carriage?"

"No."

"It goes so fast, John. And you can feel everything. The earth and stones… and when they slow down. They cheer. They cheer for you." She began to cry. John sat down and put an arm around her.

"Hey," he said in a fatherly tone, "it'll be all right. I'm sure you're innocent."

"Of course I'm innocent. They brought me here," she continued bravely, "I got to see the cow. I even tasted real milk." She brightened momentarily, "It was… I didn't think it would be so thick or sweet. I thought they lied."

He comforted her. Music flowed from his lips. His lust dissipated. Light flickered in the hallway.

"There must be a way to save you." He said at last. She looked up at him.

"Who would champion me?" she asked, weeping again. An alarm sounded in his brain.

"Who would?" he asked. She looked at him. Hazel eyes, as mixed up as his own flickered hopefully. She pulled away from him.

"Ah," he said, his heart silencing his head with a right upper cut. "I'll do it. I'll champion you."

A platter dropped. John turned. The honey haired maid stared at him, ignoring the platter and the wine she spilt onto her feet.

"You'll do it," the maid repeated, "You'll champion her against the dragon."

"Dragon?" he said. The girl's arms flung over his head and he found himself looped between her and the shackles. Her nose pressed against his. His breathing quickened. She tilted her lips. John ducked and disengaged himself, blushing furiously. The maid and girl stared at him as if he were crazy. He jammed his shirt even lower and tried to picture his mother. Her eyes were round. Flecks of tears dotted her chin and sashes. Ah, what the heck, he thought.

"I will champion you m'lady against the foul dragon," and this time, his voice did crack.

A courtier wearing maroon tights and an orange vest came down the hall.

"Ah, there you are. The regent is ready to speak with you."

"Malen"

"Yes, Hortense," said the courtier.

"John," she began.

"The prince?" he interrupted.

"Hortense?" John asked, looking at her.

"John," she continued, "has agreed to champion me in my plight against the dragon."

"Have you?" he asked, twisting a scarf between his fingers.

"Would you tell my father Gaebil Henry. I know he…" she didn't finish the thought.

"Hortense Henry?" John asked.

"Did you agree to champion her cause?"

His brain argued with his heart. His courage sided with his brain. She placed her hand on his. The maid remained studiously quiet.

"I did." He answered. "I did." He repeated more definitively.

"Oh my. I mean good for you," the courtier said finally. He walked down the hallway a short way before looking back. Finally, he said sadly, "The regent is ready for you, John." He looked the thin lad up and down. "Oh dear," he said and looked away. To the hallway in front of them the courtier asked, "Have you done this before?" John stopped in mid stride. He looked at the courtier, then turned to the worried maid with the creased forehead, and finally to Hortense. He could think of only one thing to say.

"Killed seven with one blow." He smiled. They all relaxed.

14. Jack for All Feasts

Hortense unwrapped a rainbow-colored sash and gently knotted it around John's neck. The courtier stiffened. It could not be undone now. With a stiff smile, he pivoted and turned, leading John through a maze of right and left turns. John tried to keep track, but was soon reminded why he never bought puzzle books. The layout of the castle was more confusing than a rainbow! Each hallway fielded a different color, every room more decorated with ever more ornate frivolity. John passed men wearing orange kilts, gold shirts, sky colored capes, snake patterned capes, rings, necklaces, bracelets, torcs, and tattoos. A goblet with a nipple was belted to nearly every man's side. The women wore low or high cut bodices, tight, flowing, incandescent, smoldering, brilliant gowns. A couple wore pants and a very small number displayed proudly dented breastplates. Few hands sported less than two rings per finger. John shaded his eyes a few times to escape the reflected glare of their costumes.

After an hour or so of marching, John wondered if he were being paraded or shown off to the castle instead of being taken to the regent. Passersby certainly waved often enough at him. The courtier paid no mind, but kept up the same businesslike pace, pausing only once to smile for a court artisan who wore a press card on top of his dunce's cap.

Mile after mile they circled, turned, and walked through splendor. John's eyes grew numb to it. *What good are plush pillows if you never get to sit on them!* Whenever John lagged, the courtier picked up the pace, and Hortense, all bubbles now, trotted alongside him. John feared that the castle had no end, but just as his legs began to cramp, the courtier finally stopped at a set of double doors. Each stood over a hundred feet tall. The champion's sash around John's neck tightened as if what lived beyond frightened it. The pressure choked. John coughed and gasped. His fingers reached up and he tried to unknot the silk. The thing gave apologetically, but immediately constricted when he let go, although this time it gripped him only snugly. John caught his breath as the courtier advanced. Each great double door had two handles. The courtier signaled and guards pulled a bell rope to announce their presence. John gulped at the deep bass resonance of the tolling. The silk favor tightened again as if to say *See*! or *Me too*! Voices behind the door stopped. Then, slowly, one door opened.

Murmurs restarted almost immediately. Fingers pointed. Chins lowered. Eyes inspected. The sash gleamed prominently on his neck. Some covered their eyes. Some hands pointed in shock. Others covered their mouths at the foolishness of youth.

The regent stood. He wore a burlap sack, gray tights, and a leaf patterned bronze belt. His drab clothing drew attention to him, increased him in stature somehow. It made all the others in the room look painted and overdone.

"Presenting Prince John Fasola." Trumpets blared. "Prince of…" the man turned to John and looked pleadingly. John thought. All the faces bent towards him with an equal combination of curiosity and snobbery on their faces. Suddenly, John's face lit. He could honestly name his kingdom. A kingdom he had ruled, handed down from his father whose people he had cared for. He whispered to the page who at once nodded and smiled.

"Prince of the Corporation of Ordinary Wares."

The trumpets roared. Feet stamped. Hands pounded. A man in gold lamé brocaded with emeralds and rubies was overheard as to say. "A kingdom with three names. Preposterous. Why I shall have to lengthen my homeland's name."

John stood quite still. He lifted a hand and turned to each corner of the building and then bowed his head fractionally. The applause slowed and picked up even louder as the crowd digested what that bow meant. It meant there were none in the room that John considered his equal. John, for his part, smiled graciously. He tried his best to remember what presidents did during inaugurations and how the pope looked when he toured in his pope mobile.

"Come forth, Prince John," the regent said. John climbed the dais. He waved once more at the assemblage.

The applause started to sound strained. Arms tired. The regent looked to John. John waved again. He had the urge to scream. "Are you ready to rock?" The regent stood and gave the crowd permission to stop applauding and with little ceremony motioned for John to begin his tale. The lad looked blankly at him. "What of Jeremy Tucker?" Finished the regent.

"Well," John began, "I was at…" he began again, "I went to the BEAN factory because suspicious stuff was happening and I felt responsible. I found JTL there…"

A tumult began.

"Jeremy Tucker found beans!"

"Beans!"

"I thought this was about cows?"

"Feather and spit!"

"Stop stepping on my feet."

"He wouldn't!"

"Preposterous!"

"Look, he wears a champion's ribbon!"

"The lad cries wolf!"

The itch returned to his feet. It rubbed away all the fatigue in his legs instantly. John prepared to run.

The regent shouted something, but what he said could not be overheard. He gestured sharply to his trumpeters, but their call was ignored. Finally, he motioned John into another room. John trotted, retelling the rest of his conversation with JTL.

The regent bowed his head. He picked up a quill and snapped it.

"Thank you, Prince John," he said finally, "You are a brave lad indeed. Crates full of beans…" He shook. "Well, we will…" His earnest face searched the stone facades. Ancient etched faces shone with polish. Gleaming stained glass swords burned from the light of candelabras. Wise gargoyles supported columns, but though they winked and smiled, they did not whisper. Nothing in the room offered answers. A pause breathed long between them. He said finally. "What will you require to face the dragon?"

"What about Jeremy?" John asked, uncomfortable with the sudden change of subjects.

"We will…" the regent began again, "we will… do something. But there are easier matters. What need you, Prince John? How can we reward you? What need you to do honorable battle?"

John scratched his chin. He looked about the room. The heroic figures all shouted the same answer. An image of Saint George came to mind as well. To follow tradition, he needed a sword. He faced the regent and decided against saying "sword". He didn't want to sound stupid. Saying sword would be like going to a plumber and saying, "I need a thingy." He needed something less generic. Searching, the name of a sword popped into his mind. He called it out before thinking.

"Could you get me a rapier?"

"A rapier!" The regent said, and then he looked at John. The lad was too thin to handle much more, still, a rapier against a dragon?

Both waited for the other to speak. "Prince John, I realize your honor may be compromised, but you cannot do this. You've no time to call to your castle and request your armor. Improperly fitted, you couldn't possibly be expected to… I know you have killed seven. Your legend flies like a dentity, but without your equipment, your squire…" he stopped.

John squirmed. Suddenly, the regent's plain dress did not look like a costume. John recognized him as a man chosen by a giant to do a task, chosen because he was honest, because he wanted to do good, because he was willing to try, but mostly chosen as a joke. He wasn't a regent. He was a clerk, understaffed and underfunded, asked to be aware of and solve immense problems. A man with so few resources that he looked to statues for advice. Despite this, the man pitied John. John's cheeks burned.

"I," was all he said. The regent's hands twiddled. His eyes searched the room again, but the room was lacking.

"None will call you Coward John." He continued confidentially, "A fair deal was struck. The maiden Hortense will sacrifice her life for her village and in return the dragon will not return to that county for five years. It is a good deal, John. A very good deal."

"Five years?" John asked, "Her life is worth only five years?"

"Prince John understand. Dragons…"

"Five years?"

"You don't have to do this."

"Five years!" John pounded the arm of the chair in disgust. Statues and glass swords mocked. Pursing his lips, the regent stood. He thrust his hand into John's. John remembered his father then. His father gripped his hand like this once. It felt good. It felt good to be respected.

"I understand. There are some things that are greater than what is reasonable." The regent said solemnly. "Come let us eat. I will raise a toast to you. You are the most bovine of all men I have ever met." He paused, and his eyes lit. "I shall toast you with milk! Have you ever tasted it?"

"Milk?"

"Yes," the regent said, "It does a body good!"

The honey haired maid led him back to his room. John stared at the tapestries. They depicted bloody combat.

"I was so scared," he said. The maid paused. John smiled at her. He repeated himself. She put her hand to her heart.

"Did you mean me to hear that? Princes do not often," she said flustered, "not that I would instruct one of your rank on how to..."

He interrupted.

"I was so scared the giant would be there."

"The giant? Buir O'Cassey?" she smiled indulgently and closed the door, "You're a strange lad, Prince John." She watched to see if he took offense. "You come with tales of Jeremy and beans, tomorrow you set off after a dragon, and what you're afraid of is an absent giant."

John turned sheepishly. The maid worried that she said too much. She lifted the door latch.

"What's he like?"

"The giant?" she asked. John nodded. "He's nothing to be afraid of. Buir O'Cassey is everywhere, but he doesn't really do anything. He gives away most of his work. If no one will take the work, Buir usually considers the issue so long that it becomes lost in thought. Lost in most everybody's thoughts." John smiled at that, but the maid turned pale. "What have I said," she continued, "Oh Prince John, noble Prince John say you'll not repeat what I have said."

John considered the maid. She confused him. What made her shuffle her feet and knead her hands? He patted the bed, and motioned to her to talk some more, but she shook her head and worriedly kneaded folds in her skirt.

"I'll not do that. Please ask something else for your silence. You're a champion. It would be disrespectful." John raised his hands in protest. She moved back, as if he were reaching for her. The maid turned her head. "I'll not do that, Prince John." Tears filled her eyes.

"I just wanted," He said. "I didn't mean... I wouldn't force you to." He reached out again and gently took her hand. Panic warred against his seeming sincerity. Slowly, her brow smoothed.

"Forgive me. Forgive my immodesty to think that you would be of such poor character. I should have known that you could never desire one of my rank."

"What?" John took a step away. The maid looked relieved and fatally insulted at the same time. He had lived with mother too long. How could he have gotten this bad at talking to women?

"A man of your nobility, who would champion a stranger and yet refuse even her favor." She raised her finger in sudden understanding. "Do you favor women, Prince John?"

"What?" he asked again.

"I," her eyes rounded again, "I should seal my lips with wax. Please, take no offense. I am but a simple maid. I did not mean to speak your secrets."

John chewed his lip. He held her hand. Should he attempt to seduce her? The thought that a security camera might be recording him frolicking with a hallucination disturbed him. Forcing her, when she did not want him, also stilled his thoughts. He sighed. He was so far from James Bond it was ridiculous. James would not be bothered by this moral dilemma. Then again, the maid wouldn't have refused Bond. He put a hand around her waist. She cringed. He released her and walked to the bed. The maid smiled. Somehow, she had made a prince uncomfortable and this power pleased her very much.

"You are odd, Prince John of the Corporation of Ordinary Wares." She informed him. He turned back to her. "Are you really a prince?" She continued and then realized her accusation. A look of shock exploded. "I did not mean to question your…" she stammered. "You confuse me. I have been ignored so many times. Secrets told in front of me as if I were furniture incapable of repeating. I would not question your word, Prince John. That is not what I meant to say." A second thought struck her. "I refused you," she said. John winced. The phrasing hurt. John stammered without saying anything. "I shall be hanged." She finished.

John fell back on the bed. He looked shaken. He opened his mouth. No words flowed. The maid looked at him stretched out upon the bed. With tears brimming, she undid a knot. Her skirt fell. John stood and stared at her in slip and blouse. She approached him. She put her hand on his chest. Her tears fell onto his cheeks.

"No." he shouted, "No." he repeated and rolled away from her. "Go," he said, "I won't talk about this."

"You are truly," she stammered. John strode to the window and braced himself, grateful for the night air. *She's not real,* he reminded himself, *Don't get so worked up.* He turned and watched her tie up the skirt. Knotting it took much longer than untying.

She glanced at him.

"If you were not a champion…" she said apologetically.

"I need a drink," he answered hoarsely.

The door closed.

15. Dancing Really Fast

It was a fair inn. The tables were solid and recently rebuilt. The stains on the floor had been scrubbed to a fine varnish. Some tried feathering and complained good-naturedly of sudden drafts and talk that spoiled their aim. A flutist and a drummer played. The fare was only fair, but it came at a fair price.

Jeremy Tucker sniffed the air. He smelled a rumor. It smelled juicy. The bouncy tune suggested he stay. *There's time enough*, the music said, *gossip travels quickly.* He swam to the side of his tankard and looked up. Judging by the distance to the rim, his ale was only half drunk. He could wait.

Diving, he touched bottom and began swallowing. The ale whirlpooled. Within the span of a sneeze, the drink was gone. Rubbing his hands dizzily, he grew large enough to climb the tankard. He tight-roped the rim and belly flopped onto a handkerchief.

"It's the only way to drink," he laughed, fluffing the cotton under his head.

A thought lived in the lilt of a flute. The wee man sighed contentedly, stretched, and closed his eyes to more properly attend to the music. It keened high and long. Jeremy Tucker frowned. Unpleasant thoughts wandered in that tune. Jeremy muffled his ears with folds of handkerchief. The drumbeat throbbed under his skin. *Faerie are meant to be immune to the seduction of music*, he reminded himself. *That doom is left for those foolish enough to listen ringside.* Yet, here he was not only letting his passions feel the beat and melody, but eating and drinking at the same time.

"Jeremy, you're a feathering fool," he muttered face down into the handkerchief. His heart pounded counterpoint to the military march. Dragon wings and human eyes emerged from fireplace shadows.

"Another ale," he called. To the shadows, he added, "It's not my fault that she came unprepared. I wasn't looking for her. I needed to snatch me some luck to stop the bleeding.

The blame's not on me, lads," he muttered, sipping ale from a spoon. "Wasn't looking for her at all. Not that any of you care." The patrons studiously ignored him, intent on their games, drinking, and off-tune singing.

The leprechaun drummed his fingers against his full coin purse, its sound played over him like a lover's many kisses, but somehow it did not fill him. Looking into his tankard he groused, "It's your lands that are drying- your lands, not mine. And its… by the bovine, it's him that's taking the very color from your cheek… the very children from your homes. So, what's wrong with snatching a little luck. What's wrong with trying… Maybe trying a little… to… Giants fall... that's what they do. They're meant to rise and fall. Not that any of you'd breathe a word against him… not that I'd expect you too. Easier for you… because it's my fault. I should have kept the cow hidden, then there'd be a little more in you. Then, maybe I wouldn't have to… but he's a good lad. At least he's a good lad. And what's wrong with finding a foot to trip the giant before he eats us all."

Jeremy downed another tankard.

"Nothing. Nothing's wrong with that bit of mischief, but the girl, feather and spit, I'd not planned on inviting her… risking her. Just came at the wrong time. How can you say that's not a choice? How can you fault me? She… the rainbow chose her, not me." Jeremy drained the spoon. "She'll blame me. Everyone blames me." The flute keened high like the hunting call of a predatory bird. "What's wrong with a wee man looking for a little luck? I tell you it's not my fault, not my fault at all."

"You've a lot to say today…" said a friendly drunk.

"She shouldn't have been there in the first place. Did I invite her? She made the choice."

"You're a liar, you are." The drunk smiled.

Jeremy looked up from the handkerchief. Both spit. Jeremy rolled off his napkin. The drunk fell off his chair. Laughter rose like beer foam.

"Aye, you're right. The fault's my own. It's always been my fault." Jeremy said and the drunk nodded. He raised his tankard.

"To women, may the fault always be ours."

"To women," Jeremy agreed and put both arms around his tankard's handle. The cup tipped upwards. Jeremy put his back into it. Suddenly, the drunk's tankard clinked his. Jeremy flew into the air and landed in a wad of mashed potatoes. They laughed again.

"Too salty." Jeremy snorted, carving potato angels. The innkeeper walked by and placed a fresh ale by the little man.

"Don't you make trouble," he warned, "I'll not have you ruining people's suppers."

"I'm not an imp," Jeremy Turker said with dignity, "I'm a wee man. Whee!" Jeremy pirouetted, scattering wads of potatoes across the tabletop. The innkeeper scowled.

"You're a mess, that's what you is."

"You've think I've made a mess?" Jeremy frowned, "Here?" then curled into a ball, laughing. The innkeeper shook his head. Others in the room looked at Jeremy darkly, Jeremy ignored this. He was used to them mistrusting or hating him. Instead, he looked at the friendly drunk. The innkeeper walked between them and warned, "They're never really drunk, you know. They just try to lull you. Take a warning. His kind is nothing but trouble."

Jeremy sat. They both stared at him. The friendly drunk watched the blush fade from the leprechaun's cheek. The haze vanish from behind his eyes.

"It's just that your ale is too weak." He said.

"How does he do that?" The drunk asked spilling his ale.

"Leave him be." The innkeeper answered. Jeremy dusted his jacket and shook potato drippings from his hand. He gave a wild wink and a wide smile. His toe tapped to the musician's beat.

"How does he look so?" The drunk continued, "The man looks ready to go to a ball, even with potato drippings in his hair. I saw him drink more than five times his height in brown ale." The innkeeper waved a dismissive hand and returned to swat at greedy hands who tried to change a fifth into a fourth behind his back.

"Man could go to a coronation." The flutist agreed, taking a break.

"Ah, you'll make me blush, lass." He snapped his fingers, but his hands were too slick to allow him to grow further. He blinked the salt from his eyes. Toweling himself off with a napkin, he waved the flute player over. The musician hesitated. Her instrument was half the length of her arm and had a suitable number of holes for one with talent, but who was not a virtuoso. Her skirt was plump with the padding earned from years of tavern life. Still, she was pleasant enough to look at though she was beginning to look a bit more matronly than maidenly. Jeremy waved towards her again. Shrugging, she handed her instrument to her partner, who sealed it inside a fur lined case and then handed it back. She shouldered it.

With a nod, the drummer began tapping out a random melodic beat, he was good enough to find two octaves worth of notes on the drum's skin. She was good enough to walk on beat. Jeremy surveyed the room, peering over wads of mashed potatoes and bowls of uncertain stew as she took up a seat next to his plate. She smiled at him and took a cup. With a hop, he climbed his tankard and sat on its rim. Conspiratorially, he asked,

"If you saw a rainbow coming at you, would you step through?"

"Aye. And I'd line my pockets with gold."

"Exactly my point. She made the choice to come. I tried to do right by her, but she made the choice."

"Did you?"

"Did I? That's not right. Not right at all. Listen, it's not a hard thing to call a rainbow, but you try steering it sometimes."

"Choices," said she.

It's possible that she knew what Jeremy was talking about, but much more likely that she was just familiar with tavern talk and was just nodding along.

"Be fair, dear. Imagine you put that flute up to your lips and call forth a ballad. Most in the bar nod and sway with your tune, but in the back sits a man who just lost a love. What if that man goes into a drunken rage, because of the memory that song wakes? What if it was the song of their union and their former love? Would you be responsible for bringing him pain?"

"A rainbow is a bit more tempting than a tune, wee one," the flutist teased, "but aye, I'd be responsible for what the man felt. I brought it into the world."

"No," Jeremy splashed potatoes with his feet, "You'd not be… well, you might be responsible, but you wouldn't be guilty."

"You feel guilty, do you?" asked the friendly drunk.

"No," Jeremy said very quickly. The flutist smiled wickedly and the friendly drunk narrowed his eyes.

"I thought your folk weren't cursed with mortal failings like guilt?"

"Course we aren't. Wastes too much time. Can you imagine how much baggage you'd have to carry around by your twelve hundredth birthday if you let yourself get tripped up by something as silly as guilt? We're called wee folk 'cause we just embrace the joy of life and let slide the other. Politics is a matter for…"

With a trickster's gleam, the woman put the flute to her lips. Notes torn from lost souls wailed. Jeremy opened his mouth in protest. The tip of the flute wavered in a light melody. It sung of life. A delicate flutter of laughter and an angry shriek of tears reminded all of the newborn. Toes tapped as the music bounded in the play of youth. Jeremy's mouth made an "o". Then it became sweet. First loves met. Promises and dreams wove. Men made themselves out of boys. Girls grew to women, laughing and crying at the simplicity of the men who chased them. Then the flute bent low in its range and hearts broke. Jeremy lifted a hand in protest. Lives torn by war. Loves who fell from love. Children born still. Jeremy stood in the slick potato and touched his nose. He blew a wad of potato out. The drummer stared blankly at the flute. He could add nothing. Others covered their heads.

The woman stared at her audience. She took a deep breath. Heads perked up. A wind rose to announce the hero. The melody challenged them to rise also. It danced towards the possibility of new love. It soared, dipped, dared and challenged, full of mischief.

"Now that's not fair," Jeremy accused. "I did try." The spell of the music refused to release him. Jeremy closed his ears. Others stamped, giving it a beat. Animated stories of individual heroes sprang. Drunks and patrons roared with laughter. Jeremy heard accusations in the music.

"By the bovine, I did try." He slammed his hand against the plate and shattered it. "I did more than any of you. You sit back and let the world take shape. How dare you accuse me?" Jeremy Tucker sprang to full height and struck the table again. "You can accuse me of being wrong! You can accuse me of thinking too much of myself! Feather and spit, you can blame me for the burnt pudding …" he stopped.

The room was silent. Drunken faces looked almost sober.

"I said nothing." The flutist said.

"I…" Jeremy said, "It's not my fault." He told them all.

"Did you see that? A wee man fell under the flute. It wasn't even a full harp. What does it mean?"

"I'll tell you what it means." Said the formerly friendly drunk. "It means he's vulnerable. He can be charmed. His gold is vulnerable." Jeremy spun towards the flutist. Her eyes held no sympathy.

"Look at his garb. By pudding, I want that!" A number of them reached for the leprechaun. Jeremy with a single bound landed on the stairs. The flutist put her lips to her instrument, but the wee man threw a clump of potatoes at her. It spattered across her face and into the holes of her instrument. Jeremy's eyes twinkled with rainbows and his breath smelled of beans.

"Vulnerable, am I?"

They didn't believe his boast. Drunks and patrons charged the stair.

"Stop!" pleaded the innkeeper, "He's just making mischief. That's what they do!"

Gold filled too many minds. They scrambled up the stairs. Jeremy rounded the corner and barreled into a room. He ignored the bed and the cheap stand. He gave a bottom a quick slap. A lover whooped in surprise as more drunken bodies filed in behind him. He opened the window and flipped onto the roof. Arms reached out. The friendly drunk climbed up after. Others circled on the ground, trying to keep him in sight.

Picking up speed, Jeremy threw himself at the blacksmith's roof. He landed easily and rolled to his feet. The crowd followed. Some tried the jump. Two failed, but the flutist made the spring easily. She faced him lifting her lump filled instrument. Jeremy shivered. Where could he run from that haunt? She would have him and ride him to his gold.

They climbed on barrels. Some gave boosts. Jeremy thought to attack the flutist, but that second portion of long ago eaten cow stopped him. She played the first keening note. It struck him. A hand pulled itself onto the blacksmith's roof. Jeremy grimaced. Desperately, he curled his fingers into claws and charged towards her. Her eyes widened; the flute slipped from her lips as she saw prisms sparkle within his eyes. Jeremy ran faster, he lowered his head. The flutist returned the instrument to her lips and played furiously. A moment before crashing into her, he sprang to the side. With clever fingers, he snatched the instrument away. She lunged. He rolled between her legs. A scream broke through the crowd. The flutist fell. Quick as a rabbit, the wee man's strong hands pulled long enough to make sure she didn't fall. Eyes widened in surprise.

"You saved me. You?" she said. The leprechaun looked at the flute in his hand. He'd told them too much. He could never come back and be safe. Angrily, he broke the wooden flute over his knees and took the curse. Everyone who saw took a step back afraid that lightning would strike immediately. Some actually fell.

"You forget." He said, with a lot more bravado than he felt, "I'm a wee bovine." Secretly, he hoped that all the burritos he ate would stave off the bane tiding. A minstrel's tool was all but holy. With alarm, he looked out onto the street. Something rose on fleet hooves.

Like a wave, heads turned from him. Something important raced through the cowless village. Beans were luck, both good and bad. This then, would be an amplified curse. It rode on a wave of voices, gaining velocity and volume. The scent of rumor, thick and angry, aimed her spear at his nose.

"Prince John has championed Gaebil's daughter."

"Prince John?" Jeremy said. What did that have to do with him? Who would be foolish enough to challenge a dragon to a duel? He fingered the shards of flute. Somehow, the wind drew one last keening note.

"No!" he gasped, "He wouldn't."

A splinter worked his way into his finger. Curses work quickly, he thought.

In his mind, an amused dragon picked its teeth with John's ribs. The dragon then flew to its master. Corp O'Rat boomed with laughter. Jack was dead! With abandon, the pillaging began. Corp tore rainbows from their roots and emptied their contents into his vault. Great iron shackles snapped around children and whips flailed them in poorly timbered mines. Enormous hands with a bag of gold as big as a house filled the leprechaun's head. Finally, he saw himself drawn forward on puppet strings. He was forced to feed the giant beans. Jeremy moaned, *Johnny, what have you done to my plans*? And then a worse thought struck him.

"Feather and spit, I've killed them both."

The village folk stopped muttering. Prince John's rumor now seemed all gristle and no meat. Slowly, backing away, they repeated his words. This new rumor… murder, spoken by Jeremy Tucker himself. Now, that was something to chew on. Folk ran to feed the fire and speed the wind, but mostly they ran to get away from a wee man they had once hated for stealing a cow from M. Au Paulet.

They left him alone. No attackers distracted him. He walked to the edge of the roof. They were still running. The moon grinned mockingly

"Johnny," he called out and somewhere a rainbow fell free from its foundations and shattered.

16. Shish Kabobs and the Easter Bunny

Hortense looked fetching in her flowing white tunic. Its softness worked perfectly against the hard gray of the rock. She walked meekly up a pebbly path and tried not to wince as the rocks bit into her bare feet. Three men escorted her and they carried ornamentally thin pikes that barely had ceremonial function. The blade resembled a dragon with the tip its spiked tongue. Behind them followed a small procession of others including a backup virgin in case this one escaped or leapt to her death. In the train was also Carolie, the castle seamstress. She pursed her lips and fretted. There were too many clouds in the sky to properly show off her effort and she had been sewing nonstop for two weeks. Hortense was to look like a daffodil in full bloom, the petals opening seductively to reveal the girl.

She rudely appraised the virgin and nodded. Physically, she was fine, but the seamstress doubted she had the lungs to be a proper victim. The scream was essential. In a pouch, she carried a pitch pipe, but in all their practice, no one had ever been able to get Hortense to scream more than an octave over middle C.

Well, perhaps adrenaline would do the trick.

The small procession reached the opening and the pikemen began sweeping the ground. Even the ground should look untouched. Virginal. Carolie handcuffed the girl and began examining the folds in the skimpy white tunic they had dressed the girl in. She checked the make-up, and applied a bit more rouge. And then studied her dress. The tunic was appallingly perfect. It fell in one long sweeping drop, cinched at the waist.

Carolie tsked disapprovingly. The girl was supposed to be a daffodil, but even daffodils have more than one petal. More, she just looked to… well, dragons are notoriously picky and if they think no preparation or hardship went into their meal, they might just turn their noses up to it. Presentation means a lot.

She sighed and got to work muttering,

"People just don't have pride in their work anymore."

And with a small knife, she tore the tunic. She bent down and dusted it up. "Supposed to look like there's been a struggle." She tore a few more choice areas of the tunic and then stepped back to appraise her work. "Now, you tell me," Carolie said condescendingly to her staff, "is that more tempting or what?" They bowed their heads in shame. She harrumphed. John protested, but Carolie said, "It's tradition. If you lose…" She looked disdainfully at him and the toothpick sword he carried. Even she could see he didn't know how to grip the thing. "…should the dragon lose its trophy?" John answered yes, but they laughed. The old woman patted him on the shoulder and motioned to her crew.

With large hairy brushes they basted her with honey.

"Going to be a honey barbeque tonight." Carolie said, laughing at her own joke. Hortense for her part, practiced the specific gestures and expressions a damsel in distress was supposed to wear. She clasped her hands. She got on her knees. She spread her arms wide. She turned her head, tilting it down. The crew applauded.

Carolie pressed some berries into the honey on her skin. She smelled the girl and nodded.

"Smells like an innocent to me." She announced. The crew packed up their supplies and ran. Carolie looked at the sacrifice one last time and shifted Hortense's shackles and tore one more rent in her tunic. She nodded to herself, then changed her mind and pulled out a needle and thread.

The sun rose. Carolie looked up.

"Never enough time to get it right. Well, I suppose you'll do. In my day, we had better material to work with." The old woman shuffled off. Hortense practiced looking scared.

"Is this good?" Hortence asked. John nodded. Her brows lowered as she scrutinized him. "How do you do that?" she asked, "You do it so much better. That's exactly the way the instructors said I should look. You're so helpful." John didn't answer. What could he say? He was a natural at fear.

There was something wrong about waking up and still being high. The hallucination was becoming too linear. John paced the ground. Maybe JTL wasn't a megalomaniac; maybe he was a mad scientist. If that was true, he had rented all the wrong movies.

A shadow flew overhead. Hortense vomited. Suddenly, the fear expressions came more naturally. It landed on a hillock. An arc of fire shot into the air like a poor man's rainbow. John raised his sword.

"Are you a chef?" the dragon asked delighted, "Is it to be shish kabob? Is that why you brought a skewer?"

"Champion." John barely got out.

"Really?" The dragon hopped down. He walked towards the scrawny lad. John tried to move and he did. Well, he shook. A giant claw landed on John. It lifted him, spun him around. Then gingerly placed him on the ground. "First love?" the dragon asked.

"What?" John found the courage to ask.

"Is this your first love?" the dragon lowered its head sympathetically. Their eyes met. John staggered backwards.

"No," he said.

"Not your first love?" The dragon looked bewildered. "Is she rich?" John shrugged. "And you're sure you're not a chef?" John shook his head. "Why then?"

John thought about this.

"She asked." He said, finally.

The dragon laughed. John got mad.

He thrust his rapier at the dragon's scaled belly. The rapier bent, looking even more like a poor man's rainbow than the silk around his neck. Then, the metal snapped. John looked at the stub left of the sword. He backed away, saw Hortense, and put his two inches of blade in front of him in the en garde position.

The dragon rolled over laughing. Acid tears browned the scales around its eyes. John smiled too. It was kind of ridiculous.

"I shall have to tell Corp about this." The dragon said, beating the ground. "What is your name?"

Something stilled within John. The absurdity vanished like the smile from his face. A familiar itch worked its way through his body and his stomach filled with gas.

"Jack," he said, "My name is Jack." The dragon stopped laughing. It opened one eye. With a small cough it puffed a blast of warm air at him. John dove. Head over heel he rolled all the way down the hill breaking the ceremonial crown of champions that the regent had given him. The dragon laughed again.

John lay in a thicket of thorns. He extricated himself slowly. Many of the thorns stuck. His backside hurt. So did his front side.

The dragon lifted its head and turned the day fiery. Hortense screamed. John sprinted. Halfway up, he lost his balance and rolled back down. The dragon lofted itself in the air and landed at the bottom of the hill.

"Are you really Jack?" It said. Claws rested on his chest.

"No." John said desperately.

"Good. I worked for M. Au Paulet. We all did back then. If you were Jack… Jacks are dangerous. Practically made of luck." It snorted. His shirt darkened. "Still, you are a champion. So, I should…"

"His name is Peter!" cried a voice from atop the hill. The dragon looked up. JTL stood on the side of the hill covered from head to foot in soot.

"Who said that?" the dragon said, spinning its head.

"Would you kill Peter Pan?"

The dragon paused. It lifted John. Limp limbs hung down.

"This is Peter Pan?"

"It is." Jeremy answered. The dragon seemed totally unnerved by the invisible voice. It dropped John and clambered up the hill. Jeremy stood very still. The dragon walked by him. Struggling, John gripped a root and crawled.

Dew slicked his wooden soles. He slammed his boot tips into the earth and climbed. The dragon smiled slyly.

"How can that be Peter Pan?" Its ears untufted. Jeremy turned and threw a jar of preserves. It exploded on a rock. The dragon's nose flared. It licked its lips.

"Ah, so it is you, ghost. I apologize, but I am on duty. I am to keep the tasty for myself and take the treasure back to Corp O'Rat."

"You may have the tasty."

"No!" John shouted.

"Leave me the champion. I wish to possess him."

"You would possess Peter Pan?" the dragon said.

"Take the tasty and the treasure. He is a champion unworthy of you."

"You talk too much, ghost," the dragon leered.

It pounced, landing inches from the leprechaun. Jeremy closed his eyes and held his breath. The dragon puffed, but it couldn't see or smell anything. Just a big lump of ash it had already burned. It turned.

John picked up a rock and ran towards Hortense. He wondered why he was doing this. His answers were as plentiful as the regent's had been earlier. He braced himself. *Maybe*, he prayed, he wasn't actually Jack or Peter, but David. Of course, being David would work better if he were facing a giant and if he had a sling, but he would make do with the rock somehow.

The shackles swung empty.

"Hey?" John said, pointing. "You…?" he said to Jeremy.

Standing in Hortense's place was the largest chocolate Easter bunny John had ever seen. It stood almost five foot. A white tunic was draped sloppily over its head. One ear was missing. Jeremy's mouth looked less sooty than brown. The dragon turned.

"What trickery is this!" it shouted outraged.

"Take a smell." Jeremy whispered. The dragon swiped at the voice. Jeremy rolled under it. Dragon eyes widened. Soot rubbed off on the grass. It aimed its snout.

"Two champions!" it roared with outrage. "That is against form."

Jeremy clapped himself down to his smallest size and balled himself up. The fire roared above him.

"Take a smell, dragon." Jeremy urged, "I promise it will make up for the deceit."

It stamped again towards the voice. Jeremy took a piece of coal from his pockets and quickly tried to re-darken the cleaned areas. The dragon took a whiff. Its claws curled.

"What is that?"

"It's your tasty."

"Mine?" it inhaled again and began drooling, "For me?"

"All for you. Corp O'Rat said he didn't care, didn't he? He said the tasty could be yours."

The dragon shoved John aside. The lad rolled down the hill again. Jeremy shook his head.

It extended its tongue. It stopped bare inches from the bunny.

"It's not poison, is it?" the dragon asked.

"It's chocolate. Milk chocolate!"

The dragon stared at it.

"By the bovine! *Milk* chocolate." it smiled, "and it's for me." Jeremy didn't answer. The dragon didn't wait. It sliced off the remaining ear and chewed. Lip's smacking, it pulled the rest of the bunny onto its belly and tore at it voraciously. After the meal, it purred.

"I shall fly to the village and tell them that their deal has been honored. Fare well and thank thee, Peter and ghost." Claws lifted a sacrificial chest of treasure and wings spread.

John watched the dragon fly off.

"Peter?" he asked.

"Well, look at you. Dressed all in green." The leprechaun grumped. "Did you never wonder why dragons ever befriended the black knight?" He gave the lad a kick to the shins.

"I…" John responded, wisely. "Where's the girl."

"Hortense Henry?" Jeremy didn't answer, but led his Johnny further up the hill. Shivering under a bush hid Hortense. For all the honey and berries, she smelled overwhelmingly of ginger. So did the leprechaun for that matter. Jeremy smiled. When she saw Jeremy, she ran to John.

"Did you hear? He's admitted it. Milk chocolate! He still has the cow. We must turn him in."

John comforted her, putting an arm around her sticky shoulders.

"It was goat's milk," Jeremy lied. She buried her head in John's shoulder. The leprechaun sighed. A thread of honey taffied between his cheek and hers. A berry swung limply between them drooping lower with each word. The leprechaun harrumphed.

"You've more important matters, girl. Where will you be going?"

"Going?" John asked, "She's going home." Jeremy turned away and looked up.

"I can't go home." Hortense realized. Jeremy nodded. "Oh Jeremy, why must you always ruin lives."

"Hortense, he saved you."

"Saved me? He forced me to betray my town. If I return I shall prove us to be honorless and deal breakers. They'll shun me. Jeremy, you've ruined me." Jeremy stood silently. John stroked her hair. It wasn't easy, matted as it was.

"Feather and spit!" the leprechaun said finally, "Burnt pudding and spoiled fish!"

"Watch your mouth!" Hortense blushed. Jeremy turned red. He twisted the shamrock on his lapel.

"Force you? I forced you? You could have, if you feel honor so strongly, you should have… when I ran to save the Prince here… I forced you?"

"Yes, you forced me. It is all your fault," Hortense sobbed into John's green shoulder.

"Then why did you let me, girl. Why didn't you run out and shout, 'Here I am! Eat me! Eat me!'"

"Jeremy," John hushed.

"No, I risk and I take the blame. You…" he fumed, "The milk of human kindness would have curdled in your bowels. You deserve to be cowless."

"Jeremy, you…"

Jeremy waved John off. He tramped down the hill. John started to go after the little man, but Hortense grabbed him and held him. She really did smell like Halloween. When the little man reached the bottom of the hill, his shoulders sagged. He turned and threw something at them. Both ducked.

"Take it and be wretched anyway." Jeremy shouted.

Hortense knelt and picked the thing up. The shamrock pin was the size of a maple leaf. Gold veined lined it. Dozens of perfect emeralds fit in each of the four leaves. John stood agape. He touched it. Hortense looked greedily upon it and clutched it close to her. Her eyes glittered.

"He's rich," she said.

The leprechaun turned and stamped off.

17. Lisa, the Cow?

The air screeched as a cloud made a right angle. It left tracks of wispy silver against a rain that dissipated and tasted like sweet cola. The stone goldfish steering the cloud looked back. It opened its mouth in alarm. Its scroll, parchments, and quill were already miles behind, moving at a much more studied pace. The quill flared and frayed and secretly delighted in its speed. It remembered when it knew flight or maybe it recalled a time when it created living documents. Documents designed to last and to be savored, scrutinized, and debated.

The convoy of strawberries also trailed. The sucrose of the chocolate had given the cloud a fast start, but now it lagged. Some of the confection even toppled over, landing in a sweet mess that forced some to duck and the less fastidious to tie a bib around their neck.

For the moment, the stone goldfish didn't care about his lost inventory or stock. It was being hunted. It couldn't understand why and its instinct to swim around in endless circles wasn't helping. Secretly, it hoped that in a battle between silver and gold, gold would win out, but the dentity was certainly moving faster and the stone goldfish was old enough to remember the days when dentities were much more than Corp O' Rat's servants.

Someone once wrote that it was impossible to escape a dentity, but the stone goldfish banked on the fact that typos were not uncommon.

The dentity spun and soared after the stone goldfish. She flew fast and sure, her reflective body changing with each second. At a certain angle, the pursuing shape sparkled like a sun flare. Then it became the sky, or its metallic body revealed clouds, until finally an image of the face of a stone goldfish appeared in its silver body. Martha's quarry, the stone goldfish, puffed at a billow in the cloud to keep it humming.

The stone goldfish looked down; seeing another stone goldfish identical to itself, pursuing it, the stone goldfish scribbled nervously on the parchment it had tacked to his cloud.

Martha arced, her body a perfect camouflage. Beneath the goldfish, clouds had been ripped asunder. Patting its inventory list, the stone goldfish drifted to a hollowed out horn. A magnified stiff voice echoed with something just short of authority.

"On the business of Corp O'Rat," it stuttered.

Martha didn't respond, didn't threaten, bribe, or gloat.

The silver dentity shot through the cloud. Chocolate covered strawberries rained down. Then, she set down. Soft buttery feet dimpled the surface of the goldfish's cloud. Martha folded her hands and looked imperiously down at her quarry.

"You would touch what is mine?" Martha whispered. The stone goldfish backed away. It whipped out a badge. A silver wing flashed. The badge shattered.

"I have the authority. She interfered with collection." The stone goldfish said brokenly, into the horn. The horn split into two pieces.

"You would touch what I have been ordered to retrieve?"

The goldfish stumbled off the cloud. Its flippers flapped furiously, trying to right itself. A little pile of parchment floated behind it. Martha's golden eyes glanced at the rolls. The fish tugged the parchment further behind the shield of its body. "His orders?" it questioned.

"Am I in your reports?" Her voice was barely audible. The stone goldfish gulped and shook its head, but its tail pushed the parchment under its belly. The dentity stretched her wings. They shimmered like knives.

"I am supposed to report everything."

Martha nodded, considerately. Her toes touched the surface of the cloud again. The stone goldfish failed to notice the shredded wisps she tore. With shuffling authority, it secured the parchments. "Why would you care if I include you in my report?" The dentity did not answer. The goldfish turned to her with a sly confidence. "You're not hiding something from Corp O'Rat, are you? He wouldn't like that."

Martha paused. She looked angelic, a vision of pure cloud with outstretched wings that caught all the light. The light haloed around her. The stone goldfish chuckled, "Oh no, he wouldn't like that at all. Shame on you, hiding things."

Martha stood perfectly still.

"I see," she said. Her voice was cold as metal.

"Shame on you," it chided. They stared at each other, the stone goldfish's eyes crinkled with mirth and blackmail. With a flap, the goldfish flopped onto the cloud. It shook its head, like a mayor to an angry mob. "What will he do to you, dentity? What will he do?" Rubbing flippers together it said, "You still seem to think that you have some authority… that your kind are still revered. Well, you can pretend you are still a knight protector if you want, but we know who keeps your chains." It paused to see how the dentity responded to its overtures of blackmail. A smile spread widely, when it saw her so still, as if in shock. Somehow, it missed that all the buttery softness was gone. Martha stood still, hard, sharp.

"You wouldn't want him to know what you've been up to, would you?" it continued, "Of course, I could amend my report if I could be assured…"

The dentity raised her hand slowly. From absolute stillness, the slow movement put a crack in the stone goldfish's speech.

"if I could be assured that I would…"

"Yes, I am hiding something from Corp O'Rat." She interrupted, her voice colder than a mountaintop,

"You are?" its eyes bulged. Without even noticing, the quill lifted and began writing. The stone goldfish tsked at her. "You shouldn't have said that. I can't pretend if I have proof. I always said, that the nobility of the dentities was only cover for their foolishness. That was a very dangerous thing to do."

"No, it wasn't." Martha struck three notes on her wing. She grabbed the parchment. The stone goldfish goggled. It reached for them with a flipper. Martha read calmly. She nodded. The stone goldfish blinked. She tore a tuft of cloud and threw it over her shoulder.

"You have injured a hatchling. A hatchling that O'Rat wanted."

"But…"

"Anything of the dragon is his. Anything with power is his."

"But…"

"If you casually attack his property without concern for the greater wellbeing…" she shook her head pityingly. She threw the parchment to the air. It came down like confetti. "That… will be in my report." The stone goldfish put its flippers together pleadingly. Martha vivisected the fish. Wide eyes fell landward.

The dentity shook her head. There were at least three more who saw the hatchling. She looked and smelled, but could not distinguish between the scent of the earth and the golems. She dented the cloud.

The little girl bobbed her head out. She clapped delightedly.

"Are you going to rescue me?" she asked. The dentity knelt. It cupped the girl's chin.

"No," she said. Tears welled up in the girl's eyes. She gripped Martha's wrist.

"Please."

"No." the dentity repeated. She stood. The girl dangled from Martha's arm, refusing to let go. Coarsely, the dentity threw her off. Martha sniffed her. "You are unimportant." The girl started to cry. A blank reflective face stared back.

Leaping from the cloud, the dentity slid on the moisture in the air. She stopped and hovered just above Lisa. The woman had fresh pulp on her lips. Her legs looked stronger.

A new smell, then, added to the rest. Lisa looked up. She squinted. Martha looked away from imagined judgement.

Something in the hatchling's eyes assaulted her. A strange feeling burned Martha's lungs. It was a feeling she had not felt since Au Paulet had purchased almost every cow that set hoof upon the sod. Since about a week before the giant first displayed his thirty-foot high leather sofa. Those were bitter days. Few cows escaped purchase. M. Au Paulet wanted to buy each one. He had developed a fetish. She could still see him in his leather belt, vest, and pants. Buir was younger then, and was given a gift of six token bulls in Au Paulet's name. There was that leprechaun too who had tricked the dairy farmer. When Jack toppled M. Au Paulet most cheered, but Jack was too slow to save the cows he loved.

Without milk, human kindness diminished. Selfishness and greed gathered strength. Six bulls had to do the work of hundreds of bulls and cows … things changed. Selfishness and greed grew. It made it a simple thing for the giant Corp O'Rat to take power.

For fifteen years, she had not felt her throat tighten. It had been a long time since she felt shame for doing something that didn't improve her standing or power. It had to be the hatchling, her musk. She pulled at memories and long discarded oaths. The Muscles in her legs tensed and became sharp. Lisa moaned again in her cow-like way and clutched her ribs.

"What are you accusing me of?" Martha asked.

Lisa stammered. The woman smelled thickly of cows, so much so that Martha was tempted to call her a cow. Still, the woman's eyes, the trim line of her mouth under the fangs, looked set. Martha looked up.

"Very well," she decided, "If I must." The dentity flew again.

She snagged the girl in a buttery grip and streaked downwards. Martha shot down the country road towards the pair she had set in flight. The girl shrieked. Her parents turned. Martha released the girl and sent her tumbling. Twenty, thirty feet the girl rolled. Mother and father looked up. They ran to their child. Then, carefully they waved thanks. Mother hugged daughter. All three cried. Martha returned to Lisa's side.

"Are you satisfied?" Martha asked Lisa. Lisa looked at the family and gave a strange little smile. Martha rubbed her throat as if something had caught there. The dentity blinked. Why should she have power over me? She hasn't the strength. She took a deep breath, the smell of the bovine haunted her, awakened a long suppressed part of herself.

"Perhaps, you are not a wyrm." she wondered aloud, "Perhaps, you are a cow." Her voice fluted, "What does it matter? We must hunt. You have made my decision very difficult."

"Cow? Are you calling me a cow?!" Lisa backpedaled. Pain flared from her ribs and head. She hurt too much to fight. Besides, the dentity cut rock with her bare hands. Better to be smart than to fight. Still, she refused to be called a cow or a worm. Even hatchling grated. Breathing deeply, she pointed at herself and said, "Lisa,"

The dentity stopped. It glanced at her with a smile and a bow, "Martha," it responded.

Lisa's brow furrowed.

"Martha?" she asked.

"Yes."

"That's a very strange name for someone from a different world."

The dentity laughed. "I am not from a different world. I live here." Her eyes narrowed. "You are a traveler." Lisa didn't answer. "Ah," she said and plucked a major chord on her wing. "I thought you had too many scents for a hatchling."

They walked together. Martha's hawk face watched her carefully. The bunny ears lay neatly back and almost invisible. They stumbled over farmland and roads that were bumpier than the earth and roots next to them.

Golems were nearly impossible to track by scent. Still, the ones Martha and Lisa had chased off likely headed to the mountains. The dentity pointed a silver hand to the north. Steel colored mountains twined their way up towards the clouds. A few wore them like red puffed clown hair.

"We must pursue that way," Martha said. *The hatchling, Lisa,* Martha corrected herself, *could use a healer.* Still, the wyrman nodded as if understanding how important is was find the golems before they found an engraver. A report would mean both their destructions. They had to hurry to preserve, well, to give a chance at some plans Martha didn't realize she was plotting until she smelled Lisa.

Lisa stumbled and groaned, clutching a broken scale. Martha paused, pulling her to her feet. The dentity growled; it was not certain that Lisa could be helpful. The wyrman smelled strongly of Corp as well as of cows and though she fought with vigor, she nearly fell before the weakest of the giant's tax collectors. Martha cawed angrily at the woman.

Feather her and her smell! She considered leaving Lisa behind and finding the golem herself, but suddenly, the thought of leaving behind a helpless injured hatchling rankled. Martha looked at the woman staggering behind her and growled again. The fool didn't even know how to use a walking stick properly. Lisa winced and feigned a smile. Sighing, Martha looped Lisa's arm around her shoulder and helped her walk. The hatchling shivered and kept her eyes away from the dentity.

Martha's nose flared. Lisa carried too many smells. Her fear was the only pleasant one. The others made her nauseous.

18. The Reluctant Cow

They crossed miles. Forests grew to hills. Hills sprawled into mountains. Paths turned to roads. A few scattered villages spread their way up to the mountains. Martha entered houses and demanded answers. Few had seen the golems, but everyone pointed her in a direction to get rid of her. For some reason, Martha didn't kill them even when she smelled a lie.

While interrogating, the dentity tied Lisa to a post like she would a steed. The wryman unsettled her, made it hard to remember her duty or made it hard not to remember her duty. Lisa's smell thawed the core of the dentity. Awakened shame. Martha wanted to keep Lisa a secret until she understood her power.

In a small ramshackle village of hay topped houses, Martha opened a third door. There wasn't a person who didn't tremble upon seeing her. She strode forward and lifted a barkeep into the air by the collar of his shirt.

"Where did you see the golems go!" she demanded. The man waved his hands and sweated.

"What golems? I'm paid up. There's no reason…"

She threw him into a table.

"You're lying. Someone's lying. There's a golem out there, a golem gone wild. Would you keep it safe? Would you put your families at risk?"

"But what if…" the man swallowed when he saw how quickly the dentity had spun upon him. His feet dangled from the ground.

"But what?" she demanded.

"If it's gone mad. It may attack me. I need to think of myself."

"You have a duty to your home, your hearth, and your kin." She whispered dangerously.

"Why do we pay the protection fees then?" A shaggy man in a blacksmith's apron called out, "It is your duty to protect us. I've no duty to him, or him or anyone here." The dentity discarded the one in her hand and picked up the latest voice. She tried to shake some sense into him. She shook him at any rate.

"I want to do my duty." The words echoed from a painful long ago. A hard look passed between the patrons in the tavern.

"What's in it for me?" many seemed to ask.

"Your lives." She growled barely audibly. She knew that if the golem was not destroyed, Corp would know that she lied to him. Self-preservation mixed with anger. She surveyed the meager tavern. The wood wobbled and no table stood straight. The ale smelled more of water than alcohol, and the chipped plates stacked in the cupboard appeared long unused. Worse, the man in her hands stank. His odor was entirely his own. Gone were the friendly smells of ash and hearth, of charcoal and metal smoke… even his apron looked clean. Martha tossed the man from her arms violently. His conscience weighed less than a thought. She plucked a mourning song on her wing. This stopped the men. They seemed to calculate the cost in their eyes. "Will she choose me?" They seemed to ask individually, "What chance that she will slaughter us all?" She answered these looks.

"You will not be much of a revenue loss. I can rationalize the downsizing," she threatened. One man stood and pointed.

"That way," he said, a dirty finger pointing to the north. She followed his fingers. She smelled the lie on his breath.

"How long ago?" she asked. The man scratched his ear and looked for help. He saw no kind glances, no encouraging faces. None would bail him out. They figured if he were fool enough to earn her attention, he was fool enough to take the penalty and maybe the whole price of it for them.

"A month ago?" he tried, "You better hurry."

"A month ago?" she whispered. Advancing, she sliced off his hand. "You are a thief. You steal my time and patience." Her wing arced backwards and gleamed. The men shielded their eyes. None raised their hand or took up a stool or a knife for their townsman, as they had probably sworn to do. It would have been futile, Martha knew, but she would have respected them for trying to stay the execution. She plucked the first six notes of the death march.

The hawk face lifted. Lisa's scent assaulted her. She looked at the pathetic wretch holding the stump of his hand. She blinked. The second note rang. One man, a man with brotherly resemblance took off his hat and placed it on his breast. The third note rang.

"Where is the golem?" she cried out. The scent overpowered her self-preservation. By the bovine, she was a knight protector, would she slaughter the only man who had shown any trace of nobility here? This wretch was the only one who tried to avert her wrath. Hesitantly, she struck the fourth note. Her brow creased and her bunny ears lifted slightly. The man closed his eyes. A peace fell over him. Martha lifted her beak suddenly and pretended to listen to a stir in the wind.

"Very well," she said, her voice caused many to jump. "I have been ordered by the great Giant Corp O'Rat to spare this man. Instead of his destruction, your taxes will be tripled. Should any harm come to this man or any blame be uttered in his name, the taxes for the next year will be quadrupled."

Mouths fell open.

"Be grateful for his mercy," Martha said, "be ashamed that you have delayed his noble cause."

She stamped out of the tavern. Lisa sat on the post, exactly where she was left. The dentity backhanded her. Lisa fell off the post and into the mud. The woman rubbed her jaw. She said nothing, but her look made the dentity turn away and bow her head.

"Stop bewitching me," the dentity said, quietly, "please."

Martha squared her shoulders and aimed herself at a fourth door. Before she knocked, the door opened briskly and a man strode out clutching a bag full of liniments. A woman marched after him. She wore a torn woolen dress, patched with mismatched bits of whatever scraps she could find. The man looked no better. She grabbed his arm.

"But you're not even sick yet. Your child…"

"Away witch," the man called. "If he be ill it may be catching. Should I give away the medicines I paid for so that I may suffer later? It is not right and it is not fair, wife."

"He will die, Bannedy."

"Better him than me," he said, clutching the liniments even tighter. Lisa rose to her feet.

"Are you…?" Lisa couldn't get the words out. "It's your son."

"It's none of your business."

"Not everything is business," Martha said. She blinked in surprise, hoped that no one had heard her.

"It's your child. You have to." Lisa demanded.

"I'm young enough to have another," the man said, hugging the liniments tightly.

Claws sliced the rope Martha used to tie the wyrman down. Lisa advanced on the unkind man and stood before him, hands on hips and face full of outrage. He glared back, then his moustache itched.

He wiggled his nose, rubbed it, and shook his head. Lisa lambasted him for his selfishness. The man acted as if he didn't hear. Wrinkling his nose, wasn't enough, he began to stamp his feet. Fiercely, he sneezed.

"You see," he said, but his voice lacked conviction. A tear brimmed in his eye. Lisa looked skywards as if angels would answer a call to teach him.

"…and you call yourself a father. A father must…" she continued lecturing. The wife released her husband. Both stared at Lisa for the barest instant and then at each other. They studied the other's features as if many years had passed since they could last see. Gently, the husband loosed his death grip on the liniments. The wife took a single tube.

"I'll not take them all."

"Take what you need," he countered.

"By the bovine," Martha swore, fixing her gaze on Lisa, "he'll not have you. *Not if you can restore us …me.*

The couple embraced. Lisa nodded righteously, a smile burning in her cheeks. Her fangs stood a touch shorter. Martha nodded to herself. She took the hatchling by the hand. Lisa trembled at Martha's touch, but did not resist.

"It is important," the dentity tried to explain, "Corp O'Rat must not have you. Too many others need you, Lisa."

Lisa smiled. A wind blew coldly between them, carrying on it a hint of rain. Thunder cracked distantly, cutting itself off after the first rumble. A frown crossed the dentity's face and she looked at the position of the sun.

"I am taking too much time. Will you hurry with me, Lisa?"

Lisa nodded meekly, confused why the dentity, why this monster was suddenly asking her, treating her as if she were something other than a prisoner. A smile winked across the wyrman's face, but it was a curious smile with only eyebrow raised, as if Lisa was scheming. Martha nearly returned the smile; she frowned deeply instead. The wryman tried to shrink from the dentity. Martha smiled after all.

"Where could he be? Where would the golem go?"

The husband turned, a look of helpfulness on his hungry features. He pointed east towards Carver's Path. The dentity smelled no treachery or deceit.

"There's a man who lives in the Datchery caves. An excellent potter. Supplies this village with all its wares. I suspect that a golem would go there." Lowering herself to the height of the man, she took his hand. Her buttery grip was firm.

"Thank you, may all be well with your child."

The man appeared shaken by the concern. After exchanging glances with his wife and shrugging with embarrassment, he said, "Fare well on your quest. May the wind carry you high."

The denity lost her grip. A bright smile consumed her and her body gleamed as if newly smithed and polished.

With a fierce embrace she took the two in her arms and whispered something urgently to them. They blushed. Martha returned her attention then to Lisa and with a companionable pat on the back she began ahead. Lisa waited behind. The dentity skipped, half flying along the path. It took her steps to realize that she left Lisa behind. Then, the silver woman stopped, turned, and with brows raised quizzically asked—

"Will you come?"

Questions gathered between the lines on Lisa's brow, but shaking her head she only wore the slightest of frowns. Instead of answering, Lisa began slowly walking towards the dentity. Martha smiled even more broadly.

A rumble of thunder echoed, this time it was not cut off. Martha frowned and held a hand out as if expecting something worse than rain. Grabbing Lisa's hand, she ran towards the Mountains and the Datchery Caves.

19. Sled Ride

Clear-cut grounds appeared. A silver waterfall brought life to a river. The dentity and wyrman climbed up a steep bank and wound their way upwards. Clouds thickened over the sun. Lisa sweated, at least her human parts sweated. Martha kept the pace brisk and yanked Lisa forward whenever she fell behind.

"It must be…" Lisa gasped, "time to rest."

The dentity gave her a look of impatience and pulled her hard enough that she tumbled to the ground. Lifting herself, the wyrman hurriedly got up, before the dentity started dragging her again. Martha felt a touch of guilt for pushing so hard, but also annoyance for being made to feel guilty. She looked towards the mountains and thought of the golems somewhere far ahead of her, dooming her. For the sake of the tired wyrman, she paused and pointed to a dark piece of rock half a mile distant.

"Datchery Caves," she said. Lisa groaned in her cow like way. Martha shook her head and smiled.

"That will not always work, Lisa. We will not rest."

They continued.

Martha suddenly released her hand. It had become momentarily sharp. Lisa rubbed it, but, when she looked up a moment later, the dentity was gone. Lisa collapsed gratefully on a stump. Her legs throbbed. From a distance, she heard a banging, as if a boulder was being dribbled against rock face. The wyrman groaned, *It did not sound like a cow's mooing!* And turned the corner.

A golem with knuckles stained the color of Lisa's scales hopped nervously on one spike. Its other spike-leg had been severed, cut smoothly away. Martha stood on a rock above it and glared. Moss-like eyebrows rose questioningly.

"You have interfered." She whispered to it. It threw a rock at her. Laughing, like wind chimes, she sidestepped it. "Corp O'Rat demands punishment."

"Why are you… you're planning a hostile takeover of the giant Corp O'Rat, that's why you…" Lisa declared, then covered her mouth. Martha narrowed her golden eyes. The golem opened its silent mouth in surprise. It picked up rocks and tossed scattershot at her. Martha rose. It was like trying to hit a mosquito by pitching softballs at it. From behind, the silver sliced. A shearing sound echoed. An arm fell off. One armed and one legged, the spiked thing toppled. Martha stood still for a moment. The golem tried to push itself towards the caves. Lisa turned away.

Martha crisscrossed, shallowly cutting it, time after time. Branches ripped. Plates shattered. Slowly then, she stood before it. With its arm, it grabbed at her silver leg. The fingers curled weakly around her calf. Martha struck six notes on her wing. The thing closed its eyes. Lisa grabbed her stomach. A bit of parchment stood revealed among the rocks and branches. Martha didn't hesitate. That the thing didn't scream somehow made it worse. Coldly, dispassionately, the dentity lifted its head.

"I made a mistake letting you run. I should not have let you suffer this long." She said and killed it.

"You shouldn't, didn't need to-"

Martha spun on Lisa. She gripped the wyrman's neck. Fury burned in the hawk face.

"You talk too much." She whispered. The whisper sliced courage. It shook bones. Fingers around her neck shifted between buttery soft and knife-edged.

"I'm sorry," Lisa choked. Martha considered her. She loosened her grip and Lisa slid to the ground.

"You've worked for Corp O'Rat. You stink of him." The dentity accused softly.

"For a long time," she agreed, "almost since college."

"You fought golems, too."

"They were…"

"Yes, they were, but if you are his creature…?"

Lisa's eyes hardened. She felt the itch return. Martha flared her wings as if she smelled something dangerous. The dentity plucked a piercing note from its wing.

"You're his creature." Lisa accused. "Not me."

Martha raised her arm. Lisa ducked. With a frustrated hiss, the dentity strode toward the mountain wall. Clenching her shoulders, she repeated with incredulity, "Planning a hostile takeover, she says. Planning a hostile takeover she shouts as if no one besides her has an ear. You had best be useful, very useful." Martha struck her silver leg, denting it.

Lisa bowed her head. The itched burned, but she couldn't reach it.

Calming herself, the dentity continued. "We are too near to mouth these things. I should give you to him."

"I'm sorry."

"As if that matters. He must need me. How else can I…" Martha's voice became smooth as silver. She expelled a breath.

"Do what?" Lisa asked.

"You do not like Corp attacking farmers." Martha countered, perhaps in an attempt to change the subject.

"Farmer's rights aren't exactly my passion. I'm more into…"

"Farmer's rights?" she laughed, "Even Buir O'Cassey barely pretends that there is such a thing."

"You have a bureaucracy here, too?"

"Of course, Buir O'Cassey is everywhere. This is foolishness. To talk of giants where whispers echo." A few scattered raindrops pinged off the dentity's skin. The pinging sounded familiar, but Lisa could not quite place the melody. She was sure she had heard it during Fantasia, it was…

"We must find the last one."

"Modest Mussorgsky," she interrupted.

"What?"

"A Night on Bald Mountain, that's what that is." And she began humming along with the rain's melody. Martha stroked her forehead, easing away a headache, then pointed at the divots the fleeing golems left. Most were already growing fuzzy from the rain. Droplets pattered against her scales in thick heavy blobs. They landed like small explosions on the ground. There was a melody on her scales too, but Lisa couldn't make it out. All she knew was that she didn't like it.

Dark clouds shifted. The dentity studied the craggy rocks and parched grass. Lisa rested on the displaced head of a golem. The rain left small dents in the hard earth. Martha stretched a wing to shield her hatchling. Lisa crouched under its shade.

"I know you are weary, hatchling, but if a report is made you will never see Arnold Movies again. We must move. Can you not see that he is calling for me?"

The tempo of the rain quickened to a military march. It struck wing and earth with an urgent beat. The drums pounded. Furious clouds pelted the earth with a machine gun snare beat.

The rain beaded. It bubbled and spilled. Slicks of mud began rolling down. The rare grass and shrub drank, but was not enough to absorb the water. Too many trees had been torn down. The runoff hurried towards them. Tons of mud sloshed downwards. Martha tugged at her, but she was still too heavy to lift. Her wings spread. Lisa clung to her. A wave took her from her feet. They slid. Martha's hand bit into a rock. Fiercely, the hatchling held onto her waist.

They tried to stand, but the torrent of rain pounding from above and the slickness rushing from below unsteadied them. Lisa fell, the weight of her conscience pulled Martha down to her knees.

Golden eyes blinked rapidly. Rocks were beginning to become unhinged. She stared at the wyrman. She smelled like a cow ready to stampede. Grimly, Martha lay down. She pulled Lisa on top of her. Silver mud spattered wings wrapped both of them. Mud sloshed down. It rolled over and under them. Lisa's breath steamed the silver of the dentity's face. Then, there was motion.

Sliding, rolling, banging into rocks and over them, the dentity clenched her lips. She gripped Lisa closely to her. They shooshed down the path and bumped into the air, landing with a horrible clang before they ricocheted into the side of a mountain. Mud poured through the spaces between her wings. Lisa pressed her wing flush against Martha's. The two frowned at each other. Then, the dentity pushed off again.

The silver body slid quicker and quicker, slicing roots, rocks and earth. The mud carried them. Rain fell torrentially. It drove them. Martha tried to use her feet to steer, but she was too tense. Her whole body had tightened. She could feel Lisa try to pull away. With every movement, every jostle, the hatchling felt the bite of the dentity's sharp skin try to cut through her scales.

"Stay still as you can." She cried. Thunder echoed outside. Suddenly, they dipped. A weightless feeling overtook them.

Martha unfolded her wings. They were falling. She stretched her wings and urged her feathers wide. Lisa fell. Bladed hands reached down to catch the woman. Lisa grabbed. Flesh touched silver and bled. Reflexively, her hand released.

Lisa's body tightened. She curled herself into a ball and fell.

"Feather and spit!" Martha yelled, "Use your wings."

Lisa tried. She stretched herself out like a skydiver. The ground was too close. A body streaked under her. Lisa fell atop the wings. Both forms crashed and the sledding continued.

Lisa guided Martha using her body weight to turn away from trees and rocks. Martha dug her toes in the ground. The drummer in charge of the weather took the rain to a new level. The pace became blinding. Hills smoothed out. Trees began appearing. Martha gripped one. They spun around and around, ringing the trunk. Lisa flew off and thudded against the ground. Martha tilted her body and tried to wedge herself into the tree, but she was too tense, and the tree snapped and fell over on top of her. Staggering, Lisa felt for the dentity under the pile of wood. The wyrman felt something sharp and began to remove debris. After a bit, Martha stood and put a buttery palm on Lisa's shoulder. She shouted something, but neither could hear the other. A cascade of hail pounded, dislodging pebbles. The earth cratered.

Then.

The sky cleared. Birds sang. Animals shook their heads and peered up.

"I'm late." Martha said, simply. "He's calling me to the home office." With buttery fists she began to hammer out her dents.

"You're late?" Lisa asked, "What do you mean?"

"The giant Corp O'Rat is calling for me."

"That," Lisa responded looking up, "is one impressive pager."

Martha cocked her head and opened her beak with curiosity, "a pager?" she asked, then she pointed at the clouds. "He sends them to call for me. I suppose they could be called pages, though I have not heard them called so before. Pages announce for kings, not giants."

Lisa stared at the fluffy white clouds scurrying down the horizon, flaring after few miles with thunder and sudden violence. She shook her head and pursed her lips. The storm began anew in its effort to alert Martha. Lisa blanched.

"No way," she said finally, "just no way."

The denity nodded. She agreed that it was an unreasonable show of force. Still, Corp O'Rat's calls were not one you put on hold.

"I've got to put you somewhere." Martha said, finally. Loose and uprooted trees surrounded them. Discordant notes rang from her wings. She bent them as best she could and tried to flap. Martha winced, but her feet lifted. Her skin visibly softened. Pointing towards the setting sun she said, "I know a family of bears."

"Bears!"

"Bears are sweet. They'll keep you safe until I am ready to reclaim you."

"Bears!" she repeated, alarmed.

"You are half dragon, Lisa. Why should you fear bears? Besides, it is a good family. There are three as I recall. The father's a carpenter or furniture maker or some such, though his work is… well, do not sit down too heavily on any chairs or you will break them. They will treat you well since you are not Scandinavian."

"Scandinavian? Oh no," she said, picturing a little blonde girl. "What am I doing?"

Martha's voice became cooler. "What I tell you to. Do not run."

Lisa shivered and nodded.

"But…"

"Do not run." Martha repeated, coldly.

"What about that thing that's going to report us?"

Martha hammered harder at her wings. She scraped mud off her silver body. A squirrel darted by them and ran up the bole of a tree. In the distance, another rumble of thunder shuddered. The dentity's shoulder slumped.

"Can you hunt?" the dentity asked, finally. Lisa didn't answer, but she smelled of confidence.

"I've done a lot of detective work."

The hawk face smiled. "Good. Chase then. Do not worry. I will come back for you." Thunder exploded again. "All right, all right," the dentity muttered, "I'm coming." She staggered into the air, her wings pulling slightly to the left. The dentity circled once back to face the wryman.

"Find the golem and kill it."

"Kill it?"

"I saw your sword, Lisa. A…" she thought for a moment. A light lit behind her golden eyes. "Destroy our enemy. Go. Defend the honor of your kind, the honor of all wyrmen. Kill."

Lisa had only shot her gun three times away from the practice range. Two of those were warning shots aimed straight at a wall. The third time she missed and felt great relief. She watched the dentity limp through the air on bent wing. Kill? Could she intentionally hunt something to kill it?

The itch burned hungrily.

20. Quests and The Damsel's Reward

Hortense took both of John's cheeks and kissed him. It was the sweetest kiss he had ever had.

"Honey," he said.

"Yes," she answered, "My champion." She looked at him with deluded eyes. *Hadn't she seen*? He thought, rejecting the compliment. His sword broke on the first thrust. The dragon played with him like a rag doll. Jeremy had won the day with his cleverness. Jeremy, who everyone seemed to hate and call villain, had been the hero. He saved John's life too.

"No. Honey." John said, trying to explain. It seemed to excite her. She kissed him again. A long, after-school-special, impatient, innocent kiss that tasted of honey and berries and ginger. When she finally pulled away lines of honey stretched between them like taffy. She looked at him and blushed.

"Oh," she said, "honey." And she rubbed at the honey they had thickly basted on her to tempt the dragon. John cut the honey that connected his mouth to hers with his tongue. He smacked his lips.

"I had always dreamed of the day when a champion would call me honey." She admitted, "Honey Hortense Henry." John put his arm around her. He looked into her eyes. Full vibrant youth sparkled. No dust, no cracks, no lines creased her eyes. Everything was new and possible and wonderful. He gripped her protectively. Her cheek rubbed his, stickily. Her honeyed fingers stroked the back of his neck, fiddling with his hair. He could… Reluctantly, he pulled away.

"Hortense," he said, "I'm just too old for you. It would be… illegal." Her features worked, trying to make sense of her champion. She cocked her head and touched his cheek. He stiffened, like he was torn.

"Illegal?" she said regretfully, "I don't understand. What have I done? No," she answered herself, "Oh poor little

Prince John, in some ways a man, but still so young. Do you not like women yet? Just because you do not prefer women… it does not make it illegal."

"What," John said, "I'm not…" then he smiled, remembering his reflection. He did look like a youth, but he didn't like her implication. He looked for another reasonable excuse. "I wasn't your champion. I didn't save you."

"You're wrong, Prince John. You were brave and noble in facing that dragon. You stood straight as a tree and struck fearlessly. And now you prove yourself as well with the grace and modesty of a true prince."

John stared at her. Daydreams of cheerleaders and supermodels stirred in his head. Thoughts of all the women who had turned him down or that he didn't have the nerve to ask out, wrestled with his morality. Dripping with honey that made her tunic cling to her, she reached out for him. He stared at the strategic, suggestive tears that Carolie had cut. He took a step in and embraced her and enjoyed another kiss.

Why did it feel wrong? They pulled free for air. Her cheeks were flushed. She would offer him a champion's reward if he would take it. That's what all the stories said. The man who saved the princess from the dragon got the girl… except, he didn't save the princess. He needed to be saved himself. *Besides, she really is too young. It's sick. She couldn't be more than sixteen.* He took a steadying breath as an unsteady part of him argued. *Marriageable in a medieval time period*, it proclaimed.

In the arms of a fairy tale beauty, John suddenly felt like a loser and a liar. He pulled away.

"I've got to take a cold bath." He stammered and started down the hill. She followed. It hurt to be good. She reached out to hold his hand. Was sixteen really too young for a guy in his age? He pulled away, wincing at the look of pain on her face. She stopped, pridefully.

"Why do you run from me?" He was running, he realized. Jeremy had told him to run. He should have listened. He shouldn't have stopped. Of course, had he not stopped, she would be dead. The girl called out with a tearful voice. "What have I done wrong?" John pinched the bridge of his nose.

What would James Bond do? No, he was not going to do what James Bond would do! Of course, he could do what James Bond would do. No, he would not do what James Bond would do.

"I…" he said hoarsely, "I have to find Jeremy. It is a champion's duty."

Hortense nodded bravely. She even threw another ribbon for him to wear. He bent and picked it up. He tied it between the buttons on his vest next to his chest. The hill rose steeply behind him. Hortense stood stiffly, very much like the perfect princess of a fairy tale. Tears slid down her honeyed cheeks. Stiffly, he turned away.

"Good-bye my love, my champion." She called. His shoulders hunched.

"Goodbye honey," he whispered and then added to himself, "Idiot."

He stopped at a pond and splashed water on his face, glad that the water was cold. It occurred to him that he was not high. Weren't drugs supposed to lower inhibitions? *If I'm not high*, he continued…he suddenly wished he had been into science fiction as a kid. It certainly would have given him a better frame of reference.

"That's it," he said.

Searching the ground, he began looking for a golden road. He needed that or a cabinet or… he smiled and hit himself in the head, "the guy used a lens. Lens, mirror, duh!"

When he was eight, mother had reluctantly taken him to a film revival of Disney's Alice in Wonderland. Mother had hated that movie passionately and forbid him to ever see another Disney movie. She railed against the movie's destructive message and raged that she would protect him from the vile seductions of those classics. John, a good boy, listened and never watched another cartoon. Now he wished he had. He tried to recall the movie. All he could remember was Alice getting big and small and people trying to chop her head off. There was something about being late too...

He felt honey on his cheek and blushed. Splashing more cold water, he tried to drive thoughts of Hortense away. Did he need a mirror? There was something about looking glasses. No, the looking glass had to be a lens, like a telescope lens, like the one Jeremy used.

"Alice was about opium," he distracted himself, "maybe BEAN…" but he couldn't force himself to believe he was high anymore. The dream went on too long. Besides, the animals weren't as chatty. and he was pretty sure that was an important part of Wonderland. *They did, however*, he reminded himself, *write*. At least the stag did and with a fine legible hoof too. Then again, didn't Alice and Dorothy take a blow to the head or… he smiled, "Maybe I overdosed, and this fantasy is all happening inside a coma." If that was true, he could go back and… or maybe someone found him at BEAN and whacked him with a lead pipe. He stopped.

What was he doing? Actually hoping he was in a coma so he could get with an under-aged girl?

He splashed more water on himself. Tried to scrub the red hair and puckish features off his face. In the end, he leaned against the moss, and threw the stub of his rapier as far as he could.

"No," he shouted. What finally convinced him that he was someplace real was that everything made too little sense. Dreams made sense in dreams. People rarely questioned events and debated morality in dreams. He stroked Hortense's ribbon. Smells of ginger and honey rose from it. It grounded him a little. The champion's ribbon felt soft against his chest.

Champions challenged villains. Jeremy, JTL was a villain. Everyone said so. Jeremy had something to do with mad cow's disease or endangering a species or something. Well,

Jeremy needed confronting and knew answers to his questions. Besides, John didn't have anything else to do. He told Hortense he sought Jeremy on champion's business. He might as well hold true to that. *The man will answer to me*, he thought grandly and giggled. Truth be told, the only thing that didn't frighten him between the dragons, giants, and Jeremy, was Jeremy. John Fasola rose to track the evil Jeremy.

Left alone, Hortense's mood turned. Her tears began to steam and she fumed!

"Burnt pudding and spoiled fish," Hortense called out, not the least bit ashamed. She stamped her feet. Two Champions! The dragon left satisfied? Her heroes departed uninjured and single?

She felt insulted. She felt wounded.

"This will not stand!"

Prince John and Jeremy Tucker broke all the forms. Neither fought for her. Well, Prince John sort of fought, if you called falling down and breaking your crown, fighting. Jeremy deserted her, after freeing her from the shackles and throwing her in a bush. Worse, he rubbed ginger over her body like she was a turkey ready for roasting. A champion must not touch a damsel on the day of the dragon... at least not until after. To make it worse, Jeremy then saved not her, but her champion!

"Unbearable! Intolerable!"

True, he saved her without honor and through trickery, but what could you expect from Jeremy. She pointed out how he broke form so politely too. Now, she was left homeless and did he take responsibility?

Despite all that, she offered her hand, as custom demanded, to the champion that was left. John had started properly enough at least, drawing sword and attacking. She shook her head. Feather and spit, he acted more like a buffoon than a champion. Still, she offered herself. She followed the forms. Was he grateful? Well, he was a pretty good kisser, but no, the puckish little imp pushed her away.

Hortense pivoted. He was not a good kisser. *It was awkward and he tasted of beets! His hands were weak and shook like a metronome. Did he speak poetry! Did he speak epically! Did he even bow with a flourish doffing his cap?* After all she had done! Why, she even managed not to frown at the reedy little imp after kissing him. The boy should have turned cartwheels. And what does he do? Run. Both of them ran from her. What was she to do? She needed another champion to avenge the humiliation beset her by her other two champions.

She threw clods of dirt down the hill. *At least he took my hair ribbon.* A part of her thought peaceably, *No, she would not settle for "at leasts". It was not enough.* She stamped again and one of the heels on her damsel costume broke. Stumbling, she rolled her ankle.

"No," she whimpered at the unfairness of it all. She would get revenge. They broke too many rules. They deserved punishment.

"I'll go to Buir and demand redress. I have been wronged." She shouted in the direction both had run. Buir O'Cassey would not stand for the laws of conduct being ignored. She stood straight. Her ankle burned.

"You'll see. You won't get away with this. I'm taking you to court! You'll be brought before Buir O'Cassey himself. Let him judge the merits of my champions." She took the shamrock pin and prepared to throw it. It glittered spectacularly in the sun. Its weight sung sweetly to her. A smile warmed her face. Unclasping the shamrock, the pin reminded her of John's sword. Then she pivoted and scowled, "You think you can buy me off with tokens." She flung the jewelry high into the air. The emeralds sparkled.

She watched it fly with satisfaction before common sense took the reins. Hortense covered her mouth and began to hobble down the hill. Then steeling herself, she stopped.

Sometimes, there were things of higher value even than gold and emeralds.

"I'll see you again, both of you." She threatened in a very unkind, uncowlike way.

Stiffly, with honey drying on her skin and tunic plastered to her body, she limped down the road. A trail of ants hurried after.

21. Tantrums

Jeremy arrived at the holy place and smashed toadstools. He ground the faerie ring into a fine paste. Spores hung in the air. Wide eyed, sharp eared faces thrust out of knotholes, gopher holes, and inside the bowls of tulips. Jeremy put his hands on his hips and glared, daring them. He harrumphed loudly and began jumping up and down, kicking the remnants of the ring out of its sacred shape. His eyes darted from side to side. Nothing came. Snarling, he scooped a piece of mashed toadstool and held it up for all the silent watchers to see. Then, he took a bite.

"Come and get me!" he challenged with a mixture of rage and self-pity.

A little ancient face growled and grabbed at its weedy wand. Urgent hands pulled it down. His was a beautiful broad marble bust that someone had gently cracked with a chisel. Spidering lines told his story more clearly than the glyph lines of his palm. The ancient one pointed at the ruined ring. Hands pulled and pleaded.

When Hortense condemned him for saving her life, something inside Jeremy had broken. He needed an end. All his plots and connivances, regardless of their intent, ended in some way he could not foresee. Every act of good he tried resulted in loss. A trickster should not act in serious ways. They had to stop him. He would let them.

"I'll do more!" he threatened and kicked at the sovereign earth.

Jeremy waited. Silence answered his sacrilege. Biting his lip, he began uprooting the flowers. Yanking daffodils, tearing roses, stamping daisies, spitting in tulips. His fingers trembled. Thorns pricked in defense, but found themselves shorn from the mother. Nothing was left standing. The ring was barren. It's center dead.

Still, they didn't come, but he heard a few of them buzzing. Rubbing his hands together he turned towards father Oak and mother Maple. An intake of air rippled through the ring. Jeremy paused. His hands trembled. Resolutely, he plunged a hand into father Oak's soil and took it out. Challenging them, he drew another scoop.

Father Oak stood tall and dignified. Six children would not be enough to reach around him… would be unable to hug father Oak. Jeremy's fingers felt a root. He grabbed and pulled. The wood was hard. He could not break it. Jeremy continued to dig. Another root, this one moist, touched his fingers. Jeremy stopped. His heart cried. He leaned his head on father Oak.

"Take your vengeance on me and be done with it," Jeremy asked of them. Wise, capricious, pointed, rounded, slithering, flying, crawling, climbing, airy, fiery, earthy, watery, solid, translucent, sharp, soft, beings crawled out. They studied him. Some eyes angry, some murderous, some sad, and a few amused.

"What if it be our vengeance to leave you be? It would be a punishment for you, Jeremy Tucker." A spidery thing said.

"Would you dig at father Oak until your hands bled, Jeremy Tucker? Would you dig until Father Oak fell?" asked a rose shaped insect.

"What punishment could fit your crime, Jeremy Tucker?" continued a puddle of water that gurgled with icy spikes.

"This ring birthed you, Jeremy Tucker. Was that crime worth the sentence you gave it?" asked mother Maple. Dozens of questions pressed down on him. They marched on him. Words buried their blades in his mind. None of them gave the release he wanted.

The leprechaun took off his rings one by one and threw them at the barren ground. When the voices brushed his face, he stood. Eyes closed. He waited. He hoped. He listened, but they had stopped.

"That is not the reason." The wee man croaked. Voices rumbled. He held up his hand. They silenced. As slowly as he could, he removed his forest green Armani jacket and unbuttoned his silk shirt. He threw them towards the desecrated ring. "Before. Would you even let anyone stand in the ring?"

"You are one of us," came the answer. The boots and his socks joined the pile.

"That is not the reason." He whispered, "Once, you would have struck me down before I could have put my foot down the first time. You would not let even one of your own do what I did." He unbuckled his belt and left that hanging.

Slowly, he opened one eye and winced when he saw their conflict. Cringed at the looks of worry and sympathy for him. His only relief came from the rage and anger of most. "Is it because I invited you to dinner?"

A few nodded. Some looked away. Many even dared to look ashamed.

"Why did you come? Were you so curious? Did you hope, like I did, that it would fill a hole? Doesn't matter, does it? You ate. You took your greedy little bites and we killed it together. Does it matter that we didn't realize how close it was to the last?" They hung their heads, the ones that had heads. He continued, hoping to make them… "Burnt Pudding. Did any of you care? You ate and now… by the coin, you feel my guilt." Many shuffled backwards. "I've seen what's come to us and what's come to the world. It's my fault. Because I wanted to… no, don't make excuses, Jeremy… because I slaughtered the cow and we ate. It went wrong. No matter what I do, I fail to…" His throat clenched.

Too many eyes softened. Too many sniffed and hid their faces with their hands. Jeremy tried to steel himself. This was not why he came. He unraveled a bit of yellow, blue, and red from his waist. "I beg you, for the sake of the green, stop me. Punish me. Be what you were before. Please. Kill me." He held out the streak of rainbow that tethered his soul to the world.

They hung their heads. None looked at him. Father Oak spoke,

"Jeremy, they can't."

Jeremy bowed his head and embraced the mighty tree.

"Even after all I've done. Look at the ring, you load of spoiled fish. I've done the worst thing I can imagine. None will ever be born here again."

Wind rustled through father Oak's leaves. His branches tipped and tangled themselves with mother Maple's. The two held silence. Hundreds of eyes looked for wisdom. Mother Maple pronounced judgment.

"Your punishment is this, Jeremy Tucker."

"Yes," he said eagerly.

"Isolation." She finished.

Kindness is cruelty, Jeremy Tucker thought. "But…" he said.

"I can think of no harder punishment for a kind heart. You will be forever separated from your people. They will neither care, nor tend, nor think, nor aid, nor hurt, nor speak of you. They will live in your thoughts. You will be absent from their lives."

"If malice fills you," father Oak continued, "your one grace shall be removed. Your connection to the rainbow and the pot shall be removed."

Jeremy nodded.

"I will ruin us, father. My plans…" but the tree had stiffened and all the backs had turned. Jeremy slumped and in silence re-dressed. He looked back hopefully, but not an eye watched him. He looked at the twined limbs of mother and father.

He removed his last bean. A bean he had hidden when he had purchased the chocolate Easter bunny. Gently, he scratched a small hole in the barren ring. He covered the bean and patted the earth, sending his prayer into it.

Stiffly, he rose. They were all there. They would stay there and ignore him, so he could witness their indifference. None even looked towards where the bean began stirring. With straight back and set jaw, the leprechaun walked off. Not a word was said. When he had left, a single leaf fell from mother Maple.

The Datchery Caves lined up like a series of round townhouses overlooking a cliff of red clay. There was little fauna, but what was there was thick, heavy, and kept close to the ground. A few cheery nuts wobbled on the ground. A military squad of ants marched oblivious to everything but those morsels and the mechanics of cracking that nut. Closer in, next to the caves, rested squat vases filled with muddy water.

Lisa worked her way down searching for spiked footprints and angry silver sparkles. Her solution to the impossibility of her situation was to focus on the task. It was how she had always survived. No matter what anyone asked of her if she only concentrated on the steps, on each specific action, then all the side stuff vanished. Do your job. The question of right or wrong was only really relevant for those who had too much time on their hands.

She picked up a vase. Embossed images of banana leaves, hibiscus hedge trimmings, eucalyptus, and guava marked it, but the neck was intentionally rough. It felt hard, like metal-colored sand. Lisa tried to feel impressed, but she had seen better at some craft shows and certainly superior work at the Smithsonian. Compared to everything else she witnessed in this… wherever she was… the pottery was downright ordinary and that, she realized, was an incredible relief. She strolled along a brick walkway that might have been baked by the sun, towards the caves themselves. Their state made her pause.

Half a dozen caves had collapsed and rumbled downwards, due to what looked like excessive digging. A sign hammered into the ground confirmed this. It read, *Please do not dig, unless you are making a very important mug.* The sign was covered with red fingerprints. She continued on, even after the brickwork ended. The caves that looked the most solid lay further below. On these, she even spotted some stonework. She would enter those and… best not to think of that.

Her feet sank into the moist clay. She pulled a foot free. Stride by stride, she worked her way forward leaving behind impressions of her feet. She travelled over a pond of clay: damp, eager and restive. It was thick enough to support her, but pliable enough to grab at her and cling onto her. There were depressions everywhere. Signs of digging and scratching, so that the clay pond undulated. The condition forced her to concentrate on where she planted each step.

Slap. Slap. Slccccckkkkttt. Slap. Slap. Slllkkkkt. Snap! Slkkkkttt.

She made a splashy sucking sound. Anyone tracking her would find a path impossible to miss. Did she care?

Slap. Slap. Slccccckkkkttt. Slap. Slap. Slllkkkkt. Snap! Slkkkkttt.

She lifted her head. Something was coming and it made a louder slapping, sucking, snapping sound than she did. The red clay in front of her rose in a steep hill and blocked her view of the caves. Behind her was only a few hundred feet of clay, but it taken her minutes of trudging and pulling to come this far. Even if she tried to run, she wouldn't get very far. Her infantile wings flapped. The clay practically laughed at them and if anything almost tightened its grip on her feet.

Slap. Slap. Slcccccckkkkkt. BANG! Slckkkkt. Slap. "Burnt Pudding!" Slap. "Ow!"

Whatever it was it was coming closer. She looked for a place to hide. Her itch felt restive. Lisa retreated to a small hillock and hid behind it.

A man stretched. Scratching his hair, he placed a plank on the ground. He walked over it. Placed a second plank, turned to retrieve his original plank, pried it free with a curved blade, and continued. Working his way to the edge, he untied a shovel and loosened a sack. He thrust the shovel deep. Stepped on it to push it deeper, then with a backwards look, pulled out a load of clay to dump in his bag. He repeated this action several times, only stopping when a great mound of clay broke loose and began sliding down the mountain's side. The man hurriedly scrambled away, shook his head, and hefted the sack over his shoulder.

He spotted her and nodded. She rose and glanced disapprovingly at the impression her butt left in the ground.

The man worked his way forward to the hill she had failed to hide behind. He moved unhurriedly, slapping down one plank at a time. Lisa waited, unsure what her next move should be. Her feet were caked with mud. Her stomach hurt again. For two days the only food she had eaten was a giant chocolate covered strawberry. The man advanced with an expression that darkened with each effort filled step.

Lisa decided to begin with the friendly approach.

"Hello, I wonder if I could ask…" she began.

"Thief!" he accused vehemently.

"What? Where?" she started, then "Who? Me?"

The man pointed at her feet. He dropped the heavy bag of clay. It thudded and sank several inches. Brandishing his shovel, he said, "No wonder the caves have been slipping. You've been smuggling clay on your feet."

"No, I…"

"Who said you could take our sacred clay?"

"Sacred, I didn't know."

"Wait 'til I tell Jochim that you're the one to blame for his grandfather's cave falling. The boy still grieves. They lost their home. Do you know what it's like to have to take your in-laws in?"

She looked at her feet. A few pounds of clay clung to them. The cliff rumbled again as it continued to resettle. She pointed at his bag. The bag must have weighed 50 pounds. The man glared angrily at her feet. Openhanded, she pointed at the shovel and at the spot in the cliff where the damage had just occurred. In response, the man shook his fist at her feet.

This was getting them nowhere. She tried words.

"My fault? Look at your bag?" Surveying the area, she added, "Why don't you move to the caves up there?" She pointed at a set of caves three hundred yards distant set firmly in the rock away from the clay gathered by the edge.

The man nodded.

"I see your plan. You want us to move away. You want us further, so no one will catch you smuggling clay."

"Are you a moron?"

"Moron! Why I bet you don't have the brains to be initiated. You are a smuggler. Oh, you'll take your clay, but it will dry and crack and you'll have nothing but dirt from it."

"I don't want your clay."

"The proof calls you liar."

"I'm looking for a…"

"Looking for our secrets, yes. So you would steal our ideas as well."

"Look, I'll give it back." She scraped a wad of clay off her foot and flung it down.

"All well and good, to give back the booty on your booty when you're caught."

"All I want is information."

"Aha! She admits she comes to steal our secrets. Why I bet you don't even know the secret of the snake?"

"What secret of the snake?" she said, tiredly, an itch gathering itself at the back of her throat. The man shook his shovel threateningly.

"You would smuggle and you haven't even heard of the snake?"

"Oh please. I don't care about your clay."

"If you knew the secret, you would be entitled to your information. Without knowledge, you are a thief, a smuggler, and a saboteur of homes."

"You want the secret of the snake," she said sarcastically, "You want the secret of the snake. Here." She took a wad of clay from her foot and kneaded it. Rolled it between her fingers until it became a long cylinder. Then, she tamped one end and pricked holes for eyes on the other. Letting loose a small cough, she baked it. "There's your snake!"

The man dropped his shovel. Round eyes and round mouth worked silently.

"A snake," he said, reaching for the clay, "I did not think you knew… forgive me. I did not realize you are a master."

Lisa just shook her head.

"Come. Come inside. I'll assign one of the metal workers to repair your scales." And he skipped happily down his planks of wood. The sack of clay rhythmically banged him. Lisa followed. She glanced at the snake she had made. "Who would've thought that one of Corp O'Rat's dragons would have an actual skill?"

"It is pretty good, isn't it?" she smiled, and carried it carefully with her into the Datchery caves.

"It must have been some chicken," Corp O'Rat said, studying Martha's dents. She listed to the left. "A true heroic struggle," he added, noting the dust and mud that covered her fine silver skin. He tied his de'amon stiffly and studied himself in the mirror. His cheeks dimpled approvingly. "Certainly there are none fairer than me."

"No Corp O'Rat, there are none fairer than you."

"Then why do you lie to me?" A heavy hand smashed a table. Boards splintered. Martha winced. A great hand reached for her. The dentity sped under a ladder-backed chair. It shattered.

"My Lord executive," she pleaded.

"You've…" he roared, "made a poor business decision."

Martha shot into the air. For a thing so big, Corp moved quickly. One hand pulled a lever. Bars fell between the windows. The dentity wheeled and flew towards the door. She found the giant's waiting hand. He squeezed. Her wings crumpled like tinfoil. Her eyes widened in pain and surprise. She had been caught so easily.

"Everything is strategy." He growled. Effortlessly, he broke the stitches and threw the dentity's legs into a distant corner of the room. They clanked against the edge of a wooden bowl and slowly sank into oatmeal. With dispassion, he pulled her wings off. Martha wailed. Balling up the wings, he tossed them into the fireplace.

"You return with a chicken, then leave again. You think I will not notice. Do you think me feeble, that I would not remember that smell? You insult me. You call me unobservant. I will make silverware out of you."

"Master," she wept. "I… don't, please. I am loyal. I have never even written out my resume since enlisting with you. I would never plan to…" Pain flared through her. Her body squealed, as metal rubbed metal.

The giant plodded towards the fireplace. He placed her between his tongs. Casually, Martha was shoved into the fireplace.

"Master, please."

Corp then took a one-handed bellows and heated the fire. The dentity squirmed, but the giant reinserted her into the fire and held her stiffly with his tongs. The dirt and dust sizzled against her skin. He shoved her deeper. She howled, though the heat failed to reach her yet.

"You smell of cow," he said calmly. His pointed nose flared. "Fees, Lies, Grosses, Sums. I smell a bad business decision!"

Martha hung her head, "No, not a cow. I know your order, slaughter cows on sight. Do not let the kindness fester. It is not a cow."

"Liar," The giant squeezed, "what else could it be?"

"A traveler," she said finally, "a wyrman."

The giant discarded her as if she were forgotten. Martha rolled. Clawing with her beak she edged out of the fire until she reached her boss. She wrapped her arms around the toe of Corp O'Rat. The giant kicked her into the wall. A brick split. Martha slid down. Corp sat down and frowned at the legs in his oatmeal. He hammered them flat with one strike of his meaty fist. Martha winced and gasped. Her body curled into a tight crumpled ball. Her fingers found the dents that rocks and the giant's fingers had caused.

"I think you need a sabbatical, Martha. You've been working too long. I've given you too much responsibility." Martha nodded and crawled back towards the fireplace. "No!" the giant roared. Martha froze. The fire danced over her wings. "Did I say you could still use the company jet? You are grounded until you can reprove your loyalty."

"I…"

The giant's brows lowered. She crawled to her cage. Eventually, after the mice came to clear away the morning dishes, a gossfer arrived to remove the wings from the fireplace. With a glance at the giant, it turned away from Martha's cabinet and began heading to the servants exit.

"Should I have these melted down, my lord executive?" It asked.

The giant considered. The silver dentity steeled herself.

"No, repair them and promote a dentity from the mailroom. We must capture a traveler. A wyrman." Corp glanced casually back at Martha. The gossfer crossed to Martha's cage. It opened the door. The giant's foot came down. They bounced.

"Leave the harp-y here."

The gossfer nodded. Martha smiled weakly. Corp's face clouded.

"No Martha, do not feel secure. You are not." A crease lined his forehead. Corp itched his chin. A distorted reflection glared back at him from the dentity's crumpled body, but the beak was upraised. The gossfer took the moment's distraction to grab the wings and flattened legs and quickly bowed its way out of the room. Corp paced in a short circle.

"So, you still think highly of yourself?" Corp mused, "You still see yourself as a knight protector. You forget yourself." He paced a circuit around the room, for once ignoring the daily profit sheets. Already, the broken furniture had been swept to the side. By morning, his servants would replace it and the room would look whole. Only his oatmeal remained ruined. That darkened his expression. Breakfast was the most important meal of the day! He turned back to his dear, loyal Martha with narrowed eyes. "This wyrman is a danger to my power. Our stability and growth is threatened." Loudly, he berated Martha, "Do you know what a cow would do to our profit margins! A knight's first duty is to his lord and chief executive. If there is someone you would protect before me…" He turned to a waiting gossfer. One or two always waited within earshot. This one bowed deeply showing off a finely quilled back.

"Tell the new dentity that when it finds this wyrman it must destroy it immediately."

22. The Datchery Caves

The cave Lisa and the potter entered swirled with iron and copper colored rust until the first curve. Its walls sagged naturally, as if still moist and in need of a kiln. The squat potter, who had tested Lisa with the riddle of the snake, left his planks against an upright support and patted the dust out of his beard on the threshold where mud became stone. Beneath them, the floor was tiled and glazed phosphorescently which was a good thing because after the first hundred feet it was blindingly dark in the Datchery Caves.

With a splash, the potter dipped his feet into water and scrubbed the clay from his feet and ankles. After a gesture, Lisa followed suit. Then, reshouldering his sack of moist clay he hobbled downwards.

Cold embraced them. Below promised warmth, but the tiles were cold and the stone not much kinder. Lisa saw veins of pyrite, quartz, and gypsum here and there as well as a few flecks of actual gold. The veins were raw though clearly they had been struck at some point because the Caves' shape was not natural. It was far too regular and predictable for that.

They travelled down a mosaic tiled floor with squares that alternated between metals and clay. Color too, varied. Here brown, there gold, elsewhere silver, a stretch of black next to a wave of bronze, reds and pinks warmed a distant corner, and blues and grays cooled the center.

Their route sloped gently down. A fine banister was carved from crystals in the wall. The ceiling shone with an illusion of milky translucence.

Lisa gawked. The only thing she had ever seen remotely close to the splendor of the Datchery Caves were the executive bathrooms at corporate headquarters and she had needed a keycard to enter that, not a mere clay snake.

The eyes of molded statues seemed to follow her. Light, reflecting from their crystal eyes, traced her movement. Each beam of light seemed to strike the gems studded in Lisa's wings. Whistles and murmurs followed her. Waving her to follow, the potter continued lower.

Deeper down, grim faced women bent over disks of iron and hammered. Gnarled men with shaggy coats sanded carvings for jewelry. Sweat glistened from everybody and the place stank with a thick rich odor of hard work and burnt metal. Lisa opened her mouth. The man shushed her and took the snake. He placed it on a low pedestal. The snake glimmered and came to life. It slithered up to Lisa and corded itself around her ankle, where it froze, beaded, and hung like jewelry.

A burly woman handed Lisa a flask, then took it away to take a large swallow, before handing it back. The potter nodded at her encouragingly. She eyed it. Rubbing the flask clean, and hoping it wasn't too germy, Lisa took a drink.

"Welcome to the Datchery Caves, Craftmaster dragon," yodeled the potter. The others in the room repeated his words and the words bounded and echoed as if thousands were saying it. The burly woman struck her hammer against an anvil. The echoes stopped suddenly. Lisa took her hands away from her ears.

"Yeah," the burly woman rumbled, "Can't stand it either. Men're too pudding melodramatic. Why've you come? We're paid up." Every sound on the work floor stopped. Hammers held in midair. Steam stopped rising from the cooling vats. Diggory Thomas even stopped bouncing and just held his foot. "Well," she said, "how much more is it to be this year?"

"I'm looking for a golem."

"Golem!" she spat, and the others murmured darkly. "We produce thirty a year, dragon. We're only human. Tell the Corp O'Rat we work as fast as we can."

"Tell him if he paid us a fair wage we would…" Hands clamped over Diggory's mouth.

"Forgive him," the gnarly lady groused, "he'll be punished. It just be that the workers, they've not seen an increase in so long and the giant sometimes do pay less.

Feather and spit, I couldn't afford to keep all my craftspeople this season."

"How can we produce more?" Diggory complained.

"We be knowing he must cut expenses to keep strong and do not cast blame on Corp O'Rat for our hardships." The gnarly woman explained, hammering impatiently against her anvil. Diggory faced his forge. "Report him not, dragon. I know it be the right thing to do, but he be right skilled. It'd take four men to replace him and the cost and loss of production be not worth dismissing him. He not be worth the loss in revenues." She looked hopefully up at Lisa.

"I'm looking for a golem that would have come here for healing… repairs." Lisa said, trying to use the power they thought she had.

"Aye, we be doing that without cost, as promised."

"He's a renegade. He caused damage to one of Corporate's strawberry fields."

"Why does she pronounce his name that way?"

"Feather and spit, Diggory! Will you wax your lips?" Two men grabbed and dragged the metalworker out of the cave.

"Many will starve, because…"

"Starve!" Diggory shouted from a distance, "Corp O'Rat no cares about starving folks."

"Do you love the noose so much, Diggory," the man said.

"He cares," Lisa answered, trying to cite a company line. Once again, everyone stopped and let their mouths drop. The gnarly woman pawed the ground with her cloven foot.

"It be a long time since Corp pretended to care, dragon. A long, long time. Who are you?"

"She be a craftswyrm of great skill," interrupted the potter with the clay sack. He pointed at her anklet. Hafts stamped on the floor. "Do we question craftsfolk here? She be a dragon. By contract, we must fix her scales done in battle. Do you really care why?"

The gnarly woman faced the potter. The clay sack dropped and he fingered his rasp. She lifted her hammer.

"Clay men be soft," she challenged, "They not be ordering metal workers." Each of the metal workers slammed their hammers down, kicking up dust and sparks. The clay man pounded his hands together, as if he were flattening a lump of clay. The metal workers slammed their bellows sending heat and ash billowing. Countering, the potter took out a small blade meant for slicing blocks of clay. Menace filled the air.

"You be one. You be soft like dirt." The gnarly woman insulted.

"You be dull and rusted through." Countered the potter.

The hammers rang with a constant heated beat. The two advanced towards each other.

"Duty," the clay man swore.

"Strength," the metal woman stamped.

Heat and dust swirled. Lisa backed away. The itch burned hotter than the fire. Her claws curled at the end of her fingers. She could practically feel it. Dust and ash and fire gathered in her lungs. The clay man swung and sliced into the arm of the gnarly woman. Striking heavily, the gnarly woman shattered the potter's shoulder with her heavy hammer. The hammers drummed angrily. Stabbing, the knife bit again. The hammer missed its mark, but its backswing crashed into the man's hip. He tumbled. The workers manned the bellows, making the room hotter, hotter.

Sweat slicked them. He stabbed at her calf. She aimed for his head. Lisa sneezed. A torrent of flame issued forth that made the forges seem cold. Both stopped.

Her itch blazed in her arm, smoke curled from her mouth. The gems in her wings glowed. The dragon woman stood erect with menace. Volcanic light flashed from her itch-sword. She surveyed the room. Her nose tickled. Fighting an instinct to cover her mouth, she sneezed again. She spat fire. They flinched.

"Stop!" she ordered.

They did.

The clay man rose and scampered behind her. All the others scurried as far as they could. Her eyes gleamed with orange malevolence.

"I want that golem." She said quite simply, "Where is he?"

They shivered.

"He is under the protection of Corp O'Rat. Renegade or no." the gnarly woman said with false bravado.

"I don't care. Where is he?"

They flinched.

"In the scribe's room preparing a message."

"Take me." The itch burned fiercely, demanding of her. They hesitated. She loosed a blow on an anvil. It split in two. She thought of Martha, her captor. A grin bared her fangs. Limping, with bad hip, the potter touched her shoulder.

"Follow me."

She nodded. The rest tried to push themselves against the walls. A growl rose unbidden from the bottom of her soul.

"Pray the message is not sent."

Maybe it was the heat, but many fainted.

23. Tra-la

John tripped, stumbled, and tumbled thirty times before reaching the bottom of the hill. He rolled to his feet. Grass stains marred and emphasized the green of his clothes. He looked back and waved.

"I'm okay," he called. Hortense failed to wave back.

Swallowing, John turned. First loves were difficult. A girl like that, she would get over him. Someone would come soon. In the meantime, he had to find the mad scientist, villain, wizard, or whatever Jeremy was, that brought him here.

Sprinting into the forest below, his itch suddenly lessened. He weaved between trees, leapt shrubs, and leapfrogged openmouthed wolves. He slid on a pile of leaves and leapt a falling log. A bear toddled forward. It snuffled the air. John sprang, wrapped his hands on a heavy limb and swung beyond it. The bear lifted one eyebrow and shrugged.

Bushes, berries, fish, leaves, sticks, and elephants flew by without him ever noticing. The exertion filled his body with life. It demanded more and more speed.

Memory vanished. All that remained was motion. Relief flooded through him. Even faster then, he ran, pinballing off the boles of trees, unable to see, because the speed made his eyes tear. Roots snagged, tripping him.

He continued past the weave of light. Continued through a chorus of harp and flute. Continued untouched and unharmed, through ditch, over river, around pond, and through lines of trees so dense that snakes sucked in their breath to pass.

His legs trembled violently, but still, he built up speed. Another root tripped him. Legs churned to keep him upright. His fingers clamped momentarily around a sapling, but they were ripped loose by the energy of his feet. Violently, his heart thrashed within him. Arms pumped still. It felt like he never stopped breathing in. His legs throbbed. Still, he went faster and didn't care.

Breath wouldn't come. Legs churned. His heart vibrated like a plucked string. Finally, the legs stumbled. They faltered and he sank, blinking with surprise, into a thick coppery loam.

A group of frogs watched him. Their bulbous mouths inflated. One by one they croaked, "We're princes too." They burbled laughter.

A still log, the color of bubble gum, edged its way through water. Slowly, it turned with a malicious crocodile smile. The jaw snapped in the water. Frogs pointed with one webbed-hand and announced tra-la, tra-la. The pink log swished its tail one last time and aimed itself towards John. His itch suddenly began burning in his feet again.

"You're lucky. You can reach your itch," bemoaned the log, trying to bend its wooden tail towards the middle of its trunk. After a time, it flopped over, rolled in the mud and sighed.

"What's wrong, Prince John?" the log asked.

John rose to his arms. He had run too fast, too hard. He couldn't catch his breath. The world began spinning. He tried to speak, but lacked the breath for that too. The pink-scaled log slowly clambered beyond the loam. It worked its way next to a moss covered stump and lounged against it. John wheezed.

"I see," the log responded to his wheeze, "but why should we care." The frogs laughed. John turned redder. The log rotated to see him better. It dipped its head and tumbled off the mossy stump. "Cousin Harry always was a bit pushy," it said, and frowned, when neither John nor the frogs deigned to laugh. No one got the reference. The log tried to look abashed. It spoke lowly from its knothole.

"Have you come then to see ventriloquism?" The log found itself immensely funny. A few frogs hopped away, looking for better fare.

"I'm looking for Jeremy," John said.

"Tra-la! He looks for treasure. Tra-la," sang a frog.

"Chasing rainbows and he doesn't even have a sack, still he hunts the wee. Poor, poor Jack, there'll be no gold for thee," chorused the frogs. The log whistled and the frogs silenced.

"Why are you after Jeremy, Prince John?"

John scratched his jaw. He didn't know. It seemed the right thing to do at the time. A bird landed on top of the log. It began patting grasses down. The log tried to shoo it with his tail and wound up falling down again.

"I have to find him." John said, simply after a good stew.

"As good an answer as any other," a frog told another frog." The log leaned against the stump once again and tried to strike a dignified pose.

"Prince John… Jeremy is a hero to many and the deal he struck was fair."

"He's a hero?"

"He's a monster. He's a villain. He's a trickster." The frogs disagreed.

"That too," agreed the log. The frogs smiled, appeased. "but the more important question is, why do you want to find him, Jack. Don't bother lying, you can't fool us, nature knows your nature."

"I… how do I deal with… you're real?" John said, pinching the bridge of his nose hard.

"Not my concern, my prince."

"Where's Jeremy?" he continued.

"Jeremy?" the log asked, "Who's that?"

"But you were just talking, arguing, if he was a hero or villain? How can you say that you don't know him?"

"Tra-la," applauded the frogs.

The log laughed, "He Jacks me. You weave many colors, Jack. One could get lost in your spinning. Still, I must insist. Why are you here? Why do you seek this Jeremy?" It showed its teeth. John resorted to the truth.

"I'm not high." John complained.

"No tra-la," agreed a frog, "On the ground, not high." The log swiveled on its edge and rolled towards John. It let

John smell its breath. John backed away. It reeked of moss and swamp water. The spinning was slowing. The world seemed to balance. A heaviness lay in the log's crocodile smile. Owl like eyes peered for an instant from within the knothole.

"Jeremy said he needed me to deal with a giant. He said a giant was after him." A sinister smile curled. The log nodded and nearly teetered, but John kept it upright. With a blink, the frogs leapt into the water. The log waded in.

"You, against a giant?" it laughed, "You should have said you were here to make him a meal." The log paused, its knothole just visible above the water. An armored tail slapped, making froth. John wiped the spray from his eyes. Standing atop the water, balanced on the point of its tail the pink log said, "Prince John, your Jeremy is lost… abandoned, and is trying to give up his heart."

"Help me find him." John asked. The log bobbed upwards.

"A giant has already caught him. He surrendered without even a chase. This is very unlike him."

"A giant?"

"Tra-la. Tra-la." Countered the frogs. One by one, they slipped beneath the water. The last one paused. It leaped on top of John's head. With a flick of its tongue, it knocked off the broken crown. It made lazy circles in the water. Springing into the air, the last frog said, "In the old days, we might have helped."

"Consider what was lost, Prince John. Consider what was lost," and dove without a ripple beneath the water.

"But… Tra-la," John said for it.

"Tra-la," submerged voices agreed and then they too vanished beneath the water.

24. Alexander

"Alexander?" Martha said. A sparrow head turned towards her. Wings of bronze and silver flared. The male dentity's neck feathers bristled. It looked down its sharp beak at her. Martha faced her counterpart bravely. His arms gleamed sharply.

"You have betrayed your liege, Martha," he stated flatly and turned away from her as if she were less than the ashes of a long spent fire.

"Alexander," Martha said sharply, but besides a slight tensing of its shoulder blades, the male dentity took no notice of her. Corp O'Rat fingered a man-sized chess piece. Disliking the options available to him on the board, he crushed the marble pawn and ordered a new and better chess set brought to him.

"One that works properly," he added to the scurrying server mouse. Alexander waited until Corp acknowledged him, then swept a bow with hand going from forehead to wing.

"You are the new dentity," Corp assessed unhappily, "Males are slower, both of wit and speed. What need do I have for a male dentity?"

Alexander's face did not change, though his bunny ears lifted slightly. Standing stiffly, he said, "I will do you proper service. I beg you to reconsider. I was once highly thought of."

"Arrogance leads to sloppiness, Alexander." Corp opened his palm and the dentity hopped onto it. "Martha's arrogance after years of loyal service makes me doubt any faith I might have in you."

"She was unworthy. The fair sex is fickle." Alexander stated simply.

"And you are not," Corp said smiling slightly.

"No," Alexander answered. Corp's fingers curled around the male's body, Alexander stayed still, his eyes carefully blank. "I trust you, my lord executive. Do with me as you will." Corp studied the dentity carefully, then laughed.

"Perhaps slow of wit will serve me better." It released its grip. "Alexander, there is a cow released upon the land." The giant watched carefully. A muscle in the dentity's cheek twitched. "You will find it."

"How could it have been hidden all these years?"

"Apparently," the giant said, turning away from Alexander, "it has been ensorcelled into the shape of a wyrman."

"I have not heard of a wyrman…"

"My time is not to be wasted." He said denting Alexander's waist. The sparrow head dipped apologetically. "When you find the wyrman, kill it. Do not speak with it. Do not even study it."

"I understand." Alexander wheezed between the giant's fingers.

"Martha?"

"Yes."

"Where can Alexander find this wyrman?"

Martha held her breath. She lifted her beak and blinked twice. The giant's face stood cold and hard. Her counterpart glared intentionally away from her. Her pathetic wrecked and smash body reflected back to her. The bars surrounding her were made of gilt, the one substance every champion was vulnerable to. With no wings, she had no melody, no way to soothe her CEO. The intensity of his will daunted her. The gilt wilted her. The Martha's head fell. To the side, she spotted a looking glass. Her reflection appeared differently there. It was still broken, smashed, crushed, and dented, but it was… less distant. Martha considered this and met the giant's glare if only for a second. Bowing, she lied, "The grass fields of Emma's Wart."

The giant nodded.

Alexander took to the air and began towards the window. Corp halted him with a wave.

"Did you smell that?" He asked Alexander.

"Smell what?" the male dentity asked, landing on the O'Rat's palm.

Corp O'Rat shook his head and rubbed a temple. Setting the male dentity down carefully, he said "You will find the wyrman anywhere but the grass fields of Emma's Wart. Start looking as far as you can from Emma's Wart."

Alexander nodded. His wings spread.

"And Alexander," Corp O'Rat said tiredly, "A wyrman is half wyrm, half human." The male dentity bowed.

"Thank you, my lord executive."

Alexander bowed again, this time touching beak to toe and stood. Stretching wing, he lifted gracefully from the ground. Arcing his back, he let all gaze on the magnificent glitter of his wings, then he flew out the window.

"You have done me a great disservice, Martha." The giant said, watching Alexander go. "I will not forget that."

The gossfer returned with Martha's legs slung over its sloping back. Its paws held needle and thread. Corp stared at it and gently shook his head. He pointed to the cabinet. The gossfer blinked once, but placed the restored legs in the cabinet and locked the door. Martha's eyes fixed there.

"Alexander will succeed, Martha" the giant warned, "Before you first noticed this wyrman you were still mine." He laughed mirthfully, "You are still mine. You will remember that soon enough. After all, you smelled her as a hatchling and whether hatchling or traveler, she is too newborn to have much impact. Besides, what chance does a dragon have against a dentity?"

Martha closed her eyes and refused to grab the bars, though a part of her felt the urge to shake them mightily. Corp placed a wool coverlet over her cage. Darkness closed about her.

"Months from now. When this cow has been long erased, you will return to me, Martha. You will return and beg forgiveness for forsaking your duty and nobility for this hatchling."

Martha breathed deeply and tried to hold the smell of cow deep within her core, but she knew that though Corp O'Rat might be twisting it, the giant spoke the truth. He was too powerful to bother with lies.

25. A Wyrman's Itch

The potter led Lisa down a spiraling set of twisting tunnels. As they walked, the elegant scrolled columns and fluted cornices gradually gave way to a warmer, less austere setting. The emergence of earthen colors calmed Lisa whereas the solid precision of the stone and metal masons had steeled her purpose.

A smile nearly stole her itch away as she stepped upon the umber bricks. Their warmth stole the cold from her feet. For a moment, she relaxed. Her itch all but vanished, then she shook her head and focused on her task. She needed the sword more than gecko claws. The itch responded gathering in fiery fury. Nodding grimly, she smiled. She was starting to get this magic stuff.

The clay figures and plants along the path seemed nearly alive with their puckered mouths, imperfections, and faces filled with fingerprints. Hanging over them, gently curving sienna trees with stained autumn leaves stood frozen in an imaginary wind. Fantastic earthen frogs leapt held up by thin guide wires. Mermaids playing harp overlooked scalloped benches with hands a moment away from plucking a lullaby.

Further down, the clay felt hot as if fresh baked. The wyrm in her reveled in the heat and yearned to curl. She hadn't realized how cold the metal workers and stone tunnels had been. She looked behind her, missing the fires of the forge and again ahead towards the heat that must have come from potters' ovens. She followed her guide quickly, using her pace to press his. Lisa felt sure that the potter made at least six circles to make sure she lost her bearings. She said nothing, keeping as tight a grip on her mouth as she did on her three-foot itch.

"Here," the potter said at last, showing her a wide room braced with stone, but painted in reds, yellows, and browns. The potter rubbed dirt into his hair, then frowned at the clay underneath his nails. His narrow eyes squinted and he set alight kindling in a clay fireplace.

Lisa braced herself. She pointed with her sword. The potter shook his head regretfully and pointed to a beaded curtain. A very slight tapping could be heard through it. Lisa placed her hand on the potter's shoulder in thanks. The man stared fearfully at her claws. She waved him off, but he would not move.

"Every murder should have a witness," he said quietly.

Lisa's eyes burned and he winced, but gathering his courage he turned from her and set himself on the bench. The man loosened his collar and opened several buttons on his patch coat. His hands drifted towards the fireplace, but his attention never fell from her.

"It's not murder." she muttered, "It's necessity. Self defense." She took a step forward. The weight of his eyes burdened her. "Besides," she grumbled, "it's not human."

"Why should that matter?" the potter answered, "Neither are you."

She cursed the echoes and felt weight pile on her shoulders. Martha would never be able to lift her now.

She parted the curtain. Clay beads rattled. The thing looked up. A young woman who looked a bit like the potter sat with an engravers chisel in hand. The golem tapped its foot in a coded rhythm. The woman concentrated and wrote, then asked the golem for confirmation.

"Is this what you meant? I'm sorry. It's just that when the beads shook there was an awful lot of tapping and I lost what you said." The golem didn't answer. It rose. The girl placed the chisel down. She noticed Lisa and straightened her wool sweater. "Oh hello," she said to the wyrman. The golem shoved the girl brusquely behind it as if to protect her. Lisa widened her stance. The girl's voice suddenly raised in pitch, "Is that her?" she said. The golem nodded and raised its tangled fists.

Lisa willed it to attack first, but the thing hovered protectively in front of the female potter as if Lisa was the monster and it was the only thing between her and destruction. A small stool, a writing stand, and a cubby dug into the wall described the room. The wyrman made a half swing, trying to provoke it. The golem made a move to block her blow. It stood its ground. Lisa ground her teeth. The itch burned hotly and begged to scratch.

"Break the message," Lisa told them. The golem looked down at the tablet and with a twisting of vines and a grating of stone shook its head, "No."

"If you promise to break it and not to speak of what you saw…"

Again, the thing shook its head with a sad dignity. Mossy eyebrows lifted, sockets where eyes should have stood, stared at her itch. Slowly, it bent and picked up the stool. It snapped off a leg and held it before itself.

"No one likes the tax collectors," the girl said protectively, "but leave him alone." She even tried to stand before the golem, but the golem gently shoved her behind its bulk.

Lisa blinked. Why did people keep ascribing human characteristics to these monstrosities? *Who said they could be given job titles? Since when did monsters speak in Morse code? Why does this one stand like a hero protecting the girl?* She was supposed to kill the thing to protect herself from Martha and Corporate, but if the thing was... then she was the monster.

She needed to be a monster; a spirit of self-preservation demanded it. Her itch faded. Desperately, she tried to hold onto it, but it gave her the raspberry and vanished. The moss raised its head again, questioningly. Lisa's face paled.

"I don't want to hurt you," she said. A craggy smile split its features. Its enemy had shown weakness. The golem cracked her with the leg of the stool spraying the room with splinters. Lisa fell to the side and pulled down strings of beads. It hopped on its spiked feet towards her. The girl's nose twitched fiercely. She covered her eyes and ducked from both monsters.

The golem lifted Lisa and threw her into a wall. Lisa sprawled. It reached for her again. Instinct took over. She grabbed the hand that reached for her and flipped it over her shoulder. A part of her stood apart and said, "You just flipped a ton and a half of rock, mud, and stuff." But most of her turned and launched a kick at its midsection. Pain flared in her foot. The thing grabbed her and smacked her into the wall again. Lisa clawed frantically and cut a vine. Then she hit the wall again. She scratched with her dragon nails. Her wings flapped. Again, she struck the wall. And again.

"Stop," she heard. Dizzily, she saw the potter, many potters actually, stand, "Did she not show you mercy? Did she not sheath her blade to talk? She be a master craftsman and you know your debt. I'll not be allowing any potter to touch a golem's wounds if you lay hands on her." The golem stared incredulously and jumped up and down.

"Aye, I know," the potter answered, "she provoked you and she be the enemy and all that blather, but more than that she knows the secret of the snake. Think, where will you be if potters close their doors. Within a month, your arthritis will be unbearable."

The golem hammered furiously on the floor.

"That may be as well, but that goldfish did be in the wrong as well and you know it." The golem hung its head. "Go ahead, lad. Go and file your report. We'll see that she leaves you in peace."

The golem pounded its chest, pointed to the wyrman, and then towards the tunnel.

"I say thee no, by the bovine, no. You'll go. Go and deliver your message, you pile of spoiled fish." The female potter gasped. The shale trembled. It advanced on the potter. The potter raised an eyebrow. The golem paused, then pointed again to the tunnels. The squat man shook his head no. The golem raised its arm threateningly. Sadly, the potter clucked twice.

The golem staggered backwards. All the clay and earth that sealed it and let it move suddenly dried and exploded outwards as powdery dust. Shaking his head, the female potter ran to the piles of rock, weed, branch, and moss and tried to hold it together. It fell loose and apart. The dust slipped between her fingers and drizzled the flowers of a clay garden.

"You forgot what you are," the potter said sadly. "Velma, destroy the message. This was not a creature of art. It be a tool warped by a hand who overused it and took no good care of it." He nodded, "and then bring me as much clay as you can carry. I'd not like to lose a soul today. Let's be seeing if we can remake this poor beast."

He patted Lisa on the shoulder and carried her to the bench, then he left her. He returned shortly with the gnarly woman. She bent over the wyrman and picked at things in Lisa's hair.

"You be saying true, Potter."

"Aye," the potter answered, "she needs lessons, but she is what I said."

"A champion's heart in a dragon's body."

"Aye. Too feathering many of the bat wing beasts making havoc these days, Helga, but this one hasn't sold her heart, not completely. Besides, she knows the secret of the snake." To Lisa, the potter said, "Be strong dragon, there was a day when we were all more than we are now. We remember when craftsmen were artisans. We remember when we were more than laborers forced to mass produce. We'll set you right."

Helga, the gnarly woman dragged her away.

26. Storming the Castle

John chose a road by closing his eyes and running until he fell. What use was a lifetime of beans if you didn't trust them? The grass was soft under his feet and the earth springy. Lilac and licorice scented the air. Trees mopped the top of his forehead with dew blessed leaves. His breath was surprisingly even.

This body was meant to run. In fact, it felt good to move. He widened his stride. Laughing, the wind kissed him and teased his chin. Faster then, he wondered if rocks were leaping out of his way or if animals were clearing the way for him. Life was his to command. He was the master of the bean. Nothing was insurmountable. If he just the used the beans in him, then he could conquer dragons, win the hearts of beautiful maidens, and be declared princely. Nothing would stop him. Every solution was in his grasp. Even the riddle of Jeremy would be child's pl… He tripped.

The road was broad enough to hold six lanes of traffic. It smelled of dung and mown grass. In the distance, he saw more distance. Just lots of brown road, tall amber grass, and more licorice vines that crawled along the edges. At the moment, it was mostly empty. A little man… creature, waddled slowly forward. John grabbed him by the shoulder and demanded.

"Where can I find Corp O'Rat?"

The turox sputtered.

"Wha?" Its strawberry blond eyes shifted under a turtle's face. Fox tail hung limp and unhappy. Its toes flexed as if preparing to run, but never bothered, knowing it would be futile. Instead, it bent and gnawed on licorice.

"Why do you wish to find Corp O'Rat?"

The itch scrambled like a dentity from John's feet to his throat, and wrestled his tongue away from his brain. John said, "I'm Jack."

The thing fell down, wobbling back and forth on its shell unable to right itself. John tried to right the poor thing, but it retreated under its shell forcing its spectacles to pop off and break. The turoc's four legs retreated too, hiding from the uncertainty a Jack brings. The only part of it that stayed put was its fox tail. That red and white appendage quivered with excitement.

"Can't help you," a quivering turox voice echoed from deep within the shell. It suspected what a Jack chasing giants meant. Jack bounced from foot to foot as if his feet were asleep or as if he had downed a weekend's worth of Halloween candy in a single night.

A small puckered turtle hand reached out from beneath a robe and the turox muttered. "There is a sweetling house over the next rise. Truly, a marvel, you should take a day to see it. Imagine raisin bread walls, chimneys made of goobers, window panes of frosted sugar, and shutters of peanut brittle. Doesn't that sound better than chasing after giants?" The turox smiled hopefully from under its robe, "I think the landlord even rents a room for bed and breakfast."

"Give me a break! You think I never heard of Hansel and Gretel?" John shook his head, bouncing with an eagerness buoyant enough to match a child on festival eve.

"Who?" the turox asked, wishing that it had the owl's power of flight and not its wisdom. Jacks made messes. The turox knew this first hand. He had been plain once. A Jack had mixed him up so badly that even his genes couldn't recover.

"Hansel and… you know, the bread crumb path, the witch, the oven"

"What! What have you done this time?" the frightened creature cried and tried to retreat further into itself, but its fox aspect was dancing with the opportunity to get involved with mischief.

"Nothing, I'm trying to find someone."

"Try the sweetling house. It really is very nice! I spent a two week vacation there last summer. There is indeed nothing like their mud baths or their hot chocolate Jacuzzis.

"Thanks," John said, "If I get a chance, but I have to save someone,"

"From Corp?"

John nodded. "Jeremy,"

The turox lifted his head and squinted at the red haired boy. Life and chance sparkled in him.

"Worse and worse," the turox said, kneading its fingers. The creature raised its head and puffed out its chest. "I'm sorry Jack, I can't tell you where the giant Corp O'Rat lives. I simply don't know." John opened his mouth, disappointment dulled his features, but then he smiled so brightly that the turox smiled in return.

"Thank you," he laughed.

"For what?"

"For being concerned about me."

"Jack," it smiled.

"And for telling me where to find Corp O'Rat." Jack laughed and the turox sputtered. The lad turned and faced the correct direction.

"Don't go!" the turox cried, "It's not safe. Corp O'Rat…" the turox felt a slight tugging and looked down. His fox tail, his trickster tail, was busily pointing down the corporate road. Back and forth the tail jabbed the air to tell Jack what he needed to know. "Traitor," he accused the tail and it drooped.

John smiled much like Peter Pan, or perhaps like Jack, and ran. From a distance the turtle headed man rose and dusted his robe. Pulling yet another blade of grass from the ground, it chewed nervously.

"Jack?" he said, "Oh feathers," he said, "Good luck Jack."

John ran barely a mile before he saw a sign. *Elevator to Cloud Corp O'Rat- six miles.* John chewed his lip and ran harder, letting the itch have its way with him. "Don't think," he said, "just save the man and get out."

The itch burned like fever.

After five and a half miles, two lines began and stretched towards an enormous stalk. John looked at the setting sun and hopped nervously in place looking at both lines wondering which line he should join. A woman turned to him. She eyed him suspiciously, then clutched her coin purse tightly.

"Plaintiff or defendant?" she asked. John stopped bouncing, the itch wrestled with his mouth. This time John won.

"What?" he asked.

"This line," the woman sniffed, "is for plaintiffs, that one for defendants. Which one do you need?"

"Ah," John answered astutely.

"You do have a case pending before the giant?" She sniffed, disdainfully. Everyone suddenly moved forward ten paces. "Do you have a writ?"

"A writ?"

"Feathers, the lad's a duck on a volcano." Someone else blurted.

A few laughed. John rubbed his head and shuffled his feet.

"I have a…"

"Idea lad? Do you have an idea?" someone suggested. John pounced.

"Yes, I have an action against the giant."

"Then you're a plaintiff," the woman said sharply. John looked at her dubiously, but she just shook her head and put her hand on his back to give him a little shove. "They won't see you unless you have a writ. Do you think they'll see everyone who thinks they've been wronged?"

"But Jeremy," John said, backpedaling. Jeremy's name sped up and down the line. A dragon lifted its head at the beginning of the line. Again, everyone advanced ten steps.

"I heard Jeremy murdered Prince John."

"I heard the Lady Hortense brought suit against them for feeding her ears to the dragon after Prince John valiantly championed her."

"I heard that even the faerie ring distances themselves from Jeremy now."

"No, really."

"It's true. I heard it."

John's head spun with rumors. He was listed in a quarter of them, but Jeremy's name seemed to attach itself to stories like the leprechaun was made of honey. The stories stretched like it too. John's itch hammered at him fiercely, twisting his head; he saw a sleek golden dragon approaching.

Run, it roared, *Haven't you learned anything by now!*

John, as a good Jack must, ignored it.

This dragon had whiskers like catfish except they had been waxed into a neatly upturned moustache. Its body slithered on the ground like a giant worm and though it lacked legs, two massive arms crocodile padded forward. The dragon wore a clipboard on a chain around its neck.

"Who," it rumbled, "speaks the cursed name?"

The line separated. John found himself in a sudden clearing and the focus of a dragon again. His knees shook. Cat like ears leaned forwards and gold dipped eyelids clinked. "Who," it amended, "are you?"

John's throat went dry. He opened and closed it several times, but nothing came out.

"He's not mute," yelled the sniffing woman helpfully. The dragon moved closer and encircled him within his curls. John glared at the woman who smiled back pastily. The dragon pricked someone and wrote a note on the clipboard. The plaintiff fell down and turned instantly blue. Tightening its body around John, its venomous spikes edged closer. John blew hard, trying to force the spikes to move away from him.

"The boy thinks he's a wolf. Look at him huffing and puffing."

Several laughed.

"Who," repeated the dragon, "are you?" A golden eye narrowed and a mammoth jeweler's loop appeared before the dragon's eye. "You are holding up the line. These fine people here will wait until matters are resolved." John felt the weight of angry impatience from the crowd.

"I…" he said, and decided to give over to the itch, "found a room full of beans. Hundreds. Thousands of beans."

The dragon's mouth fell agape and a few whiskers sprang apart. It mouthed "Beans" silently. The jeweler's loop popped from his eye and rolled. The crowd pressed a little closer, not close enough to press against the dragon, but close enough to hear the tale.

"I found kidney beans, pinto beans, green beans, lima beans, castor beans, soy beans, horse beans, broad beans, asparagus beans, hyacinth beans, butter beans, navy beans, civet beans, and phaseolus limensis."

The wax broke completely springing twelve ungainly whiskers. The dragon scratched its maw and repeated the names of each of the beans John had just named; then the great wyrm licked its lips. A chill breeze blew metaphorically. The crowd shivered in unison. The dragon blinked uncertainly, coils throbbing as if its heart churned mightily. Something felt different. It searched up, down, and around looking for that damnable sense of… chaos? No, it was far more off-kilter than mere chaos. It inhaled mightily, bringing everyone a step closer. The smell was earthy. Heavy. Slightly salty. The smell was…

"Sustenance." The golden beast murmured. Then looked around quickly.

Too late to take it back. The word was already on the wind and in the vines. It flew off the tongues of people who were empty. Several fell immediately. They hadn't been aware of their loss. Still, that wasn't the greatest danger. The greatest danger was that this… stranger knew of such a treasure trove. Such a great store of sustenance and the dragon realized that it too was starving.

That the lad before it was telling the truth was obvious to taste and smell. The very air around him resonated in a very fickle way. It closed its eyes and breathed in memory. The dragon had never tasted a bean of course. She was strictly a carnivore and proud of it, but there once had been other sources. Beans were, of course, the most magical, but there was also… Where was he?

John had stepped away. He looked green and indecisive. *What would he taste like? Would he taste as he smelled?* The dragon sniffed again. It was a hearty smell. *Well, that's disappointing.* The golden dragon preferred sweet. Still, a memory spoke very loudly.

Remember the goose! Remember the GOOSE!

It paused.

John wasn't sure what to do. The itch had left him. He could still feel it kind of, but it certainly wasn't in his feet and so it wasn't time to run yet. The golden dragon was oddly beautiful and somehow terrifyingly serene. Men, women, and beasts gave way and yet tried to press in. Only its massive coils prevented them from pressing in on him. Instinctively, John knew he had to wait on the wyrm. In a way, he was glad. Now that the itch was gone he felt dreadfully uncertain and his momentary burst of confidence dispersed.

The dragon coiled around him again though it kept its scales carefully distant. A decision must have been made.

Scribbling furiously on his clipboard, the wyrm pretended to regain its composure.

"So you are looking for a merchant's license?" the wyrm finally declared.

John blinked and then nodded.

"But surely you know what so many beans would do?" It was clear from John's face that he either didn't or didn't care. The dragon paused, "You don't know do you?"

"I could deal with Corp directly," John answered, "Let him control the distribution and rights." The dragon blinked again.

"How are you called?" it pointed to his clipboard, "What name should I make the appointment under?" The lad smiled almost like James Bond.

"John, Prince John."

"Prince John?"

"Of the Corporation of Ordinary Wares." He nodded.

The great golden wyrm winked at John. Actually, it closed one eye to reveal a seal that had been branded on the golden lid. The dragon pressed the lid on the parchment and rolled it. Then it tore off a leaf and twiddled his fingers. The parchment shrunk to man sized proportions.

John caught it easily.

"This is your writ, Prince John. My name is upon it. Should a good deal be made, I shall be subject to a grand commission. If, on the other hand, there is a deception, I will look the fool." It waited for John to speak, but the lad looked unable again. "Go to the elevator on the left and take it to the penthouse cloud. It will open to a golden bricked road. Stay on the road or you will fall through the cloud. Your writ will entitle you to a meeting with the Lord Executive himself." John furrowed his brow and the dragon repeated his directions.

Smiling, John set off. The dragon escorted him to the stalk and saw to it that John received a private elevator car.

The ride up the fibrous stalk was smooth. Fireflies flitted about when the door opened. Puffs of whip cream or marshmallow tempted on either side of a long golden bricked road. Above, the sky was a deep navy, just a shade or two bluer than midnight black. John took a step forward and instantly the fireflies dove at him. Trying to shoo them away, John accidentally lit his writ on fire. He blew on it, but fireflies, being vengeful insects kept landing on it, "Mmm, very interesting," one would say until its spark would go off and the writ would start to burn again. Alarmed, the lad waved the parchment vigorously in the air. John didn't notice it, but his itch returned.

"Get away," John said and chased the winged pyromaniacs. They tittered and led him off while others circled him and ignited what was left of the writ. By the time John tired of chasing fireflies, the writ was a crumbly black mess. Insects laughed at John, especially after he set down the golden brick road anyway.

"You should turn back," they offered. John wished he had companions. You should never have to journey down a golden road towards the enemy with neither writ nor companions. He looked at the charred parchment, then up the road towards the looming castle. Maybe with a little spit he could.... The writ crumbled. He dropped the pieces. Maybe he could explain and they'd still let him in.

The castle brick was gray and hard. It twisted with savage gargoyles, jagged spires, and spiked gates, but the scariest part was that the entire front facade was in the process of being replaced with large flat mirrored panes that took away from its gothic darkness, and tried to suppress the elegant, spooky dark lines of the castle into a box that showed you your own face. The mirrors seemed to proclaim, *All the world is a reflection of me and you are mine.*

John figured they wouldn't just let him in. He began to turn, but then wondered what the dragon would do if he spoiled its commission. If John could find Jeremy, he was certain they could at least get to the beans. Sighing, he squeezed between the gates and marched up to the castle wall.

Somehow, conveniently, a ladder sat abandoned by the mirrored facade. Panes of glass leaned near it. John crept to the ladder watching himself in the mirrors to make sure he was being sneaky enough. He noted a sign. "Ye Olde Union Workers on break," it read. The sign looked a little dusty. A few spider webs trailed from the sign to the ladder. Feeling guilty, John took the ladder and shouldered it around the first corner.

The ladder almost reached to the lowest window. He set it and breathed deeply. He wanted to turn back, but didn't know where to turn back to. Hunching his shoulders and looking down he smirked at himself.

"Okay Jack," he said to himself, "It's time to be Bond."

27. Fees, Lies, Grosses, Sums, and The Harp

John levered himself over a window and fell into a swimming pool. Greasy liquid weighed down his arms and he grabbed at bobbing wheels of carrot slices and celery. The pool smelled of chicken. It was also getting very warm.

He was in the soup! Literally.

He breast stroked through the broth. It reminded him of his youth. Of course, he was always on the shore back then, but he'd been quite envious of the kids who got to swim in the polluted Tarris River. Their ability to dodge tires and cans were impressive, but he most enjoyed how they emerged from the waters green, would scream, and go off playing super heroes. Oh, the carnage they could wreck.

A potato bonked him in the head bringing him back to today. He tried to grab it, but it was slick, and the effort pulled him under. He pushed off against a piece of… he didn't want to think about what kind of raw meat that was… he pushed off to regain the surface. It was definitely getting warmer. *Run… errr Swim,* the now familiar itch demanded, dividing its attention between his arms and legs.

In the distance, he saw a curving black metal edge. Sweat and chicken fat burned his eyes. Luckily, the giant seemed to be watching his salt. Logs of celery shifted and bumped him. He latched onto one and began kicking. *How long 'til boil*, he worried.

The edge was not smooth, but even with the ridges the vegetable was not easy to grasp. For one thing it was hot. For another, it was curving the wrong direction, but stubbornness prevailed and he began making progress. The water shifted from warm to hot. So, using common sense, he tried surfing on the celery. Balance and steering proved the fatal flaw to that theory. He wobbled atop the green stalk and not even his itch could save him. Pin wheeling, he belly flopped over the side. On his second attempt, he flopped backwards and nearly lost the celery altogether. Worse than that, a surfer, it turns out, is victim to the current. Normally, waves push to the shore, so that's okay, but in a soup pot the currents moved less helpfully. In his efforts to ride the waves, John actually lost ground. He huffed, then smiled. The chicken soup cleared his sinuses. Refocusing, he decided to ditch his James Bond style and, although less cool… and far less Fonz-like, he decided to paddle on the celery as if it were a raft. In this way, he reached the rim.

The metal wall curved slightly towards him with no obvious handholds or grips. It was cauldron black. He kicked hard to maintain his position. He reached out tentatively and nodded, it was not too hot to touch yet. Even better, all his sprawling was keeping the rest of the flotsam away. He tried again. The metal rejected him. There just weren't any good handholds. At least none that he could hold onto long enough to propel himself upwards.

He treaded water. The itch needed to find its way into his head, he thought. Then he realized how lucky he was that no chef had come to taste or check his work yet. That gave him a second deadline. Turning in the fatty water, he looked. There must be a prop, something he could use. The friendly celery bumped into him again sending him over.

This'll have to do.

Teetering, he climbed onto the celery and held his arms wide apart for balance. With a deep breath, he thrust forward to try to jerk the celery forward, but his momentum banged him into a boulder-sized potato. John circled his arms, but felt himself slipping. He jumped from the celery, but landed well short of the rim. Swimming hard, he climbed onto a potato. A bubble spurted into the air.

"Help!" he called. If his voice were louder than the fire or if there were people who heard, none stirred. None even came to stir the broth. Visions of being rescued in a giant ladle disappeared.

The potato was still stiff, but was made slick by moisture. He paced a step and nearly fell back into the broth. Looking over the sea of bobbing vegetables, he searched for an idea. A smile quirked and he raised a finger. He slowly lowered himself and fished out a giant carrot. Keeping the carrot to his side with his left arm, he began to gnaw at the potato.

"Too much pepper," he spat after the third bite. He tried to break pieces off with his right hand, but the motion unsettled him too much. Another bubble exploded from the broth. Within minutes a healthy boil would begin. Heartily biting, spitting, and sneezing he dug a hole. The itch ran from his feet to his teeth as if the itch understood his need. His teeth sent shards of potato flying, like he was a fierce beaver cutting through a log.

The hole in the potato was of goodly size. *Would a diner notice?* John decided that wasn't an important consideration for him right now. He carefully lifted the carrot and bit a notch in the top, before setting it in the hole. Twisting, he set it as tightly as he could. The potato began rocking to the broth's sporadic beat. Pursing his lips and spitting over his shoulder, he rubbed his hands together. He looked back guiltily. He really shouldn't spit into other people's soup.

With a mighty leap, he launched himself onto the carrot. The stalk teetered. The potato rolled in the roiling waters, but by the bean's grace managed not to overturn. John scissored higher, squeezing his legs and arms alternately. The carrot fell with his weight, but the tip of the carrot hooked onto the rim of the cauldron. John smiled fiercely. His luck was holding. The potato swayed, rocking John, the carrot, and its notch precariously. Blanking his mind and closing his eyes, his itch took him to his feet. When he looked, he was running with arms outstretched up the slick knobby carrot.

Almost there, he sighed. Thank god this isn't a Bond film, if it were… the potato and carrot gave a lunge and the carrot bounced. John leapt. The carrot fell off the rim. It passed him and fell into a mass of boiling flesh and vegetables.

Landing on the rim was no good either; it was hot too. He sprang from the burning metal without looking and landed on the window ledge.

"This is where I started," John complained. Breathing carefully, he worked, hand over hand, to the curtain. Sliding down, he felt a little like Errol Flynn, but he was getting closer to James Bond. The fabric he shimmied did him the favor of drying him at least a little.

He landed on a chopping table and ran to a puddle of water to dip his feet.

"Ah," he sighed, "that was hot."

Vegetable and fruit smells lingered, making his stomach growl. Nibbling table scraps, he filled his belly and sat down contentedly. His itch jabbered at him, but what finally got him up was that he couldn't tongue out some food between his teeth. Walking to his right, he saw a thatched box marked toothpicks and opened it. Inside were dozens of rapiers. Swinging a few, he picked one and clipped it to the belt the regent had given him. His face flushed when he saw that each of the toothpick rapiers had a name engraved in them; his own read, *Sir Bravearm.* The itch chastised him for staying still where others might find him. John agreed with it and with a running leap, reached and slid down a chair leg.

The wooden kitchen floor stretched for acres.

He steeled himself. Before him stood a table the size of a small house. Guessing from the height of the furniture, the giant must stand over a hundred feet. He unsheathed his toothpick and held it before him. The size of everything struck him again. Sir Bravearm's rapier looked like a toothpick even to him. Dismissively, he sheathed it. What did he think he was going to do with it, blind the giant like he was Odysseus reborn?

He smiled, that could work.

Then he frowned; was he seriously considering injuring another person? *Giant*, he reminded himself, but he looked at the ordinary, if magnified, room and his conscience prevailed. Sense whispered, "Whatever you do Jack do it quickly. I'd not like to be here when the giant comes for breakfast." Why his sense spoke with Jeremy's voice, he didn't know, but he agreed with it.

Jeremy wanted him to topple the giant, but the giant controlled dragons like tame pets. How could he beat up someone that could cow and control monsters? John shrugged and did the only thing that Jeremy ever told him too. He ran and passed mops as long as trees, dishes of gold the size of observatory lenses, and forks of silver the size of fence posts.

Pushing his way through a doggy door, he entered a dimly lit hallway. Gray granite bricks, unadorned and rough, lined the sides. The floor was cobbled with the same stuff. A thick carpet of red and purple velvet lay over the cold stone. John pressed himself against the wall and thought. "Why would Corp O'Rat keep such an austere headquarters? He needs to hire an interior decorator. This place has got to work against his PR." He touched a hollow suit of armor. It creaked and dropped its axe. The visor seemed to curve oddly, almost as if it were smiling. John patted the spiked shoulder plate and thanked it for reminding him that delay was an enemy.

"Where would he keep Jeremy?" he asked no one, but this time no one answered. The hallway stretched into darkness in both directions. "A lifetime full of beans," he remembered hearing Jeremy say. Well, he would trust to the beans. Let luck guide him. "Luck is a fickle mistress, Johnny" he imagined Jeremy warning. Still, who else walked with him?

He chose a direction and ran.

Silk tapestries hung from several sections of wall. Columns of smooth timber bracketed with more timber braced old walls. Flower petals burned in small clay jars, scenting the halls pleasantly. John listened, but heard nothing stirring. His luck seemed to be holding, the castle seemed asleep. He imagined it would take most of the night to cook a swimming pool worth of soup using a simple fire, but felt somewhat bothered by the fact that there were no cooks at all who attended it.

"Can't find good help anywhere, I guess." John clichéd.

A room opened before him. Wooden debris lie on the ground, as well as more monstrous chairs, a cubby full of abacuses, paintings of rich color and chests, endless stacks of chests that brimmed with so much gold that it made Fort Knox look like one of Miss Hannigan's pockets.

John stared open mouthed. His pockets suddenly felt very light. Carefully, he worked his way past the gilded cage, tables, and fireplace tools to look around. Only the moon watched. Undoing his shirt, he tied it like a bag.

This is wrong, he reminded himself. *Shush*, his itch seemed to say, *Remember when you felt like Eroll Flynn. Yes*, he answered himself. *Well, Look at you. Dressed all in green and with a rapier. Go with it, Johnny. Just pretend you're Robin Hood.* His conscience fought as John shoveled money into his pockets and shirt. When the interior debate finished, his conscience conceded, *Well, I suppose as long as you give some of it away, it isn't too wrong. Of course*, John nodded absently, *I'm not a thief.* Corp O'Rat, on the other hand, stole this money. He was sure of it. He paused and fingered the weight of the bag. Did that make his actions any better? John shouldered the bag and told himself to shut up.

His hands shook. He put half the money back. Glancing at an accounting sheet, he noticed an error. He straightened. *If this goes unchecked, why the giant might be guilty of underreporting. That would be wrong.* He began to walk away, but turned back. Bad conscience or no, he couldn't just let something like that stand, could he? He sat on a bench and began to make corrections.

He corrected twelve mistakes by the fourth page. The errors were strikingly similar, almost as if they were intentional. John tsked, and gripped his shirtful of money tighter. *Corp O'Rat is a thief*, he said justifyingly, but a guilty frown fought the slight itch at his lips. Yawning, he looked out the window. The moon had fallen out of sight. Alarmed, he looked to the fire. Only ashes burned.

"What am I doing?" he said, slapping his forehead. Then he heard chimes.

"Morning chimes?" he fretted. Standing, he stretched quickly and prepared to go. He would come back for Jeremy. The sound was too quiet. They tinkled like water. John stood and walked towards their source. Taking a breath, he removed the coverlet from the gilded cage.

"Wow," he said, "An Egyptian bust." At least it looked Egyptian. It had a woman's torso and arms with a hawk's head. The antique was in pretty bad shape though. It was dinged, scuffed and even mashed in quite a few places. He reached forward knowing that if he ever got back home he would never get a chance to touch an Egyptian antiquity. The hand was soft and warm, not like metal at all. He had heard that the Egyptians were fantastic artisans and had incorporated.... It moved.

John screamed. Martha turned a battered face.

"Lisa," the dentity said, then it saw a boy in front of her and shook her head to clear her thoughts.

"Lisa," John said, his throat tightened. A woman from Homeland Security with that name had scared him into this. If it were not for Lisa Fischer he would never have broken into BEAN and he would have lived a happier... he paused.... Saner, he nodded, life. "Lisa?" he whispered urgently. She might actually be James Bond! "Where?" The dentity sniffed.

"You know her," she nodded, "Of course, you smell of the cow, too. Are they returned?"

An idea winked in John's head.

"I'm John," he said.

"John," she said, her voice echoed strangely, as if it had to pass through many chambers before reaching her mouth. "John, would you get me my legs?" A confused frown crossed his features. The dentity squeezed his hand. "They should be in the cabinet." John looked to the window, the fireplace, and the hallway door. Bustling sounds came from the kitchen and began to work their way through the hall. The soup should have certainly cooked thick and well by now. John swallowed. He looked at her dented face.

"You're a prisoner too, aren't you?" he asked stupidly. She nodded and pointed again to the cabinet.

"If you get my legs," she said simply, because he seemed to need it that way, "I can lead us out of here." John measured her with eyes that didn't look quite so foolish as his actions. With a brusque nod, he opened the cabinet.

Two silver legs leaned against the back wall.

"Yes," she called when he pointed to them, "bring the needle and thread too." John dragged the legs to her cage, leaving behind him a white mark where the legs noisily scratched the floor. Martha winced. Shrugging apologetically, he lifted them and staggered the rest of the way to the cage. Martha petted her legs while John ran and retrieved the needle and thread.

After diligent sewing, Martha stood and walked. When she bent she creaked as metal pushed against metal. Then glaring intensely at the bars, she Judo chopped. Her wrists slid through the hard metal cutting almost soundlessly. One more chop and she created an opening to hop through. John now understood why the Egyptian dynasties were so powerful and lasted so long. She motioned him to follow, a pleased expression on her face.

Gliding on restored legs, she headed towards a small block of stone. John pointed furiously towards the hall. Kitchen sounds grew more insistent. Balling his fists, John followed her.

Martha levered the block with straining, crumpled arms and pushed it backwards. The two slipped beneath and then Martha and John shoved the block furiously back in place. The room echoed with the sounds of a monstrous yawn. Platters clattered down. The hawk's eyes were big. She held John still, muffled his mouth with a hand that kept shifting nervously from soft to sharp. She released him when he motioned that he was calm. They waited in darkness. They heard the creaking of timber, the ring of a silver platter being lifted, then a mighty whiff to smell a breakfast.

They heard a sound similar to trees toppling. Martha covered John's mouth just in time. He bit down on her palm. She petted him, trying to calm him with her free hand.

"Not an idiot," she murmured to herself, "just a fool." John stared at the block in front of him. Another huge intake of air was heard.

"Fees, Lies, Grosses, Sums," the giant roared, "I smell the blood of a bad business man." The giant stamped. Coins clattered. "Someone has taken my gold." He roared. Martha shook her head and noticed the bundled shirt by John's shoulder.

"A large fool." She decided.

"Someone has altered my accounting." Corp O'Rat fumed. The giant stopped. Feet pounded away from their block then came nearer. More quietly, the giant said, "Someone has stolen my dentity." Pandemonium broke out. Dishes clattered, metal clanged, and Corp ordered, "Find the thief. Bring back my dentity."

John smiled. Finally, he felt like James Bond. Rescuing the girl, under a megalomaniac's nose. Martha nipped the air and waited. A great stirring rose outside, lots of running and shouting and bumping. With calm dignity she heard Corp say, "They are still here. In the castle." The scurrying intensified. Dishes clattered and pots shattered. Sneezes rose, probably from overturned carpets and rising dust. Sounds of chaos rose until, the giant shouted, "Do you think they would stay here under my nose? Do you think so little of Martha? Go! Find her!"

Martha smiled and breathed deeply. John turned to her and saw a look of pride on her reflective face. She had been recognized. He smiled and she frowned back, shaking her beak. John understood; this was not a time to feel good. This was another time to run. Did people ever have the opportunity to walk in this world?

She led him down a narrow corridor that was actually a long crack between bricks.

"Can we…" John began. Martha shook her head and shushed him. The light grew brighter. She pointed and began climbing creakily down the backside of a support beam. John lowered himself after, vaguely insulted that she was leading. After all, didn't he rescue her?

They landed in a storeroom of sorts. A blacksmith's forge lay at one end. Even better, tongs and hammer rested in a bucket. John eyed the numerous swords, bows, and a series of sharp and blunt weapons he couldn't recognize. Martha nodded and walked to a door. She pulled. It was locked. Frowning, she rammed her shoulder into it. The door held.

John picked up a broadsword. An itch tickled his arm, than ran away and clung to his feet. He ignored the implications. He swung the blade cavalierly. His imagined opponents backing away from the ferocity of his attack. Martha shook her head and said "No." John turned to see what she was upset about. His sword thrust banged into its hanging brethren. The swords clattered and rang like morning bells inviting a city to mass. John dropped the sword. Martha closed her eyes and lifted her beak to the heavens.

One after another, the swords banged into each other violently. John tried to calm them, but was afraid to touch the swinging sharp metal. He watched helplessly, as they dominoed their way down the line. The last sword swung out and tapped a pile of shields. The shields edged forward. John reached forward as if his hand could reach across the many feet and stop it. Then all at once…

The door opened. The shields fell. A head peered in the room, it yelled "Aha!" drew a mace, and reeled forward, as the first shield struck him. The intruder shook his head and took another step. Ten more shields wobbled. He looked up as the next ten landed on his noggin. The man lie buried under shields, the only part of him visible was his heavy blacksmith's apron. Martha blinked. John mouthed the word "beans" and shrugged. Martha nodded.

She hurried over and pulled from the fallen smith a key ring and with amazing speed, fit one key after another into the lock. Finally, one clicked. Peering over her shoulder, she watched the doorway. John stood guard with his feeble rapier and poorer grip.

"You'll get your wrist broken that way," she said critically, studying him, but made no effort to correct the lad. John tried to look fierce. She stepped into the closet.

She embraced her wings tightly and walked back out.

"You must have eaten more than one bean," she said admiringly, "the whole castle should be here by now." Easily, Martha dragged the blacksmith inside the room and locked the door. "Tie him," Martha ordered, and walked to the forge. Pumping the billows, she stoked flames. With the tongs she plunged a set of scavenged wings into the fire. John looked back to find three other sets hanging next to a set of maces.

"You will have to attach these to my back." Martha explained.

John spread his hands.

"I know you do not know how to." She said grimly, "but if we are to live, I must recover my wings. You should be able to see how they fit. Don't fret, lad, make yourself useful. Pump the bellows." John finished tying the smith and took over at the bellows.

John pumped. Martha began piling objects against the door. After a time, Martha pulled out one wing from the flame and handed the tongs to John.

Martha screamed. Her back arced, but she forced herself stiff. Her brow bent and she gasped. John tried to stop, but she flung a hand backwards and kept his grip on the tongs. Their eyes met. John gulped. He pressed harder and she screamed again. Weakly, the wing shifted. It shivered with Martha's pain.

"That's enough," she wheezed, "Now the other one." The dentity staggered to a basin and tumbled in. Steam hissed. Hands pounded on the door and shifted the stack

Martha had placed in front of it while John had worked the bellows. The man stirred. John clunked him with another shield and he fell back to sleep. The dentity shook as with fever in the basin. Still, imperiously, she pointed to the fire. Wincing, John put the second wing in the fire. Afterwards, both hurried to the door and threw anything of weight they could find against it.

The second wing was, if anything, worse, but somehow the dentity withstood the soldering pain. The former knight protector endured it with strength and silence. John lowered her to the ground, pumped water into a bucket, and poured loads of water onto her back. She gasped.

Not knowing what he was doing, he picked her up. His legs tottered. He staggered onto the smith's worktable. An axe blade broke through the door. John reached up and boosting with all his strength, helped the dentity clamber up through the ceiling's hole, before scrambling after. Together, they replaced the stone that hid the passageway. Breathing hard, they looked at each other and gripped hands.

Sometime later, the rest of the door shattered and pieces were moved away. The only thing alive in there was a smith with a nasty concussion. John and Martha crawled. Martha led and John didn't mind. Finally, they reached a place where a cold wind blew on them. Martha gathered John in her arms and stood.

"You have a lighter conscience than the wyrman," she said, sounding surprised. John closed his eyes. "You better pray, lad, that you have some skill at smithing." Martha leapt.

They fell like a stone. They hurtled towards the stiff whipped cream of Corp O'Rat's cloud. Buttresses of stone jutted out and the remnants of gargoyles lifted their stumps to watch them. John caught his reflection in the paneled mirrors that had been set into the gothic brick. John didn't like the way his face looked when he screamed. Martha stretched her wings and flapped mightily. They pulled upwards in a furious arc. A sense of exhilaration washed through him. Martha's face filled with pain and concentration.

"We can run." John said. The dentity laughed coldly, her eyes looking back. They made it only a little way before John felt a burst of heat and cowered in her arms.

"Dragons?" Martha said disdainfully, "You send dragons against me?" Insult seethed in her eyes. She turned and whisked through the air, between the clumsy monsters. Flames crisscrossed. Deftly, she spun between the checkerboard of fire. Precisely, she pivoted and used her wings to cut through a dragon's wing. The surprised beast jerked once and spiraled down. She aimed herself at three more and sent each tumbling. Twenty dragons hovered around her, their necks twining desperately to try to keep pace with her. Her speed amazed John. She flew so fast it felt like winter.

Like a silver bullet, she aimed herself at the dragons. They gave way and she was through. Muscles in her neck corded. She muttered rage against the dragons. John wiggled in her arms, trying to improve his grip. She turned once more. Racing, with the beasts pursuing, she screeched. Dragons collided into each other trying to keep pace. They looked dizzy and roasted the air in frustration. John gave her wrist a panicked squeeze and the dentity glared down at him. The severity of her hawk's beak scared him, but he shook his head no. She opened her mouth. For a moment, John feared she might snap him in two, but Martha reluctantly nodded and twirled away from her pursuers.

She outdistanced them quickly. They dove through a break in the clouds and the sky lightened to a Caribbean blue. The air mellowed and along with it so did Martha's mood.

"They didn't burn you too badly, did they?" She asked in a dulcet voice.

John didn't answer. She looked down, the lad was a bit red, but hardly blackened. She rotated his body so that the speed struck the back of his head. He breathed a little easier. The dentity laughed. "You did a fair job. Nay, it was a job well done indeed. Now rest, I must put some distance on the dragons, so that the more fearsome creatures will have a more difficult time tracking us." John nodded, tears streaked down his face and his mouth dried, but he managed to breathe and not complain. The dragons behind him became tiny dots.

"Where…" he rasped.

"Where I left the wyrman Lisa, of course."

Martha smiled fiercely.

28. A Grass Roots Movement

Wide cumulous clouds shaded a hot summer sun. Mountains of rusty iron, greenish copper, and red clay sloped downwards. Yucca plants and Joshua trees stood in long rows and from a distance looked like a vast army surrendering. Rolling brush with sharply textured veins sat still, eagerly awaiting the wind. Hard packed earth tight with suppressed memories lay littered with soft blues, warm oranges, and dull yellows.

"I thought deserts had no color?" John asked.

The dentity didn't answer, but continued her sweeping arc towards the mountains. Long green waterways wended their way down from the rocky slopes and fed startlingly clear cobalt blue lakes. Peacefully, animals sipped by the rim of the water. By their side, lizards, normal and magical, drank. A truce between natural enemies held at the water's edge. Then man came. Man chased and waved his hands as if the water was a deeded possession. The animals fled, but not in the way one might expect. They fled, tempting man by staying just out of his reach, and as man chased and waved his arms the elderly, sick, and young crept out from hiding places to drink. John smiled approval. Martha dipped lower to swing beneath a flock of birds.

The green began abruptly with a startling richness and warmth. Waves of turquoise grass swept and golden, umber, and sienna trees climbed. The color deepened beyond the mountains, bringing to sight a rich valley of farmlands, lush forests, and ancient woods.

"I agree," said the dentity to John's awestruck expression. Her voice was tight with pain, but he failed to notice; he just nodded and tried to absorb the beauty of this world.

Martha flared her wings to slow her descent. Her beak curled in pain and she hugged John tightly with one hand. With the other, she grabbed her ulnare and tried to hold the bone bracing the wing in place. Off balance, she aimed for the mountain road. The patchwork seemed to be failing and

Martha's wings twitched between every downward stroke. Bumps of concentration sharpened her broken body. The arm holding John lost its grip. She reached forward to try and catch him, but when she released her wing she heard a snap and began to spiral out of control. The ground met her like a giant's fist. Martha stood for the barest moment, then collapsed, her right wing attached only by the smallest of silver tendons.

John rolled to his feet without a cut or a hair out of place, although even beans could not prevent his Peter Panesque costume from getting torn and clay stained. Martha staggered upwards surprised to see John already at her side, ready to give her a hand. He winced when she folded her wings and revealed the damage she had borne for miles and miles. He spoke strange cryptic words that Martha had never heard before.

"Metal fatigue." and fingered the sharp wings tenderly, "You flew all this way on broken wings." He massaged his shoulders in sympathy. She waved his words off.

"If I did something of note, it was less than a lad breaking into a giant's castle." With long practiced discipline, she vanquished the pain from her face, though not from her body, and brushed aside John's hand. Her beak reflected the remnants of an austere sunset. A falcon circled above and called a greeting. With a sharp breath, Martha tapped her damaged wings and called forth a bright tune on her one still whole wing. The music soared with a bright, hopeful message that made the falcon's beak sway and bounce.

Her strength made John feel terrible. That she would gift the world when she was in pain and hammer her own broken wings to do it made him feel small. John smiled; she wanted him to smile. The weight on his back, the weight of stolen gold he had made her carry for all those miles, weighed heavily on his conscience. When the last echoed note faded, he promised himself he would give away all the money he had stolen from the giant.

"They're worth fighting for, aren't they," he heard the ghost of his father say. "That's the biggest shame of it and you'll get nothing from it." John opened his mouth, but his father cut him off, "All you've gotten so far is a shirt full of gold, audits from the IRS and subpoenas from everyone else." John nodded and stared across the vista.

"But how do you fight a giant?" he asked the ghost. His father's memory laughed. The ghost considered his son, measured his resolve and leaned down to whisper a vital secret.

"You don't," he answered, "If you're really lucky you'll find a really big axe." John Sr. gave John Jr. a level look. John gripped his rapier and nodded.

"A hatchet would be better." He agreed, even if it was not a weapon suitable for Errol Flynn or James Bond. His father laughed an unencumbered laugh. His spirit ruffled his hair. "Better run, John. You're better off running from all of it. If you start, they'll be fitting you into all their stories and all their problems."

"But,"

"Hush boy, don't talk when I'm talking. You better go, John, your ride's leaving without you. I didn't listen to my Pa either. You better hurry up."

"What?" John's daydream, or his father, vanished. Martha was half a mile ahead, walking steadily on perfect legs, broken wings, and battered body. The itch raced eagerly down every corner in his body. What else could he do? He ran after Martha with the thought that if he ever returned home he would be in shape to enter and win the Boston Marathon.

Her beak pointed to a row of caves. "She's here," she said excitedly and cawed. Quickly, she covered her mouth, embarrassed. John pursued quickly enough to keep her in sight, barely. He called out three times, before she realized how far she outpaced him. She waited. John caught up and collapsed against her shoulder, puffing. She ruffled his hair.

"I'll not leave my squire behind." Martha said, fondly.

"Squire?" he asked, blankly. "I thought a squire was a fat guy who chased after really skinny men and told them not to go charging at windmills."

Martha looked to see if he joked, then gave him another look; one just like mother used to give him.

They entered the Datchery Caves. The opening was so rough, uneven, and craggy it had to be artificial. John heard Martha's steady insistent sniffing and tried to follow that. Blindly, he stumbled into a wall, rebounded into a pointed metal gargoyle, tripped forward and fell into a fountain. Sighing, the dentity took his hand and led him through the cave.

"How did you break into a castle at night, avoid all the guardsmen, and enter Corp O'Rat's executive dining room?" she asked incredulously. John turned an impish smile on her and said,

"There were guards?"

She pulled him along.

Rude caves quickly opened up into polished hallways. The checkerboard metal tiles and elegant scrollwork were accompanied by low phosphorescent tiles and the smell of burning metal. Martha's eyes widened and narrowed. She threw off John's hand and rushed forward.

"Unhand her," she whispered fiercely into the forge room.

The gnarly woman looked up and dropped her hammer onto her foot. The smiths fell to their knees. Lisa rose from a pile of pallets. A dozen other smiths gawked.

"Burnt Pudding and Spoiled fish," the gnarly woman yelled, "You broke me foot."

"Martha?" Lisa asked.

"Are you well, Lisa?" said the dentity, as she rushed to her side and sniffed her hand. Her brow smoothed as she stood. She took one last sniff to make sure and sighed, "It's still there. The essence is still there." Lisa raised a brow and began to speak when John interrupted. John, looking like a twelve-year-old waif, pointed at Lisa's half dragon form and said.

"That's Lisa?"

"Who's that?" asked Lisa, pointing back at John. The smiths seemed not to care. Instead, they sprang forward, shoved John aside and surrounded the dentity to study every ding, tear, and rent on her body. Their brows lowered with worry. Pulling, they drew her forward to a flat basalt pedestal. A calloused hand tried to touch her. The hawk beak snapped. One smith backed away, but the ones behind her began stroking her damaged wings. Martha raised a hand in protest. Her features darkened.

"Look what they've done to her," said a smith urgently. The gnarly woman advanced, frowning. Martha shoved several smiths back. The beak snapped warningly, again. Shaking her head with disgust, the gnarly woman slapped her hands together. There was a sudden absence of music, of sound. Martha hissed, but the sound came out emptily. With her hammer returned to her hand, the gnarly woman paced around the silver champion, her brow growing more furrowed with each step.

"Burnt pudding and spoiled fish." She admonished, "Feathers!" she continued causing some of her fellow smiths to blush. Though in truth it was hard to tell with their ruddy complexions and the heat from the furnaces and hearths.

"What have they done to you? What have you done to you?"

The dentity found herself unable to take her eyes from the gnarly woman. Many hands tugged at Martha and urged her toward a worn pedestal of smooth basalt. Her wings sharpened, but the gnarly woman clapped again and Martha lost her concentration. A confused look crossed her eyes. One of the smiths crossed to John and took his sack of gold and held it up to the gnarly woman. John tried to grab it back, but a smith walked between him and his gold-filled shirt.

"They can even pay," the smith said happily, counting Corp's gold.

"Repairs and more repairs," grumbled the gnarly woman, "Soon you'll be having me fixing wagon wheels. Well, set her down." They clamped the startled dentity down. Martha blinked with surprise and then thrashed violently. The gnarly woman walked up to her and slapped her cheek with her hammer. John drew his rapier and shouted, "Hey!" The smiths laughed and pointed to the ceiling. John looked up to see what they were pointing at and they disarmed him. Then almost carelessly, they tied him to a bench next to Lisa, who looked uncertain if she should be concerned or happy that Martha had been chained. John studied the scaled lizard woman next to him.

"Lisa? Is that really you?"

She studied him without recognition. They began battering Martha loudly. Her skin rang and shook. Lisa rose, but a gentle potter's held her down and shook his head. She questioned with a lift of her eyebrow.

"Your new scales are not well set. If you move now they will settle painfully."

"But?" Lisa said.

"Is it really you?" John said, hearing something echo in her voice. Lisa frowned at him.

"Who are you?" she asked.

"It's me," he said, shaking his twelve year old red haired head, as if it were obvious, "John, John Fasola."

"John?" she asked. He nodded. Her features darkened and steam came from her nose. "How come you get to look human!" she roared. John shrunk from her and tried to edge away, but the chains held secure. "How come he gets to be human!" she demanded. The smiths shrugged and looked away, whistling. Lisa fumed, literally.

Martha did not yelp or scream; she made no noise. The workshop roared with fire and pulsed with the beat of hammers.

"They're killing her," he told Lisa, wishing his chains would allow him to turn and see. Lisa rose, her itch lost somewhere beyond her reach. She tried to force herself to cough. A smith with a glowing white metal scale held by tongs approached the wyrman next. John's eyes widened, he closed his eyes, and held his breath. Lisa grimaced and sat down. Three smiths held wyrman down. A heavyset smith pried her scales apart. She whimpered.

"Monsters," John accused. The man held the plates separate by hammering with a chisel. Lisa screamed. Martha made no sound. John clutched his chains tightly, twisting to try to break the metal. Lisa's smith slid the white-hot scale in. The metal sizzled against her like a frying egg. Lisa bared her teeth and hissed a painful breath. Two smiths leaned their full body weight on her while another approached with a gloppy brush. Smells of burning meat combined with acidic, metallic, and carbon odors flooded the room. Lisa flailed wildly and more smiths pounced on her to keep her still. John jerked back and forth, trying to at least loosen the chains. He needed to help! Lisa fainted. A grinding sound grew behind him, hammers beat with purer and purer rings. He smelled sparks. John tried everything he could think of, he wished desperately that he had a hairclip. Nothing opened a lock better than hairclips in the movies, not even keys. The smith with the tongs came back with another white-hot sliver of metal. John began to cry.

At the end of four excruciating hours, they released John. He charged the first smith he saw and knocked him down. Furiously, he struck. The man covered his face. Blows rained down with frightening speed. Three smiths circled John, but the lad's wild blows struck everything near, and while the blows were not powerful, they were many and by the bean, they were well placed.

"Monsters," he yelled, striking his target again and again. They yelled at him to stop. They shouted many things he couldn't hear through his rage. Hands grabbed him. Like a berserker, blindly he swung. A jaw popped. A stomach lost air. A knee buckled. The hands left. Crawling, the smith that first drew his rage tried to flee. John leapt for him.

He stopped in midair. Kicking, he tried to swim or remind gravity to let him fall. The heavily muscled smith cowered in a fetal position and tried to push himself through a wall to get away. John, impish four foot, ninety pound John, swiped boldly. The thing that was holding him up didn't let go. Eventually, adrenaline wore off and the thrashing of his legs and flailing of his arms stopped. John hung limply in midair. The gnarly woman nodded. Martha stood behind him, her beak curved in a smile. John blinked as the madness left him, then leapt to his feet to hug the dentity. "You're alive," he shouted. Her silver beak bronzed for a moment, as if blushing.

"Martha," he said with a wave of relief. She looked as polished and pretty as a tinman after a trip to the Emerald City. He gaped. Slowly, reality dawned on him.

"Oh," he said sheepishly, "they were fixing you," then added sincerely to the smiths, "I'm so sorry." To his surprise, they laughed and advanced to clap him on the back, even the smith he had jumped. Afterwards, the gnarly woman pointed a stubby, blackened finger at him and motioned for him to come near her.

"You," she said, "are not a master. Your work was poor, shoddy, and incomplete."

"But," John stammered.

"How dare you be risking a dentity's life that way?"

"I…" he interjected.

"I should be breaking your hands to see you never lay them on another set of tools. You feathering layman." She slapped his face. "You be owing us a mighty price for setting on Garlan Martin over there. A big strong strapping lad like you ought to know to watch his temper. What chance does a smith have against a big brute of a monster like you?" At the end, the gnarly woman couldn't contain herself and laughed. Puny little John dipped his head in shame. As sure as his blows had landed, he missed the gnarly woman's punchline.

As for the smith, Garlan Martin's face crimsoned deeply and the smiths laughed again, although they politely turned from facing him so as not to laugh directly in his face.

John offered the man his hand in apology. Garlan Martin rubbed his jaw and was about to shake his head, when he saw Lisa beginning to rise. A look of frustration warred within him, but he swallowed it and shook John's hand. A cheer rose.

The new plates fit stylishly and well along the scales of Lisa's body. She flexed and stretched and seemed entirely without pain. John struck his head against a wall and called himself an idiot.

Soon after, the beating of hammers began again. Orders still needed filling, after all. The gnarly woman smirked at her workman and smiled at John as he winced and sat down. Garlan Martin left the room unable to stand by a boy that had manhandled him, a boy that looked lighter than some of his hammers.

A slight itch touched the bottom of John's feet, when Garlan passed. Martha's beak raised and she smelled the air urgently. Surprise led her to John's foot. She grabbed him and lifted him above her head and sniffed, then sniffed Lisa's arm.

"You're a traveler too? A hatchling?" the dentity asked.

"A traveler?" the gnarly woman appraised him, "Impossible, that boy would get lost tying his own shoes."

"Why does he get to be human?" Lisa asked again, still upset. The room exploded in quite unfair laughter. When the mirth died, Martha lowered the boy to his feet. She kept her grip on him though.

"I am Martha, dentity, and knight protector," she said to John and waited. John looked at her blankly, "How may I address my savior," she added finally.

"Oh," he said, and the gnarly woman nodded that her assessment of his aptitude was accurate. "Prince John of the Corporation of Ordinary Wares." He answered, finally.

"A prince," Martha and the gnarly woman said with surprise.

"The Corporation of Ordinary Wares?" Lisa accused, "You sold that. Didn't you? Or were you lying to me when you said you were just a shareholder in BEAN?"

"I sold it," he admitted, "I'm sorry, I didn't mean to lie. I… it's just that it's been with my family for years and I still feel…"

"Lisa," Martha chided, "Show compassion. It is no shame if your kingdom is overrun and conquered. He will still be Prince John to me, if he wishes it, whether his kingdom was conquered or no."

Lisa rolled her eyes.

"This be unimportant," the gnarly woman said, "What be mattering is that you have three debts counting. The repair of a dentity, Prince John. That be a high price, silver is an expensive raw material. Especially a silver that can live and bend and be hard when it has to. Second, you have stained Martin's honor, be it true that he should have held you up like a pup and spanked you, but you still attacked a journeyman smith and that requires a price, whether he set it or I. Lastly, since you know the master dragon, I will lay her debt on you."

"What?" Lisa interjected, "I thought because I knew the mystery of the snake…"

"Silence, we do be haggling."

The dentity put her hands on her hips and glared at the gnarly woman.

"Knowing the secret only means you have access to the guild. It does not provide free…" The dentity appeared red in the forge firelight, her stillness brought a promise of quick movement.

"Fine," the gnarly woman said, "fine, fine, we'll forget the one debt. She gave us a snake, though she did keep it." The dentity nodded imperceptibly. "But the other debts," the gnarly woman continued, "those are real and must be paid."

"You took Prince John's gold in exchange for healing me," the dentity said.

"No," John said, both looked at him in surprise, "it wasn't my gold to give. I'll pay your debt. Both debts. What is it you want?" John gestured with a royal grace and waited. The gnarly woman hesitated and then spoke quickly.

"We want the dragon, my Prince. She is a craftsmaster and we want her."

"No," Martha hissed, "she is mine."

"I can't give her. She's not mine to give."

"I'm not a slave." Lisa contributed.

"We want her. This be erasing all debts and it be fair. She should be working off her debt. Her screaming drove the boy mad and made him attack poor Martin and from what she be telling, the dentity brought the boy here because the dentity be wanting to find her."

"There is truth in what you say," Martha said flatly, "but still you will not have her."

"I thought dentity's honored truth." The gnarly woman challenged.

"Wait," Lisa called, "You can't make a deal without both sides knowing what the compensation is. There was no bargain about me. I was told this service is owed me. I will not stay here to be your pet or your servant. It wouldn't be right."

"Right?" the gnarly woman said. Lisa lay a clawed hand gently on the burly, gnarly woman. They faced each other for only a few moments, but there was something about the wyrman that melted resolve. The gnarly woman brushed something from her eye. She blinked rapidly and put her hand on the wyrman's wrist.

"Feathering lawyer," she groused and then pleaded, "But you awaken things in us, Lisa. Things we want to remember. Things we be not wanting to lose again."

Martha sighed.

"Then you have to let her come with us." John intervened and laid his hands over both of theirs. The gnarly woman shook her head "no" as if she would not listen. John continued anyway, "Jeremy brought me here because he said you needed help. He said there was a problem with giants and a problem with cows. If he was right, you can't hold onto someone who can help. Look what your world did to her. It made her into something that… does something. She's got to be important. You can't be selfish."

"Tis the worst speech I ever be hearing, Prince John." The gnarly woman said. The smiths laughed and loudly agreed. "We be selfish once she be gone. As for giants, she be not enough and you be not enough. You do be needing more practice in making speeches."

The dentity stood quite still and said, "This prince stormed the castle of Corp O'Rat," she paused to let that sink in, "broke through the castle's defenses single handedly, made his way to the executive dining room, rescued me, took on and held off a castle that was on the hunt for him. You saw my condition. I could not help much. Do not tell me the lad is incapable."

Lisa gaped at him. So did the smiths. Martha's simple inflectionless speech allowed no dispute. She nodded at him and her beak turned up in a grin.

"The lad is a living bean." Martha rested her case. John's cheeks reddened. He sat beside Martha and said simply...

"Still," the gnarly woman interjected.

"She's not safe here." John said. They turned to him. "Corp O'Rat sent someone hunting for her."

"An unawakened dentity," Martha confirmed, "He is to kill her without speaking."

"The more reason for her to stay." A smith said, pounding a table, "If it be a metal thing after her, then we be her best defense." The smiths nodded agreement.

"True," Martha agreed, John and Lisa opened their mouths, "but after the dentity, Corp will pile his resources against you. You are a small manufactory, how long will you stand against the giant Corp O'Rat alone?"

"And what will you do with her?" The gnarly woman asked.

"The question is not what we will do with her. The real question is- What will you do for her," John said, pointing to Lisa and sounding very much like John Kennedy. The smiths shuffled their feet.

"Prince John is correct. She is valuable to us all. Name a new price," Plinking a low note, she added, "John, you can have. He can work off his debts as apprentice."

"What?" John asked.

"It would be fairer." Martha said, "She is mine. He is in your debt."

"Martha," Lisa scolded, "you don't really believe in…" she hunted for words, "indentured servitude. It's not like they're asking him to wash dishes to pay a restaurant bill."

"I say he pay his debts and we go."

"But…" said the gnarly woman.

"I can't believe you think that way."

"It is fair."

"But…"

"It's wrong."

"Who are you to tell a knight protector of right and wrong?"

"But…"

"I live the law…"

The gnarly woman clapped her hands. The dentity froze and Lisa's lips became blue as if something inside her had grown very cold.

"But," and the gnarly woman looked to see if any would dare interrupt her again, "we do not want him. The lad be useless." She jutted her jaw, trying to push away the look of kindness Lisa's presence instilled in her, "but it be clear that the master craftsdragon be not wanting to stay. And I'll not force her when her debt be so small. I shall therefore set a new debt," she paused dramatically, "Prince John of the Corporation of Ordinary Wares to restore your name and clear your debt you must retrieve for us a broom."

"A broom?" John stammered, "A witch's broom?"

"No," the gnarly woman chuckled kindly, "Did ye no look at this floor. There be ashes and scraps on the floor and by every corner. We be needing a broom right badly and all of us be claiming our time be too important to find one. You be a man without skill, so this task be worthy of you John. Do you think you are up to it?"

John fought futilely against the insult. Instead of speaking, he nodded. Martha and Lisa smiled.

Minutes later, Martha returned with a broom from one of the valley villages. The gnarly woman declared all debts void and even told John that he had some hope as a smith, though she assured him that was not an invitation to join the Datchery Caves Union of Craftsman and Artisans.

John was amazed that there was no catch. He shook the gnarly woman's hand and thanked her. His itch buzzed. The gnarly woman looked up, her eyes wide and startled. Her voice sounded surprised as she said,

"You did prove yourself an honorable man, Prince John, paying your debts and all with such speed. Further, you be showing that there be those that would hold to friendship when following their own path be easier. I be declaring that we too, should be holding true to such a man. Prince John, from this day, this be a home to you and more, should ye be having a need, we be yours."

Diggory Thomas grumbled. "You be promising allegiance?"

The gnarly woman rubbed her hands together and clapped the fellow on the back. She cleaned some soot from her forehead and pointed to the great molds and fine tools. Petting a great sculpture, she strode over to John and stared down into the thin waif's eyes.

"I be meaning what I be saying. He named a higher honor price than ever could I be setting. The lad be taking on a giant for us. He be a traveler with no roots and no foundation, yet he be going after giants. Fool he may be, but he be understanding what it is to be a prince, to care for his people, and I pledge us to stand by his cause."

"Thank you," John said, his throat and chest tight.

"Do you know what this means?" Martha asked.

"Corp O'Rat gone would be meaning a lot less money for we artisans." The smith groused.

"Aye, there's that too," the gnarly woman smiled and kicked a chunk of coal towards the forge, "but… never mind, you're too young to remember what we'd gain in the bargain. Besides, if you ever listened to any of me teachings you'd know never to cross a Jack."

"He's Jack?" the smith asked.

"You be living too long in a cave," the gnarly woman added quietly, "he be the spitting image of his da'. Good luck to ya, Jack and courage to you, Lisa, you'll always have a home with craftsfolk." She gave the wyrman a friendly punch. John said nothing more, but he shook as a burden of responsibility fell upon his shoulders. The dentity smelled the additional weight and smiled, it didn't stagger the lad at all. "If they win, oh by the bovine, you'll see a world you only heard tales about."

"Come with us then," Lisa said, not really wanting to be left alone with Martha. To everyone's surprise, they agreed. The gnarly woman and the potter only asked that they be given time to get prepared. The smiths and potters fled to various chambers and returned in a dazzling display of fresh clean clothing. In answer to Martha's unasked question, the potter and the gnarly woman answered almost simultaneously, "You don't expect us to go out after Corp O'Rat without preparing our best suits?"

"By the bean," Martha answered, "Our hostile takeover has an army."

After a hearty feast, Martha, Lisa, and John jogged down the mountainside accompanied by an army of twenty-two smiths and four potters. Their full bellies reveled in the briskness of the night air and they clanked merrily downwards gathering the attention of the village folk, who for the most part shuttered their windows and hid. The army sang loud off-key songs and issued challenges to village folk. "Join us," they shouted and some of those who saw Lisa did. John wanted to leave the army. He said he had to rescue Jeremy from the giant before the… he had a difficult time saying the word war. He still hoped he could convince them to do a sit-in or sign a petition or file suit against Corp O'Rat. By now they had some very fine suits, he argued. The idea of taking up arms against the giant and his army of dragons, dentities, and other monstrosities chilled him. He did not want to lead his people into slaughter.

Martha convinced him to stay with the army until it gained enough strength to defend itself. She promised she would go with him afterwards, but his duty as Prince was to his subjects first and all of these had sworn allegiance under his flag. John argued fruitlessly that it was Lisa and not he who mattered in the building of an army, but Lisa insisted there was as much talk of "Jack" as of her. Martha added that his luck was all that protected them right now. John dismissed that, saying that he wasn't really all that lucky and besides he wasn't magical.

Martha won the argument by saying. "But you do have luck, that's why Jeremy wanted you. You must decide which duty is more important - the lives of Lisa and the men and women gathered under our flag or Jeremy. We need you more right now." John disliked Martha for saying that, her argument cowed him.

A rumor began to spread. It coursed up mountainsides and down through valleys. No man or woman could resist the charms of Lisa. Soon folk started looking for the wyrman just to see for themselves. Seasoned veterans, vagabonds, merchants, shoemakers, elves, and small children eager for adventure, filled their ranks. Lisa nearly swooned at the numbers that demanded to see her so that they could swear fealty. Within a month, the army stopped moving in order to let more people find them. The rumors continued until it could be honestly said that Lisa's was the smell that launched a thousand suits.

29. Warrants and Lawsuits

Wending through the army, a man walked towards John. Actually, the ghost of a man walked towards him. The ghost was frail, so thin you could practically look through it. It was as if he hadn't eaten since his death, but its skin stretched tautly against its neck and its face was gaunt to the point of appearing hollow. Its billowing robes were embroidered with scales, not dragon scales, mind you, but weights and measures. Rose tinted John Lennon spectacles hung askew from his nose. The ghost waited to make sure it had been seen and then raised a rattling hand.

"John?" the whining voice echoed. The dentity shook her head, cuing him to say "no".

"Yes," John said, raising an eyebrow to the dentity.

"Prince John of the Corporation of Ordinary Wares?"

"Yes," John confirmed. Martha threw up her hands in exasperation.

"Good," the ghost said. Ghostly chains snaked around the lad from head to foot. Lisa took a step forward. Martha held her back, shaking her head vigorously.

"There's nothing you can do," Martha warned. The ghost gave her a wry look from beneath its spectacles. Reluctantly, the dentity amended, "There's nothing you should do." and turned away unable to meet the ghost's eye. The chain links clunked around John, each solid despite their spectral appearance. John tipped over. A musty breeze stuffed John's nose. The metal smelled of moldering stacks of paper.

Martha, Lisa, and the assembled army of suits watched numbly as the ghost attached the chain to a harness and hook beneath its robes. They caught an unsightly peek at protruding spectral ribs. A connection made, the links reeled in until John hung above their heads. The ghost then spread its arm wide and made an announcement.

"Prince John of the Corporation of Ordinary Wares you are hearby served with this warrant for arrest. You are accused of breaking the spirit of the law." John mumbled something, but the chains gagged him. The metal seemed to shift size at the ghost's discretion. John protested again, but taking an ethereal end, jerked him into silence.

"What is he accused of," Lisa asked.

The ghost continued spooling. John felt a jerk. It occurred to him that he couldn't breathe and the world had gone red. Everything felt heavy.

Fearful of the spirit, the army backed away from their Prince, turned their heads, and whistled as if they saw nothing out of the ordinary. The ghost knelt and whispered something to John. John blinked. It took a link into its mouth and slurped it down. Lisa's itch erupted into life. She strode forward threateningly. Martha put her hand on the wyrman's wrist to try to hold the heavy wyrman back. Strangely enough, Lisa felt lighter since eating, repairs, and being swept up into their cause. She fell backwards and her itch scored Martha's shin, but the dentity refused to let go.

"Did you think he could escape his crime?" the ghost said to Lisa while its body began expanding. The spirit gave one last mighty slurp against the chains, sucking them in like spaghetti, and John fell inside the gelatinous thing.

John sank into liquid oxygen, at least he guessed that's what the ghost was filled with, because it soothed the burning of his muscles and he could still breathe.

"How?" he gasped, with his first regained breath.

"There is no one who is not linked to Buir O'Cassey." A voice spoke in his mind, "You have defied the law. Specifically, Section 1,232,944,543 of subsection 32,498,532 part C."

"What?" John bobbed as the thing began moving. Its speed was imperceptibly slow.

"Ignorance of the law is no excuse. Be aware that I have amended your list of crimes. You are further accused of rapid breathing."

"What?"

"Again, I will inform you that ignorance is no excuse. This is a thirty breath per minute zone when inside a servant of the courts. I have recorded your breathing rate at 65. You may wish to be silent, Prince John of the Corporation of Ordinary Wares. You endanger yourself. Already, you are dangerously close to breaking the repetition code."

"What?"

The gelatinous thing tsked. The sound reverberated in his mind like a migraine. Then, it sloshed, snail-like, forward. Trying to show mercy, it refused to talk to John, but being a creature of the Buir O'Cassic law, it recorded all the lad's offenses. By the time, they reached the elevator to the castle of Buir O'Cassey. John was accused of breaking four hundred and thirty codes and of being a 3rd degree repetition violator. Lisa and Martha followed, hoping to at least act as character witnesses.

30. Toppling a Giant

Buir O'Cassey was an immovable ancient blob that towered over one hundred and twenty feet with rolls of fat tumbling down his body. He wore a simple white tunic decorated with innumerable buttons, pins, and clasps. His swollen feet and ankles rested in a swimming pool full of cool water. Every movement creased his face with pain, so Buir O'Cassey moved very little. His features were greasy, though vaguely honest. Wisps of white hair lay matted to his scalp, patterned like a laurel wreath. Two mammoth eyes remained closed, but as John, Lisa, and Martha entered, he leaned forward. Unfortunately, that level of exertion tired him and he fell asleep. Beside him, a dapper giant dressed in elegant black walked up to the great Buir O'Cassey and kissed his swollen hand. Milky eyes flicked up for a moment and a small smile touched the ancient giant's face before a fit of coughing made his features sag again. A snore soon echoed in the cavernous chamber.

John knew nothing but the itch, could hear, feel, nothing but the itch. He could even feel Lisa's itch resonating in tune with his own. Martha stood with hands behind her back, very much a soldier at ease. Attendants and audience filled a vast amphitheater that circled them. A whisper from one of them rode on a perfect echo back to the travelers.

"I thought this John would be taller and, you know, more charming."

Someone shushed and place which looked a bit more like an arena than a courtroom silenced.

Lisa wore a worried look. Her right hand kept opening and closing as if trying to grasp something. Martha kept slapping her hand as if she were a disobedient and troublesome child. Everyone else seemed to wait until three spirits entered carrying a small man.

Jeremy's mouth was bound with tape. The spirits carrying him were more of a smudge than transparent or translucent, and their heavy chains scraped the floor. Grimly, the ghosts deposited the wee man on the floor besides John. The leprechaun wiggled indignantly.

John knelt and tried to tear the tape from Jeremy. The tape resisted. It was a very strong and sticky red tape. By the time he had undone the wee man's mouth, the dapper giant had checked his briefs and began walking towards them. Jeremy's eyes widened and John fought the urge to spring wildly into the air. The lad wished he had an axe. Staring at the giant, John asked, "Who's that?"

"That's Buirs' boy, Kinspear." Jeremy answered.

"Oh."

"Kinspear O'Cassey?" Lisa questioned with a slight roll of the eye.

"Aye, you'll find him sniffing under every bush expecting to find something." Jeremy said.

"He looks so different."

"Only giant I ever met you could call a sneak, Johnny. Beware that giant, he's quicker on his feet than a dentity in a rainstorm."

"Why's he skipping?" Lisa asked.

"Kinspear O'Cassey is always skipping or jumping," Jeremy answered, "especially to conclusions." He added wryly to himself.

"Have they treated you well?" Martha asked the wee man stiffly. Jeremy sputtered at the whispery voice and turned to see Martha.

"No," Jeremy admitted nervously, "I'm not too well loved in a house of giants. They keep wrapping me up in tape and playing handball. At least these giants have little love for their French cousins. I think that's the only thing that's kept my skin whole." He looked to John and kneaded his hands. "By the bovine, they sent a dentity to collect you, Johnny? That's bad."

"She's a friend," John said, shaking his head. Then added, "Why're we here?"

Jeremy laughed. He rubbed a bruised jaw and put his thumb under his a sweat stained t-shirt. They stripped him of his fine clothes, but somehow, somewhere he retained his polish, though it took much of his willpower not to scratch himself while dressed in coarse, flea ridden prison garb.

"Why are we here, Johnny?" he smiled ruefully, "You think I can keep up with the laws of Buir O'Cassey. I'd be better off trying to count grains of sand."

The ghosts parted and Kinspear O'Cassey approached them. Dressed in a crisp black jacket, gold buttons and a simple starched white shirt, the giant looked the picture of propriety. He wore the kind of beautiful face that seemed all veneer to Lisa, a face that suggested trust if you didn't study it carefully, but was littered with traces of paranoia in the set of his eyes… as well a mouth that was too facile.

Kinspear bowed to Lisa and Martha before turning a shaming look on John and Jeremy. Lisa blushed and felt an irresistible urge to tell him her secrets. The giant nodded with a rye smile and both Martha and Lisa looked away blushing. Unconsciously, Lisa played with her hair. Martha preened her feathers. Jeremy darkened, but wore a playful face. John tore the last piece of tape off Jeremy and made a fist.

"You're to be honored, my father will attend your case personally. I will preside. Do you have anything you wish to tell me?" His rich baritone rolled across the room with an almost hypnotic chant. The giant smiled and Lisa felt her knees weaken. She slapped herself. She was not a schoolgirl; she needed to keep her wits about her to save Jeremy. Without Jeremy, how would she ever get home?

Jeremy stiffened; his face became as hard to read as a rainbow was to catch. From deep within his pot, he leveled a trickster's smile at the giant. The ghosts edged closer to him, making sure that they nulled his trickeries, but the wee man ignored them. His foot tapped impatiently on the thick carpet before him. Seeing this, the giant's smile faded and a frown deepened his beauty. Kinspear looked on Prince John and Jeremy with disgust, as if they must be diseased if they somehow were not immediately charmed by him.

"Nothing at all," the giant sighed. "Well, it will all come out in the court. May the spirits of law be fair today!" He said the words as rote, but the ghosts that guarded John and Jeremy blushed and their chains rattled happily. "Bring them."

The courtroom was decorated only with vases and thickly padded carpets. The carpets' bristles rose to John's knees and the lad picked his way carefully to avoid falling between the shag. Martha flew Lisa to the gallery benches to the left of the raised podium in front of Buir O'Cassey's dais.

On the walls were quotes or histories or something. John tried to read the writing on the wall, but found himself getting dizzy. Every time he began to read, the words switched around as if the laws were constantly changing their meanings. All he knew for sure was that the engraver used a garish style of cursive with many long loops.

Set on a blue slab of chalk, John and Jeremy waited. Trumpets blared and the people in the court began yelling, "Bring in the cow! Bring in the cow!" Within moments, a side door opened and they led out a black and white bull. Everyone's face seemed to soften at the sight of the cow, except for Kinspear's. His face became more suspicious.

"Johnny, when you speak, keep your hand on the cow. If you let go of it for any reason when you're answering their questions, they'll think you're lying."

"It's a bull." John said, remembering what bulls did to people in rodeos and bullfights he had seen on TV.

"It's not just a bull. It's the embodiment of this world's kindness. One of only six left. Be grateful they brought it out. Kindness is an endangered species."

They paraded the animal in a slow wide circle around the chamber, letting all breathe deeply and feel the invigoration and deepening of life that comes from bull. At the end of its parade the bull stood between John and Jeremy on the blue chalk.

"Giants, mortals, and faerie, know that you are here to preside in judgment and mercy," Kinspear began, "Yes, mercy even for Jeremy Tucker, the being responsible for the disappearance of Jack Spratt's cow. Yes, even mercy for that monster. But what is mercy? Is mercy bull?" Kinspear O'Cassey said, pointing at the cow, "Is mercy, letting a heart grow pained and leaving a conscience burdened or is mercy punishment." There was a murmur of approval followed by an undercurrent of boredom. One brave gossfer even whispered, "Haven't we heard that before?" which elicited some giggles from the stands. The giant feigned deafness and instead spun abruptly towards the leprechaun and pointed.

"Jeremy Tucker how do you plead?"

Jeremy stood straight and kissed the bull. The trumpeters, clerks, and even Kinspear smiled. Placing his hand on the bull he said with his brightest smile, "I could not have broken the law. You are what you eat."

The audience gasped and Kinspear glared at him.

"You think that will protect you, Jeremy Tucker. The crime you have been accused of is among the most serious."

"I should like to know then," he said, "what I am accused of, for though I know I have been guilty of many things, I should like to know which thing I am facing."

"Very well," Kinspear said, "but know this. Upon seeing the face of your accuser all mercy leaves both of you. We must instead invest our mercy in her and her victimhood. Mercy shall only lie in the retribution and reparation doled out!"

"Take the lad out of the court first then," Jeremy asked, "He is not…"

"His crime is the same as yours…"

"Johnny?" the leprechaun seemed startled.

"I knew it." Lisa whispered. "There's no way fifteen million dollars just falls into your lap."

Martha shook her head and mouthed the name "Jack" as if that explained all. Aloud she said, "I'dve not believed it of him."

"Bring the accuser out. He, the accused, wishes to hear the accusation."

Lisa winced at the redundancy.

Jeremy began to say "no", but John put his hand over the leprechaun's mouth. The wee man closed his eyes and took a deep breath. He began patting his thigh to the beat of a comforting song that once the faerie used to sing to him. A tear welled up in him at the thought of the ring.

A door opened, a burly set of guards marched in a protective circle around their accuser, Hortense Henry. John opened his mouth and closed it, then opened his mouth and closed it again. He held up her scarf still knotted around one of his shirt's buttonholes.

Hortense?" John stammered.

"Indeed." said Kinspear sinisterly.

Hortense was lifted gently onto a giant-sized seat. She stood there furiously. Her face had been scrubbed, but John could still smell the honey. Her gaze flicked away from him with a tremendous amount of hurt. *Is breaking a heart a crime here*, John wondered. Kinspear made sympathetic sounds and the people in the courtroom murmured their support for Hortense. Even Buir's snore's sounded comforting.

"They wish to hear it from you, Hortense," Kinspear said, "They act as if they are innocent babes unaware of wronging." Hortense reached forward and with shaking hands put her finger on the horn of the cow.

"That one," she said, pointing to Jeremy, "that one," an uncertain look passed over her eyes and she removed her hand from the bull to point emphatically at the leprechaun, "He broke the forms. I was to be a sacrifice to a dragon. He hid me and stole my honor and he prevented my champion from championing me. And that one," she pointed to John, "he abandoned me and failed to either fulfill his role as champion or die." She stopped and waited for the crowd to curse those who did this to her.

They responded not with cheers or silence, but concerned whispers. Though her accusation was severe, most noticed that she needed to remove her hand from the cow before making the accusation. Some whispered that an inability to hold onto the bull in court suggested that the case could be frivolous. Kinspear slammed an open fist on a pile of parchments nearly the size of his father. The people looked at the piled laws of Buir O'Cassey and tried to silence each other.

"So, you see, Jeremy Tucker. Yours is a crime magnified by breaking numerous customs. You interfered with contractual law between a dragon and a village. You disregarded the convention of one champion per trial…"

"Magnified?" John said, and he looked at the bull.

"Yes, a magnified perversion." Kinspear declared.

John looked at Jeremy and scratched his ear. "Magnified?" he repeated.

"They took everything from me," Hortense bemoaned, refusing to let this descend into a battle over word choice. John's attention returned to the teenager.

"Hortense," Jeremy began sweetly. "I saved your life. You brought me up on charges for saving your life?" Mutters began anew because she didn't refute him. To sue someone who saved your life had certainly been done before, but the ethic of it was questionable.

"Saved her life?" Kinspear chided, "Saved her to what? A damsel who flees her duty is unhomed and unfriended because all know that she abandoned her people. Jeremy Tucker saved her, but took from her all that matters."

"Except that the dragon agreed that its conditions were met and would neither seek retribution nor do anything further against her people. Hortense Henry, I saved your life and preserved your homeland for five years. Again, I ask you, is this a cause which you feel warrants damages?"

The gallery whispers grew louder. Kinspear grew darker and his veneer of beauty cracked.

"Dragons must be defeated with weapons. That is clear in the code." Jeremy laughed in response to this and none could miss that the wee man leapt to sit on the bull as he said, "Kinspear, what other weapon does a wee man use. A wee man's weapons are his mind, tricks, and magic. If you accuse me of attacking without a weapon your case has no merit."

The giant roared and looked for those who must be feeding the leprechaun answers in an attempt to make him look bad. He marched up to the wee man with such fury that the spirits faded backwards. Just before striking him, he pulled up and put his thumbs behind the lapels.

"Isn't it true that the lady Hortense already had a champion? How can she have two champions? Surely, that is not only unfair, but illegal?" He turned a wicked gotcha-grin on Jeremy. Jeremy shuffled his hands, but stayed on the bull.

"Well, I suppose you're right," he conceded. The crowd gasped and the whispers quieted. Kinspear O'Casssey pounded further.

"Wasn't it your plan to undermine our entire system of laws, Jeremy Tucker? Haven't you shown disdain for our laws every day of your life? Why should we show you any mercy?"

"You shouldn't," Jeremy answered, "but of this, I'm not to blame." His smile infuriated the giant and the wee man's polish gleamed so brightly that the gallery could almost see rainbows forming in his eyes. In comparison, Kinspear O'Cassey's seductive whispers seemed bleak. "To Hortense," Jeremy said, quieting the crowd, "I admit I'm guilty of saving her life, but I'm not guilty of being a second champion. While I defeated the dragon, the person I was championing was Johnny. You see," he said, turning to address the crowd while never for a moment stepping off the bull, "I brought him here and I do believe that as his host the laws demand of me certain responsibilities. So, the truth is that I saved the girl and the village in order to do my duty to my guest." His smile was perfect. The giant staggered backwards and Jeremy leaned forward to whisper almost inaudibly, "There is a reason that they never brought me here before, Kinspear. We tricksters were the first lawyers." Aloud he added, "I'll admit to this," he embraced the bull, "this time the only thing I am guilty of is kindness."

The bull mooed affectionately. The gallery did something they never expected to. They cheered Jeremy Tucker. This cow forgave him and supported him. That a bull would allow his embrace, even though the wee man's greatest known revilement was against cows moved everyone in the room deeply. Kinspear O'Cassey knew something was askew; he suspected dirty play and demanded justice.

"Father?" pleaded the giant knowing that the public had turned against Kinspear O'Cassey. Buir stirred for a moment and raised an eye.

"Send it to committee." He mumbled and went to sleep.

"No father," Kinspear roared, knowing that meant he could not even legally decide the case, but that the case would be decided by all those who had heard them. He turned venomously on John.

"State your full name."

John gasped. Jeremy placed John's hand on the bull. John wasn't as used to bull as Jeremy and his hand shook, but the animal's hide felt warm and comforting. His itch even lessened. He straightened himself and loosened his collar.

"John Spratt Fasola."

"Spratt," the giant spat. The faerie whizzed over his head and landed on his shoulders. They inspected him with wispy calipers and weedlike tape measures, then wordlessly returned to their seats.

"John Spratt," Martha breathed oddly.

"Father loved Mother so much he took her name when they got married. I called myself John Spratt for a while when I was in my rebellious teenage years, but mother cowed me. I usually use her last name."

"She cowed him." applauded the gallery, "A Jack with Cows!" John turned away from their approval and blushed, further endearing him to the crowd. Unconsciously, because the itch still demanded, he absently scratched the bull's shoulder. The bull's tail swished with pleasure. Kinspear could not believe it, neither could Hortense. The giant's eyes turned bloody.

"Spratt?" Kinspear O'Cassey screeched and even Buir O'Cassey stirred. "Your father was John Sprat!" The giant hopped back and forth. John and the bull bounced lightly. Barely controlling his rage the giant asked, "Was your father a thin man, John Spratt Fasoma?"

"My dad ate no fat. He was very health conscious."

"You are Jack Spratt Jr?"

Jeremy winced, but knew John would answer.

"Yes sir," John answered.

Buir O'Cassey stood. His son froze in shock. The ancient blob took a ponderous step and knelt before John. His milky eyes sharpened for a moment. John felt his heart go into hummingbird mode. The bull even began clawing the chalk nervously.

"You…" Buir O'Cassey began, "you dare to come into my court?" the giant blasted, "and you brought him?" Jeremy watched the ghosts shrink back. "You… I'll kill you myself." The strain of lifting his enormous arm burned on the giant's face and veins protruded from his neck. Sweat beaded on his face. The giant was so unused to doing anything for himself, was so unused to not delegating, that the bare half dozen steps that took him to where John stood made his breath raspy and broken. Kinspear advanced, but Buir shook him off. The spirits of law fled. Looking at Buir O'Cassey, they knew the giant was not interested in law.

The giant swiped at John. The lad leapt and found himself swinging between the giant's fingers as if they were parallel bars. The giant squeezed his meaty paws together, but too late. Already, the lad had propelled himself up amongst the matted wisps of the ancient giant's hair. Buir growled and clubbed himself on the head. John skittered downwards. The giant's breath came in tortured heaves. Still, he swung heavy blows. Martha found herself cheering. She was not the only one. No one in court had ever seen a Jack in action before. Buir O'Cassey twisted trying to swat the gnat that was Jack, but John slid down the greasy arm and tumbled beyond his reach.

"No Jack will… I'll get you," Buir O'Cassey gasped. John slipped and rolled under a giant foot. Buir staggered, his face was red with fury. The giant dove, which with his weight looked like Buir was toppling forward. John closed his eyes and twisted, the itch roared in merciless delight. The bull mooed joyously. Somehow, John found himself atop the giant's back again. The giant rolled over and John dove into a swimming pool that smelled of Buir's swollen feet.

Even underwater he could hear the giant's ragged breathing. Scissoring his legs, the lad pushed himself to the far end of the pool. With squirrel-like quickness, he darted through the water and upwards. Standing on a velvet cushion that stretched fifteen feet to either side of him he suddenly realized that he didn't hear pursuit. He stopped for an instant and looked.

Buir O'Cassey's face was no longer red. It was blue. He grabbed his chest with a meaty fist and knelt on one knee. His breath sounded ragged and choked. Suddenly, John felt a tremendous urge to run over to the giant and perform CPR, though he had no idea how he could ever do mouth to mouth with a mouth that was longer than his body.

"Father!" Kinspear wailed. Buir O'Cassey fell over. Jeremy rushed over and grabbed John's arm, holding him back.

"I've got to help," John sad desperately. Jeremy slapped him. John jerked with enough force that both leprechaun and boy fell off Buir's throne and back into the pool. Jeremy slapped him again.

"They'll kill you!" Jeremy shouted, but John was beyond hearing. In fact, so was Lisa. The wyrman had run over to the giant and worked her way between Kinspear's hands to listen to the giant's heart.

"It's not beating!" she shouted.

"Can't kill Buir O'Cassey, can't be done." Jeremy said, pulling on John's shoulders.

"Martha," John shouted, the dentity turned towards him. "Fly up and strike him in the chest as hard as you can. Right by the heart."

"You have felled him already, Prince John," said Martha flying to the edge of the pool. "We must leave here or our cause is done."

Buir O'Cassey fell to the ground. His arm rolled limply downwards.

"Do what he says, Martha, please." Lisa cried.

"Father!" Kinspear sobbed, "I should have known Jeremy's plan. Why else would he bring a Jack? Father! Come back!"

"Martha," John said, grabbing the dentity with such intensity that he hurt his fingers. Warm golden eyes turned on him. "We can save him. Trust me. Don't make me a murderer." Martha raised her chin.

"It was defense, John. In truth, you struck not a single blow. Feel no guilt."

"You said you owed me a debt," John tried desperately, "Do this for me. Hit him as hard as you can in the chest." His eyes held something that lacked foolishness. Martha nodded, a knight protector paid her debts. "Then keep doing it!" The dentity flew away at a speed so fast that the air shattered.

"She broke the speed barrier," Lisa said wonderingly. Then the wyrman quickly turned to Kinspear. Could she get the giant to understand mouth to mouth? "Keep yourself soft," Lisa yelled vigorously.

The dentity crashed into Buir O'Cassey's ribs and ricocheted off, bouncing off three walls thousands of feet apart before she could regain control. Then she hurtled herself at the fallen giant again. She heard a rib crack and was impressed with herself. Twice more she pounded his chest. She aimed herself again, but Lisa placed herself in the dentity's path and Martha veered away. Kinspear charged towards the dentity. His hands cupped to try to capture her.

Lisa listened at Buir's chest.

"Again." She shouted. Kinspear ran back towards his father again, but knew he was too slow. John, dragging Jeremy behind him, climbed up the dapper giant's suit and leapt onto his hair until he climbed high enough to be next to his ear.

"You have to save your father, Kinspear. You must breathe life into him."

This, however, was the wrong thing to do. The giant seemed to stir and reached for John shouting, "Monster."

John swung on the giant's hair like it was a movie chandelier and hurtled down the massive back. Spinning, the giant tried to swat Martha away, but Kinspear O'Cassey lacked Corp O'Rat's timing.

Again Martha struck. On the eighth blow, the massive giant lurched.

"His heart!" Lisa declared. Kinspear froze. Everyone froze, even John as he twisted in midair. Buir O'Cassey coughed. The itch vanished. John's hands began pinwheeling wildly in the air and he landed tangled within the laces of Kinspear's boots.

"You saved Buir O'Cassey's life," Jeremy said, a lone voice too quiet to hear amongst the tumult, "What were you thinking?"

31. I Beg your Pardon?

The volume increased to the level of white noise. Beings, monsters, and whatsits shouted and screamed and waved maniacally, but somehow the power of bull compelled them to stay in their seats. Barely. The gallery shook as they witnessed Buir O'Cassey fall. They clung to their seats as the world suddenly bent in an impossible direction. Would life be lead only by Kinspear O'Cassey. Even the most radical had to admit that distasteful.

Then there was life, because a dentity, a killer, a once-knight brought everything back by attacking, hurtling herself at the unconscious and unbreathing giant. The spirits of law were indecisively translucent. They jangled in confusion.

Then, the son stood. He voiced the chaos within him.

"You attack him and then save him?" Kinspear mused, "You bring him to his knees and then bring him back to life? It must be a plot! What are you planning?"

From somewhere, Jeremy found a box to stand on. He placed his thumbs where suspenders should have been and gave such a wink that all were mesmerized. Court artisans tore up their renderings. Jeremy was not in beggarly clothes. This was no supplicant. He was a man above. A man of polish. He cleared his throat and all the shouting stilled. As much as they feared, loathed, and wanted Jeremy punished or gone, they suspected that he knew something. That answers resided like coins behind that rainbow smile.

Dismissively, the leprechaun waved.

"John never laid a hand on your da'. You and he were the ones who acted like a pile of spoiled fish." Jeremy chided, "You and your theories, Kinspear."

"You call me spoiled fish!" Kinspear jumped up and down, fanatically outraged. The floor shook and the leprechaun shrugged apologetically. Well, perhaps his words weren't as polished as his appearance. John thrashed back and forth enmeshed in the giant's laces. "I'll…" Kinspear choked and began to chase Jeremy.

The moment of quiet and peace dissolved. Jeremy laughed. He delighted in the chase.

The faerie court argued angrily with each other. The libelous nature of Jeremy's words versus the debt of saving a life was the main topic. Sly tricksters began preparing briefs to exploit the insult for money. Others, hangers on and committee members mostly, circled Buir O'Cassey for instructions on how to think and act. Buir blinked slowly and tried to regain his strength. His son kicked and screamed and carried on.

Jeremy climbed wooden braces and sped under furniture. Kinspear's fist was always close behind. A trickster glee helped renew Jeremy's spirit and the wee man taunted the giant with laughter. Outside, a rainbow began to burble forth from a spring. Jeremy felt it and embraced the luck and energy. The spirits were small now. When they released the leprechaun to flee the falling giant, they also loosened his burden. His back felt lighter. With a malicious twinkle, the wee man shrunk himself and scurried up the giant's arm.

"You… a peasant… touch me!" Kinspear said, shocked. Jeremy ran into the giant's nose. "You will not touch my royal person!" The giant's fist slammed into his own nose. Jeremy whooshed down even as the giant clamped both of his hands over his hurt.

"Ow!" the giant said.

Jeremy laughed and ran through a crack in the wall. The giant rammed the wall in a berserker rage. John bounced dumbstruck wondering if he should play a role in this… or if he should take notes from Jeremy's master class.

Kinspear pounded again on the wall.

Wooden braces shifted. Cobbles loosened and the ceiling began to creak. Dust sprinkled down. Jeremy, a bundle of rabbit quickness, hurried between Kinspear's legs and dislodged a ceremonial sword from a plaque. Kinspear bounded after him.

"I'm getting nauseous," said John, as the room continued to bounce.

Lisa drew her itch and backed a pace away from a group of confused ethereal forms. Their eyes beseeched, drawing pity from the wyrman. Lost, the spirits of law hovered uncertainly, looking to and fro for direction. A few seemed to be sucked upwards, threads of ghost material being spooled like fishing line, into the ever changing laws engraved on Buir O'Cassey's wall.

Lisa's eyes widened when the ghost's chain flared outwards. A flash of memory of Red, Yellow, and violent battering, ripping, and biting slapped at her. It drove her to her knees. She gasped, raising her head to see the spirits anew. The spirits were weighted not by chains, but snakes..

Venomous snakes that tried to drink your soul within rainbows.

"They're prisoners," she shouted and with vigor brought her itch to its sharpest point against the chains that shackled the spirits of law to the whims of giants. The links cracked as her human arm and itch sword struck. The spirits mouths opened in a look of horror… hope? A blare of trumpets, of fife and drum whispered from within them as Lisa struck three times in quick succession at the bonds. She hurtled all the might of dragon and cow within her until the ethereal metal broke. The shattering rang like an anthem. Even Kinspear froze then. He looked back with incredulity as the spirits trembled and then grew voluminously.

Kindly faces evolved from the tortured faces of spirits of law. Free after years of enslavement, the spirits charged the miles of Buir O'Cassic law and where they touched, the laws pages erupted in blue flame. The tomes of parchment sizzled selectively. The laws shrunk and became legible.

"Ah," said a faerie in an orange top hat, "that's what he meant."

In the confusion… or perhaps in the clarity, Jeremy cut John free from the giant's shoelace and a kick sent both high into the air. Martha swept upwards and caught one of the lad's flailing limbs, before ducking a new set of spirits.

Angry spirits, spirits of justice found swords that glimmered with their own itches. They surrounded and spun around Lisa. Their menace mesmerized the wyrman. In the dance, within the vortex of law and justice, Lisa bowed to every choice she made for the sake of expedience, selfishness, or pettiness. Her legs staggered and she fell beneath the anchors of the lives she had ruined for the sake of money. Her heart spasmed in the memory of the destructive lies she had pieced together to better her reputation. Her wings failed to shield her from every poor choice in her life and each rationalizing lie she had comforted herself with. The spirits bore her down with heavy chains of her own making. The core of Lisa, a core bundled down and nearly mummified by thousands of chains itched. The spirits seemed to ask, are you worthy. And she looked at the myriad of chains and ties and could not rise. She could never cut all those threads. She could never sever herself from her past or from all the choices that connected her to her wrongs. A very tiny voice rang out. It was a child's voice, innocent, but strong.

"Leave her alone."

With a tremendous effort the wyrman's itch flared to blazing life, but it proved ineffectual against the chains. It was impotent against the steel of her own history. Lisa choked.

A spirit of law tugged at the bonds dropping Lisa easily to her knees. It was impossible to tell if it felt the heat of Lisa's itch, but a moment of life sparkled through its translucent eyes. The spirit seemed amused.

"You cannot sever, wyrman. You must untangle... unknot the threads."

"Why…" she asked tearfully.

"We often ask this of the accused."

Lisa gripped each heavy chain. They were rough and sharp simultaneously. The accumulation of all her wrongs, all her self-accusations, weighed her down. No wonder Martha could never lift her. She wondered if the pressure would kill her. Something swept through her. A ghost? A thought? Whatever it was it drove her from her knees to the floor. She pressed her eyes shut and searched for it. There must be a way to unknot these things… to escape regret and guilt.

Inside the courtroom, it was quiet, but Lisa was aware only of the weight, of the heat of her itch, and of a mounting pressure inside her. She searched, but found nothing. No easy answers. Her head was hurting too much to concentrate. She gasped afraid of the dimness of her own thoughts.

When she opened her eyes, she saw that John too was bound on the floor. Jeremy's chains were iron and nearly a solid weld around him . Martha also was held frozen by the threads and chains of her mistakes. Buir O'Cassey somehow had no chains upon him though the chains of many were linked securely to him. His weariness seemed to be bound within the burden of carrying other's chains. His son was strangling. He struggled as a new heavy chain grew from John and corded itself around the giant.

With an effort that strained his puckish face, John tottered towards Buir's son. He gripped the chains around Kinspear's nose and mouth.

"You're killing him," John screamed. The spirits nodded.

"He is killing himself."

"You've no right."

"We are justice, Jack Spratt. They have years of crimes to answer for. These chains are their own judgments."

"Justice must be tempered with mercy…" Martha's countered "…must be tempered with bull and cow."

The spirits drifted to her.

"Too often is justice tempered by the bull," said an impassioned spirit, "Did you need to join Corp O'Rat. You have murdered in his name and in the name of self-interest." The dentity's chains tightened and she fell from her feet.

"No," Jeremy said.

"You would dare speak, you who stole from every living being. You who are guilty of creating this?"

"I…" Jeremy fell.

"Your pursuit of self-interest will crush you." The spirits observed.

"Enough," Buir O'Cassey said.

"You…" the spirits' mouths fell to the floor. "You are not burdened."

"Without the cows I stayed the hand of war. I kept… I did what I thought best. The only thing I am guilty of is wasting time." Buir's rye grin sparkled, "Besides spirits, did you think I did not study you. I am immune to your power. Buir O'Cassey never feels guilt. He delegates it. He sends it to committee. I owe Jack Spratt my life and I will not allow him to be guilty here today. A man who rushes to his enemies' rescue as he does should be spared."

The spirits conferred. Enormous Buir O'Cassey shuddered and rose to his feet. He grabbed his chest and staggered again to his throne. He poured himself a goblet of wine and sipped. A spirit of law lifted John by his chains. It read the words burned onto the chains that bound him. John was neither wise enough nor self-aware enough to understand these words. None the less, even their unintelligible utterance cowed him.

"Have him," the spirit said and tossed John Spratt Fasola to the giant. All John's chains evaporated. John's eyes widened and his smile brightened. It caught those who saw it like a wave and carried them. Jeremy returned the smile and felt his burden lessen.

"I too," the leprechaun said with pure sincerity, "tried only to help my people. M. Au Paulet took away the cows. Corp O'Rat killed what was left." He looked about but his chains didn't lighten or loosen. Shrugging, the leprechaun said, "I tried." Spirits of Justice rattled his chains.

"We will take these. They have condemned themselves."

"No," grated Lisa and she stood. A ghost touched one of the wyrman's threads. The vibration toppled her.

"Buir," John said. The giant turned hate filled eyes upon the lad.

"Do not presume that…"

"Why did you imprison these spirits?" The giant struck his throne and coughed. The spirits looked to the giant and trembled. "Why?" John insisted.

"Jack," he said hoarsely, "What is law and justice without kindness? A cold law protects no one." John pointed to the imprisoned giants, faerie, and friends. They flopped like caught fish.

"What has changed?" John asked. Buir looked at the meager bull mooing emphatically at the spirits and then to the multitude of vengeful spirits. Hunching his shoulders, Buir O'Cassey gritted his teeth. All in the gallery lie bound, strangling. A grimace of pain closed his eyes and he caught his throne for balance. The giant squeezed his fists shut and struck his thighs. The music of the spirits marched with no sharps or minor chords. Buir nodded slowly, then hung his head.

"One day I shall make it a capital offense for a Jack to enter a giant's castle." The giant said slowly.

John backed away from the plodding steps. The giant shuddered and sweated, bowed his head under the strain of walking, but managed to reach the stack of laws. He placed a heavy hand on them and they ballooned to three times their density. Several chains dispersed. Buir coughed again and collapsed near the wall where the words began shifting again. He combed wisps of hair with a pudgy hand, and with dignity, strode to the wall behind his throne. There he put his hands on an enormous mirror. He hesitated. John stared at the huge mirror and thought again of the BEAN factory.

"Magnified…" he whispered.

"I had hoped for a vacation." When he lifted the mirror free of its peg, the spirits shied backwards. With heavy heart and strong conscience, Buir O'Cassey walked towards them. When a spirit saw its reflection, heavy chains sagged around its neck and waist. It shrunk, a wizened creature, to the ground. Howling, the other spirits tried to flee, but Buir conscientiously exposed every Spirit of Law and Justice to its own merciless reflection. Each staggered under the weight of what it was without cows. When the giant finished, he set the mirror on the ground and settled himself on the ground. The mirror clattered heavily behind him, discarded.

With a wistful sigh, the giant massaged his temples.

"I, as the chief spirit of law in this land…" a fit of coughing cost him his breath. Buir continued with reluctance and a dark look of hate aimed at John, "declare all those guilty in this room to be pardoned."

Chains failed to dissipate, but they became invisible and their weight returned to within the consciences and souls of those who wore them. Breathing slowly and with eyes beginning to close, the mighty giant said, "By pudding Jeremy, how many beans did you give Jack this time?"

Jeremy smiled. Buir's eyes closed. A low rich snore filled the chamber.

Kinspear O'Cassey rose and bared his teeth to Jeremy and John, but he had heard his father's words and turned his back to them. Tenderly, he lifted his father and laid him on the velvet throne. Carefully, he set each of Buir's swollen feet in the cool water of the swimming pool. Rubbing his father with a cool silk, his shoulders slumped. With a voice filled with rage and distrust, but still charming, the giant roared, "Get out."

32. A Corp O'Rat War

John left with a light heart and the belief that maybe he could deal with people calling him Jack, even though the spirit of his dad began pulling out his astral hair when the younger Spratt-Fasola voiced that particular thought. The grounds outside the castle of Buir O'Cassey were dark. Rain spattered and plinked against Martha's metal skin. The dentity looked at the wyrman worriedly and her forehead wrinkled. Jeremy's nose flared and he cupped his hands. He tasted the droplets.

"What have you been up to, Johnny?" Jeremy asked.

"We kind of gathered an army."

"Against Corp O'Rat?"

John nodded.

"Feathers and spit! Burnt pudding and spoiled fish! Curds and whey, boy! By the very luck, Johnny! Do you have a brain in there at all?"

"Your language is unsuitable, leprechaun," the dentity warned.

"I…"

"It just sort of happened, Jeremy." Lisa tried to explain.

"I told you you're no knight, so you decide you're a feathering general. Waiters spit, lad…"

"I shall get soap," Martha threatened, "he did no wrong."

"I told you you're no… Johnny, you can't… didn't your ma ever read you any fairy tales. Jacks are saboteurs. Terrorists. Tricksters. They aren't generals! You'll get them… you'll get your army killed. An army needs more than luck!"

"I am a knight protector!" Martha whispered severely.

"Aye, you are a champion," he said turning on her, "but have you ever led a battle. You…were born to uphold honor. What in the name of spit does honor have to do with war." he looked to the skies and spit out rain, "They're going to blame me for this too!"

"But Jeremy," Lisa interrupted, "you haven't seen. A thousand people joined us."

"A thousand people," Jeremy stared incredulously, but then dismissed it, "What will your people do against fire coursing down from the sky! Lightning strikes! Feather and spit…"

"I fear no dragons," Martha interrupted.

"What will you do against a hundred dragons?"

"Corp O'Rat doesn't have one hundred dragons," she countered, but her voice became slightly less sure.

"How many?"

"Eighty-three."

"Burnt pudding!"

Martha flared her wings and grabbed the little man. She turned him over her knee and spanked him.

"You will learn to guard your tongue. We must be civil."

"Civil… ow… during a war! Spoiled fish, woman… Stop that! That hurts!"

"He's gathering his troops?" John asked quietly. Lightning lit the sky. Jeremy stopped kicking and wiggled free. Lisa looked at John and agreed. She spoke for them.

"They're our responsibility. We made them do what they're doing."

"You're all mad."

"Please," John added, "I don't want another chain."

They all stopped.

"Follow me," Jeremy said, quietly. The wee man grabbed his own neck as if he could already feel the burden of another chain weighing down his soul. He ran towards the spring he had seen earlier from the window. Clapping his hands, a sound of drums resonated. Wind started blowing towards them. "Take my hands and close your eyes." He snagged John's hand, just as the lad claimed the dentity's. Lisa descended from the air to hold Martha's hand. Then she stopped. She tried to pull away, the rainbow overwhelmed her with its horrors, but found the hand holding hers iron. Her wings heaved backwards lifting the three of them into the air. Above them a bolt of light disrupted the sky. Jeremy whistled and the light curved.

"No," Lisa screamed and covered her eyes.

"Stand near. It will be a near fit."

The rainbow swallowed them.

They felt the motion, but no turbulence. Under a leprechaun's stewardship they sailed easily. Their bodies felt invigorated and fed on the light. John gasped. Lisa squeezed hard enough to break a human hand. Then, she felt water and wind and rage.

They opened their eyes on a field. A thousand people all dressed in their best suits stood with pitchforks, rocks, sticks, and bare hands at the ready. Marching to meet them came an army of moving rocks. Above them an air force of dentity and dragon. Great gouts of earth erupted and the chunks that came down were coated with a harsh acid. Above and below ground, horse headed snakes slithered. Martha ripped her hand free and covered her mouth.

"Oh no." she said.

"What? What are they?" Lisa demanded.

"I didn't think he would dare."

"What?"

Martha pointed at the snake like things, "He sent out the loan officers."

John felt an urge to laugh. Martha shook him. "You don't understand," she said, "he plans to take it all back. Corp will take everything from them." Jeremy winced.

The army fidgeted, their nerves fraying. Many eyes turned to their leaders. Most began trying to edge away and began to whistle as if they had just been innocent.

"Form ranks," Martha ordered. The suits lined up looked impressively fashionable. Soaring from the air, a silver and bronze sparrow streaked. Martha continued ordering the troops, trying to align them in some sort of defensive posture. She ordered them to take off their dinner jackets. Jeremy sighed and kept a hold of the rainbow.

The bronze dentity attacked. John dove, but he was far too slow. Too late, he tried to scream a warning.

Alexander, Corp's replacement dentity, swept down and slashed at Lisa. Her scales squealed horribly. Lisa spun to the ground. Martha snapped her beak shut. The bronze and silver dentity wheeled around to strike again. He smiled as the wyrman returned to her feet. Lisa drew her itch.

The rainbow attached to Jeremy exploded in brilliance. Even Jeremy shaded his eyes. Orange sunset covered the land and the dragons trumpeted in response to the call. The dragon fire looked dull in the glow of itch and rainbow.

Lisa turned to face her opponent with outstretched wings. Her feet braced in a ready posture. Her eyes tracked the male dentity. The itch hungered in her grip, but she held it as if it were a baseball bat and not a sword.

Alexander paused and cocked his head towards the three and a half foot blaze of color. Screams erupted around them. The earth itself rumbled. The two ignored it, their focus too intent.

Lisa squinted as the dentity's metal hide reflected her itch's light back at her. John scrambled to stand next to her, but the wyrman pushed him out of his way. John fell backwards and hit his head. He closed his eyes. Alexander shot towards Lisa and sent the wyrman sprawling. He was too quick. Again, Lisa stood. Jeremy clasped his hands together.

Faster then, Alexander raised his hands, the dragons moved with his signal. Lisa glanced for a moment at the thunderous clap of eighty-three dragons moving. Martha, caught between Lisa and her army, looked terribly conflicted.

"Who do I protect?" worried the knight protector.

"You can't wait, Martha." Jeremy warned. Nodding, the female dentity launched herself after dragons, an angry hawk against a flock. Lisa's army saw its leaders' unconscious, in desperate one on one combat or elsewhere and began to panic. Gouts of fire broke between them. They fled then, randomly and in whichever way their smoke-filled eyes heard fewer monstrous sounds.

Lisa spun and began swinging the itch frantically, the rubies on her wings glittered fiercely. Alexander aimed again for her back. Lisa anticipated the maneuver and spun violently. Alexander cawed. Her itch met the dentity.

A shower of sparks flew in the air. Lisa landed on her back, a blinding pain in her shoulder blades. The itch trembled, flickering as if it lacked the strength to continue.

"It's not fair." She complained and climbed to her feet. Everything was too fast or too strong. Wildly, she kept spinning trying to find where Alexander would come from next. Fire billowed upwards next to her. She coughed her own fire in return.

Jeremy ducked and called the rainbow back. He began to climb back in.

"No," he heard. John crawled towards him, an ugly gash at the base of his head. Jeremy looked at the dragons, dentities, golems, and loan officers and yelled back.

"I'm no knight, either, Johnny. There's nothing I can do."

John reached forward with an unsteady hand. Jeremy pinched the bridge of his nose and cursed himself for waiting.

"Wait for me," John ordered. Jeremy waited. "I know how to do it." Jeremy frowned as John took his hand and forced him into the rainbow." I know how to do it."

On the ground beside her, Lisa spotted Alexander's hand. It lie shorn and separate on the ground. The sight encouraged her to rise.

"Thank God," she said, "I finally hit something." The dentity walked towards her.

"You nothing," Alexander roared, "You think you are worthy to do battle with one of my station. You pitiful untrained buffoon, I shall shame you first. Then, I will lay your soul to waste."

Lisa didn't stare or goggle or back away. Instead, her mouth clamped closed and she swallowed fire. She widened her stance. Alexander approached slowly. It motioned for Lisa to swing. Lisa attacked. The dentity barked laughter and blocked her blow, but then his eyes widened. Lisa pivoted, shot her leg into his sternum and in one fluid motion twisted and sent him to the ground behind her. The dentity shook its head in surprise and screamed a blood oath. Lisa didn't bother listening. If it wanted to waste time threatening, it could. As Alexander pontificated on the exquisite torture it would subject her to, Lisa turned and severed one of its wings.

"Maybe I don't know how to fence..." she growled and spit flame on him. She knew it would be harmless, but it felt good. "but..." and she raised the itch as high as she could. Alexander aimed a bronze wing at her throat. Her itch crashed down and severed it. The rainbow reflected in the silver feathers turned orange. The wyrman bathed in flames and with scales aglow looked demonic. Alexander emitted a tiny frightened chirp.

"...I know how to fight" Lisa finished, and let the itch fly.

33. To the Rescue

John felt fat, slow, and old.

He tumbled out of the rainbow onto the floor of the empty BEAN warehouse. Security tape covered the entrance. Litter lined the room and the windows were all broken as if kids spent their afternoons throwing rocks. He looked at his middle aged soft hands and sighed. Jeremy stepped neatly out of the rainbow.

"They took the tungsten lamps and the tripod!" the wee man groused.

Other than a few scraps of paper and discarded soda cans, the BEAN Factory floor was empty. Echoes filled the room and the doors above hung lazily open. Even the rooftop bay was left open.

"Someone even took the fire extinguishers!" Jeremy groused. John looked. There were puddles on the floor from drying rain and some signs that mice had taken up residence. *It looks*, his father's memory cried, *deserted.* A lump moved up in John's throat and halted him. This body felt so less capable, so less ready, so less real… and yet the problems he saw through it had a heaviness that stifled him and left him all but paralyzed.

"I never should have sold the business," John said firmly and then he caught the wink of a rainbow from one of the puddles. He took a deep breath. Even his breathing felt abnormal to him.

Shut up. He told himself.

He took another deep breath.

"Okay, then." He turned to Jeremy and took the leprechaun's hand and ran slowly towards the police tape.

"We need a phone,"

"Why?"

If John had seen himself in a mirror in that moment even he might have called himself Jack.

"We're not stopping 'til the cows come home."

"What?" Jeremy stopped. "I told you. It can't be done."

"You were thinking too small, trying to save too much money." He looked disdainfully at the tiny chalk x's where the tripod once stood. Jeremy opened his mouth, but John ducked under the tape and ran again. The man was puffing. He reached into the remnants of his black slacks and pulled out a ski mask and his wallet. Jeremy caught up with him as he dialed the first three numbers on the business card at a pay phone.

"Cows are too big." Jeremy protested. John ignored him.

"Hey Terry," he said into the receiver, "yeah, I know. I'd be going crazy too. I'll call mother and let her know I'm alive." John waded through three minutes of questions, none of which he answered, instead he said, "Terry, I need you to tell me where the nearest livestock auction is." John listened for an answer. "Okay. How big are the lots? For cows?" The former owner of COW shook his head in frustration. "What else would I be interested in, Terry?" John listened and paled, "Okay, listen I'm going to need proxies for several auctions. How much are cows going for today... No, for God's sake, Terry, I don't care what they're going for by the pound. By the head, man, I need them by the head." Jeremy complained loudly that it was useless. "What do you mean?" He turned to Jeremy, "What's better Angus, Hereford, Corriente, Scottish Highland, Parthenais?"

"What are those?" Jeremy asked.

"The names of cows, Jeremy."

"You mean there's more than one type of cow?" Jeremy asked, stunned.

"By the bovine," John said, and looked down at the receiver nervously. "I don't think it matters?" he told Terry. "Okay, you can get twenty Angus commercial cows for eight hundred dollars per at an online auction? Do it, Terry. Don't worry what I'm going to do with them... yes, I'll have plenty of grazing land and no, I do not sound like a lunatic." He looked at Jeremy and stuffed his green feathered cap under his rope belt. "How many Jeremy. No, not you, Terry, how many do we need, Jeremy? How many cows?" Jeremy scratched his jaw. John's voice lowered, "No Terry, I don't want to just get one and see how it works out."

John hung up the receiver and told Jeremy they were flying to Texas. Cows were being offered at $720 dollars a head. At auction, John bought every lot he could at a price ranging between one thousand and twelve hundred and fifty dollars a head. At first, the ranchers laughed at him, called him a stupid Yankee. At the end, they were convinced he knew something they did not and started bidding madly. The auctioneer hammered happily when the last lot of cows sold at thirteen hundred dollars a head. Jeremy practically swooned. Almost feverish with the frenzy of the auction, John shook the hands of hooting ranchers.

"Boy, you done did so much the blamed commodity price rose three cents." John felt his chest swell with an obscure pride. "Why sir, we even have media coverage."

"You do?" John asked, his eyes wild. The man backed off and twiddled his moustache. John gave the auctioneer a strange look which caused him to back away.

"Son," he said, carefully.

"Where are they?"

The reporter stood next to a pen of animals and made such a horrific pun that John was sure that the cows responded with a "boo" instead of a "moo." Her cameraman nodded them off air and rested. He wore jeans and the hand-me-downs of a freelancer who hadn't gotten many calls. A small pen held the just auctioned off cattle. Up close, the animals looked small and lacked vibrancy, but Jeremy was dumbstruck and even looked a little dull next to them. John strode past the gate and straight up to the correspondent, who was packing away her mic. She was intimidatingly lovely and smiled when the auctioneer pointed John out as the man who had initiated this price surge. She took a step towards John and said into her Channel 7 microphone,

"... and here's the man of the hour..." her voice strained for Standard English, but held too many hints of twang to pass. The tech shouldered his camera and captured in his sights a red faced middle aged man dressed from head to foot in torn black. The reporter smiled and began as soon as she was given the wave.

"And here is the… hey!" the reporter said, as John shouldered past her towards the crew.

"I need to rent or buy lights. Big lights."

"What do you need them for?"

"John Fasola?" the reporter interrupted, "You have caused quite a stir. Do you have…"

John ignored her and focused on the freelancer. Her perfect face lined with agitation.

"For…" John paused to think up a suitable lie, "A rock concert."

"A rock concert," said the cameraman with a disconcerted look, "Is that why you needed all them cows?"

"Please."

"You may have trouble with the ASPCA and God knows what if you all are planning to do something with them cows in a rock concert."

"Cows and concerts! What is the BEAN man up to!" said the reporter, proud of the info her producer had told her and how she slipped the info into the segment.

"I won't do anything to them! I just need cows and light and…" he grabbed the cameraman with passion and asked, "Where is the nearest astronomical observatory?"

"Well, there's Mount Palomar in California?" said the man nervously.

"You don't have to go to California. There are some right fine Observatories in Arizona. The National Solar Observatory this time of year'll give you the greatest look at the Taurus constellation."

"Why in the world would you go to Arizona when you got the best darn observatory right around the block in Austin. The McDonald Observatory up back in the Davis Mountains has got four, listen to me, four operating telescopes."

"Are they big?"

"Are they big? Son, you're in Texas. The McDonald has the 9.2 meter Hobby-Eberly Telescope."

"I thought that scope was only 2.7 meters?" challenged the auctioneer.

"Nope, you're thinking of the Harlan J. Smith. That's the one that's only 2.7 meters."

"Of course if you don't need a Texas-sized scope, they might just let you look at the .8 meter one or the Otto Struve." Added a janitor from around the corner.

"They also got one that's less than a meter, but it's usually for student use." Piped in the auction's registrar.

"Yeah, but sometimes the McDonald's really busy. Why don't you check out the D. Nelson Limber Memorial Observatory near San Antonio. Lens ain't quite as big, think it's only point four meters, but…" drawled a cowboy.

"What is this, an astronomy convention? How do you people know all this?" the reporter asked.

"He's Jack." Said the leprechaun, as if that explained everything.

John asked if anyone knew who he could call for permission to use the observatory. Fourteen people rushed to be the first to answer the question. Somehow, it seemed that near everyone who attended this cattle auction was an astronomy buff. It left the reporter bewildered, but she gamely reported to her viewers that a John Fasola had just purchased at auction 2,300 head of cattle for a little under three million dollars and though he failed to consent to an interview, the eccentric millionaire seemed determined to promote some kind of rock concert concerning the cows and an observatory.

John sped to another pay phone. No one could understand why he just didn't use his cell or how the first place John looked he found not only a phone booth, but an operating one. Shrugging, Jeremy chased after.

He dialed up the McDonald Observatory and asked how much it would cost to rent the use of their biggest telescope. Jeremy shook his head. John shouted an outrageous number into the telephone. Turning, he nearly toppled a man coming to receive the bank check John needed for the deposit. John handed him a large check and told him to mail him back the change and to make sure that all the cows were shipped to the McDonald Observatory immediately. The man balked.

"I'll pay double if you can get them there by 3:00."

They agreed. The reporter lingered, pestering him with questions, but John shooed the woman away. He didn't have time. Lisa, Martha, and their army could be dying at any moment. He just hoped that time was not linear there, that it did some kind of contortionist elongation. To get rid of her, he said, "Miss, I'm an illusionist. I'm going to make all these cows disappear." John could have sworn he felt an itch.

The woman announced it. Jeremy kneaded his hands together worriedly. After a series of phone calls to rent lighting and construction equipment, John had promised to different people eleven of his fifteen million dollars. Jeremy cried to see so much money spent at once.

Somehow, the cows, machinery, and equipment all arrived by 3:00. Jeremy shook his head. Even a Jack's luck should not have been able to make construction workers arrive on a timely basis. A large crowd gathered outside the observatory to witness the rock magic spectacular John Spratt Fasola had promised. John strode into the McDonald Observervatory as if he were a billionaire and ordered the 30 foot lens moved. The professors protested. John marched up to them.

"How dare you!" he strode within inches of the chief astronomer's nose and began a verbal tirade about the safety of the world and compassion and the man's lack of proprieties and principles causing unending doom. He ranted with such passion and insanity that the man fell down and began to weep. With the sternness of a businessman whose industry survived for ten years selling products that practically no one used, John orchestrated the re-angling of lens and ordered the observatory ceiling opened. Cranes lowered in giant spotlights. The scientists fretted, but John ignored them and waved his rental agreement in front of their faces.

"Are the generators on?" He shouted over the diesel engines. The crowd had grown even larger during the minutes John had spent inside. John gulped and looked frantically over at Jeremy. The leprechaun stuck the eraser of a pencil in his mouth and chewed. He looked over the diagram and his equations again. One of the astronomers looking over his shoulder began typing maniacally.

"This is so exciting," said the man swept up in the obvious momentousness, but oblivious to the event. Jeremy listened to the whir of the computer and looked up. The astronomer had projected his formulas into the computer. Jeremy frowned and explained with hands and words what he needed to happen. The scientist nodded eagerly. John motioned to the trucks to keep the cattle calm. 2,300 cattle waited in a line of trucks on the border of the observatory campus.

Jeremy and the astronomers high-fived. The cranes reset the lights and engineers angled them. Bending his fingers back until they popped, the leprechaun stretched out his hands. The wee man nodded. The scientists cheered, feeling for some reason like they were part of a NASA project. John ran to a truck and without thinking leapt on to the back of a jersey milking cow.

"Easy Bossy," he said uneasily. He shouted for Jeremy to begin and the word was passed along. Jeremy began rhythmically clapping. The scientists thought it was a cheering thing and began clapping too. The crowd outside caught on and joined in. Jeremy quickened the pace. People began shouting and hollering. The stench of cow was unbearable. John clenched his teeth. The crowd clapped and stomped to Jeremy's rhythm.

"Clap! If you believe in bull! Clap! Damn you! Clap if you believe in BULL" And the crowd, after a lifetime of Texas politics clapped like you wouldn't believe.

Sweating, the leprechaun ordered the lights turned on. The spots blazed and blinded everyone in the observatory. Jeremy clapped harder and added a snap between his claps. John reached over and unhinged the barrier. The cows ambled forward. John couldn't resist it. He yelled to the clapping, stomping crowd.

"Are you ready to rock!"

Pandemonium broke loose. The crowd tossed their hats in the air and roared. Bossy got spooked. The cows began charging towards the observatory. John held on for dear life. The television reporter couldn't hear herself. In the middle of it all, a mall man wearing a gray suit failed to gain any ground. He shouted loudly that he needed to check permits, but no one heard him over the clapping, stomping, cheering, and mooing.

On the thirty foot lens, colors began to shimmer. Harder, the leprechaun clapped, unaware of the screaming. Louder, the scientists slapped their palms together unaware of the two thousand head of cattle charging towards them. Maniacally, the crowd screamed and clapped until the steer got really close. They began to panic, but the bulls stampeded ever faster towards them.

Then—

Colors streamed forth from the lens and a dazzle fueled by the force of hundreds clapping streaked forward. People stopped. Children oohed. So did grandparents.

"Rainbow," emerged as the first word spoken by more than one baby.

Within the brilliance, every clap brought a faerie back to life. Jeremy whistled and leaped onto the colors and rode it like a surfer. The rainbow arched, a dazzling prism that erased apathy in every eye it touched. The crowd stopped fleeing. The cows paused and as one looked up.

"Moo?" they asked, twenty three hundred strong in unison. John closed his eyes. Jeremy slid downwards and the rainbow crashed over all of them. The explosion of color for the barest moment looked like a newborn ring.

They vanished.

No sign of cow, John or Jeremy remained anywhere, except for the broken ground and hoof prints they left behind. The crowd became deeply quiet and then roared its approval. Someone thought to launch a firework, but it exploded dim and pathetic next to the rainbow. Somewhere in the middle of the rainbow, a tiny voice rang out.

"Moo."

And for the barest moment, people thought they knew what the cow meant.

34. The Cows are Coming Home

In a triumphant blaze of glory, the cattle stampeded up the slopes striped hue. Most stayed in their lanes, though a few blinked their right or left eyes to change lanes. They climbed seemingly forever, but once the rainbow reached its apex and began curving down the cows took on even more speed. Gripping Bossy tightly around the neck, John opened his eyes and saw colors blur by him. He knew nothing other to say than, "Yippee."

As the rainbow swept inside his lungs and heart, John knew Jack emerged beneath him. He felt his hair and eye change color, watched his hands and arms shrink and tighten and heard his cry become more resonant and full. The cows changed too. A rainbow glaze coated them. Soon, red cows, orange cows, yellow cows, green cows, blue cows, indigo cows, and violet cows charged. Cattle that changed lanes became either striped or muddied a deep brown. Cows who suffered from road rage and had to pass every other cow became the color of all colors combined. But it wasn't just color. The cattle grew. How they grew!

Enormous Paul Bunyan sized cattle trotted forward, bustling, thrusting, running, sometimes mewling, down the rainbow. They followed a little man, a bit disheveled, but still polished, a leprechaun, whose present smile made every rainbow look ordinary. His feet gripped the tide of color and shot forward. With hands extended, he studied the color contours as one would map.

"Are we almost there?" the lad Jack yelled, but Jeremy couldn't hear him over the sound of the animals. If he had, he might have told him to stop complaining. He had never seen a rainbow this size since the days of Saint Dorothy and most believed she was strictly myth.

Leaning, he slashed through the rainbow and vanished. John screamed and clamped harder onto the ear of the massive cow he rode. He flopped around as the cattle, as one, turned and exploded into the world.

The ground was black. Trees were charred or shorn from their roots. Loan officers looked fat and recently fed, but nowhere near sated. Golems lay strewn on the ground like remnants of an avalanche struggling to stand. Lisa flew with the dragons and seemed to be leading them in a charge. Somehow, it appeared she had become their queen. Only twenty majestic wyrms still flew. Martha appeared only for instants at a time as she darted here and there issuing orders and attacking. Creatures struggled for life or struggled to end life.

A cloud of dust bloomed over the rage of war. Stampeding through the rainbow charged twenty three hundred cattle of every shape and color. With a fearsome moo they shook the earth and caused every combatant to stop and look up. Horns speared the air as hooves crushed the ground beneath. Jack sat on the head of the lead cow and lifted a feathered hat into the air.

Steering the steers, the animals charged straight into the front line. Fat, horse headed loan officers who had just taken the arms and legs off their victims suddenly stopped chewing. Gossfer's puckers puckered. Dragons took a deep intake of breath. Within feet now of the battle, the cows all suddenly stopped. Horns raised, they sniffed the air warningly and snorted.

All waited.

And then the cows did it.

They dropped their heads and began to graze. Dragons, gossfers, potters, smiths, swordmen, dentities, golems, and faerie all blinked and shook their heads. John scratched his nose and sneezed from all the dust the cattle had stirred up. Shrugging, the monsters, faerie, and humans looked at each other and then one by one they saw.

"By the bovine," the two forces said simultaneously.

The land was emerald and rich with a golden sun that embraced the world with warmth. Even Corp O'Rat's rain only worked to sustain the abundance. Chocolate strawberries, marshmallow fields, and carrots the size of water towers filled their eyes. The armies returned their attention to cows contentedly grazing and felt ashamed. This was a land of plenty, a perfect beautiful and enabling land of possibilities. A cow lifted her head and mooed at them. They bowed their heads. Beneath their feet was char and ruin. Flying creatures landed, flooded with uncertainty. Bovine heads lifted and winked at the dragons. The dragons blushed and turned their heads away. Bulls pawed the earth at the dentities, but then simply walked over to a new patch of grass. Gossfers retracted their poisonous quills and bent themselves into the lotus position. .

"The war is over, Johnny. You did it." Jeremy laughed, incredulously.

"It's over?" John said. "But..."

"The huge powerful cows disdained to join the killing. Don't you see, they ignored the advantage of their strength and simply ate?" Jeremy explained.

"But they're cows. They're cows eating grass." John continued.

"Exactly." Jeremy said in a mystic sort of way.

Dragons plucked strawberries. Loan officers harvested carrots. Dentities stood numbly and pretended to supervise. Faeries dusted the burned earth with dust which immediately responded with sprouts of mint and licorice grass. Men and women planted seeds.

"But?" John repeated. Bossy ambled over to John and grazed the ground near him as if to aid Jeremy's explanation.

"Have some milk, Johnny. The time for fighting is over."

"But? You were trying to... I'm confused. " He threw up his hands.

"You are Jack," a dragon nodded, "If a Jack knew what he was doing, he wouldn't be Jack." John scowled and sat on a broken log and grudgingly accepted a marshmallow from a golem. He had envisioned a much more heroic climax, possibly even a speech or some manifestation of the divine. He looked about and saw some of the cows wandering off. The herd slowly dissolved as they headed in smaller groups across the land.

"There are so many," Martha said. Her face had gone from silver to white and she looked dazed. "Can you not feel it, Prince John?" Lisa jogged over to them.

"That was amazing. We were… I was… and then there were thousands of cows. Out of nowhere. You did it, Jeremy."

"No," he blushed, "I can't take the blame this time. It was Johnny."

Thunder bellowed angrily above. John looked up. Dragons trembled. Bossy mooed and gnawed more grass. Grimly, John stood and shook his fist at the clouds. Heroically, he leaped onto Bossy's neck. The cow didn't even have the courtesy to rear dramatically. Embarrassed, John lowered his hat and placed it firmly on his head to protect his eyes from the suddenly hammering rain.

"He'll drown the world." Martha said.

"We're not done." John realized, his eyes agleam with beans.

35. You're Not Putting That Cow in My Elevator

Bossy ambled down the road to Corp's cloud. The line to petition was short. Either the rain had driven many away or they knew that the giant was in more of a foul than a bovine mood today. Above John, twenty dragons led by a wyrman with a blazing orange sword soared. The golems had stayed behind to rebuild, farm and tend to the cows. The gossfers simply had burrowed into the ground and disappeared. The loan officers apologized, but declined to join the march, informing all that they had too many approvals to make and homes to un-foreclose on if the people here were to rebuild their lives successfully before winter. John felt an odd catch to his throat as he watched the great horse headed snakes slither off, but although he watched them go with a smile, he still didn't trust them.

At his station, in front of the beanstalk elevator, the great golden dragon stiffened when he saw their army. Lightning bellowed as the giant's deluge continued. It planted its feet in a wide stance against the road's slick paving stones. Countless droplets made its golden scales more dazzling than usual. It sniffed at the approaching group and glanced up at the angry rain. Licorice and wild marshmallows grew thick and swollen. Matted and sodden stragglers and petitioners parted for John and his make-shift army. They were a damp bunch with surprisingly upbeat expressions and a cow. Martha landed by their Jack's side and placed hands on hips.

"Join us wyrm," she ordered. The dragon cocked its head and studied Bossy.

"Barbecued beef," it said, smacking its lips.

"It's a cow," John stammered, "don't you want to… just… I don't know… go off and have a picnic or visit someone or something."

"I was a mean old hoarder before the cows left," the golden wyrm informed them, "and I'm still feeling cranky."

"Dragon," Lisa spat, flames sparking between her fangs. She stood before the great wyrm, bruised, scarred and battered. Her itch flamed hotly in her hand.

"Yes, my queen," the great wyrm answered.

"We need an appointment with your master."

"My queen?" John asked. Jeremy shushed him.

"He has no slots available in the foreseeable future, my queen."

"We will enter," whispered Martha dangerously.

"Moo," added the cow emphatically.

"You know he'll kill the cow," the great wyrm said.

"I am the great dragon cow of legend!" Lisa roared, "You will do as I say!"

John laughed and repeated, "Dragon cow?" Lisa bit her lip and was caught between a smile and a glare. Twenty-one dragons' gazes scored John. He patted Bossy's neck and the cow looked up nervously. Quickly, with stumbling tongue, he apologized to Lisa. That he apologized while sitting on a cow proved his sincerity to most of the dragons and they turned away mollified.

"You will let us in!" Martha and Lisa demanded.

"You are not getting a cow in my elevator!" the great golden wyrm roared, it added belatedly, "my queen." The twenty dragons bared their teeth and smoke curled upwards. The great wyrm stood proudly and stiffly and billowed its own smoke. Martha preened her wings. The golden dragon's composure faded a little. "You don't know what that cow will do to the elevator's floor!" it cried, "I'm responsible for its maintenance and…" the great wyrm met very hard stares, "do you know how expensive overtime is. I'll need a full crew to clean and repair and…"

"One last chance, dragon." Martha whispered coldly. Looking back and forth, the dragon kneaded its foreclaws. Corp O'Rat's deluge continued. Rain gathered in deep puddles around their feet.

"My queen, consider my job! I'll lose my job if I let you up!" the dragon pleaded, "Please." he begged to the dentity, "You know how he feels about cows."

Martha softened and felt a kindly sympathy towards the dragon. The twenty dragons behind her shuffled their feet uncertainly. Lisa grabbed her itch tightly and advanced a step, but in truth felt daunted by the dragon's monstrous size.

"Thank you," the great wyrm giggled with relief. "I…" The dragon shut its mouth. Bossy had just lifted her head and snorted. She lazily looked back at the dragons and dentity, and then, wearing an expression remarkably similar to John's, charged and burrowed its head into the dragon's belly. The dragon expelled a huge breath, its eyes popped, spun twice and then the great wyrm fell to the ground. Bossy snorted again and nodded as if to say, "Well, that's that!"

Martha and the dragons shook. They never imagined they would actually witness bovine wrath. Stepping around the unconscious dragon, Bossy delicately entered the beanstalk's elevator. Lisa entered behind and pointed for the dragons to meet them above. They nodded, but their eyes stayed worriedly upon the collapsed form of the golden wyrm. John, of all people, explained.

"Sometimes the greater kindness is not allowing atrocities to go on."

The dragons nodded, saluted their queen, and took off. Martha eyed John suspiciously, but didn't question him. How could she? The lad sat on a cow. He must be speaking bull and that is of great worth.

The elevator played a harmless sort of music. It slid quickly through the slick inner core of the plant. It stopped on the third floor and opened to show a broad leaf. Three worker mice wearing hardhats waited. They studied the occupants with jittering noses. With a careful wave, they motioned that they'd wait for the next car. Martha hit the close button.

John tapped Bossy's coat and swayed his head to the beat of the androgenized music being piped in. Martha sharpened.

Lisa gripped her itch with white knuckles. Jeremy hid as small as he could be within bossy's tail. Bossy flicked her tail as if she thought that Jeremy was a fly. As they climbed, the sounds of music quickly became drowned out by the sounds of combat. John pinched his cheeks and took deep breaths. Bossy's tail swayed vigorously on the strength of Jeremy's shaking.

The door opened. Dragons fought in pitched battles against indescribable cloud shapes. Lightning flared upwards. Martha shot forward and ripped through a piece of cloud. She arced and cut and soon was lost between the blasts of fire and lightning. Lisa, with a frightened, but determined look, took three strides and launched herself into the air to defend her subjects. She too struck at clouds.

John urged Bossy forward. The cow seemed reluctant.

"No," Lisa screamed, "to the castle. Go." She took a blow and severed a piece of cottony muscle.

"You're no knight, Johnny. We must protect the cow." Jeremy agreed. A war of elements tore gaping holes through the clouds. A dragon fell. John chewed his lip. "Johnny." Jeremy screamed. Indecision gripped John as he watched dragons and allies fight for their lives. He couldn't leave them, but what could he do. He shook Bossy hard and shouted into the cow's ear.

"What do you want to do?" John asked the cow.

The cow shook its head and looked dismally at the barren cloud. Perhaps it thought it could find something to eat in the castle's garden or perhaps it understood John, but in either case it began running towards the castle. Immediately, clouds disengaged to attack the cow. The dragons countered ferociously, dissipating the clouds into mist with their flames, and tearing with their claws. Lisa savagely leapt to engage three misty puffs at once. Martha blurred, slicing everything in her path.

His hair frizzed, but somehow, because he was Jack, he reached the castle steps without the lightning doing more than that. For the barest moment, John wondered how they could possibly gain entry, but suddenly a crack of thunder startled Bossy, who very reasonably butted the door with her head in full panic in response. The great wooden door fell backwards. Shaking her head woozily, Bossy ambled inside and aimed herself towards the potted plants.

Corp O'Rat stood on a granite stairwell. He clutched a dilapidated banister with one hand and with the other a woodsman's hatchet. John gaped at the axe and felt his itch screech to a halt. Calmly, the giant walked towards the cow. He splintered a rosewood stand with a single blow. The giant's guest book crashed downwards. John pointed at the axe.

"I thought it only fair," the giant said smoothly, "Jack, I presume." The giant took a deep inward sniff.

"Moo?" the cow asked.

"Fees, Lies, Grosses, Sums," Corp said shaking his head, "I smell two poor businessmen." Jeremy peaked from beneath the cow's tail. John sat paralyzed with fright, his finger pointed straight at the giant's axe.

"It takes more than profits to make a good businessman." The Jeremy argued. The giant quirked an eyebrow and the leprechaun blushed. "I meant to say…" The giant cut him off with a laugh.

"Fees, Lies, Grosses, Sums. You've made your last bad business decision." A crew of gossfer waddled forward, but Corp waved them off and fingered the axe blade with his thumb. "Mmm, very sharp," he smiled, "I must thank you, Jack, for bringing me a cow to slaughter. M. Au Paulet looked quite impressive in his leather vest."

"You can't." John stuttered. The giant leaned against the wall.

"Why?" he asked.

"They're valuable." John answered.

"Valuable?" the giant turned his back on them, "Do you know what kindness does to a business. It corrupts it. It destroys it. The only thing to do when a kind impulse overwhelms you is to crush it. Do you understand me?" The giant waved expansively at the vases, tapestries, gilt laced rugs, and other signs of wealth before them. "The bottom line is the only line. You, you stink of conscience and sympathy. Where did that lead you," Corp sneered derisively, "I'll bet you ran your business into the ground. I'll bet it had less life to it in the end than a dry fish."

John pointed his finger. The cow chewed on a flower.

"Cows consume too much, Jack. They will absorb the land and what will be left? Why do you think there are wolves? Kindness will murder the earth. Loose, it will eat everything and leave us all to starve. You, you and Jeremy keep making these decisions for everybody. You don't think. You don't plan." Corp O'Rat choked on self-righteousness, "The leprechaun, at least, is a trickster. If his plans cause chaos he is happy, but you… you're just a fool."

John Spratt-Fasola slid off the cow and strode up to the giant Corp O'Rat. He reached only to the giant's ankles, but squared his shoulders and said, "You're wrong" and nodded. The giant paused and knelt to examine John. He lifted the lad up and turned him around. He waited, but it seemed John had summed up his arguments in those two words. Strangely, the lad wasn't shivering. Didn't seem afraid in the least. The cow chewed. With a discordant high pitched laugh, the giant tossed John into the air. John flipped twice and landed on the giant's outstretched palm. Bossy barely deigned to acknowledge the feat.

"I'm wrong," the giant repeated, laughing. "I never thought about it that way before. What a marvelous argument. How could I have ever have been so naïve?"

John blushed and tried to turn away from the giant's inspection. Still chortling, the giant placed him in Martha's gilded cage and locked the door. Pocketing the key, he motioned for the gossfers to get Jeremy. The leprechaun scurried, darted and ducked and eventually found his way to the window and hopped out.

"You see, Jack," the giant said sympathetically, "in the end, the tricksters leave you and all you have left is your foolishness. Now, I have put this off too long." The giant hefted the hatchet and turned towards Bossy.

"Fees, foes, lies, sums," John shouted through the cage. Corp O'Rat turned, raising an eyebrow. "I smell a poor business decision." The giant did a double take, then laughed, a full booming laugh. Tears leaked from his eyes and then he burst out in a second fit of laughing. When finally he could control himself, he said,

"Oh, do tell. What bad business decision do you see?" and he wiped a tear from his eye. John waited, his cherub cheeks fiery, but his eyes calm. Pacing up and down the wall of the cage, John put his hand to his chin and looked thoughtful. The giant lifted the cage and placed it on a table so he could see the lad's face. A smile kept bursting from Corp's lips, but he waited.

"The way I see it…" John began, earnestly.

Corp O'Rat began laughing again. He slapped his thigh and leaned backwards kicking the table in delight.

John looked back undaunted.

"The way I see it, you'll be bankrupt within three years." The giant stopped laughing. He leaned forward, a smile still lit his features, but his brows lowered.

"How?" he snickered.

"I released twenty three hundred cows," John explained.

"So?" asked the giant, but his smile faded.

"Think about it, Corp O'Rat. Cows everywhere."

"Not a worry, I'll just…"

"No you won't," John countered, "your army won't be able to kill that many. The herds themselves will stop them."

"Then I'll simply…" This time John interrupted the giant by laughing. "What?" Corp O'Rat demanded.

"You'll kill them all yourself." John smirked, the giant nodded and John laughed again, "How long will it take you to hunt down and kill twenty three hundred cows."

The giant's face grew pensive.

"And," John continued, "Who will ever do business with the man who killed all those cows."

"I will…"

"No, you won't," John cut him off fiercely. The giant bowed his head.

"Why?" he asked.

"Because in the months or years it takes you to kill all the cows think about what will happen."

"What?" the giant's voice trembled.

"Every business will make kind and fair deals with each other. Every business will look out for the growth and good being of its neighbor, all except for one. Your business will dry like that fish you were talking about. By the time the cows are dead, every other business will be stronger than yours, and at that moment of your greatest fiscal weakness, when you will need loans and kindness to get restarted, Corp O'Rat…"

"Yes," said the giant, seeing the future John painted.

"Where will the murderer of the cows find the kindness to restart his enterprise?"

"By the bovine," Corp O'Rat whispered and the axe slid from his fingers and fell to the floor. "I'm doomed." He clutched the bars of John's cage and bent them. "What can I do?" he demanded, "You've cut the foundation from my stock. My company will fall." John fell to the back of the cage as the giant shook it. "What can I do? Tell me! What can I do?"

John thought. His itch made him scratch and he caught the gaze of Bossy. The cow winked and he thought of Carnations. Seeing the smile on his face, the giant relaxed a bit. Placing his hand on the giant's finger, the lad pointed to Bossy.

"Adopt her," John advised. The giant backpedaled and fell onto his back. The cage crashed to the ground and Jack tumbled out through the broken bars. He dusted himself and walked to the room where he had once found the giant's fudged books. Lifting one, he began correcting some of the math again. The giant followed. For some reason, he waited at arm's distance. John tilted his hat like it was a visor and he was about to charge into battle with his enemies. Corp's foot tapped pensively. Crumpling paper, and copying down a few figures, John finally nodded and returned his attention to the anxious giant.

"Yup, that's the only way I can see it working out for you."

"What?" the giant said on the verge of losing its temper again.

"Adopt her and make her your mascot," Jack wore a sly smile.

"Why?" Corp asked. The cow met his gaze with an unsettling clarity.

"People don't blame you for the disappearance of the cows. They blame M. Au Paulet or Jeremy, right? Right. Good. Now, once the cows do their thing, everyone will have to give you the benefit of the doubt. They'll figure you were affected by the… well, they'll figure you acted the way you did because there were no cows."

"I see," said the giant, though he didn't.

"Then, if you use the cow as your mascot. They'll see you as the business accepted by the bovine. And…"

"They'll never believe it." The giant said sourly.

"Your business model will be bovine, Corp."

The giant paced down the hall, studying the treasures he'd accumulated. Fingered ivory and marble busts of himself that were perfectly idealized. He sighed at his accumulations. It was inconceivable that a Jack could threaten what he had built. A Jack that didn't even wield an axe!

A life sized portrait gazed sternly back at him. It had taken the artist seventeen years to complete and Corp had refused to pay because he found one of the painter's hairs in the dried pigment. The giant sighed wistfully. Such good days. His wandering took him back to Bossy who looked at him with the hugest of brown eyes. Its fur was mottled, spotted and nearly golden yellow. His favorite color.

The weight of the axe felt right in Corp's hand.

The cow mooed.

"But," Corp pleaded, "I've worked so hard!"

"Drink milk," John countered harshly. The giant winced and frowned with distaste. "Drink a lot of milk and you'll do business with the rest of them."

For a moment, John pictured not his father, but his mother.

"Don't be an idiot." Jack Sprat Jr. finished.

The giant considered, he gnashed his teeth, but in the end he closed his eyes and leaned into his hands.

"It won't work. I'm still doomed," he conceded.

"You'll have to change." Jack agreed, "It's a new marketplace out there," The part of him that was still John S. Fasola winced thinking of his beloved turntable needles and record albums. "Or you'll just be a giant who was remembered as someone who was once powerful. Do you want to be just another fallen giant?" John climbed an intricately carved jewelry box and rose to his full diminutive height. He gestured towards the window, towards the greater world.

"Are you ready?"

The giant listened to the crackle of fire and sizzle of lightning, absently, he nodded and heavy hearted he slumped over to the window. He turned back with puppy dog eyes to John and said, "Must I?"

"It's time to prove yourself. You must do an act of kindness. If you are to reject obsolescence, you must become bovine."

The giant gagged. Clutching his suddenly hurting tummy, he pushed his head out the window and screamed.

"This conflict is ended. Any violence now will be heavily fined."

The combatants paused and glanced in the giant's direction. Corp O'Rat nodded with fierce authority. With a suddenness that sent chills down John's spine and made his ears pop, all the battle screams and sounds of combat died.

"We..." Corp O'Rat said slowly and with great reluctance, "have entered the age of the cow. And we shall live in the bovine manner." All paused, then slowly a cheer rose. "And further…" Corp continued, making the applause wait for him, "I declare we will be glad of it… or else!" With a swift motion he pointed to the gossfer and to his goblet. Stunned silence followed as all watched Corp O'Rat drink his first glass of milk.

36. And They Lived…

For the first time in a long time, John took an easy breath. His limbs felt heavy with the exhaustion of constant running and he collapsed. He knew he could stop running because his itch was finally and completely gone. From the window ledge, Jeremy kicked his heels in the air and did a jig.

Jeremy Tucker walked through the front door of Corp O'Rat's headquarters with a drunk expression. What he found there, he didn't expect.

"Johnny!" he cried in alarm. The lad looked at him with a desolate expression.

"Come on, m'boy. We've won. What's wrong with you?" Jeremy offered a grin. John's face fell and sagged. For him, the world turned bleak and horrible as the most horrid of all monsters rose in his mind. He entered and edged to the back of the cage. Jeremy grabbed his hand and pulled, but the lad braced himself on bent bars and refused to go. The leprechaun's face crinkled with sudden worry.

"What is it, Johnny? The giant wouldn't dare lay a hand on you now. Listen. By pudding, you can hear dragons and dentities dancing with each other. That is a mighty strange and wonderful thing." John looped his arm around the cage and locked his arms together. The chiming of dentity music sprung to life and though John's attitude worried him, the leprechaun felt his foot start to tap.

""I'm not going," John insisted. He clamped his hands over his ears as if the music outside were the haunt of dread sea sirens. It wasn't a bad hypothesis, Jeremy worried, when Corp O'Rat started to hum along. The wee man stepped into the cage. John repeated himself. "I said I'm not going."

The wee man lifted a pile of dentity feed and sifted it through his fingers. Corp harrumphed when he noticed server mice listening to him hum and hunched over a desk to begin crunching numbers and accounts.

"Pudding," the giant groused, "milk tastes just like burnt pudding. Knew it would." With jittering noses, the servant mice agreed and rushed off to tend to some duty. Scratching, and breaking pencil points the giant went over and over the numbers.

"Look what your Jack's going to do to my margins." The giant wailed, shoving a piece of parchment towards Jeremy. Jeremy whistled, as he looked over how much less money Corp O'Rat expected to make.

"You could perhaps…" began Jeremy with a trickster smile.

"No, I couldn't," grumped the giant, "Ruined, I tell you, I'm ruined." And the giant went over to the cow and fixed himself another glass of milk. Leaning his head against the cow's back, the giant Corp O'Rat wept, "I'm practically, a beggar. I'll hardly be able to afford gold leaf garbage bags. Dealing bovine, I'll barely pull in four billion coins a year."

Jeremy left John's side and patted the giant on the back.

"Ah well," he consoled the mighty Corp O'Rat, "you could always hire me."

"Hire you?"

"Well, if you'll be running a good and kind business now, a few leprechauns working sales and figuring out what you owe tax wise might be a good thought."

"Leprechauns," said the giant hopefully, "tricksters?" An evil grin took the giant. "Agreed leprechaun." Jeremy shook the giant's fingertip.

"Partners," Jeremy affirmed.

"Partners?" Corp stood and grabbed the wee man and looked dourly at him. "How about a vice presidency?"

"That would be fine," Jeremy squeaked.

"Good, I'll need a proper miser in charge of payroll," Corp laughed and then sighed when the cow mooed sternly, "but make sure they're paid a fair wage."

"Surely," the leprechaun agreed, "but not too fair. We must keep viable."

The giant brightened and told Jeremy he was going outside to dance. "It's been too long since I've danced," he declared. Happily, the giant trotted out of the castle. Jeremy hopped back to the cage.

"Did you see that, Johnny? I'm going to be a part of remaking it all. I'll be making it as fair and good as I can too. Don't you bet I won't!" John looked as despondent as a turkey on the Wednesday before Thanksgiving. Sitting down, the leprechaun pretended to conduct the music with his hands, but John didn't even bat an eye. If anything, his face grew more grave.

"That was your plan all along, wasn't it?"

"What, to be able to dip my hand and hold the reins of the richest…?" the leprechaun looked up innocently, "Never thought of it. Johnny. Never thought of it. Ah lad, brighten up. Corp brought enough rain already, just think how much money everyone will make… why the business the lithographers will get alone… just for changing Corp's business cards to include my name, will make them all rich."

"I'm happy for you," John responded, dully.

"On my business cards?" Corp O'Rat griped… the giant had unfortunately good hearing, but then he sipped more milk and nodded. Outside, a folksy tune blossomed as people picked up long discarded instruments or just slapped their knees. Jeremy quickened his dance steps and tugged on John's arm, but the lad continued to look as sullenly morose as a man awaiting a tax audit. Jeremy stopped dancing and his brow wrinkled. He tapped his lip and looked thoughtful trying to uncover the reason for John's mood. Clucking his tongue and blinking quickly, he ran through every possibility he could think of and his mind remained blank. Finally, he said, "What is it, lad?"

"Jeremy…" John breathed, "How am I going to explain it to mother?"

"Oh."

"I spent eleven million dollars in one day."

The leprechaun slumped and looked out of the cage. His shoulders fell and his back slumped.

"She'll kill you; she will," the wee man agreed. Bleakly, John nodded. Jeremy fielded a weak smile, "She still has two million. That's not bad, Johnny." John turned a weathering look on the leprechaun. "Feather and spit," the leprechaun growled and rose to pace the cage, "It's not fair."

"I'm an idiot," John agreed.

"What if…" Jeremy began, John looked up hopefully, "No, I suppose you shouldn't have her killed. Corp might have a few he could lend…"

John gave the leprechaun a horrified look.

"No," Jeremy smiled, waving his hands. "I didn't think so."

"Well," John said rising, "if I have to."

"What did you say, lad?"

"I said I might as well go if I have to. Let's get it over with."

Jeremy laughed suddenly with a bright mirth and did a twirl in the air. "That's it, Johnny. You've named the solution and it's a good one it is."

"What?" John said, not holding much hope.

"Why do you have to tell her, Johnny? If you say nothing, if you just vanish in that bovine spectacle they'll be reporting about in Texas, why she'll be a rich woman with two million…"

"I can't just hide."

"You're not listening to me," he said pulling John towards him, "I'm saying never go home. Stay here. You're more a Jack than a John now anyways. She'll have what she wants and you can find here, whatever it is a Jack needs."

"Stay?"

"She'll be rich. With two million what worries will your ma have? It's time to leave the nest, Johnny."

"Are you selling me a load of beans, Jeremy?"

Jeremy laughed, "Ah Johnny, you're doomed," Jeremy laughed, "Never was a Jack who could resist buying beans from me." The wee man clapped him on the back and began teaching John the steps to the most intricate dance the lad had ever seen.

Acknowledgments

A Climbing Stock took a strange path to print as I suppose all Jack stories must. The book began humbly enough inspired by a writing prompt suggested by Al Lefkowitz, a director, playwright and friend. His thought- revisit a classic tale and modernize it- resulted in something that looked a bit like the first chapter. When he read it, it tickled him so much I decided to see where the story might go.

From there, the story both clung too and sprang away from its roots. I had a host of beta readers and editors who helped me. First and foremost, Alicia Hiller-Mahmoudov and her husband Vadim who climbed the stalk and found where many gold laying geese were hidden without killing a single one of them; my father, who argued that wordplay should only be deleted if you feel it can't stand without apology; and much more recently Henry Sienkiewicz. Their sharp eyes brought wisdom to a foolish tale.

I also want to thank Max Beaver who directed the first play I wrote that ever hit a stage. He provided me with confidence and a wealth of tips and David Furst, the best radio host, producer, and mentor a young journalist and commentator could ask for.

Finally, I need to thank Dave Goelz who respected me enough to be blunt, honest, and critical. His commentary, kindly given, took time to digest, but his lessons can be found in this text and other works.

About the Author

Andrew Hiller is a writer, playwright, and radio personality living in Maryland. His commentaries have been selected best of the year four times on public radio's Metro Connection. As the host of the Prism and Under America's Armour his work has been broadcast in over 45 countries. He is especially proud of his Cobblestones series of documentaries about Jim Henson… the experience of interviewing, writing, and working with the original Henson Muppet crew, Hiller describes as "geek heaven." In addition to **A Climbing Stock**, he is also the author of **A Halo of Mushrooms**.

To discover more about Andrew and his work go to www.andrewhiller.net.